"BECOME MY MISTRESS,"

Lucas offered angrily. "Do you accept?"

"With all my heart," she whispered.

"Well, I don't." He slammed his fist onto the bed. "I want you for my wife, Tatiana."

"No." She swallowed a sob. "I cannot aspire to such a position. It would not be right. I would not make you happy."

"Damn! Would you stop thinking of *me*?" He broke off, seeing her tears start to flow. "I'm sorry," he said more gently, brushing them away. "But you may as well know this. I have some scraps of honor in me, too. Indeed, you bring them out in me. . . . Marry me, Tatiana."

This was all she had ever dreamed of. But she'd sworn that he deserved better. "God, Lucas. No. Please . . ."

He had pushed back her robe, and was kissing her bared shoulders, her throat. "I want you—as I have never wanted anything, anyone." He put his mouth to hers. At his hungry touch, she felt her resistance melting like snow beneath a midday sun.

"Milord." Against all odds, she found the strength to fight him off. "Milord, I beg you. Do not force me!"

He let her go, so suddenly that she staggered back against the door. "Force you? Oh, Tatiana. Tell me honestly that you don't love me, and I'll never touch you again. . . ."

A Most Reckless Lady

SANDY HINGSTON

A Dell Book

Published by
Dell Publishing
a division of
Bantam Doubleday Dell Publishing Group, Inc.
1540 Broadway
New York, New York 10036

ISBN: 0-440-22368-7

Printed in the United States of America

Published simultaneously in Canada

July 1998

10 9 8 7 6 5 4 3 2 1

OPM

For Ruth Hallman Hood,
and the pleasures of old friends refound.

"He makes a solitude, and calls it—peace!"
—George Gordon, Lord Byron
The Bride of Abydos

Prologue

LUCAS KIMBALL STRATHMERE, fourth earl of Somerleigh, stared in dismay at the tops of his close-fitting Hessians. They were leaking, by damn. He was sure of it now. Well, he couldn't fault Hoby's, not when the pair must be ten years old. Fault the snow instead—great swaths of the stuff that lofted as high as his breeches buttons. There was never snow like this in Dorset. *I should have stayed there*, he mused, urging the horse on through the endless drifts. Mid-March. The bushes would be starting to swell now. Time for pruning. *Hope to hell Timkins has got the smudge pots lit if it's snowing back—*

Whoa! The damned bloody nag he'd hired stumbled, nearly sending him headlong. He hauled at the reins, turning in the saddle to scan the vast, silent reaches of nothingness behind him. His sight felt sharpened by those two rogues he'd left behind in the post carriage at Lipovsk. There'd been something off about them, with their kerchiefs full of sausage and flasks of spirits. Too willing to share for a country so barren as this.

Russia. Haven't missed you one whit, White Lady, he thought grimly, steering the plodding mare forward. *Nothing personal, mind you, but I'd have been just as keen if I'd never had the pleasure again.*

His stockings were wet. Every cape on his coat was sopping. He was going to sneeze, too. He reached for his handkerchief, felt the crackle of parchment tucked into his waistcoat. That was where the fault lay—with Casimir Molitzyn. But one mustn't think ill of the dead.

Something howled up ahead in the distance. Wolf, he thought, his new-sharp eyes narrowing. Plumes of gray smoke there, on the horizon. Had he come ten miles from Lipovsk? Hard to gauge in such a morass of white. He urged the nag on, sensing an end to this futility—then pulled her up sharply, twisting in the saddle again.

Nothing there. No one was following. He shook off the foreboding, almost laughing, his breath hanging stark in the air. Impossible, anyway—hadn't he watched the carriage from atop a hill for three-quarters of an hour at least after it pulled out from Lipovsk, just to make sure those two ruffians didn't decamp? Who would be after him anyway? Five years since he was in Russia last; five years of peace and what passed for domesticity in Dorset. No one in Moscow or St. Petersburg even remembered him now.

Still, those two in the coach—not quite Johnny Raws, despite their bumpkin accents, hail-fellow-well-met. Too ready with the vodka. And something in their eyes that had raised the latent sharpness in his.

You're too suspicious by half, Lucas, he chided himself. After all, Bonaparte was marching on Moscow. No one in the halls of government gave a cat's damn about . . . what the hell was the name of the place? He pictured the parchment Casimir had pressed on him. *Mizhakovsk*. It had taken him half a day to find the damned spot on his maps. And he had *good* maps.

You've sent me barking up an odd tree, Casimir Nikolayevich Molitzyn, he thought, with a pang of sadness at the memories the name and this bleak winter setting evoked. Christ, they had had times! That first year in St. Petersburg—when Lucas had been so angry over what he still viewed as exile—it was Casimir who drew him out, showed him the city, taught him the Byzantine intricacies of etiquette at the Tsar's court. He'd saved Lucas's life once, when a bit of business regarding a certain French courier had gone awry, and Lucas had repaid the favor six months later, when the two of them had inadvertently stumbled onto a deadly brawl on the Neva docks. Half a decade of working with Casimir on behalf of their nations had built more than trust—it had created a friendship closer than any Lucas had formed since his years at school.

Against the backdrop of white he again saw Casimir's broad, swart face, his intensity as he offered the parchment, coercing the promise: "You will not open it, Lucas, unless . . . until . . . you have word I am dead?" Lucas had laughed. They were both young and hale, and Casimir had been heading for a quite prestigious posting in Paris. Five years past . . . 1806. Tsar Alexander had just then allied himself with Bonaparte against England, despite all Lucas's efforts on behalf of the Foreign Office—efforts overt and surreptitious—to prevent the pact. "Why should you die, Casimir?" he remembered asking. He remembered, too, the look on the Russian's face as he whispered the answer: "They will come for me, in time. They *will* come."

Blind, unholy terror. Casimir hadn't looked that frightened when Lucas snatched him back from death at the hands of those dockyard assassins. You had to respect fear like that, had to let it drag you away from the roses and smudge pots in Dorset, even so far as this: the White Lady. Russia in winter. And his senses were alert in ways he had not asked of them in five long years.

Up ahead he could see chimneys now, and the thatch roofs. A dozen houses, perhaps—hovels, really. Outbuildings. Barns. A thin patch of trees—and then the vast nothingness again. God, what a country. But the thought of a fire spurred him to spur the nag. Just to get his feet warm! He'd forgotten this sort of cold, had reckoned happily never to feel it again.

Another half mile or so slogging through the drifts, and he heard the voices. Disoriented by the ride's long silence, he turned, hand on his pistol, trying to pinpoint them. His fist uncurled as he saw only emptiness behind him. Where, then? There. Atop a slope to his left. Splotches of dark on the white. And the voices were those of children, high, giddy, with something furtive and illicit to them.

Then he saw the dog, heard it howl again. A huge thing, a wolfhound, size of a pony—and strapped like a pony to the staves of a sleigh. He rode closer, saw the splotches resolve into six or eight figures, one carrying a basket, one swathed in dark wool and fur clambering into the sleigh. Its voice rang out in Russian, loud, commanding: "Go ahead, go ahead!" But the others in the tableau were reluctant to assent to his—her?—will. Curiosity mildly engaged, Lucas watched as she—he?—leaned from the sleigh, spewing an admirable string of expletives, and wrenched the basket from protesting hands. The figure reached inside and yanked out something that, once flung into the snow, proved unmistakably feline by its outraged yowl. The wolfhound sprang forward like a shot. For one snowbound instant the sleigh stayed behind, quivering. Then it whipped out, skidding and slithering, hauled by the slavering hound, its occupant laughing deliriously.

"Christ," Lucas said under his breath. What a lunatic! The flimsy craft shimmied, slid, skittered; the terrified cat bounded, hell-bent, for the nearest barn, pursued by the huge, howling hound. The children on the slope were motionless, frozen at the spectacle. But the rider—the rider had a crop, by God, and was plying it happily across the hound's haunches. Unfair advantage, really, Lucas's English mind registered, even as he found himself admiring the sheer bravado. The sleigh was heading straight for the barn. The rider was going to die.

But out of the shadows of the barn a shape loomed up—another wolfhound, this one untrammeled by reins and a sleigh. The cat let out a desperate hiss and abruptly reversed its course, forsaking the barn for . . . for what? Lucas turned, saw the outcrop of pines just behind him. His eyes widened as he realized what was coming at him.

He hauled at the nag, who was standing transfixed by the sight: one cat, two hounds, and the rickety sleigh with its frenzied rider still whipping away. "Move, damn you!" Lucas snapped, pulling again. The horse moved then. It reared up with a spiritedness it had shown no sign of whatsoever on the ride from Lipovsk.

Caught by surprise, Lucas felt himself rise, pitch back, and become airborne. He flew from the saddle, and landed with a surprising lack of impact in a large, cold drift.

"Whoa! Whoa!" he heard the rider bark with blithe assurance. Then the cat came scrambling over his knees, his waist. It raked a long gash down his throat as it sprang past him; he felt blood welling. "Damn," he muttered, struggling to sit up and attaining his goal just in time to be thumped in the chest with a sledge stave. Blindly he raised his shoulder to block the runners, ducking his head low. The sleigh abruptly upended, crashing in the drift beside him and enmeshing him in a web of leather strapping and wet dog flesh.

Indignant, the hounds growled ferociously, baring their teeth.

A few yards to the side, the snow was moving, heaving, as the rider who'd been pitched there surfaced. "Boris! Sascha!" that imperious voice roared. *"Down!"* The whip cracked, licking at their hind flanks. They backed off, not exactly willingly.

One hand on his pistol—those dogs had mean eyes— Lucas floundered for footing, fighting free of the reins and rigging. The rider rose, dusting off snow, hood falling back. Lucas, about to give this idiot a piece of his mind, stopped in mid-breath. The idiot, trying hard to look repentant, was the most singularly beautiful girl he had ever seen: fine-boned, fair, with Eastern, slanting eyes green as grass and a red mouth bowed in contrition beneath a haloed braid of thick hair nearly as pale as the snow. *White Lady*, he thought, and realized he'd said it aloud only when she cocked that unspeakably lovely head at him.

"Do you find yourself hurt, sir?" she asked, and he shook his own head slowly, struck by the incongruity between her pale, patrician beauty and the coarse rural Russian. Like finding a Bourbon bloom on a hedge rose . . . One of the dogs snarled again, and she kneed it soundly, adding a few choice oaths as she grasped both hounds by their collars— they stood nearly as tall as she—and wrestled them to the barn. Lucas stood and watched her, noting that the rest of the children had melted off into the snowbanks. She tramped back in her fur-lined coat; she'd pulled the hood up, but from within the nest of stone marten he could see those disconcertingly clear green eyes alight with inquisitiveness. "You are a stranger," she said in her raw accent, "and we have not given you good welcome to Mizhakovsk. For that I am sorry." Only a slight frown at the corners of her mouth hinted she was more sorry that her sport had been spoiled. "Can I help you in your business, good sir?"

Lucas had meant to be more circumspect, but the indecorous tumble in the snow, not to mention her ruthless handling of the dogs, had left him off-guard. "I am looking for someone," he answered in her language, straightening his hat with belated dignity. "Someone called Tatiana."

The green eyes widened. "Why, sir. That is my name."

An hour later, in her parents' cottage, Lucas had been warmed, more and less effectively, by a peat fire, gruel, and vodka so raw that the worst London gin sot would have choked on it. The parents were wary—and little wonder, Lucas thought, meeting the father's suspicious gaze. The girl clearly was no blood kin to them. They had the broad, stumped build of centuries of serfdom; Tatiana, freed of her mass of furs, was lithe as a whippet, standing out in the dim hovel like a bright gem. Shaking off with effusive politeness an offer of more vodka, Lucas fought its potent effect and his aching weariness to listen as the father demanded, on the edge of rudeness, exactly why he had come.

How much to tell him? He was stolid, but not stupid. The White Lady stripped stupidity even from her peasants; fools simply did not survive here. He thought of the parchment drying in his waistcoat, with no more on it than the name of the village and the girl's name. *Casimir, what did you want me to do in this place?* If Lucas had expected to find anything, it was, perhaps, an aging lover of his friend. But Tatiana was young enough to be the Cossack's daughter— though she showed about as much resemblance to Casimir's dark looks as she did to her foster parents. So he answered with small talk, told half-lies: An old friend from the wars told him of Mizhakovsk, mentioned Tatiana. What old friend? From which war? the father wanted to know.

Lucas skirted the questions and posed his own, turning the tables: Did *they* know why?

The woman, busy with her samovar, rattled the teacups. The father paused, considering his daughter, then brusquely sent her to the barn. She went without demur. Not stupid, Lucas thought, observing her quick obedience, but ofttimes brutal. Was she so free with the whip because she'd tasted it herself?

With her gone, the father sat on a stool, thick legs planted. "Seventeen years past," he said without emotion, "a man rode into Mizhakovsk with a child, an infant. By the will of God, the woman and I had no children of our own. He asked if we would foster her. We took her into our care." His wife's hands were trembling as she brought Lucas tea.

"Did you know his name?" Lucas asked quietly.

"I know the name he told me. Ivan Ivanyevich." The Russian equivalent of "John Smith."

"Did he come again?"

"He came once a year. *Dyed*, he had the girl call him. *Dyed* Ivan."

"Uncle," Lucas echoed thoughtfully. "He comes no more?"

"Georgi," the woman implored her husband.

But he answered Lucas: "Not for the past five years."

His wife had begun crying. "Tatiana is ours," she whimpered. "She is all we have."

The subject of the conversation ducked back through the door then, tugging one hound with her, reporting that the other had got loose. "Fetch him," her foster father said roughly. She vanished into the cold. The remaining hound curled against Georgi's knee, regarding Lucas no less suspiciously. Lucas wished hopelessly for a brandy. The situation required delicacy and tact, two qualities he'd not had much call for of late. "I suppose he gave you money," he said, making his tone indicate that anyone would expect it. After a moment, the father nodded. "Has the money stopped coming?"

"It stopped when he stopped." The Russian straightened on his stool. "But you must not think we were wasteful with what he gave us. There is more than enough for her dower. She is betrothed to Pietr, son of the chief of the village." There was pride in his voice. "She is assured of a good life. I have seen to that. There is no need for you to concern yourself with her."

Lucas was about to agree when a sharp rap at the door made him reach for his pistol. The men from the coach, he thought. Georgi bellowed nonchalantly, "Come in," and the door burst open. Lucas had the gun cocked. But the tall, fair young man on the threshold was a stranger to him.

Not to the wife. Her furrowed brow cleared, and she quickly wiped her eyes on her apron. "Pietr!" she cried happily, glancing at Lucas. So this was the fortunate groom. Lucas let go of the pistol and rose to his feet. Pietr was eyeing him as though he were an apparition. Were visitors that infrequent? Probably so. It was time to leave.

The father cleared his throat. "Pietr. *Dobry vyecher.*" Good evening. "This is . . . this is . . ." He gestured at Lucas uncertainly.

"Lord Strathmere, attaché to the British embassy in Moscow," Lucas said suavely, bowing. Pietr's blue eyes blinked. "Just passing through on my way to—" He searched the map in his mind rapidly. "Archangel. Official business. I was nearly run down, though, by an angel. One riding a sleigh."

The wife shot Lucas a grateful glance. Pietr's face creased in a smile. "Up to her tricks, is my Tanya? Never fear, milord. I shall keep her well in hand once we are wed."

There was an indelicate snort from the doorway. "So you think, Pietr," the bride-to-be said archly, grappling the second wolfhound.

His smile widened fondly. "So I know, Tatiana." She kicked the door shut behind her. There was a little silence. Then Pietr reached into the inner depths of his coat and tossed a small paper-wrapped bundle at his betrothed. "For you, *lyubov*. For your bridal gown."

She pulled at the paper, eager as a child at Christmas, red mouth pursed in excitement. Her breath came out in a wondrous sigh. "Oh, Pietr! *Mater*, see what he has brought!" She held them out on her palm: a sprinkling of seed pearls.

"All the way from Nadvollsk," Pietr said with complacence. "You see how I take care of you."

"She sees." Her foster father's glance at Lucas signified the stranger must, too. And Lucas was impressed. The pearls would have made no more than an inch of bodicework on any fashionable woman of the ton. But for a bridegroom in Mizhakovsk, they must have come dear.

"So come and give me what I want," Pietr told Tatiana. Blushing, she crossed the room to kiss him swiftly on the cheek. He caught her by the waist, held her fast there, put his lips to hers, watching Lucas defiantly over her shoulder. The chief's son. The best catch in all Mizhakovsk. *Casimir, what in hell did you want from me?*

Lucas stood up abruptly. "Well! I had best be going. No bones broken. But mind, young man, that you hold to your word—keep her away from that sleigh!"

"But you cannot leave now," Tatiana protested, puzzled. "The night . . . the cold. And it has started to snow." Pietr's arm tightened around her; her father's gaze was quelling.

"I seem to recall," Lucas said swiftly, "another village, not fifteen miles from here—"

"Lalsk," Pietr and the father said in unison, and vied in their eagerness to give him directions. Lucas dutifully noted them in his pen book, thanked the woman for the meal and the tea, the father for the spirits. They let him see his own way to the barn. Lucas saddled the mare swiftly and rode off west, in case they were watching. There was no reason on earth for me to come here, he thought. *Sorry, Casimir.*

He turned south again as he passed the pines. He'd gone less than a mile when he heard the explosion—heard it and felt it, for it rocked him in the saddle. He stood in the stirrups, staring back. In the light of the fat half-moon, smoke was rising from the village. He saw flames now among the smoke plumes, and sparks hurtling skyward.

He rode back in a fury, whipping the bewildered mare. As he cleared the pine thicket again, he saw the girl, Tatiana, standing stone-struck, the cat in her arms. She looked at him as he spurred up, those green eyes uncomprehending. "I came back for her," she said, nodding at the cat. "Is it . . . the end of the world?"

Lucas hushed her with a wave of his hand, and then he saw what she did not: two figures on horseback emerging from the burning village, headed west, following his trail. She started to cry. He leaned down, scooping her into the saddle before him. The cat gave a yowl, and he swatted it away. "Kitty!" she cried. "You've hurt Kitty!" She struggled against him. He was drawing his pistol, and her frantic movements threatened his aim. Reluctantly, he brought the weapon down against her smooth, pale temple—hard. She went slack in his grip.

The first rider had reached the point where Lucas had turned south. He called to his comrade, gesturing at the trees: "There!"

Lucas fired once, silencing him forever, then drew a bead on the second. "Lord Strathmere!" the man called, wheeling his mount. Surprise nearly made Lucas lose his target. "There is no use in this! You cannot keep her hidden!"

Lucas answered with a shot. The man dropped like a stone. Leaving Tatiana slung across his saddle, Lucas dismounted and trudged forward through the deep snow.

He knew he'd killed them. He wanted to know *why* he'd

killed them. Closer examination confirmed they were the pair from the coach to Lipovsk. He rifled through their pockets and purses. Nothing but sausages and matches— though the purses stank of sulfur. Explosives. Odd he hadn't noticed that in the coach. Or perhaps some small part of him had. He glanced back at the trees, saw Tatiana stirring. Damn. He should have hit her harder. Rushing now, he headed for the cottage, feeling the heat of the flames.

The door dissolved as he crashed against it. Kerchief over his mouth, he took care to make certain all three of those within were dead. The gaping shot-holes in their foreheads were clue enough, but he felt for pulses. For some reason that seemed important to him.

He emerged from the carnage to find Tatiana stumbling toward the house. "Pietr!" she cried. "I must find Pietr!"

Lucas yanked her back toward his horse. "He is dead," he said, more roughly than he meant to. "All of them are dead."

"Dead?" she echoed in utter bewilderment. "*Dead?* Why should they be dead?" Lucas, pulling her through the snow, did not know what to say. But she reasoned it out, cried in terrible anger, "It is because of you! It is because you came here!"

He paused, hands clenching her wrists, up to his thighs in snow. "Tatiana." What could he tell her of why, when he himself did not know? So he simply took her in his arms, carrying her as she cried, lifting her—light as snow she was, eiderdown—into the saddle with him. Sobs wrenched her cocoon of soft marten as they rode away from the smoking ruins. Casimir Nikolayevich Molitzyn had damned well better have had good reasons for this, Lucas thought angrily.

She was trembling. Lucas let his arm tighten around her, wishing he knew what to say or do to comfort her. But what could, really? He fell back on convention. "It will be all right," he murmured as he spurred across the cold breast of the White Lady. "Everything will be all right. Believe me. You'll see."

One

Everything was, most emphatically, not all right.

Lucas sighed heavily, staring from the window of his upstairs study onto the yard below, where Tatiana, clad in a stableboy's cast-off breeches, was wrestling with his two mastiffs—and getting the better of them. Mrs. Smithers was appalled by the breeches. They were *all* appalled by the breeches. But Mrs. Smithers had been a good deal more appalled when Lucas had attempted to settle the girl on her. "See if you can make something of her. Understairs maid, perhaps?" he recalled saying tentatively.

It had taken Lucas nearly two months to get the chit out of Russia and across war-torn Europe to home. The housekeeper had glared at the bedraggled creature on the threshold of her parlor, then snapped, "Christ, if ye ain't a sight! Go on to the pump, then, 'n' draw water for a bath. We'll see how much o' that comes off ye." Tatiana had stood silent, still as marble. Mrs. Smithers moved abruptly to smack her for effrontery, but Lucas stayed her hand.

"She doesn't speak English."

"Don't speak—" The housekeeper boggled. "Well, how in hell's bells am I to—"

"As always, Mrs. Smithers, I have great confidence in your ingenuity."

"In my—here, now, where d'ye think ye're—Good God, m'lord!" But Lucas had escaped, gratefully, to the stairs.

So far as he knew, the redoubtable Mrs. Smithers never had got the girl to bathe. Three days after undertaking the assignment, the housekeeper had reported to Lucas in his study, her gray hair literally on end. "There's no makin' no understairs maid nor nothin' else out o' that 'un," she'd muttered darkly. " 'N' if ye don't relieve me o' the duty for her . . . well, m'lord, it's with regret, but I resign my post." Mrs. Smithers and her husband had served the earls of Somerleigh for thirty years with great distinction. Lucas relieved her of the duty. He'd tried Cook next, but, fore-warned by Mrs. Smithers, she'd flat out refused him. Cook, too, was very fine at her work. That left Timkins, in the garden, and Costner, in the stables. Mrs. Smithers's brief but poignant recounting of the havoc Tatiana had wreaked among the linens in her perfectly aligned closets—the sets all mismatched, splotches of grime on the sheets the house-keeper was so proud of—ruled out Timkins; Lucas could not bear to think of the chit let loose on the roses. So she'd fallen to Costner, who'd somehow come to terms with his exotic new underling over the horses and dogs.

Thus the breeches—and thus, too, Lucas's sense that he had failed Casimir Molitzyn. True, he'd got the girl safely away from her incinerated village, but to what purpose? To wrestle dogs in his drive? Surely she was meant for some-thing more, he thought, watching the late-summer sun set fire to her disheveled gilt hair and make shadows on her cheekbones as the mastiffs slathered her with their tongues. The sight made him flush slightly, and reach for the brandy on his desk.

All in all, he mused, pouring himself a long one, she was no worse off in his stable than in her foster father's barn. But that was a lie. In Mizhakovsk she'd had Pietr, and a handful of seed pearls, and the prospect of contentment, children, her own hearth. Mayhaps Costner would wed her. But just then the stablemaster came from the stables and bellowed something at her as she knelt in the dirt. At the sound of his voice, she turned and thrust her tongue out at him. He shook a fist, but he retreated. Costner wasn't a match for her, and Costner knew it, even better than Lucas did.

The trouble, he thought, lolling the brandy on his tongue, was that she was neither flesh nor fowl. Too hopelessly proud to serve in proper fashion, she was too uncouth for any other possibility. He swallowed, and felt his head ache. The four months since his return to Somerleigh House had marked a definite increase in his brandy intake.

Despite the muddle of his thoughts, one fact stood out clearly: Someone, somewhere in Russia, had considered her important enough to raze a village.

For the hundredth time since their return in May, he yanked out the box in which he kept Casimir's correspondence. He'd read the letters over so often he knew them by heart, and no clue lay there. Frustrated, he looked down again into the courtyard. She'd vanished from the drive. Memories of the holocaust at Mizhakovsk made his head positively throb. He hurried outside.

Costner had lost track of her, and didn't seem inclined to worry over the fact. Lucas checked with Cook—there was naught wrong with the chit's appetite—but she hadn't been there. He found Timkins in the shed, mixing potash and bonemeal for the season's last feeding. "Nah," he responded to his master's question. "But there's somethin' eatin' at the Gallicas. Not that ye can be bothered, I'm sure."

"Shut up, Timkins," Lucas said briefly, not needing the reminder; he had been negligent of the roses of late. Then, considering the gardener's hurt face—and he *had* done a fine job with the smudge pots while Lucas was in Russia, through three late frosts—he said, "All right. I'll have a look at them."

The Gallicas weren't his favorites; they were too bold, too wild, and their palette was a gaudy range of violets and crimsons. They had fragrance, though, and toughness, and they stood him well as rootstock. It was from a mingling of those qualities with *Rosa indica*, he suspected, that he'd created the rose that was his masterpiece, the exquisite Lady Innisford. It would have made a fortune on the market, but he'd shared it with no one. Gillian's namesake was for him alone.

He went through the arbor beneath the dangling tendrils of a yellow *chinensis* sent by a colleague in the Foreign Office. Even with the waning of summer, his private Eden was glorious. Timkins had charge of the lesser plants that edged the Holland-brick walkways—alyssum and thyme and a host of stuff that Lucas couldn't even name. It was the roses he had made his own, in those first dark days after his return from Russia five years past, when Bonaparte's alliance with the Tsar had made Lucas's diplomatic abilities obsolete.

They'd been his companions then, silent and uncomplaining as he wandered among them. They had suffered badly in the family's long absences from the estate. Somewhere in his memory were stored visions of the place from his childhood, when his grandmother had had their tending. The glimpses were tantalizingly lovely, hazy with sunlight and scent, the residue of a simpler time. He'd sensed, considering the neglected bushes, that here was something once grand that had gone awry—rather like his life. Only the garden was small enough, unlike his life, to be put right again.

There hadn't even been a gardener, Smithers had informed him, for nigh on eight years. The Admiral hadn't had much patience for such frippery as roses; he'd thought his son's new avocation daft. But Lucas hadn't cared. He'd learned what he could from books, the best that could be had. On a tip from his mother he'd hired Timkins, who'd lost one eye as well as his sense of smell from a head wound suffered at Trafalgar under the Admiral. The man had been pitifully grateful for the post.

Remembering that made Lucas even more regretful of his rude words. He hurried to the Gallicas and pulled at the leaf tips. Timkins was right; something had been nibbling. Lucas went on probing, patiently, and was rewarded at last by the sight of a pair of small striped caterpillars hiding among the foliage. He crushed them flat beneath the toe of his new Hessians. Russia had ruined his last pair.

There—he'd done his duty, and was able to continue his search for Tatiana. But here, now, in this peaceable corner, the marauding Russians he'd imagined coming to seize her seemed patently absurd. Maybe he should send her to a convent—though she didn't seem a whit religious. That scandalized the servants as well—that she never went to St. Aidan's. Perhaps with what she had seen, Lucas reflected, she had no faith left in God. There was a darkness to her green eyes now that he hadn't seen in Mizhakovsk.

He heard Timkins coming. Lucas turned to give him the glad news about the caterpillars' demise—then stopped. It was, instead, Tatiana, the breeches low on her slim hips, her secondhand linen shirt open at the throat. She saw him at the same instant, eyes flickering wide, and froze beneath the archway. Framed in roses. Her pale hair floated, loose, on the wind. Lucas swallowed a thick lump of regret. In Mizhakovsk, Pietr would have brought her to her bridebed by now. He pictured her wrestling her groom as she did the dogs. Those slim, brown arms were strong.

He spoke to her in Russian. "It's all right. I am leaving." She wouldn't stay if he did; he knew that by now. She moved to one side, lowering her head as he passed. As always, she said nothing. So far as he knew, she had not spoken one word to him or any other human being since they'd left her village. The power of will such lengthy silence signified put him in awe.

Three things she loved: his dogs, his horses, and the roses. He would never forget the first time he found her in the garden, in early June, running headlong from bush to bush, burying her face, her hands, in the surfeit of blossoms in their full summer glory. Nothing in her experience had prepared her, clearly, for the possibility of such beauty in the world.

Remembering that moment softened his heart. He turned to glance back through the archway and saw her standing motionless, watching him, waiting for him to be gone. She preferred to keep her pleasures as private as her pain. And what was she . . . sixteen? Seventeen? Scarcely more than a child. Her self-containment rattled him. Worse, it reminded him of himself.

I must do something about her. He'd thought that often enough, but seeing her waiting there, proud and silent, crystallized his resolve.

The obvious answer—the only answer, really—was to call on his mother.

But to bring in the Dowager Countess of Somerleigh would just complicate the situation more. It was only in these past two years, since his father's death, that Lucas and his mother had struck an uneasy peace: She stayed out of his life, and he did not rebuke her for the outrageous expenses of her own.

In truth, he admired Dulcibella. Somehow she'd managed to cope with perfect aplomb with all the vagaries Lucas's father's career in the Foreign Office had entailed—the long, frequent absences abroad, the unsavory midnight visitors, the general air of mystery. It must have put a strain between man and wife. Yet through it all, she'd maintained an absolutely impeccable position in the very highest circles of society, and without—so far as Lucas knew, and he was *nearly* certain he did—the commonplace recourse of taking a lover. Her grief upon the Admiral's death had been utter and genuine.

Besides, she was a woman, and Lucas dimly realized that a woman's resources in regard to Tatiana were badly needed. Lady Strathmere might succeed in managing the girl where he had not simply by virtue of her sex.

Lucas could feel the rightness of the argument. Why, then, did he hesitate?

Because, dammit, for a grown man to have to call in his mother was impossibly demeaning. Because the peace they'd made since the Admiral's death was tentative at best. Because Lucas *knew* his mother refused to believe he was content stuck away in Dorset, tending to his roses. She still thought he was hiding—and she knew what, or whom, he was hiding from.

Even with all that considered, and it was, did he really have any choice?

"M'lord?" Timkins, hauling two pails full of bonemeal and potash, was standing on the pathway, staring. Lucas roused himself with reluctance. "Did ye see the trouble then, m'lord?"

Lucas foresaw nothing but trouble. "Caterpillars," he said briefly. "I crushed them."

Timkins's scarred face creased in a grin. "Pity, ain't it, all life's trials can't be dealt with so easy?"

"Timkins," Lucas said with feeling, "you have no idea."

Two

THIRTY DAYS LATER, the dowager countess arrived at Somerleigh House with a baggage train consisting of three coaches, four carts, a dozen servants on horseback, six spaniels—several of which were in heat—and seven pack animals loaded nigh up to the sky. "Darling," she said, kissing Lucas's cheek as he helped her down from her post chaise. "I came the *instant* I got your note."

"So I see." He eyed the line of vehicles and critters stretching back nearly to the gates. "Just threw a few things in a valise and hurried right off, did you?"

"Exactly," she agreed, and only the glint in her eyes—like his, ice-blue ringed with black, winter moons against dark skies—let him know the irony was mutual. With a complacent hand, she patted the midnight curls beneath her jaunty chip hat. "I imagine I must look a sight."

"You look lovely. As always."

She smiled at him, head cocked. "Well, I *have* got the most marvelous new facial recipe from Marianne Cuthbert's maid. Almond milk and oil of wintergreen and crushed pearls."

Lucas arched a brow, letting her precede him through the doors in her powder-blue damask cloak and peach kid Roman boots. "I trust you aren't pulverizing the family jewels."

"Oh, no, you use those tiny little Scotch ones. How are you, Smithers?" She greeted the butler warmly. "I hear you've yet another grandchild! Dorcas's, was it? A boy?"

"Aye, milady. Named—"

"Jonathan. I know. Lovely name, that. Give Dorcas my best, will you, when you see her? And do bring sherry and biscuits to my rooms. We had a most indescribable luncheon at the Green Man in Cranborne."

"Aye, milady. You have my sympathy." The butler hurried off, preening, and Lucas was left wondering how on earth Dulcie learned of, much less remembered, such things. He would have been hard put to name any one of Smithers's many children, much less *their* children. But that was part of Dulcie's magic: She took notice of folk, high or low.

In her sitting room she took off the hat and ran a hand through her curls—Lucas had that hair, too, thick and black and waving without the aid of pomade or dressing. He noticed, though, the first inroad's of white toward her temples, and calculated her age: twenty-two when she'd birthed him, and so past fifty. She didn't look it. He could think of no graceful way of telling her so. She surveyed the appointments with a studied eye, noting that her gilt pearwood vanity was freshly waxed and laid out with her mirrors and brushes, that the yellow organdy drapes were pulled back to the angle she preferred at that time of day. "I see you've let the place go to pot," she observed.

"All but your rooms, Mother."

She threw him another smile, tugging off her gloves—though not before running one finger over the very top of the turned leg of the writing table. It came away spotless. Lucas fought off an impulse to make a face at her. "So," she said, settling gracefully onto her chaise longue, "what exactly is this urgent matter as to which you require my advice?"

"I never said it was urgent," he protested—faintly.

"Come now, let's not pretend. You've neither sought nor heeded my advice since you were born—quite the opposite, really. I cannot in my wildest imaginings apprehend what dire calamity could have brought you to this end. To consult your mummy!"

"Oh, really, Mother. Must you—" Smithers's entrance with a tray brought Lucas to a stop. His mother poured herself sherry, held the decanter out to him.

He waved it off, and Dulcie clucked her tongue. "Lord. It must be bad."

"It's the same Cordova Father always bought," Lucas said, bristling.

She laughed. "Not the wine, pet. Your trouble. If you require stone sobriety even to discuss it." Defiantly, Lucas sent Smithers for brandy. Drunk or sober, this was going to be just as difficult.

As Smithers deposited the decanter and a snifter at Lucas's elbow, loud, raucous barking erupted from the yard. Lady Strathmere arched her head on its elegant neck. "Dear me, Smithers. Have we been invaded?"

"No, milady." His expression was inscrutable. "That would be the girl. With the dogs."

Lucas saw the way his mother's blue eyes narrowed, though the motion was minute. "The girl?" she echoed, perfectly pleasantly.

"The foreigner, milady."

"That will be all for now, Smithers," she told the butler, and waited until he had left them to say, like a cat pouncing on a mouse, "The *foreign girl?*" Rousing herself from the chaise, she crossed to the window. "Dear Lord in heaven." Reluctantly Lucas joined her, and saw Tatiana rolling in the dust with the mastiffs in the October sunlight, her loose blond hair flying like a jezebel's. "Who *is* that?"

Lucas yanked the drapes closed with a *whoosh*. "If I knew the answer to that question, Mother, you wouldn't be here."

The dowager countess sank back onto the chaise, bright eyes betraying her fascination. "Darling. Do tell *all*."

An hour later, with the help of much brandy, Lucas had told—not all, precisely, but as much as he could within the limits of national security, constraints his mother well understood. He could not, for example, name Casimir Molitzyn, but could say only that he'd been a trusted ally and friend. Nor could he tell the country from which he'd fetched the girl home—though, "Pish," said Dulcie knowingly, "it had to be Russia. And you say she won't speak to you?"

"Nor to anyone else."

"No wonder Smithers looked as though he'd got a toad on his tongue. It really isn't fair to him and the others, you know, thrusting such an anomaly into their midst."

Lucas snorted into his snifter. "It hasn't exactly been a custard pie for me, either, Mother. Besides the difficulty of smuggling the wench through Bonaparte's sphere of war—"

"Oh, darling, I didn't mean to underestimate the inconvenience to *you*. After all, you've so much here that demands your valuable attention and time."

Lucas stiffened. "As it happens, I do."

Dulcie picked delicately at one of the upholstery buttons. "Well, dear, I've always maintained, if you're satisfied to live out your life piddling with your little shrubberies—"

"Would you care to see the account books, Mother? I

made enough in wool and roses last season to keep you in crushed pearls through the next bloody century."

"Someone has to uphold the family's obligations," Dulcie said tartly.

"If you mean by *that* paying attendance on that fat greasy pig of an excuse for a regent—"

But Dulcie had clapped her hands over her ears. Lucas took a breath, counted to ten, then to thirty, then to fifty. Then he said slowly, loudly, "I'm sorry, Mother, that I haven't fulfilled your lifelong dream for me. I'm sorry I haven't given you grandchildren. There. Does that do it?"

Dulcie took her hands away from her face. "It isn't for me that I want you to marry, Lucas. If you could only understand the satisfaction, the sublime contentment of sharing your life with someone *respectable*, someone *appropriate* . . ." But they'd danced this dance too often; she saw it in his expression, and sighed. "Well. Be that as it may. You've called on me in your hour of need, and I'm delighted to oblige. If you will tell me what it is you want."

Lucas let out his breath. That could have been worse, he supposed. He stood up and paced to the hearth. "I don't know what to do with her, Mother. I'm responsible for her. Yet she clearly doesn't want me to be."

"She must have relatives, relations, *somewhere*. Have you made inquiries?"

"I've tried. But I'm hampered, as you must see, by what happened at Miz—at her village. Those men were searching for her. I hardly want the world to know I have her here."

"Did you write the ambassador to Ru—to her country of origin?"

"Write him what? That I've got a peasant girl holed up in Dorset, and has anyone reported one missing?"

The countess's blue eyes were shrewd. "You said the killer called you by name. You don't suppose that you're in any danger? Harboring her, I mean."

"I don't know. I don't think so. After all, it has been seven months."

"Mm. Quite. Then again, your friend—the one who gave you the note—he, too, is dead."

"I looked into that. Dysentery. Nothing untoward at all about it, my contacts insist."

Lady Strathmere sighed. It wasn't, Lord knows, what she'd expected or hoped for. A disgraced Dorsetshire shepherdess—now, *that* she could have dealt with. It would have been a sign, at least, that Lucas was coming to his senses, coming out of his funk over Gillian Innisford.

She looked at him as he stood leaning on the mantel. He had the Admiral's masculine poise, and his dignity as well, despite what that red-haired bitch had done to unman him. He was asking for her help. This was a first in all his life, that she could recall. "Why *did* you go and get her?" she asked softly.

"It's not as though I went there to *get* her! I went because I felt I owed Casi—I had an obligation. To an old friend. The rest of it just . . . happened." His handsome face showed frank traces of the tension he felt. "My friend was not the sort to exact such a duty from me whimsically. He must have sent me for some reason. And I could hardly abandon her to those thugs who'd just murdered her entire village."

Some men would have, Dulcie mused. Some never would have gone in the first place, would have concluded that an obligation to a dead man was no duty at all. But not her Lucas. The Admiral's blood ran thick in him indeed; neither one of the infuriating males she'd loved in her life could ever stand to leave a debt unpaid. Still, this . . . it was an ineludible morass. And just as the new London season was set to begin. . . . For a moment her heart yearned for the bright gaiety of the capital, the easy familiarity of her circle of friends, the gaming tables and soirées and gossip.

But only for a moment. The Strathmere sense of duty was not limited to the masculine side.

The mastiffs howled beyond the organdy-draped windows. Dulcie set down her sherry glass, pushed aside a half-nibbled biscuit. "Suppose," she said, with an equanimity she did not entirely feel, "I have a closer look at the girl."

Three

ONE HUNDRED AND twenty-three minutes later, Lucas
stood in the corridor outside his mother's rooms, fighting off
an overwhelming urge to put his ear to the door. Somerleigh
House was distressingly well-built, with stout stone walls
and close-fitted appointments. Not a single sound had issued through the portal's oak panels since he'd dragged the
girl from the stables and deposited her there.

He was growing more and more anxious. Who knew
what Tatiana was capable of? She blamed him, didn't she,
for the deaths of her family? What if she took it into her
head to repay the debt at Dulcie's cost? He was just imagining his mother slumped motionless on the blood-spattered
chaise when a voice at his elbow said, "Beg pardon, milord."
Lucas whirled and saw Smithers bearing a tea tray. The
butler knocked and entered, leaving Lucas craning for a

glimpse of the salon's interior while trying hard not to be seen doing so. At least Dulcie hadn't been murdered. She could not have rung for tea if she had.

He checked his pocket watch again. What on God's green earth might they be doing? He knew damned well his mother didn't speak a word of Russian; he could hardly picture Tatiana playing pantomime for hours. When Smithers backed through the door, Lucas blurted out, "What exactly is going on in there?"

"The countess is giving her tea," the butler said in a highly disgruntled tone. His stiff back as he paraded off down the hallway showed he found the notion just as unsettling as Lucas did.

Not until another three-quarters of an hour had passed— by which point Lucas was leaning on the door in bewildered weariness—did it suddenly fly open, sending him stumbling into his mother's rooms. Tatiana brushed by in her breeches and shirt, her small chin upraised, shoulders squared in such an attitude of exalted sangfroid that Lucas wondered how he'd ever thought she might suit for an understairs maid. She did not spare him a glance; Lucas was left to stare after her in amazement before coming to his senses and hastily closing the door.

His mother was folding up a napkin, her blue eyes unreadable. "Tea, dear?" she asked, reaching for the handsome Adams service. "I daresay it's still warm. Or I could send for more."

"Damn the tea," he growled. "What the devil went on here?"

"You needn't take that tone with me, Lucas Kimball Strathmere!" And defiantly she took the time to pour herself a cup before answering, "We had a nice little chat."

"A *chat*? How in God's name could you chat? The chit doesn't speak English!"

"Ah, but she does, passably. Though she shows a distressing tendency to lapse into stable language. A habit, I trust, she's acquired from Costner, not you."

Lucas worked his gaping jaw loose. "She speaks English? But . . . how—"

"She told me she'd worn her 'dog's ears.' Is that some sort of quaint Russian idiom? She meant, I presume, that she'd listened and learned. She's bright as a pin, Lucas. Don't ever underestimate that."

Seven months of watching and listening . . . it was possible, he supposed. Nay, more than possible for a creature with the strength of will to go without speaking for so long. But that raised a question. "How did you ever manage to get her started talking?"

Dulcie smiled a little. "I simply asked whether she'd prefer to marry Costner or a grand duke. She said a grand duke, of course, because that would be more like Pietr."

Lucas laughed, nearly giddy with relief. "A grand duke, like Pietr? She has no idea."

"She'll learn," his mother said complacently. "She has a great deal of spirit, that little one. I don't suppose you'll have noticed, but she's remarkably lovely underneath all that grime—though, granted, in a most exotic way. She should make quite a splash when you present her."

Lucas was in the process of discovering that the brandy decanter still held enough for a celebratory snifter. "Present her?" he echoed absently.

"To society," Dulcie said.

Lucas made a splash himself, with the brandy, across the Savonnerie carpet. *"What?"*

She met his eyes that were her eyes and went on, her voice steady and even. "That's the bargain we made, the recompense she finds acceptable for the tragedy you caused."

"The tragedy I—Christ, I saved her life!"

Dulcie wagged a finger at him. "According to her, her life was in no danger until you arrived in Mizhakovsk."

"You're not supposed to know she's from—" But what she was proposing was enough to make Lucas forget national security for once. "You had no bloody right to offer such a deal!"

"Since you have ruined her life," Dulcie continued relentlessly, "it seems only fair that you provide her with another. Lord knows we have the means for it."

"Impossible!" Lucas declared. "Why, she's a polecat, a hellion! Ask Mrs. Smithers about her linen closet! She couldn't make a satisfactory servant out of her—and you want to present her at Almack's?" The notion made him shudder.

"Understairs maid is a far cry from wife to a grand duke," Dulcie noted, and took a sip of tea before adding, "Besides, *you* will be presenting her, not I."

Lucas saw through her then. He backed off across the stained carpet, holding out a hand. "Oh, no, Mother. I know what you're up to. You think you can use this as an excuse to force me back into the ton. Well, you can just forget it. Not a chance in hell."

Dulcie set down her cup. "She cried when she spoke of Pietr. It was most affecting. 'The love of my life,' she called him." She dabbed at her eyes with her napkin edge. "And the tears she shed over the cat!"

"What bloody cat?"

"The one you pushed out of her arms and made her leave behind."

Lucas had had enough. "You've gone straight over the edge, Mother. Honestly, you have. All that champagne and crushed pearls has made you quite dotty."

Dulcie never faltered. "We'll have to move fast, of course. She's nearly of a marriageable age. Fortunately, I am at loose ends at the moment, and shall take the poor thing under my wing. Properly fitted out, and with a smattering of learning, I daresay she'll be ready in, oh, two years."

Lucas groaned, from his heart. Yet the timetable set by the dowager countess was his first ray of hope. Two years was a very long time for Dulcibella, Lady Strathmere, to stick to anything.

"In the meantime, you might put your mind to fabricating a plausible background for her. I don't imagine we'll ever completely erase the accent. Some sort of Continental cousin, perhaps."

The Strathmeres hadn't made a foreign marriage in half a century. But Lucas had regained his equanimity. This was a whim, like those his mother occasionally acquired for temperance, or a new card game, or a cut of sleeve. She might try and do with Tatiana what she liked, but she could no more make him go to London than she could change the past.

"Where precisely do you propose to perform this miracle, Mother, may I ask?"

"Oh, not here. I wouldn't dream of imposing on your hospitality for such a length of time. Not when you are so dreadfully busy with those shrubberies. I think the cottage in the Cotswolds."

Lucas laughed out loud. "The Cotswolds? You'll be bored senseless within a week!"

"I can't afford that luxury," she said frostily. "I have a duty to fulfill."

He raised his glass. "Well, go to it, Mother! Best of luck!"

"I do hope, Lucas, you will do your part. After all, this muddle's of your making. And I would hate for you to be the first earl of Somerleigh ever to shirk a duty."

He bowed to her, the elegant motion an unconscious remnant of the gay young London blade he had once been. "I will, of course, fulfill my obligation to the lady—once you have tamed her." His voice held only the merest hint of the bemusement he felt at the prospects of that.

Lady Strathmere nodded in satisfaction. "Thank you, Lucas. I knew you would see it that way."

Four

LUCAS STARED IN disbelief at the lavender-corded letter atop the sheaf of correspondence on his escritoire. *Another* bill from Madame Descoux? He slit it open with his pruning knife and nearly gasped aloud. The mantua-maker's grasp of English spelling was negligible, but the total at the bottom of the page was written plainly enough: three hundred sixty pounds. He yanked at the drawer where he kept his account book, found the page he sought, and added this latest number to the astronomical figure already noted there.

Lucas's black brows knotted. It had been nearly a year and a half since Dulcie and the girl had decamped for the Cotswolds. He'd heard not one word from his mother in all that time. But two months past, the extraordinary deluge of bills had begun.

Dulcie's long silence had fairly convinced him she'd given up on her protégée. Now he was not so sure. The dowager countess was profligate, certes, but she was not one to throw good money after bad. He cocked his head at Bellerophon, the brindled mastiff who was sprawled on the hearth rug. "You don't suppose . . ." The dog let out an enormous yawn. "No. You're right. It isn't possible. Mother must just be consoling herself for her failure with this orgy of spending."

The mastiff pricked his ears, just as Lucas, too, heard the clatter of hooves on the front drive. "What the bloody hell . . ." No one called on him here; he'd taken pains to discourage visitors from the start. He briefly considered slipping out by the back stairs, but astonishment kept him rooted at his desk. After a few moments, Smithers knocked and entered, with a card on a tray. "Mr. Dauntley, milord," he announced. Lucas blinked at him, and the butler expounded. "Mr. Trenton Dauntley. Nephew and heir to old Lord Dauntley, who has the manor just across the Bentford stream."

"Oh, God. What a bother. I suppose the old man's dead."

Smithers cleared his throat. "I shouldn't think so, milord. Not unless the fashions in mourning-wear have changed considerably."

Lucas grinned a little. "A tulip, Smithers? Do show him up. It is instructive to be informed from time to time of fashion's latest careens."

The creature ushered into the study more than fulfilled Lucas's expectations. He wore a pair of gamboge breeches that might have been painted on, a peacock superfine coat that must have taken three men to ease him into, and a cravat tumbling in intricate cascades down a waistcoat of blue and green patterned silk. His fair hair was cut in some monstrous sequence of terraces that put Lucas strongly in mind of the Hanging Gardens of Babylon.

The young man smiled eagerly. Lucas raised a brow. "Mr. Dauntley. Have we met?"

"No, milord. Beg you forgive the imposition. But I was

riding by, and it occurred to me I might as well stop in and deliver personally my most honored acceptance for the seventeenth."

"The seventeenth." It meant naught to Lucas. "The seventeenth *what?*"

Dauntley laughed with delight. "There, I knew you'd prove a funner! Trayhorne said—you do have the acquaintance of James Trayhorne, I believe—you were a cross old Tartar, but I refused to believe it, having had the pleasure of your mother's company more than once in London, at the theater and such. These past seasons have proved quite desolate without Lady Strathmere to brighten them. We are all so relieved that she is well again."

Lucas inclined his head slightly, gathering from this flood of palaver that his mother had used the pretext of illness to explain her long absence from the ton. Young Dauntley rushed on: "My uncle sends his most regretful excuses, I'm afraid. Gout's got him quite in its grip. I know he'd make the effort if he possibly could."

"Make the effort to . . ."

"The seventeenth, of course."

Lucas cast a quick glance at Smithers, who lifted his brows, as much in the dark as his master. "You must forgive me, Dauntley. We cross old Tartars have such wretched memories. What, precisely, is the seventeenth?"

Perplexed, Dauntley reached—with some trouble—into his breath-constricting coat. "Why, and, I've got the invitation right here." He pulled out a sheet of vellum and gave it to Lucas, who read the engraved message with astonishment:

. . . of Strathmere
. . . Leigh House, Dorset
. . . urday, 17 April, 1813
7 o'clock P.M.
Supper, dancing, cards

Managing to conceal his emotions, Lucas passed the card back. "Ah, yes. The seventeenth. How could I have forgotten?"

"It's all the talk of the county," Dauntley assured him. "After all, it's been some number of years, my uncle tells me, since you've entertained."

"So it has." And so it would continue to be. Whatever Dulcie had up her sleeve—and it had to be her doing—Lucas planned to make a quick end of it. Just the thought of a host of strangers traipsing through the house, rolling back the carpets, satiating their appetites at his table, made him reach for the brandy. "Care for a drink, Dauntley?" he asked with tardy politeness.

"Thanks ever so much, I would. I had a thirsty ride. Got a new hunter at Tattersall's last autumn. Lovely thing. Shoulders laid back like Wellington's. Still breaking her in."

He talked horses for a time while he sipped his brandy. Lucas downed his and poured another, barely listening, trying to discern what scheme was in his mother's mind. His silence eventually made the intended impression on Dauntley, who put his glass aside. "But forgive me, milord. I've taken too much of your valuable time."

Gratitude for this advance notice, however scanty—the seventeenth was less than a month away—compelled Lucas to manage a small smile. "Good of you to stop in, Dauntley."

"Not at all, not at all. I say, if you'd like to have a look at that hunter . . ." Lucas wasn't *that* grateful; he explained he'd just been on his way the rose beds. "I won't impose any longer, then." Dauntley loaded for the door, turned back. "You know, there was one more thing . . ."

Lucas arched a brow. Dauntley re a bit and went on: I ran into a fellow—a close friend mother's—last rday at Mrs. Rose's gaming house the most amazing stories about Lyme Regis. was. All about the time you bested Brummell on the Holloway Road, and took eleven straight hands at White's against old Sheffington . . ." His voice trailed away, squelched by his host's blank stare. Then Dauntley bravely pressed on. "He also let drop a few hints about this Continental cousin of yours. Quite the stunner, by his account. I hope, milord, you'll forgive the impertinence. But as one man of the world to another . . . well, one wants to know the lay of the land, if you get my drift."

"I'm not at all sure I do."

The flush deepened. "I'll be blunt, then. Is there any sort of settlement on her?"

"Oh, yes," Lucas said after a moment. "Quite a hefty one."

Dauntley's furrowed forehead cleared. "Well! Beauty *and* a fortune—a rare combination! Hope you don't mind me speaking so baldly. But, as I said, as one man of the world to—"

"Quite."

With his mission fulfilled, Dauntley at long last was ready to take his departure. Smithers saw him out, then returned to the study to find his master standing just where he'd left him, staring straight ahead. "Milord," he began.

Lucas turned to him. "My God, Smithers. You don't honestly suppose—"

The butler wagged his head. "I am very much afraid, milord, that Her Ladyship intends to make a go of it."

Exactly one week later, the dowager countess arrived in Dorset, accompanied by a train fully twice as long as the last time she'd come. Lucas stood at the window and watched the endless stream of baggage being hauled into the house. He'd had only a glimpse of Tatiana as she alighted from the post chaise, clad in a yellow habit and ribbon-strewn poke bonnet whose price he knew to the penny. He gave his mother ten minutes before summoning Smithers. "Ask Lady Strathmere," he said with admirable restraint, "if she would be so kind as to meet with me immediately." The butler went off with a cheerful air that seemed to imply he knew precisely what this meeting was to be about, and that he heartily approved.

The countess, never one for punctiliousness, kept him waiting an hour. He put the time to good use, rechecking the remarkable string of figures in his account book again.

"Lucas, dear!" His mother's voice was gay as May as she entered, resplendent in a half-dress of pearl-gray Berlin silk and a rich Norwich shawl. "How unlike you to make a stranger of yourself on our arrival! One would scarce know you were in residence here."

"One might assume it," he said darkly, "from the absence of duns on the doorstep."

The countess blinked at him, settling herself by the fire. "I beg your pardon?"

"I refer, Mother, to this." He shoved the account book at her, and she took it as though it were a five-day-old fish.

"Oh, Lucas. You know I have no head for figures."

"You've no head at all, from what I can see! Six hundred pounds at Madame Descoux's, another two hundred at Loch's, a hundred fifty at Hallowby's—"

"You can scarcely expect the girl to come out in leather breeches!"

"You've spent nigh a thousand pounds of my money on that chit's wardrobe!"

"And spent it thoughtfully and well. You are out of touch, dear. If you'd pay the least mind to your own attire, you'd realize prices are not what they were the last time you shopped."

"Never mind my clothes," he growled. "If you think I

intend to allow you to bankrupt me for a load of baubles that will never even see the light of day in London—"

"And what precisely do you mean by that?"

"I mean this whimsied campaign of yours hasn't got the faintest chance of success!"

"You only say that because you've made yourself such a stranger. One would think that after all the havoc you wreaked in that poor child's life, you might make at least *one* trip to visit us in our exile. After all, I only undertook this 'campaign' in response to your desperate plea."

Lucas chose to ignore that. "I've been working," he said shortly. "And a dashed lucky thing I have been, since you clearly intend to run the family fortune to the ground in pursuit of this bacon-brained scheme."

Dulcie straightened her slim shoulders. "I may not have a head for figures, Lucas, but I am not a babe. Your father always kept me well advised of the estate's affairs. You could readily absorb a thousand pounds a *month* without making a dent in the Strathmere principal."

That this was true only served to infuriate her son. "Is that what she figures to cost me?"

"Not at all. The bulk of her wardrobe is already in place. There are only a few minor items—shoes, half-boots, reticules, gloves, stockings—that remain on my list. I thought to allow her to choose them herself once we rejoin civilization. So far she has shown a most uncanny sense of fashion. And it might give her pleasure—something her life has had very little of so far."

This play on Lucas's sympathies was, alas, misguided. "Oh, I do beg pardon, Mother. I'd forgotten your set's guiding light is pleasure."

"There is nothing illicit in enjoying one's self. *You*, I recall, were not averse to it once."

"Aye. And see where it got me."

Lady Strathmere stood abruptly, shaking out her skirts.

"Where it has got you, apparently, is where you're content to play the skinflint to no purpose and wallow in self-pity. If that Innisford creature could see you now, she'd laugh herself to death—an outcome, by the by, devoutly to be wished! And as for my 'bacon-brained scheme,' if you wish to observe its progress, you might join us at supper, rather than secreting yourself here while I attempt to repair the damage that *you* wreaked!" Dulcie swept grandly toward the doorway. "A Strathmere earl, quibbling over a few dresses!" She put her elegant nose in the air and departed the room.

Lucas looked to Bellerophon, who'd observed the encounter from his place on the hearth rug through barely open eyes. "Hmph! Might have known you'd take the chit's part. She's had you wound around her finger since the day she got here. But I've news for you. Even if by some miracle she makes it to London, you won't be going along." At that, the mastiff sat up with alarm in his velvet eyes. "That's right, m'boy. You and I will be staying right here." Bellerophon bounded for the door and let out an imploring howl. Lucas opened it, scowling foully. "Go on, then. Go to her, you Judas." Cropped tail wagging, the dog bounded off toward the west wing.

Lucas poured himself more brandy. He could not deny a rising curiosity as to what his mother and the girl had been doing closeted in the Cotswolds for all these months. He thought again of her wrestling with the mastiffs in her leather breeches, hair wild with wind. Could his mother actually have subdued her? Common sense revolted at the mere possibility.

Still . . . "Time I got a glimpse of what a thousand pounds has bought me," he told Bellerophon—then remembered that the dog had absconded. Clearly, matters were so far out of hand as to require the firm imposition of reality. Dulcie might be persuaded there was hope for the chit. Lucas, though, was sure there was not.

The notion of pricking the bubble of his mother's fancy was decidedly appealing. He rang for Smithers and informed him, "I'll be joining the ladies at dinner tonight."

The butler, clearly fearing the imminent loss of all reason in Somerleigh House, nodded in resignation. "As you wish, milord."

Five

$\mathcal{A}$ QUARTER HOUR AFTER eight, Lucas was still struggling to master an Osbaldeston in his neckcloth—a feat that once was second nature to him. Now, however, the folds eluded his fingers despite his best efforts. Might almost think I were the one on trial, he brooded, and with an angry yank on the linen he created an acceptable, if unanticipated, result. He took the stairs at an even pace, found the salon deserted, and deduced from the soft sounds of chinking porcelain that the countess and her improbable ward had preceded him into the dining room.

Dulcie glanced up from her soup plate as he entered. "Darling! We'd quite given up on you. What a very interesting thing you've done with your cravat."

So that was how it was going to be. "Forgive me, Mother, and Miss . . ." Lord! What the devil was he to call her?

"It was *your* job," Dulcie said, faintly accusing, "to come up with an identity."

"So it was." For the first time, he contemplated the girl who was perched on the edge of her chair. She was dressed in a gown of some shimmery emerald stuff, cut low and gathered across the bodice, with braided sleeves and an ornament of artificial cherries at the cleft of her—Christ. Lucas didn't remember her bosom being so lush and full, nor her waist so slim. Her green eyes were downcast; her cheekbones were a sweep of winter-white flushed with rose, long lashes laid against them. Painted, he realized, and with a flash of wicked inspiration proposed, "Well, then. Miss Grimaldi, shall we say?"

"I think not," the countess said sharply. "And I must add, I find your humor *de trop*."

The girl stirred her soup with a wrist, Lucas could not help noting, far more pale and delicate than he'd recalled. "I don't see why, milady," she told Dulcie in a low, silken voice that held only the barest accent. "Besides the current famed master of the pantomime stage, there is a prior claimant to that name who was of great distinction. I refer, of course, to the fresco painter who adorned the Louvre for Cardinal Mazarin. You have been to Rome no doubt, milord. Perhaps you had the opportunity to view his landscapes in the Colonna Gallery?"

Lucas forced his open jaw shut. His mother sat for a moment in stunned silence, then burst out laughing. "Touché, my dear! Grimaldi it shall be. Do eat, Lucas, before your soup grows cold."

Lucas, still thunderstruck, took his place. Tatiana delicately set her spoon against her plate at precisely the correct angle and sat back a few inches in her chair. Her thick blond hair was taken up in a weighty chignon at the nape of her long, swanlike neck, and little downy wisps had escaped the pins just at the hollows of her throat.

His mother, following his gaze, smiled a little. "What think you, Lucas, of my Turner's handiwork with regard to Miss Grimaldi?"

Lucas rallied himself. Really, it would not do to let the baggage think one lucky facer was enough to gain passage into high society. "Frankly, I'd not have recognized her."

"Milord is too kind," the girl said in that satin-smooth voice, and folded her hands in her lap just as properly as the formidable Lady Jersey herself might have done. "Lady Strathmere, this soup is remarkably good."

"Thank you, my dear. Cook always does well by sorrel. How do you find it, Lucas?"

He took a belated sip. "Very tasty. Very tasty indeed." Christ, he sounded as stuffy as the cross old Tartar Dauntley had called him. He'd been taken by surprise, that was all. Hadn't expected the chit to have got half so far. But there would be weak points, vulnerable spots; he only had to pinpoint them. He finished his soup, then gathered his wits as the servants cleared away.

"I read in the *Gazette*, Mother, that all the town talk is again of the Corn Laws. Have you an opinion on the controversy, Miss Grimaldi?"

Lucas thought he saw a glimmer of apprehension in Dulcie's blue gaze. He hid a grin of satisfaction. Politics, eh? One might expect such a sticky wicket as the export of grain to be beyond the girl's grasp. She took a breath—making, he noted, the bunch of cherries on her bodice rise and fall most becomingly—and then said softly, "I am certain the Parliament will do what most behooves the nation. But it is a hard thing to me, it seems, that while they ponder their course the poor should go lacking bread."

Dulcie, who had taken some time to explain the Corn Law controversy to her charge, only to be dismayed by Tatiana's fury at the notion that peasants were starving while the battle between Whig and Tory played itself out, contented her relieved soul by saying only, "Oh, hear, hear! You would not argue, Lucas, surely, with such a summation."

He shook his head, his wintry eyes narrowed. "Indeed, Mother, I don't see how anyone could. Miss Grimaldi, may I offer you a slice of this joint?"

Her green gaze flickered questioningly toward the countess, who grimaced. "Quite right, Tatiana. Of course he *ought* to have offered first to me. But I've found it best when in the presence of those whose manners are not top-notch not to call attention to the fact."

"I was not aware," Lucas said between set teeth, "that we were so wont to stand on ceremony in this house."

The countess shrugged. "You may do as you please. But Tatiana will do what is correct."

Irked by his own lapse, however minor, Lucas broached the widest possible array of conversational gambits over the next two courses: music; literature; the Royals; even, in desperation, horse racing. Miss Grimaldi was, to his perturbation, utterly unflappable. If there was a hole in his mother's education of her, he could not discern it. Even more alarming, her manners at table were unexceptionable. Straight through a menu that included green goose, stuffed pigeon, orange soufflé, crab in a béchamel sauce, Celerata cream, leeks braised in butter, pomegranate jelly, and assorted pastries, she handled the complicated sequences of table- and glassware without a single faux pas. By the time Smithers brought the cheese 'round, Lucas was in a funk.

Beginner's luck, he thought darkly, glowering at her as she nibbled a ratafia biscuit. Even the no-names brought to run at Oaks and the derbies occasionally took a prize. But only thoroughbreds had the stamina to last through the season. Indeed, he already detected signs of fatigue in this filly. The English consonants that had tripped off her tongue so readily an hour and a half before were beginning

to fade back toward Russian. A typical evening in town—
the theater, late supper, then a rout or ball—would have put
a hasty end to her charade.

He wondered whether Dulcie had noted the same signs,
for when Smithers brought in coffee she said lightly, "Alas,
a liking for the fragrant bean is the sole nicety that remains
beyond Miss Grimaldi's grasp. Smithers, see that tea is
brought to her rooms. Tatiana, my pet, I have some business
to discuss with Lucas that I greatly fear you'll find a crashing
bore."

The girl rose from her place with a shy, grateful smile.
"Thank you, milady." She dropped a curtsy to Lucas that
caught him rising, tardily, from his chair. "And thank you,
milord, for your company this evening, and for my new
name. I shall endeavor to live up to it."

He bowed from the waist, searching her eyes, made more
brilliant by the brilliant green gown. They had not been
affected by her evident fatigue; their expression was as un-
fathomable as ever. "I have no doubt you will, Miss Grimaldi." Then he watched as she left them, the light from
the chandeliers shifting and shimmering over her gleaming
blond hair.

He let his gaze linger longer than he'd meant to, and his
mother chuckled, stirring cream into her coffee. "Quite
fetching, isn't she, once out of leather?"

Lucas laughed too, though not particularly nicely. "Dress
any Cyprian in a thousand pounds' worth of silks and I
daresay she'd present herself as well."

Lady Strathmere stiffened. "That remark is unworthy of
you, Lucas, after all her hard work. Nearly as unworthy as
giving her the name of a stage clown."

"She did not seem to take offense," he said thoughtfully.

"That is because her manners, however recently acquired, are far finer than yours. I tell you, I would not quib-
ble to present her to the Regent himself!"

Lucas shrugged. "Well, we all know the sort of feminine company he enjoys."

Dulcie slapped her napkin onto the table. " 'Fess it, Lucas! You were astonished. And you are only being so disagreeable because it irks you no end to have been proved wrong! Did you remark anything at all in her comportment that seemed amiss?"

"No," he acknowledged. "Not until the end there, when she nearly 'danked' me." He took a long draught of claret, then eyed his mother above the goblet's rim. "Have you ever stopped to consider that this game you are playing with her is not in very good taste?"

She stared, taken aback. "I've not the slightest notion what you mean!"

"Let us say, for argument's sake, that your efforts succeed beyond your wildest expectations. That you take her to London or Brighton. That she makes a sensation. And that the love-struck son of one of your boon companions—Lady Sefton, say, or another of the Almack's tigresses—makes an offer for her. What do you propose to do then?"

"Why, I should give them my blessing!"

"Really, Mother? You would knowingly condemn one of the pinks of the ton to marriage with a nameless chit from Mizhakovsk?"

Lady Strathmere faltered, albeit slightly. "Of course I should! That is to say . . . if they were truly in love . . . and you've already agreed that you will give her a portion. So long as there's a decent dowry, there's really no deception."

"No?" he demanded. "I distinctly recall a time not so very long ago when I wished to offer for a girl whose family, upon investigation by you and Father, was found at least to be a known quantity, though it might have borne the whiff—heaven forfend—of trade."

Dulcie took a deep breath. "I really fail to see any connection whatsoever between—"

"Don't you?" His voice was dangerously tight.

"No, I don't!" the countess declared roundly. "Because Tatiana, whatever her provenance, has proven herself to be bright, and good-natured, and kind, and possessed of an extremely discriminating taste. None of which could possibly be said for that vulgar, brass-faced—" Lucas shoved back his chair. Dulcie lunged for his hand. "Oh, darling, if you could only *see* her now! Surrounded always by the worst sorts of here-and-thereians, and all her coarse tendencies given full play by having old Innisford's millions at her disposal!"

"You are speaking," Lucas said through his teeth, "of the woman I love."

"You haven't even laid eyes on her in twelve whole years!"

"And shall love," he added implacably, "until I die."

The countess shook her head sadly. "You are such a fool. She's been a free woman for all this time. If she had feelings for you, don't you think she'd have shown them?"

He'd long since yanked his hand away. "I made that rather difficult for her when I murdered her husband. As for Miss Grimaldi, I've no doubt you'll manage to assuage your conscience over the fate of whatever pliant swain you palm her off on. Neither you nor Father ever showed the least compunction at ruining *my* life."

"Just one minute," the countess said brusquely. "I'm not finished with you yet." Despite his rage, he waited, checking his impulse to slam the door in her face. "I feel I ought to apprise you of plans I've made to hold a small dinner party here in a week or so. Since you've become such a curmudgeon about budgeting, it seems prudent to ask your permission."

Blessing Trenton Dauntley's timely visit, Lucas simply shrugged. "Do as you like."

Dulcie, prepared for further battle, was taken aback. "You haven't any objections?"

"None whatsoever. Particularly since I don't mean to attend." He stomped toward the door. On the threshold he paused, glaring back. "A party. She'll have to play cards."

"I am pleased to report that Miss Grimaldi is a wizard at cards. Interestingly, she was already familiar with a number of the current rages, though in somewhat altered forms. Makes one ponder, does it not, the universality of mankind's attempts at amusement?" Having nothing to say to that, Lucas turned away again. His mother's voice arrested him. "There is one thing more. There will also be dancing. I shall engage the Lambert boys, I think. Lady Trayhorne assures me they do very well. Not a whit countrified."

"Bully for them. Now, if you will excuse me—"

"But, Lucas, I've not taught her to dance. This knee of mine . . . you recall I wrote you that I wrenched it rather famously at Lady Villiers' three springs past."

It might well have been true. Lucas scarcely scanned her letters, full as they were of gossip and the weather and her blasted spaniels. "Engage a dancing master," he said indifferently.

"I looked into that. And I must say, the wages any decent ones command are quite outré. That Gascon everyone speaks of so highly asks five guineas a lesson! And even more, of course, if one is required to import him from Brighton."

He shrugged again. "Find someone local."

"But that's the knot of it, Lucas. I don't see how I can. Granted, a Continental cousin might be expected not to know the current dances to a T. But no relation of ours could possibly be so in the woods as not to reckon a quadrille from a polonaise."

Lucas could hardly credit he was engaged in this conversation. "You must do as you think best," he told the countess, hastening to make his exit.

"I think it best, darling, that she be tutored by you." He whirled on her, black brows forming an incredulous arc. "All things considered—the expense particularly—don't you agree?"

"I think it is the height of asininity for you to suggest it," he said, scowling. "Surely there is some presentable soul here in Dorset. What about James Trayhorne? He's staying with his mother, and you've bent my ear often enough about what a Corinthian he is."

"Which is precisely why I cannot present a leaden-footed country lass to him to educate! Tatiana would instantly lose all possibility of future distinction!"

"I haven't danced in years," Lucas pointed out.

"But you won't deny you were once accounted the finest-turned shin in England."

If the countess hadn't already played the wrenched-knee card, he would have been tempted to. The realization put him even more out of sorts. Dulcie's tone softened. "Is it really so very much that I ask of you?"

It wasn't, of course. True, he could insist that Dulcie engage a dancing master. But who knew when such a desirable—not to mention expensive—sort might be free to heel it all the way to Dorset? Delay only meant a prolongation of his mother's—and Miss Grimaldi's—stay at Somerleigh House, a prospect he was increasingly convinced would lead to liver damage, if not full-fledged gout. He faced his mother resolutely. "Very well. If you think it so necessary as that."

"And would it be too great an imposition to ask that we begin this evening? Granted, Tatiana has cleared every hurdle I have set for her. But this . . ."

Lucas, confronted with that image of the girl in shirt-sleeves, wrestling the mastiffs, barked a laugh. "Oh, I understand." Perhaps, he thought with satisfaction, this would prove the weak point he'd been searching for, that would persuade the countess to abandon her ridiculous machinations. He brightened, relishing the prospect. "As you wish, Mother dearest."

Dulcie glanced at him askant, but then rang for Smithers. "Please inform Miss Grimaldi that her dancing lessons will begin in three-quarters of an hour in the drawing room."

Six

FORTIFIED IN BLESSED seclusion by several brandies and a Cuban cigar, Lucas bowed as he rejoined the countess, who was running her hands over the keys of the elderly spinet in a corner of the room. "Evening, Mother. And where is our tender Terpsichore?"

She shot him a withering look, then winced as she feathered a trill. "This instrument is appallingly out of tune. I have been meaning to speak to you, Lucas, about the help. That silly Junkins overturned a sauceboat in Miss Grimaldi's lap at tea today."

Lucas tsked in sympathy. "And what was Miss Grimaldi's reaction to this disaster?"

"She held herself with perfect aplomb. Did you expect her to scold and demand Junkins's immediate dismissal?"

"It would have made an opportunity," Lucas said with

frank humor. "None of my servants seems to hold our houseguest in much esteem."

"Why should they, when they follow their master's example?" Dulcie demanded sharply. "Those who were with me in the Cotswolds do not, I am pleased to say, share the native opinion. My Turner is quite taken with the girl. And I do not flatter myself that *she* is too easy to please."

"Oh, no, your Turner is a veritable dragon," Lucas agreed, and when the countess glared at him, grinned. "What? All I did was acquiesce."

"There are ways and ways of doing things," Lady Strathmere said darkly. The cloud vanished from her brow as Tatiana appeared in the doorway. "Do come in, my child! How ravishing you look!"

Lucas, turning to see the girl standing uncertainly on the threshold, was forced to conclude that the description was apt. The filmy green gown floated around her like a wind-raised sea; her gloves were sea-foam, ecru lace, their length emphasizing the delicate curves of her arms. The cherries at her bosom were gone; instead, his mother's amethysts dangled from her ears and at her throat, catching the candlelight and throwing it back against her shining hair. Amethysts were Russian stones, he recalled vaguely. Little wonder they suited her so well. "Ravishing indeed," he said, bowing, and was gratified to see her evident uneasiness increase.

"Milady," she said in a small voice, "I think I have the headache." She shifted in her kid shoes. "I beg that you excuse me for this evening."

Lady Strathmere turned resolutely toward the spinet. "That won't do, Tatiana. Lord Strathmere has been kind enough to take time from his busy schedule for this purpose."

"Yes, I know of this, but—"

"We've already kept him waiting. Come, come, my girl! I myself find dancing most soothing to the constitution."

Still Tatiana hesitated, her bosom rising and falling against the emerald silk. Lucas, encouraged by her obvious reluctance, held out his hand. "I daresay you won't credit it by what you've seen, Miss Grimaldi, but the chance to take a turn with me was once held in much esteem."

She ignored the hand. "Of that I have no doubt. Milady has regaled me with countless tales of your . . . expertise."

The way she paused to search for the word might have been put down to her unfamiliarity with English. But Lucas, observing the very slight sneer that curled her full upper lip, was not at all sure. Hackles rising, he said gaily, "What do we start with, Mother?"

"Something simple. The polonaise, in slow four-four."

He nodded, crossing the floor to Tatiana, sketching out the steps for her on the bright parquet. She was staring at his boots, spots of color high in her cheeks. So that blush was natural. Lucas found he was enjoying himself immensely. Again he offered his arm. "Shall we?"

"I think," said Tatiana, "I must use my hands to raise my skirts, so that I can see."

He shrugged as she gracefully did so. "If you like. Begin anew, Mother!" He listened as she did, on the sadly dissonant spinet. To his chagrin, Tatiana stayed with him perfectly. "Miss Grimaldi," he accused with a forced laugh, "you have been practicing on the sly!"

She shook her head. "No. But it is not so unlike a dance we do in—where I come from."

"Fancy that," said Lady Strathmere, intrigued. "Just like the card games. Oh, it is verily as the Preacher says, isn't it? There *is* nothing new under the sun."

"We'd best try it again, just to be sure you have it," Lucas said genially, though inwardly he was beginning to seethe. Was there nothing at which this baggage didn't excel?

Not, it seemed, in the field of dancing. They ran through the whole list of popular hops, from the bolero to the volta, with Tatiana needing scarcely more than three or four exposures to each to prove herself adept. She continued to hold up her skirts, keeping her eyes fixed on Lucas's feet—and he, gamely squiring at her side, could not help wondering what, if not a fear of failure, might have occasioned her attempt to cry off lessons with him.

He had his answer soon enough. "Well! There's nothing left but the waltz," Lady Strathmere decreed, glowing more than the dancers at this proof of her charge's fitness for society.

Lucas, torn between vexation and intrigue, held up a hand. "Some refreshment first. I've a powerful thirst. Miss Grimaldi, some lemonade?"

"If you will excuse it, I should rather have this over with."

He looked at her askance, but she had her head down, daintily tracing out the steps to the cotillion. "Mother?"

The countess, too, was contemplating Tatiana. "Such a long evening it has been for you, pet. I do think something cooling to drink—"

"No, thank you. I wish nothing."

"Well, I'll have a claret," said Lucas, heading for the sideboard. "Sherry, Mother?" She nodded, and he took it to her, then tossed back his wine.

"You'll find the waltz a tad different from the other dances," the countess was telling Tatiana. "Rather newfangled, and I must admit the first time I saw it, I was quite taken aback. But Mr. Brummell gave it his approval, and so it seems must we all! It is in three-four time." She rattled off a few bars of "Ach du lieber" as an example. "So, Lucas. Will you take her in arm?"

He set down his glass, approached, and grasped Tatiana's gloved hand in one of his, setting the other on her waist.

She went worse than rigid at his touch. Her back arched; her teeth bared; the pulse at her temples stood out in stark blue lines. Lucas, looking down at her, glimpsed what had so far escaped him in the depths of her exquisite green eyes: a hatred for him so intense it was palpable. He released her abruptly, standing back a pace.

His mother glanced at him. "Did you lose the beat? It's this abominable instrument."

But Lucas's confoundment had naught to owe the spinet. Tatiana, freed of his hands, rearranged her lovely features in a neutral expression, eyes once again downcast. Only the heave of that shapely bosom gave any evidence of the storm of loathing he'd just witnessed.

He felt breathless. Like any other man, he'd been disliked on occasion—even, one might say, abhorred, particularly by the dandies who long ago envied his title and fortune. He'd fought several duels, two with outraged husbands. Yet even on their faces he had never beheld such hostility. You curious minx, he thought, why should I so repel you? He considered ending the lesson; then interest took the upper hand. What might happen if he took her in his arms again?

"Beg pardon, Mother," he said smoothly. "My tails were disarranged. Give us the start once more. One, two, three. One, two, three." Tatiana raised her gaze to him at last. Was her remarkable will enough to conquer such hatred? Apparently so. The emerald eyes were smoldering, but she let him lay his hands on her. Lucas could not resist. "The prospect of a grand duke must be powerfully alluring to you," he murmured, his voice masked by the music.

"On the contrary, milord," she replied, the undercurrent of Russian very thick indeed. "It is the prospect of being free of you that makes me work so hard."

"Then I must endeavor to match your efforts with my

own," he said, and whirled her off so suddenly that she gasped.

She followed him. He had to grant her that. Even in her evident discomfiture, even though her teeth were gritted, she did not miss a beat as he swung her about at a dizzying pace. Lady Strathmere, glancing over her shoulder, obligingly quickened her playing to match his expert display. Lucas had never in his life had such a partner. She was stiff in his arms to the point of rigor mortis, yet she never faltered. His mother, watching with some alarm, cried out, "Lucas, do take heed! Mind the board; mind that chair!"

But Lucas, as perturbed by this peculiar creature's grace as he'd been by her display of rancor, only clasped Tatiana tighter, as though he could break her self-control by the force of his fingers. There had arisen in his loins a heat he'd never thought to experience again; the small, inflexible figure clutching his coat somehow had awakened all the rapacity of his flagrant youth. And yet no chit of the ton had ever flouted him this way. *Yield.* His heart pounded against hers as he spun her over the floor. *Yield to me, by damn!*

The music broke off abruptly. "Lucas," his mother chided, "you must let her breathe!"

He released her so suddenly that she stumbled, and had to clutch at the wall. "Lucas!" Dulcie cried. "I'm in horror at your manners! Has he hurt you, pet?" Tatiana shook her head mutely, steadying herself, reaching for a strap of her sandal that had worked itself free.

Lucas was in horror, too—at the sudden bulge in the front of his breeches, at the dizzying rate of his heartbeat, but even more at the repugnant longings that had crowded in on him as they danced. *And shall love until I die*, he'd sworn to his mother regarding Gillian. Now here he was, reduced to boyish quivers by this chit's pretty bosom, the invincible disdain in her jewel-bright eyes.

He made a bow, curt and formal. "Miss Grimaldi. Do

accept my apologies. You've learned all I have to teach you. For the rest, you must rely on the many partners you will certainly attract. I bid you good evening. And to you as well, Mother." Then he stalked past them and through the doors.

Seven

THE SEVENTEENTH OF April dawned overcast and glowering, a perfect match for Lucas's mood. He'd spent much of the past few weeks brooding over that strange waltz with Miss Grimaldi, and had come to the conclusion that his lamentable lapse in self-control was natural enough. It had been years, literally, since he had held a woman. The body had its own needs, which he had over the past decade—with the exception of a few flirtations in Russia that were really in the line of duty—held in check quite admirably. It was beneath him to have behaved as he had, but altogether understandable. Contemplating the grim, gray sky, he began to wonder whether it might not be wise to procure an amiable bit o' muslin. Not a true mistress, God forbid, but some petticoat in one of the outlying towns, someone he might visit when he felt the urge but who would not make demands—or conversation, which would be even worse.

As disgusted by his thoughts as by the lowering weather, he rang for breakfast and spent the rest of the morning resolutely going over the accounts. When, toward noon, he once again glanced at the window, he was appalled to see it had begun to snow. He ran for the rose beds and found his leather gloves—though no sign of Timkins—in the gardening shed. Cursing the sky no less than the errant gardener, he hurried through the gate, intent on thoughts of smudge pots and quilting and mounding dirt against the threatening flakes.

As he cleared the trellises he was brought up short by the sight of Timkins, sweating despite the cold, heaving an armload of heavy iron pots out of the wheelbarrow. "Let me help you with those!" Lucas cried, regretting his doubts regarding Timkins's sense of duty.

"Got help, don't I?" the former sailor grunted, hoisting the pots to the ground. "Aye, there's some will keep an eye on the weather, ain't there, even when there's others take no notice o' the plain signs o' inclemency!" Lucas suffered the rebuke willingly, especially since he saw that nearly all the Gallicas, the centifolias, and the damasks were already swathed in bunting.

"You *have* been hard at it, haven't you, Timkins? Forgive me. I had other matters—" He broke off in his survey of the beds, realizing they were alone. "But who is your helper?"

"Timkins!" a voice called just then. Lucas turned toward the arbor and saw a huge bundle of linen staggering across the frozen ground, subordinated by a pair of buck breeches and, incongruously, lavender kid boots. "This is all I dared take, with the countess expecting houseguests this evening." The bundle dropped in a heap, revealing the exquisite face of Miss Grimaldi, arranged in a devastating, impish grin. That died, however, the instant she glimpsed Lucas. Their eyes met for a space, neither moving.

Then Timkins said sharply, "Best get a move to it, Yer Lordship, if ye want 'em covered."

Lucas roused himself. "Of course. Forgive me, Miss Grimaldi. It seems my absentmindedness has occasioned your being impressed into heavy labor." He moved toward the bundled bedclothes, and Tatiana took a sudden step back. "Good God." Lucas stared at the embroidered sheets and coverlets. "You've fetched the heirlooms out."

That clear green gaze considered him coolly. "Have I? I merely chose what seemed most unused and thus most likely unmissed."

"Aye, unless the Regent plans to make an attendance."

"Does he?" Miss Grimaldi inquired, suddenly looking nervous.

"I wouldn't put it past Mother. Timkins, what's become of those two hundred yards of bast I ordered from Antwerp?"

The snow was falling heavily now, coating the bare brown earth. "Corn Laws," the gardener said succinctly.

Lucas raised a brow. "I fail to apprehend how the embargo on grain—"

"She'll explain it to ye," Timkins said, savagely thrusting the tripod of a pot hold deep into the ground.

"Balance of trade," Miss Grimaldi said brightly. "The Emperor is determined that unless England loosens its restrictions on imports there'll be no further commerce—"

"I *meant* she would explain it later," Timkins growled. "Spread them sheets, m'lord, or find me somewhat else to use instead."

Torn between amusement and horror, Lucas dutifully reached for the edge of an antique damascene cloth bespangled with his family's arms and initials. "I suppose they might as well serve for something. It's been a good two decades since royalty graced us here."

"Cow's dung and sour milk will bleach them fair again, even if they should stain," Miss Grimaldi assured him.

He stared at her. "Did my mother teach you *that*?"

Her full red mouth curved a little. "No. I learned it at home . . . from my Spanish nurse."

Timkins frankly guffawed. Lucas shot him a warning glance. The acquiesence of the Somerleigh servants was, of course, essential to the success of his mother's plan. Clearly the gardener hadn't been informed of that, and Lucas resolved to have a word with the sailor as soon as Miss Grimaldi left them—something she seemed quite eager to do.

Miss Grimaldi shook out a sheet and moved toward the beds. "Not that one!" Lucas said suddenly, seeing her about to lay the covering over Gillian's namesake. She drew back, astonished by his vehement tone, and Lucas hurried to take the linen from her. "I only mean . . . I've a particular fancy for that bush. I'd rather tend it myself."

"Tendin' 'em all perfectly well, she's been, while ye were about yer business," Timkins muttered darkly.

"And I am grateful for her help," Lucas said very firmly. "But I'll see to that bush."

She made way for him as he tucked the linen lovingly over Lady Innisford's thorny branches. "That would be the yellowy-orange one—bronze, really," she mused, considering the bush. "Altogether too flashy for my taste. I much prefer the pinks and whites." Timkins made a noise in his throat. "But I see my services are unneeded. Thank you, Timkins. I enjoyed being of assistance." She turned on her heel and left them, striding back through the arbor in her skin breeches and dainty boots, her pale braid slashing the air.

As soon as she'd gone, Lucas approached the gardener. "Timkins, I should have spoken to you before. Despite the circumstances of Miss Grimaldi's arrival, you should know my mother has taken her under her wing. She intends to present her to society." He gave a deprecating laugh.

Timkins stared back at him, stone-faced. "I don't know what else Lady Strathmere would have done with her, m'lord. She's quality through 'n' through, ain't she? Any cove can see that."

Lucas was glad the dark of the storm hid his sudden flush. "Well! That's good," he said with false heartiness. "Any casualties so far?"

"Lost a branch on that 'un." Timkins, lighting the smudge pots, nodded toward the Princesse d'Orleans, a rather spindly China.

"Such a delicate wench. I'll move her inward in the autumn." Carefully Lucas pegged the cover down over Lady Innisford. "Thank you again, Timkins, for your vigilance."

"My job, ain't it?" the sailor said with a shrug. "Be a rum thing, though, if this lot turns to ice. Ice—that's the worst enemy there be."

"Worse than Bonaparte?" Lucas asked, bemused.

"Worse for roses," the gardener said stoutly. "Say what ye will o' the Frogs; they know their roses. Look at that garden the Empress Josephine made at Malmaison. Nothin' but roses."

"Ah, but the Emperor has cast her off, hasn't he?" Lucas ran his gloved hand tenderly over Lady Innisford's shroud. "Difficult to believe, is it not, Timkins, that an ardor so fierce as his for her could change?"

"There's no accountin' for the whims o' the lofty, m'lord." Then, not perceiving the affront in his train of thought, he added, "I thought ye was plannin' on headin' out to Kenton for a look at that hunter this mornin'."

"So I was." Lucas scanned the white-clad garden. "But I have it on a whim to stay. Give me that broom, will you, Timkins, and go and fetch more charcoal. Those pots could glow a bit more hotly, I think."

* * *

At five that afternoon, the first carriage rolled into the yards at Somerleigh. Tatiana, clad in a resplendent gown of white peau de soie, the countess's own matchless Orient pearls clasped at her throat with emeralds, leaned on the sill as Turner brushed out the shimmering curtain of her hair. "Here they come!" the abigail said cheerily, pulling at a tangle. "Are you ready?"

Tatiana nodded, then winced as Turner took the iron from the fire. "I thought we had agreed there is no sense in that."

"Thought I'd have one last try at it. Seeing as all the other ladies will be in curls." Biting her lip in concentration, Turner selected a long blond strand, wound it deftly around the iron, held it there for a moment, and then slid it off. The tress fell without so much as a ripple. "Devil take it," the maid muttered angrily. "Whoever heard of hair that won't curl?"

"I told you there was no sense—"

"All right, all right. I'll pin it up, then. How do you want it?"

Tatiana, watching as a knot of fur-swathed figures emerged from the carriage, shrugged. "Whatever you think best."

"I'll do twin coronets, then, over your ears. Do come back to the dressing table." Tatiana followed meekly, and sat like a stone while Turner fussed with the nets and pins. "Nervous?" the maid asked. Tatiana shrugged. "Faith, you'll do fine. The countess wouldn't risk her own reputation—what with her passing you off as her cousin—if she wasn't sure of you."

"I suppose not."

Turner hesitated, her mouth filled with pins. Then she reached up to remove them. "Listen here, miss. I've seen a lot of young ladies in my time with the countess—seen those that catch the ton's fancy and those that don't. And there's one thing I'd say to you, even if it's not my place."

"I'd be grateful for your advice," Tatiana murmured.

"Well, then, here it is: Don't be so all-fired sweet and retiring. You want to scratch out a name for yourself, not get lost in the crowd. Do you see what I mean?"

"I would hate to do anything to attract undue attention, Turner."

"I'm not saying you should act improper! I'm just saying . . . well, pretty faces are common as dust every season. Personality—that's what makes a girl shine."

Tatiana met her earnest gaze in the pier glass. "I shall keep what you've said in mind."

"There, now, that's what I mean! You've got it all down pat now, the talk, the walk, the forks and knives—but where's the spark, eh? That's what I'd like to know." Tatiana lowered her eyes with another faint shrug. Turner sighed and set to work with the pins, then stood back to examine the results. "I've done all I can," she said darkly. "The rest is up to you."

"Thank you kindly, Turner, for your hard work. And for your advice."

"Well, I'd hate to see the countess's expectations crushed just on account of your lack of spirit." Tatiana said nothing more, so the maid sighed and left.

Tatiana sat very still while her footsteps faded in the distance. Then she hurled the hairbrush all the way across the room, making Bellerophon, who'd been dozing on the rug, bark halfheartedly. "Sorry, *lyubov*," she murmured, and returned to the window to observe the arrival of another coach. So this was the night. Everything had been leading up to this from the moment she'd first met Lucas Strathmere in the snow at Mizhakovsk, when her sledge stave had, most regrettably, missed bashing in his head. Bastard, she thought, her lip curling. It was a word she'd learned from Costner, one of the first words she'd mastered in this crude, stupid tongue, and she liked the sound of it. *Bastard*. It was what she'd called Lucas Strathmere in her mind long before she'd any notion what it meant—and what she called him there still.

She blessed whatever blind, unknowing instinct had urged her not to run from him on their weary journey from her country, the good sense that had counseled her to bide her time, acquiesce to all he told her to do. That had gained her entry here, to his house. From that it had only been a matter of cunning—the intractability with Mrs. Smithers, the refusal to speak or bathe, the unacceptable temporary alliance with Costner—all meant to force him into doing *something* that would give her an opening, an edge.

In her wildest hopes, she'd never reached this high.

Fingers curled over the emerald clasp at her throat, Tatiana unwillingly felt a pang of conscience at the thought of the countess. She seemed a good enough sort, for a foreigner; she'd treated Tatiana well. But the *son*—oh, for the man who'd killed Pietr, who'd been the instrument of destruction for her entire village, no fate was evil enough.

Even after all this time, thinking of Pietr still brought a sob to her throat. By now, she thought with restless regret, they would have been long married. She would have given him the son he wanted so badly . . . and she would have spent this winter with his body against hers, warm within their bed.

Oh, he'd been strong, handsome! His arms had held her on the banks of the river; his whispered words had been as sweet as honey, and his kisses sweeter still—

Enough! she told herself savagely, with the strength of will that had stood her against her foster father's beatings, against the endless snows of the Russian plains, against the

fear she'd always harbored that life would never mean anything more than what Mizhakovsk had to offer: the ekeing
out of an existence, the numbing repetition of chores, the
grim scramble for daily bread. Lucas Strathmere had taken
her away from all that—but at the cost of Pietr.

It was a presumption on his part for which she meant
him to pay dear.

She was not the sort to be led astray by fancy food and
fine wine and silk gowns. She knew what was important.
Revenge. Revenge against Lucas Strathmere.

She turned back to the glass, contemplating the demure
white gown, the high white gloves, her hair bound up in
Turner's tortured coronets. By Christ, I have had enough
white to stand me for a lifetime! she thought bitterly, as the
falling snow mounded up on the windowpanes. What if this
was the outfit the countess had chosen for her presentation?
Hadn't Turner just urged her to give way to her spirit? She
gave the pier glass a shove that sent it spinning in mad
circles, then rose and went to her wardrobe, eyeing the rows
of costly garments there. She ran them through her hands,
the precious velvets and damasks and silks, considering
each, rejecting them, the storm in her soul needing some
outward display they were lacking. In the very back she
found a gown all in black: an overskirt of sheer black mousseline atop black watered silk. She let her pale fingers rest
against the bodice. Black. A widow's weeds.

I'll wear this for you tonight, Pietr, she vowed, and unfastened the ribbons of the fluttering white peau de soie with
steady hands.

A brief time later she stood before the glass again, nodding in satisfaction. The gown was cut tight and low at the
bodice; against the resultant expanse of her white bosom,
the high, poufed sleeves made as dramatic a midnight slash
as the opposing squares of a chessboard. But the pearls—the
pearls were not the thing. She rummaged in her jewel box,

found the countess's silver-and-amethyst set, and fastened the necklace at her throat and the drops at her ears.

Almost . . . but not quite. The trouble was her hair, which over these past months had driven Turner to despair. *All the other ladies will be in curls* . . . And the devil take them, too, Tatiana thought bitterly. Pietr had loved her hair, had always been after her to unloosen her braids so he could let his hands play in that thick curtain of white. . . .

The notion that came to her as she stared at her reflection was so daring that she caught her breath. It was an unheard-of breach of etiquette, and might cause an irremediable breach with the countess. But suddenly Tatiana did not care. *Not get lost in the crowd*—that was what Turner had counseled. This should surely do the trick.

She pulled out the pins one by one, then retrieved the hairbrush from the rug, where Bellerophon, lost in dreams, had it clasped between his paws.

Eight

HER LAST-MINUTE change of attire had made her late; she heard a clamor of voices as she came down the stairs. Smithers was posted in the doorway to the salon; he took one look at her and went pale. "You shameless chit, what the devil do you mean—"

"Announce me," Tatiana said calmly.

"I'll be damned if I will! You look a proper strumpet!"

"Announce me," she repeated, "or I'll go in without."

"Do as you please, hussy," the butler said dourly.

Tatiana stepped over the threshold. The conversational din died to naught.

"Lord-a-mercy," murmured a young man just beside the entrance, and another, a few feet on, whistled beneath his breath.

The countess, standing beside a portly figure with a quizzing glass at his neck, registered a moment's shock at her protégée's appearance, at the dazzling, dead-straight sheen of blond hair hanging loose down her back. Then she swallowed it abruptly and moved toward the door. Tatiana went to meet her, a smile that smacked of defiance teasing the corners of her fine red mouth. "Forgive my tardiness, dear cousin. On my way down the stairs, I ripped the hem of my gown. As you see, I exchanged it."

The men in the room had surged forward en masse, like soldiers called to battle. Dulcie held out her cheek to be kissed; Tatiana felt her trembling. But she composed herself admirably. "No matter. The same has happened to me more than once. Permit me, Your Graces, to present to you my cousin, Miss Grimaldi." She steered Tatiana through the barricade to where the man with the quizzing glass was standing, with a gray-haired woman in blue satin at his side. "The Duke and Duchess of Mourne. Miss Grimaldi."

The duke had brought the quizzing glass up and was employing it at rather close range. Tatiana took care to make her curtsy more in his wife's direction. After what seemed like eons, the duchess stretched out her hand. "My dear girl, it is a pleasure to meet you. And what, pray tell, do they call on the Continent that very fetching thing you've done with your hair?"

"*La Cascade Chinoise*," Tatiana lied, so audaciously that the countess had to bite her tongue. Then Tatiana cast a despairing glance at the company. "I perceive, however, that the fashion has not yet alighted here. Am I to be held in disrepute, Your Grace, I wonder?"

"I shouldn't doubt it." The duchess smiled. "But only by those unable to effect it so becomingly. Don't you agree, Maurice?"

The duke cupped a hand at his ear. "What's that, Arabella?"

"I was congratulating Miss Grimaldi on being an innovator of fashion!" the duchess said loudly.

"Hrumph! Absolutely! Never in my life saw a lovelier lass—except, my pet," the duke added in belated loyalty, "for you."

The countess then led her on a round of the company, ladies first. Tatiana took special care to compliment their gowns, take note of their jewels, and ask directions to reticule- and shoemakers. The men were left waiting, but Tatiana could feel their eyes on her as she gossiped and giggled with her own sex. She had already noted with a sidelong glance that Lucas was present, standing by the mantel, silent and glowering. She did not look in his direction again.

"Dinner is served," Smithers intoned from the doorway. When the guests were seated, Tatiana found herself between the Duke of Mourne and his none-too-young heir, both of whom seemed most anxious to further their acquaintance with the hostess's cousin. Lucas, she saw, had been placed between one Horatia Cummings and Miss Alberly, who was prone to giggles. He didn't say much to either; the countess directed the conversation, which ran to politics and gossip. Tatiana participated eagerly and knowledgeably; this was what she had spent all those months in training for.

The Rubicon, though, she knew, would come at the withdrawing. Freed of the moderating masculine influence, might not the ladies—even the Duchess of Mourne, who'd observed her husband's attentions to Miss Grimaldi with astonishment—turn into cats? The countess must have been wondering as well; she took the precaution of obtaining Tatiana's elbow as they passed into the drawing room and whispering, "How are you holding up, my dear?"

"Tolerably well, Cousin Dulcie," Tatiana said sweetly. "The black—was it a faux pas?"

"On anyone else, Lord, yes. But you, apparently, can do no wrong. Where in God's name did you get it?"

"Don't you recall? You bade me have something made up in case we should be called on to attend . . . obsequies. Is that the proper word?"

"Unexceptionably. But I cannot comprehend what possessed you to—what's that, Horatia? Oh, my Turner does for her for now. Why? Do you know of someone reliable in search of a position?" The chance for tête-à-tête was lost, but Tatiana recognized that Miss Cummings's offer of her own abigail's sister to attend her was an excellent sign.

When they were rejoined by the men an hour later, Tatiana was pleased to see that Lucas was still among them, leaning against the mantel with his arms draped across its gilt overhang, like an angry god.

But he was still here. The countess, leading Tatiana through the bevy of suitors, raised her hand to the musicians, who waited for her cue. "My dear," she announced, "I've promised you first to His Grace the duke." A howl went up from the disappointed swains, and Dulcie wagged her head at them. "Gentlemen, where are your manners? Go and fetch yourself partners." The duke was coming forward, licking the rim of his white mustache. Tatiana watched as Dulcie stole a glance at her son, then called gaily to Charles Lambert and his brothers, "A waltz, good fellows, if you please!"

Lucas sat at his desk, a half-filled snifter of brandy by his hand, a cigar burnt to ash in its crystal tray. Unable to sleep, he'd started adding up the costs of the evening's entertainment: shrimp, foie gras, caviar, the endless trays of champagne. But he knew the source of his unrest had naught to do with money. He sipped the brandy, letting his mind run over the events of the night.

He hadn't meant to attend. He really, truly hadn't. But in the end, as the house filled with guests, as conversation and laughter floated up the stairs toward the rooms where he'd barricaded himself with claret and books, he found he couldn't stay away. He'd felt precisely as he had when, as a child banished to the nursery, he'd stood with his nose pressed to the window glass and watched the grand carriages rolling up the drive for one of his mother's balls. Here he was, stuck with his hobbyhorse and jacks, while something splendid and mysterious went on downstairs.

An understandable emotion in a child of seven. The question was, why had he felt it tonight? Because he'd been away from all of that so long. Because he'd been—did he dare say it?—lonely. But hadn't he treasured his isolation? It was what had brought him back to Dorset—the chance to be alone, never to hear again, or imagine hearing, the whispers that began the instant his back was turned. *Innisford's killer, you know. They let him off scot-free.* And the surety he would not encounter Gillian . . . He could never face Gillian. Not after what he'd done.

But no man was an island. Who'd penned that? Not Shakespeare. Skelton? Donne? He might go and ask Miss Grimaldi; no doubt the baggage knew.

He didn't want to think of Miss Grimaldi. He was aware, even in his half-sotted state, that something about her lay at the heart of his odd restlessness. His mother would be pleased with what she'd wrought that night—and so she should, he admitted grudgingly. By all appearances, Miss Grimaldi was on her way to becoming a sensation. She'd be off his hands by the end of another season, just as he'd wished her to be.

And he had spent the evening in the company of friends—well, acquaintances, really, but they knew him well enough. There'd been no hint in anyone's manner that he was *persona non grata*. To the contrary, they'd seemed delighted to see him. The Duchess of Mourne and he had talked for nearly an hour on roses. James Trayhorne had begged him to come shooting. And Dauntley had issued a standing invitation for billiards or cards.

Why, then, did he feel more bereft than before?

Perhaps it was the very absence of those whispers and glances. They all knew what he had done. Had society become so dissolute that it didn't care? If so, he wanted no part of it.

But that wasn't what his heart had told him as he stood in his chambers, watching the carriages roll up the drive.

You couldn't kill a man and have it count for nothing. And even if someday the true reason for his actions became known—a happenstance he very much doubted, being all too acquainted with the Regent's penchant for protecting his cronies—there would still remain the cold, incontrovertible fact of what he'd done to Gillian: deprived her of her helpmate, her spouse, the man she'd chosen over him. Looking back, he could not say even now what had been uppermost in his mind that fog-swathed dawn on the banks of the Thames—England's security, or his gnawing jealousy.

Whichever it was, the decision he'd made in the space of an instant had brought those whispers down on his head, propelled him to Russia to evade them, entangled him with Casimir Molitzyn—and led to the presence at Somerleigh House this evening of his mother's Continental cousin. *I really ought to see about having her name added to the peerage rolls,* he thought wearily. But that would require substantial tampering with the family tree. And she'd be out of his life by the end of the season. Even he, who'd been so dubious at the prospects of his mother's venture, couldn't deny that now. Good God, they'd all—even the antique Duke of Mourne—been licking their chops at the sight of her.

Out of his life. Drawn to the window, he looked down on the snow, remembering with startling clarity the way he'd first beheld her: bundled in her coarse furs, whipping the wolfhound on, careening down that frozen hill. And how she'd risen from the bank after smashing into him, a half-contrite Aphrodite, cheeks aflame with the cold, her emerald eyes a-dance . . .

She's nothing, he told himself brusquely, smothering the candle. Nothing but a too-clever chit with an ear for language he'd never seen equaled, and looks to rival a goddess, and the bearing of a duchess . . .

And willpower beyond human imagining, he thought, climbing into his bed. God, what went on in her head? What had she thought tonight of the slavering suitors, the gilded women, the expanse of delicacies whose cost would have fed all Mizhakovsk for a year?

He had, he discovered, an erection, rock-hard and damned inconvenient. A most unaccustomed state of affairs, what with his liquor intake. What the hell use was brandy, if not to keep a man flaccid?

Out of his life. He couldn't wait, he told himself—and then thrashed and turned in the darkness until his untoward rod finally gave up all hope and, blessedly, let him sleep.

Nine

Brighton, 1813

"AND THEN," WHISPERED Lady Bournemouth, as Viscount Salisbury saluted her in passing, "he had the nerve—the *audacity*—to tell Selma that as far as he was concerned, there never had been any official betrothal! In all my days I've never—how *do* you do, Major Conway; delightful to see you." Her bonnet bobbed.

Lady Shelton hurried her on. "But, Anthea, admit it. Selma is well quit of him, now that he's shown his true colors."

"I suppose so." Lady Bournemouth fanned herself despairingly. "But, Jane, we must face facts. Captain Rawleigh had fine prospects. And the worst of it is that poor Clothilda's romance with Lord Edgerton's son has come to naught. He got besotted over the winter with some little chit straight out of the schoolroom. Maisie Cunningham. Of the Sheffield branch of the family."

"The Sheffield Cunninghams! Oh, Anthea! You can't mean—"

Lady Bournemouth nodded grimly. "Yes indeed. The father is in *trade*."

The awesome implications of this reduced both women to silence, just as a commotion at the far end of the promenade, near the statue of Lord Nelson, drew their attention. Craning her neck, Lady Bournemouth glimpsed a slim, dainty figure in a sprigged muslin gown of ravishing cut and drape tripping along the path, a jaunty chip hat shading her face. The ruckus had been caused by the immediate mobilization in her direction of every male in the vicinity. "Good God, Jane! Is it one of the princesses?"

"With that waist?" Lady Shelton laughed, delighted to show off her savoir faire to her friend, who had only just arrived in town. "No, Anthea. That is Miss Tatiana Grimaldi. And if you ever hope to find husbands for those girls of yours, pray she settles soon on one of those gadflies swarming about her—for until she does, every maid in Brighton is doomed to spinsterhood!"

Lady Bournemouth moved on, trying for a better view. "Grimaldi? Can't say I know the name—except from the theater, of course. And I *hope* matters have not sunk so low that actresses are free to mix here!"

"No relation to the clown. But she's foreign," Lady Shelton hissed, reveling in the reaction this disclosure caused. "Italian. Or Austrian, is it? I never can recall."

Lady Bournemouth raised her lorgnette and contemplated the girl, who was laughing as she let Freddy Whittles take her arm. "But who the devil is she?"

"Oh, she has immaculate credentials. Second cousin twice removed to the Countess of Somerleigh."

"To Dulcibella! No one ever mentioned such a cousin to me!"

"As I understand it," Lady Shelton said, warming to her subject, "Dulcie's mother's sister's youngest daughter ran off with an Italian—or was it Austrian—soldier whom she met on holiday abroad. He was the younger son of a nobleman of some consequence, but nonetheless, under the circumstances, the family kept it all hushed up."

"That would have been Olivia. But we all heard she'd *died*."

Lady Shelton nodded sagely. "Very hushed indeed."

"But what brought the creature to England?"

"Apparently—I had this from Marianne Cuthbert, and you *know* she and Dulcie are thick as thieves—the chit was going through some papers after her parents died, of something tragic that I can't recall, and came upon her grandparents' marriage certificate. She traced the family, and tracked Dulcie down."

"Fortune-hunter," Lady Bournemouth said succinctly.

"No, no, not a bit! She has an income all her own of *thousands* a year. Marianne swears!"

"A likely tale."

"Come, Anthea. Do you think Dulcibella Strathmere would allow herself to be humbugged by a common swindler?"

Lady Bournemouth considered it carefully. "Not on the face of it. But you said yourself the fellow was a younger son—"

"All the older ones died. As it turns out, while we were mourning Olivia, she was wallowing in wealth—and not a penny from . . ." She mouthed a certain word beginning with *T*.

Just then the Countess of Somerleigh herself sailed into sight, looking very trim in a walking dress of navy blue with ruches of jonquil silk. Lady Bournemouth watched as Tatiana Grimaldi broke through the ranks of her admirers to greet her with delighted kisses on both cheeks. "A fetching little thing," she admitted reluctantly. "And I daresay Dulcie deserves some happiness in life, after what she's been through with that son."

"Oh, you haven't heard the best of it, Anthea. *He* is here."

"Lucas Strathmere!" Lady Bournemouth reached for her hartshorn. "Lucas Strathmere, here! Have you seen him?"

Her friend nodded, flushed with importance. "Several times. He's escorted the cousin to the assembly rooms more than once. They've taken Admiral Butterly's house on Crescent Street for the season."

"And is he . . . received?" Lady Bournemouth queried delicately.

Lady Shelton rolled her eyes. "Received? Land sakes, Anthea! An eligible bachelor worth as much as he is?"

"How times have changed," Lady Bournemouth intoned. Then her expression changed to curiousness. "How does he look after all these years?"

"Handsome as ever. He's the spit and image of the Admiral."

"Well," said her companion. "As I said, you can't begrudge any pleasure to Dulcibella, after all she has suffered. Though I can hardly believe Lucas Strathmere having the cheek to show his face—"

"Time moves on, Anthea," Lady Shelton said indulgently. "Prison couldn't be worse than what the man has put himself through. Removed from all of *this*"— her wide-swept arm took in the whole promenade, crowded with the cream of the ton—"for years and years!"

"You have a point, Jane. And I always did say more than half the blame ought to be laid at the feet of that outrageous Innisford creature." She began to muse on what chances her

Selma might have with a very rich reformed rake. "How old is he now, do you reckon?"

"Thirty-four," her friend said promptly.

"A very suitable age for marrying," Lady Bournemouth noted, eyes narrowing. "Shall we go and pay our respects, Jane, to Dulcibella and this cousin of hers?"

Ten

"WHO'S *THAT* ONE from?" Lucas asked, not looking up from his breakfast as Tatiana sailed across the room to install a nosegay of pansies and sweet violets among the host of bouquets already lined up on the mantel.

"Freddy Whittles. 'Pansies for remembrance,' the card says, but he's got that wrong. It's pansies for thoughts. From the French *penser*. Rosemary for remembrance. Ophelia says so in *Hamlet*." She buried her face in the flowers.

Against his will, Lucas raised his head from the sirloin and *oeufs brouillés* to watch her, saw the curve of her high, slanting cheekbones against the bright blossoms. Quickly he looked down again.

"It's a pity you couldn't have come with us to watch Braxton as Hamlet last week," Tatiana went on. "It's quite a wonderful play."

"I've seen it," Lucas said dryly, and rang for more toast. "What are violets for?"

" 'Violets dim and sweeter than the lids of Juno's eyes,' " intoned his mother from the doorway. He glanced up, wondering how long she'd been standing there.

Tatiana raised her nose from the corsage to scrunch it. "*Cymbeline?*" she hazarded.

"*A Winter's Tale,*" said the countess. "But I'll venture no one in your crowd would naysay you. Freddy Whittles again?" Tatiana nodded. "Persistent creature, isn't he?"

The girl's green gaze widened. "Have I encouraged him unduly, milady?"

"No, no. It's in his family's nature. Do you recall, Lucas, what an idiot his brother Ned made of himself over Cynthia Stanhope? He used to go to her window at night with a mandolin and serenade her. Until her father took to emptying chamber pots over his head."

Tatiana giggled. "I do hope, Cousin Lucas, I can rely on you for such desperate measures should they become necessary."

"Nothing would please me more than to dash that little fop with cold piss."

"Lucas!" his mother said sharply.

"I beg your pardon. What's the current euphemism—exudation? Excretia?"

"It's a marvel to me you find anyone willing to converse with you," declared the countess, settling herself at the table.

"To me too," Lucas admitted grimly. "But everyone in Brighton seems eager enough."

"You're rich," said Tatiana, delicate fingers rearranging the violets. "And you've got a title. From what I've observed, those two facts go a long way toward excusing a boor."

His storm-ringed eyes narrowed. "Is that what I am?"

The countess rapped a knife against her plate. "Both of you, stop! Honestly, you're as bad as siblings. If I'd wanted you to have a sister, Lucas, I'd have provided you one."

"Instead you found me a cousin."

"*She* found?" Tatiana began.

"Enough!" Dulcie cried wearily. "Tatiana, do come eat."

"I had chocolate and biscuits in my room. I haven't time for anything more. Susannah Cuthbert and I are going shopping."

Lucas took out his wallet and ostentatiously dumped its contents on the table. "Will that be enough? Or shall I write you a draft on my bank?"

"Why, you—milady, you said yourself I should choose a new reticule and shawl to go with the celadon mousseline!"

"So I did. Don't be so tightfisted, Lucas. Put those notes back in their place."

"What's the point, when it all ends up at the mantua-maker's? Or the milliner's, or the—"

"Lucas!"

"Never mind, milady. It's no more than what one would expect, is it, from a man so miserly it takes him three months to decide on the purchase of a horse."

That stung. Lucas was only too aware that the excuse he'd given for accompanying his mother and her charge to Brighton for the summer season—the search for a new hunter—had long since worn thin. "Mayhaps I only stay," he said, tight-lipped, "to be sure I'll have brass enough to make the purchase should I come upon a suitable mount."

"If you found Alexander's own warhorse you wouldn't give your precious pennies to buy her," Tatiana said with disdain.

He rose to his feet, palms flat against the table. "I'd have you remember, *Cousin* Tatiana, precisely where every item of clothing you've got on your back, as well as the roof over your head, the bed you sleep in, your chocolate and biscuits, your opera box, your—"

"Lucas! Tatiana!" The countess clapped her hands. "Stop this bickering!"

Tatiana's green eyes glittered. "How could I possibly forget, *Cousin* Lucas, when you remind me at every opportunity?"

The door knocker temporarily distracted the combatants. "Miss Cuthbert for Miss Grimaldi," Smithers announced dourly.

"I've just got to run up to fetch my hat," Tatiana said after a pause. "What plans do you have, milady, for today?"

"Nothing, thank God, until Lady Bournemouth's reception." She made a moue. "Six o'clock, of all the uncouth hours. You will be ready?"

"Promise," the girl said with a smile. Then one last barb at Lucas: "And if I see a particularly hip-sprung hack horse, I'll send it 'round for your inspection, shall I?" He growled in his throat as she tripped toward the stairs.

For a few moments, Dulcie said nothing. Then she looked sidelong at her son. "She really isn't at all extravagant, you know."

"Hah! Not by your standards, perhaps!"

"No, really, Lucas. That girl can make more of a plain muslin frock than most could manage with silk. It's in her bearing, her carriage. She carries everything off so splendidly."

"I know she carries off my income with great flair."

"If it pains you so to watch, you could—" Dulcie broke off sharply.

"Go home?" he finished for her. "Don't think it doesn't tempt me. Lady Shelton told me yesterday she looked forward to seeing me here on the fourteenth. What was that about?"

"Oh, nothing much. Dinner for a few friends. A spot of dancing."

"How many friends?" Lucas demanded.

"Well, darling, one can't impose on the hospitality of others without occasionally returning the favor. At least," she added pointedly, "most folk can't."

"How many friends?" he asked again.

"I believe the list stands at one hundred and thirty. *Not*," she put in quickly, "all for the dinner, of course."

Damn you, Casimir Molitzyn. "Will there never be an end to this, Mother?" His voice was oddly plaintive.

"That's up to Tatiana. It might help, though, if you wouldn't make such untoward remarks about her suitors. Freddy Whittles is a perfectly respectable—"

"Ass."

Dulcie calmly folded her napkin. "I must say, I scarcely see why that would matter to you. Isn't it enough that you settle her on someone and let the thing go?"

"There's one small, basic flaw in your scheme, Mother. Has it ever occurred to you what might happen if Tatiana chooses a husband she later finds unsuitable—and knowing her, I wouldn't expect anything less—then decides to make known to him precisely how he's been gulled?"

Dulcie blanched, discomfited. "Oh, Lucas. She wouldn't. Not after all that we have done for her." But her eyes betrayed her dismay.

"So the next time you ask yourself why I'm not home in Dorset—and Christ alone knows how I wish I were—you might bear in mind that thanks to your marvelous planning, we are stuck in the position of making absolutely certain that whomever Tatiana weds will *always* keep her happy. For perpetuity."

"Good God," the countess murmured.

"Exactly," said Lucas. "So no more talk of Freddy Whittles. Pass the butter, please."

* * *

"What do you think of this?" Susannah Cuthbert demanded, laying a pair of rose-colored ribbons against her pale glove.

"Perfect—for Selma Bournemouth," Tatiana told her.

Susannah stifled a burst of laughter. "Oh, Tat! You can be such a cat! I'll be pickled in vinegar before I dress like that on-the-shelf country spinster. What of these, then?" She plucked another set, these scarlet, from the display.

"Better," Tatiana mused. "Hold them against your hair." Then she shook her head. "No. Altogether wrong. Try these." She reached for vivid yellow.

Susannah looked dubious. "Mother says yellow is only for brunettes."

"Does your mother know everything?"

"Well . . ." Tatiana's companion held them against her chestnut curls. "I'll have to think on it. What are you getting?"

"The peacock blue."

"Oh, Lord, I wish I dared! But Mother says—"

"Good heavens, Sue, haven't you a mind of your own?"

"Not like yours," her friend said wistfully. "You always know what you want—and the countess never, ever naysays you."

"No, but her son does, at every hand." Tatiana paid for her blue ribbons while Susannah still stood contemplating the display. Her hesitation made Tatiana impatient. "It is only a two-shilling purchase!"

Susannah gingerly took up the yellow. "I can always give them to my abigail when Mother has a fit."

Their choices made, the two girls strolled onto Queen Street, with Carruthers, Tatiana's recently acquired maid, following close behind. "Chocolate now?" Susannah asked hopefully as they passed a tearoom, its windows piled high with pastries.

"If you wish." Tatiana turned to add her ribbons to Carruthers's already substantial pile of packages. "Do take these 'round to the house for me."

"But Her Ladyship said I was never to leave yer side when we was out o' doors," the maid, a short, stout girl with curling red hair, protested faintly.

Tatiana rolled her eyes. "We aren't going to be out of doors. We'll be right in this shop here. And we won't stir outside again until you return."

"Oh. Well, I guess it's all right, then." The maid trotted cheerfully toward home.

"You're so lucky," Susannah murmured as they entered the tearoom. "Our Tesserly never lets me out of her sight."

"I took a great deal of care in choosing Carruthers," Tatiana said archly as the headwaiter, frowning slightly at the two unaccompanied young ladies, led them to a table in the rear. "My main requirement was that she be too timid to ever dare cross me! What are you going to have?"

"Mocha frappe and a napoleon. Oh, I know it isn't patriotic of me, but I love 'em."

"And for you, miss?" asked the imperious headwaiter.

"Hot chocolate and a hazelnut biscuit."

"One hazelnut biscuit." Susannah sighed, gray eyes taking in her friend's dainty waist. "No wonder you've that figure! How can you shop all day long on a single biscuit?"

"There's the chocolate too," Tatiana pointed out, forbearing to tell her friend that in some corners of the world a cup of frothy chocolate and a crisp biscuit would sustain a soul for a good deal longer than one morning of shopping. "But how do matters stand with Mr. Hyde Parker?"

"I hardly know. He did ask me to dance at Lady Pendleton's last evening. Though if you'd been there, I daresay he wouldn't have."

"Fiddlesticks," said Tatiana. "Mr. Hyde Parker is one of the few sensible men I have met here. He realizes more than a nodding acquaintance is necessary to kindle a lifelong affinity."

"You talk like Mr. Johnson's dictionary sometimes," Susannah noted, cocking her head. "Whatever do you mean?"

"Only that a fellow ought to know something about a girl before pledging his love!"

"Clifford knows too much about me," Susannah noted glumly. "He was a friend of my brother's. He's seen me with my knees skinned and my skirts torn and muddied—oh, I do think it's hopeless. He'll never think of me as anything but a scrubby child."

"Was your dance with him a waltz?" Susannah nodded. "Then you've naught to fret about. A man does not ask a waltz of a girl he considers a scrubby child. It's very *intime*, the waltz, don't you think?"

"It is only a dance."

"When he must hold you so, and so?" Tatiana's gloved hand, snaking 'round to grasp her own back, made the waiter bringing their refreshments rattle his tray. The girls dissolved in giggles, and the headwaiter frowned from across the room.

"It *is* rather exciting, isn't it, when you are pressed against him?" Susannah whispered when the fellow had gone.

Tatiana sipped her chocolate. "That depends on who is doing the pressing, goose."

"When Clifford does it, then. Does Freddy Whittles make you feel that way?" Tatiana's answer was a bubble of laughter. "I cannot understand you, Tat. All those men dancing attendance on you every night and all day—isn't there anyone special whom you care for at all?"

Pietr, Tatiana thought fleetingly. But that memory was so distant from this place and time—from the fashionable girl who perched here nibbling a biscuit in a simple crepe day dress worth fifty times more than her wedding gown—that it seemed unreal. It did remind her, however, of why she'd risked angering the countess by sending Carruthers home. Her introduction to Brighton society—a sort of dress rehearsal for London—had been sufficiently diverting, and taxing, to occupy her mind for the past few months. But Lucas Strathmere was clearly chomping at the bit to be gone from this town, and she could not let him leave before she'd settled their score. She intended to make him suffer, as he had made her suffer. She simply had not yet determined how.

She was aware of the general buzz that had accompanied his reentry into the ton. What puzzled her still was its cause—a question to which her best hints dropped to the countess and assorted other ladies had provided no answer. "May I ask you something, Sue?" she said now, tentatively. "It regards my cousin Lucas. What do you know about him?"

Susannah looked surprised. "Why—nothing, really. I mean to say, he's always very polite to me." She stopped, reconsidered. "Well, not polite exactly. Cordial. No, not cordial, either. Gracious, what do I mean?"

"His behavior is acceptable," Tatiana said dryly. "Tell me, do you find him . . . grim?"

"I suppose I do."

"Have you any notion why he should be?"

Her friend shrugged, mouth full of pastry cream. "Born that way, I reckon."

"You don't know of any . . . any sort of scandal in his past?"

"Good Lord, Tat, you're his cousin. Do you?"

"No," Tatiana said, frowning. "Neither he nor the countess ever speaks of such matters to me. Yet I can't help wondering why he seems so unhappy."

Susannah wiped a corner of her mouth delicately. "He's of a different generation from us, remember. I would have been five when he was twenty. I do gather from what I've overheard that he was all the crack then. The best dancer in England—that's what Lady Hyde Parker said of him at the assembly room the other night. But I understand he hasn't been to Brighton—or to London even—in a decade or more."

"No, he hasn't. And why not? That's what I'd like to know."

"He was some sort of diplomat, wasn't he?" Susannah asked, stirring her frappe.

"Not for the past five years. He's been down in Dorset, playing with rosebushes."

"I don't think he likes women very well," Susannah said thoughtfully. "Look how old he is and still unmarried! If you think there is a scandal about him, I could ask Mamma."

"Better not. She might think you'd formed a tendresse for him!"

The notion was enough to reduce them both to giggles again—though Tatiana's laughter hid a disappointed heart. Susannah had been her best hope to learn about Lucas Strathmere's past. To whom else could she even broach the subject, when, as Susannah said, she was a member of the man's family? It wasn't seemly for his own cousin to pry publicly into his secrets. Every time she brought up the subject, always with the utmost delicacy, she met only polite, blank stares.

And she was growing impatient. If Lucas went back to Dorset, he'd be far beyond her reach—and there wasn't any earthly reason for a girl enjoying the sort of summer she was to suggest going with him. All she needed was an opening, a bit more information.

Someone must be willing to talk of it, she thought, crunching a hazelnut between her teeth. It was simply a matter of discovering who.

Eleven

TATIANA PUT HER head to the question as she dressed for Lady Bournemouth's rout that evening. Her own peers were too far removed from Lucas Strathmere's former circle to be of much help. What she needed was a gossip, an elderly gossip. But she couldn't venture into the fray without a bit more ammunition.

"What do ye think o' that, miss?" Carruthers asked tentatively of the chignon she'd painstakingly formed from Tatiana's thick hair.

"Very nice," her mistress declared. "But I'd best have Turner's opinion of it—she is such a dragon. Could you fetch her, please, and then run and see if my gloves are pressed?"

"Yes, miss." Carruthers went off without the least sign of offense.

I chose well indeed, Tatiana reflected, hiding a smile. By the time Turner arrived, she'd managed to pull enough of her blond hair free to make Carruthers's chignon appear truly appalling. "God in heaven," Turner sniffed, lunging for the brushes. "I don't know how you put up with that girl! You should have heard what Smithers had to say when she showed up this afternoon with your parcels, and you left God knows where with no chaperone!"

"The fault in that is mine. She had so many parcels—"

"Then let her send the stuff back here in a hack!" Turner ripped hairpins out furiously. "You're entirely too patient with her, miss. Teach her nothing but bad habits that way. Now, let's see if I can put this to rights." She set to work, while Tatiana congratulated herself on having earned a temporary ally in Her Ladyship's maid, who twisted and pinned until she ended up with a chignon nearly identical to Carruthers's first efforts. "What do you think of *that*?"

"Absolutely perfect," Tatiana said, and Turner beamed with pride.

"I'd best get back to milady, then. I trust that dolt can get you into your gown."

"Oh, Turner." The woman turned back from the door. "By the by . . . while Susannah and I were shopping at Bartlett's this afternoon, Lady Hyde Parker and Lady Shelton came in. They stood not far from us. And I had the most peculiar feeling they were whispering about me. I don't dare mention it to Her Ladyship, but—do you know of anything I might have done that could be construed amiss?"

"Not unless they'd seen you sipping chocolate at a public house unchaperoned."

"No. This was long after. Carruthers had rejoined us by then. Oh, Turner, you know I'd sooner die than bring disgrace on the countess after she has been so good to me."

Turner waved a hand. "I wouldn't think no more of it,

miss. More'n likely those two old biddies were nattering about the young master showing his face here again."

"I do believe I *did* hear them mention his name," Tatiana admitted. "And that of a woman . . ."

"Gillian Innisford." Turner said it as though she'd just bitten into an unripe quince.

"That was it. So you don't think I've committed any faux pas?"

Turner patted her shoulder. "If you had, milady would ship you back to Dorset posthaste. Nay, you've been good as gold, love. Don't worry your pretty head."

"I won't, then, since *you* tell me not to." Tatiana smiled enchantingly. "And thank you so much for mending my hair. I only wish you had a twin, to be *my* lady's maid."

Gillian Innisford. The unfamiliar name spun in Tatiana's mind all the time she was greeting Lady Bournemouth and her two dreary daughters, satisfying the need to pay her extravagant compliments of her suitors, and making polite conversation at dinner with elderly General Nash and the bedazzled young Bournemouth she'd been seated between. Who could she be? And why, when speaking of her, had Turner made that face?

When the ladies withdrew, she sat beside Susannah, who was playing the pianoforte, and considered her options. Lady Shelton was here, and she was inclined to chatter. But she was also exceedingly harebrained, not to mention deferential to the countess; she might not tell any tales out of school. Lady Hyde Parker? But she was Susannah's would-be beau's mother, and it would be awkward if Tatiana brought disgrace on her friend with her inquiries. She scanned the room, smiling at Dulcie, who arched a brow at the obsequious attention being paid her by their hostess.

Their hostess. Lady Bournemouth, with her two unmarried daughters. The countess had come this evening, Tatiana suddenly recalled, only because Lady Bournemouth had been so persistent in her invitations. Dulcie thought the woman was angling for Selma or the other one—what was her name? Clotie?—as a wife for Lucas.

Perfect, thought Tatiana, and subtly shifted her gown so its skirts lay beneath one leg of her gilt chair. She was turning the music for Susannah, and as she rose she pushed the chair back—to be rewarded with an audible ripping sound. "Oh, dear," Tatiana murmured.

Lady Bournemouth sprang to her feet. "Is there a problem, Miss Grimaldi?"

"Clumsy me! I've made a tear in my gown!"

Tatiana was sure she heard dowdy Selma snigger. That, of course, steeled her resolve.

"Have you pins?" her hostess asked with concern.

Ruefully, Tatiana held up the damage. "I rather think this goes beyond pins."

"Oh, my Bertram can stitch that for you in the wink of an eye. Selma, why don't you—" Selma's plain face bore a distinctly mulish look. "Clotie—"

"Oh, Mamma, not now! The gentlemen will be rejoining us at any moment!"

Lady Bournemouth frowned at her daughters. "I'll take you up myself, Miss Grimaldi."

"I couldn't *think* of inconveniencing you so!"

"Nonsense. Clotie's quite right; the gentlemen will soon arrive." Tatiana could almost see the calculations in her hostess's dark eyes: *If the toast of the town is delayed, it can only bode well for Clotie—and mayhaps I can put in a good word with this cousin for Selma.* She bustled forward to take Tatiana's arm. "We'll be back before the first dance ends, never you fear."

Upstairs, Bertram went to work on the ruined hem, ignoring Lady Bournemouth's steady stream of instructions.

Tatiana bided her time, waiting for an opening. When the hem had been mended, her hostess dismissed the maid, then fussed for a few moments at the pier glass with her shawl. "Dreadfully chilly weather we're having this summer, Miss Grimaldi, don't you agree?"

"Atrocious," Tatiana agreed. "I must say, it suits your daughters, though. I can't recall when I've seen them look more lovely than they do tonight."

Lady Bournemouth could not quite disguise her surprise. "Do you think so?"

"Absolutely. That perfect English skin . . ." Tatiana touched her own cheek deprecatingly. "You don't know how we envy that on the Continent!"

"Well, neither of them is a natural beauty, Miss Grimaldi, but—"

"Oh, I disagree! I would kill for your Selma's eyes. I do adore dark eyes; they have such *depth* to them. My cousin Lucas was remarking on it to me just the other day."

"He *was?*" Then her hostess regained her composure. "Well, Lord Bournemouth, rest his soul, always said he fell in love with my eyes, and Selma is the image of me."

"I cannot comprehend why she hasn't been snapped up by some lucky gentleman," Tatiana went on, patting her chignon at the glass.

"I've wondered that myself," Lady Bournemouth confessed. "I fear sometimes I've made her too choosy. There is the matter of station, you know. I had fond hopes for Captain Rawleigh, but he seems to have . . . moved on."

Tatiana searched her memory. "Captain James Rawleigh? An awkward, gangly fellow?" She'd danced with him at the assemblies once or twice, and subsequently had had a steady stream of bouquets from him. "I hardly think he's worthy."

"Well, he *is* only a second son. . . . Still, Selma's not as young as she might be."

"On the Continent," said Tatiana, adjusting the emeralds she'd borrowed from the countess, "a girl isn't considered to have come into her own until at *least* twenty-three."

"Is that so?" That sharp, dark gaze beside hers in the pier glass had narrowed. "You mentioned, I believe, that the earl had complimented Selma's eyes. Is your cousin in the marriage market, do you think?"

"Oh, yes, indeed. What else would have brought him back into society after all this time? The countess had a hard go of it, but she finally convinced him"— Tatiana took a blind leap—"that one mustn't allow one unfortunate experience to ruin one's whole life."

"Oh, my, yes," Lady Bournemouth agreed. "Why, none of us ever believed the fault could lie with him—especially with the spectacle she's subsequently made of herself."

"You mean Gillian Innisford," Tatiana said knowledgeably.

"Who else? Breeding will out, that's what I say. And that 'un showed from the start that she was utterly unbred. You know she was working in a gaming house when he first met her."

Tatiana looked suitably shocked. "I hadn't heard of *that*."

"She most assuredly was. At Mrs. Cuttleby's. I had it from Lord Bournemouth himself. *Not*, of course, that *he* frequented such establishments. He'd only had it on hearsay. And I won't deny she was a beauty. But even then, one knew it wasn't a beauty that *held*."

"Not like Selma's."

"No, not like Selma's. I mean, once the first flush of youth is gone—that is when you get a glimpse of true character."

Tatiana smiled. "That's very like what my cousin Lucas said about your daughter."

"Is it *really*?" Lady Bournemouth ushered Tatiana toward a boudoir chair, most willing that this conversation should go on.

Tatiana took another leap, since things were going so well. "You wouldn't feel, then, that Cousin Lucas's attentions to Selma might be . . . unwelcome?"

"Because of the murder, do you mean?"

Tatiana started—a fact she quickly hid by examining her stocking. "Do you know, I believe I've got a ladder in this." She tore one surreptitiously with her fingernail.

"Oh, that won't show a bit. There *is* that," Lady Bournemouth charged on, "and I daresay it might make some girls squeamish. But I hope my Selma would show more sense than that. After all, he *was* acquitted. Though it was a grand scandal at the time."

"The countess has told me often enough," said Tatiana, holding her breath, "how much the tragedy pained her."

"And no wonder! What none of us could ever figure was what your cousin was doing out there on Lord Innisford's estate at the crack of dawn if it wasn't a duel—and it can't have been, for then there would have been a doctor and seconds, and even the Somerleigh fortune couldn't hush all that up. *Not*," Lady Bournemouth said abruptly, paling, "that the Admiral would have!"

"Of course not," Tatiana soothed her.

"But you do see how peculiar it looked! Why, the whole world knew Lucas Strathmere was head over heels with that hoyden. And there she was, no more than three months married to Lord Innisford instead, and her bridegroom lying dead in the garden—with the bullet in his *back!*"

"It does appear suspicious," Tatiana acknowledged.

"To say the least! And it didn't make matters look any better that your cousin rushed off to Russia so precipitously. It did make it seem he was running away. After all, there was no sign she wouldn't have been willing, if he was determined to have her despite her marriage—at least not from her subsequent conduct. Oh, she may have gained some sympathy at first as the young, bereaved widow. But no one of note has received her in a decade."

The young, bereaved widow. Tatiana took one last leap. "You seem a woman of estimable sense, Lady Bournemouth. What do you think really happened?"

Her hostess pursed up her mouth. "All I know is what the coroner found at the inquest. An accidental shooting."

"You are very charitable, ma'am," Tatiana said humbly, not believing a word of it. Even more incredible than the transparent lie was the fact this woman was eager to embrace Lucas Strathmere as a suitor for her daughter even though she was convinced he'd committed a murder. How coldhearted could a mother be?

"I'll say one thing more," Lady Bournemouth declared. "Gillian Innisford may have wept and carried on at the time, but her husband being killed was the best thing could have happened to her. I had it from Lady Shelton even then that Gillian was playing fast and loose with the very worst sort—expatriate Frenchmen and who knows what else! And associating with foreigners will never lead to aught but ruin!" She nodded decisively, apparently forgetting she was speaking to a foreigner—which nearly made Tatiana giggle despite her loathing of this unnatural lady.

"Truer words were never spoken," she said solemnly. "But I must not keep you from your guests any longer. Shall we?" She offered her arm.

"I can see very well why you have proven such a comfort to the countess," Lady Bournemouth said with approval as they headed to the stairs. "But tell me true: Do you think my Selma stands a chance with your cousin?"

"I'd stake my life on it," said Tatiana, all her fingers crossed.

Twelve

LUCAS HADN'T ACCOMPANIED his mother and cousin to Lady Bournemouth's; when they returned home he was sitting by the fire in the blue salon, a book on his lap. "A delightful time, I trust?" he said in greeting.

"Bah. Do pour me a sherry, Tatiana. A long one." The countess collapsed onto the sofa. "That woman! Fussing over me as though I were in my dotage. . . . I really do believe, Lucas, she's set her cap for you to marry her dismal daughter."

"Has she a daughter?" Lucas asked disinterestedly.

"Two of 'em—and not a jot of brains or beauty between 'em. Thank you, dear." She took the glass Tatiana offered. "And the company! Antique war heroes and dog-faced scions and simpering misses—all with pedigrees impeccable, of course. But, Lord, for a breath of fashion! For a scrap of spirit! It reminded me anew of all I dislike about Brighton society."

"What thought you of the rout, cousin?" Lucas inquired of Tatiana, staring at his book.

She considered him through veiled eyes. Had he always looked so dangerous, and she just hadn't noticed? "I found it most . . . instructive." There was a heavy touch of accent to her words, and his dark head swiveled toward her.

"Really? Learn a new dance, did you?"

"More a variation on one I already knew."

He raised his claret cup. He had such big hands. Tatiana could see them cocked on the trigger of a pistol, about to shoot a man in the back. "Then your evening was not a total loss."

"*Nyet,*" said Tatiana, breath coming fast, and quickly turned it to, "Not . . . completely." She turned to pour herself sherry, then whirled back; facing a murderer was less disturbing than giving one the shoulder. She compromised, twisting to ask the countess, "Can I pour you more?"

"Oh, no, I'm to bed. I will say one thing for such a wearisome crowd, Tatiana: It only makes you shine more brightly. I don't know how you manage it. She was seated between General Nash and that mooncalf Andrew Bournemouth at supper, Lucas. Can you imagine anything more distasteful? An old bore and a young fool."

Lucas didn't answer. He took a swallow of claret, eyes still on Tatiana.

"I had to laugh, though, when you tore your hem so adroitly," the countess went on, smiling. "Hoping for a few moments of respite upstairs—and then to have Anthea herself insist on accompanying you! That's when I began to suspect, Lucas, she was angling after you. It must have been a good hour before Tatiana broke free again. I very nearly came looking for you, dear."

"That wasn't necessary. And the tear—I assure you, that was sheer clumsiness."

"Pish. You've not a clumsy bone in your body. I saw how neatly it was done. So tell me: Did she bend your ear about Lucas?"

"She . . ." Tatiana was regretting her insouciant plotting. A vein on Lucas Strathmere's forehead had sprung out, etched in shadowy relief. His stormy eyes were startlingly cold. "She spoke of him, yes. She seems to imagine her eldest daughter would suit him well."

"That silly Selma! I might have known. Poor Lucas! But at least I need not fear you'll be caught in whatever snares Anthea sets you."

"No," her son agreed, closing the book with a snap that made Tatiana jump. "But what think you, dear cousin, of myself as a husband to Selma?" His voice was a purr, low and soft. She'd never heard him use that tone before; it made her shiver inside.

She collected herself, made her own voice that of the nattering tease he'd come to know. "Oh, I daresay she'd suit you admirably. With her long face, she could pass for that horse you've been so diligently searching for."

Dulcie snickered. "Tatiana! How *can* you?"

"It must be the influence of this gay evening." She offered the countess her arm, and was grateful when it was accepted. "Let's to sleep, by all means."

Carruthers was still brushing out her mistress's hair when a knock sounded at the bedchamber door. "Don't," Tatiana began, but the maid had already moved to open it. Even Carruthers was taken aback, though, to see not the countess but the master on the threshold.

"Ooh, m'lord," she said, glancing at Tatiana in her nightdress. "Beggin' yer pardon—"

"Go fetch your lady some warm milk," Lucas said abruptly.

Carruthers bobbed a dutiful curtsy. "Aye, m'lord, I will." She backed out fearfully.

He shut the door behind him. "One disadvantage, Miss Grimaldi, to engaging a ninny for your abigail. She may jump at your orders—but you see, she jumps at mine as well."

Tatiana stood, reaching for a dressing gown. "You have no right—"

"Leave off the false modesty. I've seen you in breeches, with your blouse unbuttoned. You don't give a fig for propriety, and I know it. What I don't understand is what game you are playing—and why."

She pulled the gown on anyway over her bared shoulders. "I rather thought it was your mother who is playing a game."

"Oh, she is. But you are something more, aren't you, than a pliant pawn. Do they play chess in Mizhakovsk on those long winter nights?"

"Chess?" she echoed.

"I diverted myself for many evenings in St. Petersburg across a chessboard. I know your people to be masters at it. I think you mean to check me, Miss Grimaldi. What was it Lady Bournemouth said that has made you so fearful of me?"

"I am not afraid of you."

"No?" He took a sudden step forward with his hand raised. She willed herself not to flinch. He let the hand slip to his side, and she let out her breath. "But perhaps you should be."

Tatiana had been thinking, fast. It was useless to deny what he already sensed. She should have been more careful there in the salon; it was too late now. "Afraid?" she said, mouth curling in a sneer. "Of a man who would shoot another in the back?"

"I've shot enough in the front, too."

It wasn't what she expected. Where was the inebriate dilettante who fiddled with roses? This was another man confronting her—the man, she suddenly realized, who'd talked his way out of war-torn Russia with a mute, bedraggled girl at his side. She'd never given him sufficient credit for that. Strangely enough, she found the realization exhilarating. The game—and he was right; it was a game—had been too easy until now. That he recognized she had her own reasons for playing along with Dulcie's plans leveled the field; they were equals now, pitted against each other.

Carruthers came barging through the door with the milk on a tray, her expression indicating somebody downstairs had given her an earful about the unseemliness of abandoning her mistress in her bedchamber with the master there. "Beg yer pardon, miss, to have left ye so—"

"Don't give it a thought," Tatiana said softly. "My cousin and I are just like brother and sister. Didn't the countess say as much, Cousin Lucas, only this morning?"

"Brother and sister," he agreed. "Just like Cleopatra and Ptolemy."

"What made 'em famous, then?" the maid asked nervously.

"She poisoned him," Lucas said. Then his gaze skewered Tatiana once more. "Freddy Whittles stopped by this evening to ask your hand in marriage. I thought you should know of it."

"How very gracious of you," she managed to say. "And did you grant it to him?"

"Nay. I've a notion you and he would not suit in the long run."

She smiled obliquely. "Yet had you given your permission, you might have gone to search for that hunter in more agreeable climes."

"I find Brighton congenial enough for the moment. But

do tell me, cousin—did I do wrong? Has Freddy won your heart?"

With what she'd learned that night, the temptation to call a halt to their charade, even at the cost of marrying Freddy, was powerful. But she shook her head slowly.

"Fair enough," he said. "But in case more love-struck swains come to park themselves in my house and make asses of themselves declaring their unalterable passion, perhaps you might be so kind as to inform me which of them you *would* care to marry."

"None," Tatiana said.

He arched one black brow. "Not a one among all your conquests?"

"No. Forgive me, cousin, but it can hardly be surprising that a girl with my very limited experience of the world should spend no haste in choosing. Why, I've not even been to London yet. I daresay it will be years before I make up my mind on so weighty a matter as marriage." She had the distinct satisfaction of seeing him pale. "Of course," she reminded him coolly, "it is well within your rights, and your mother's, to encourage me to wed any man of your choosing. Though I can always wait until I am of age and then pick whom I like."

"Of age." He passed a hand over his forehead. "My damnable memory—precisely how old, Cousin Tatiana, are you now?"

"Why, Cousin Lucas! How often has your mother impressed on me that a gentleman never inquires a lady's age! Still, I shall overlook the impertinence. I am nineteen. So for the next two years, you and your mother are free to pose me any candidates you choose."

He turned abruptly, heading for the door. "I will bear that in mind."

"No doubt by then you'll have found a hunter to your

liking," she could not resist adding—and then was sorry for it, as she saw the sudden clenching of his fists.

"At the risk of once again appearing impertinent, cousin, let me say: There are times when I devoutly wish I'd never met you."

"How odd," said Tatiana, ignoring Carruthers's startled gaze. "There are times I feel precisely the same."

Thirteen

"GOOD NEWS!" THE countess declared, bustling into the upstairs parlor, where Tatiana was perusing the latest issue of the *Post*. "Oh, my dear girl, *will* you put off poring over such dull reading matter? Next you'll take up Mistress More's wretched works."

"I tried *Hints toward Forming the Character of a Young Princess*," Tatiana confessed. "It made me long to lower the necklines on all of my gowns."

Dulcie laughed with delight. "Huzzah! There's the true spirit. All those pious lady writers propel me in the same direction. Oh, thank you, Lucas." He'd come in after her, laden with parcels. "I found the most *exquisite* length of chinoise silk at Hartin's, pet—pale sea-green, embroidered over with silver. It will be perfect for your gown for the fourteenth."

"Twenty pounds a yard," her son growled, dumping his bundles in a heap on the console.

"But we must have Madame set to work at once," the countess went on, taking no notice. "*And* have shoes dyed to match it, and a new headpiece. I thought silver filigree over satin, with silver ostrich plumes. I saw just the thing the other day at Charconte's, though it was ever so dear."

"Why should that matter to either of you?" Lucas headed for the sideboard for brandy, then to the newspaper Tatiana had set aside. "Any news of note?"

"They say the Russian army is recovering from the winter campaign." Tatiana could not quite keep the eagerness from her voice. "Do you think it is true?"

"I think it will be a very long time before the Tsar dares show his face in Europe again."

Her lovely mouth hardened. "You will never forgive him his alliance with Napoleon."

"Should I? He set the stage by it for Bonaparte's conquests of Poland and Lithuania."

"And subsequently proved his mettle at the siege of Moscow, when he stood against the Emperor."

"Too little, too late," Lucas said succinctly. "The damage had been done."

Her green eyes slanted toward him. "Even the best of men might be forgiven one mistake in life, cousin, do you not think so?"

"A private man, perhaps," he answered nonchalantly. "A public one, no."

"Oh, politics and more politics!" the countess cried, clapping her hands at them. "You never will agree, so why must you discuss them? You have not heard my news yet, Tatiana. I'll venture it will put any thought of Boney and the Tsar from your mind. The Regent is coming to Brighton! Now, I daresay, we shall see some entertainment worthy of you!"

"What more could we expect?" asked Lucas, turning the page of his paper. "Europe a shambles, the papacy in tatters, the armistice between Austria and France set to expire, and Prinny comes to take the waters. There is leadership for you!"

"Oh, pish," said Dulcie. "He has not acquitted himself so terribly in these wars."

"Did you know," Lucas mentioned to Tatiana, "that our Prince Regent affects the uniform of a general and covers his fat chest with medals, when he has yet to even cross the Channel?"

"He has worked a very witty blockade," the countess said, affronted.

"The Navy worked it for him."

"There should be some credit, surely, in a ruler choosing wise officials."

"Choosing! He hadn't even the guts to put the Whigs in office, with all he owes them!"

The countess smiled at Tatiana. "Your cousin has never forgiven poor old George the Third for going mad, thus raising Prinny to power."

"Forgiven! Christ, I cannot blame him! Nine sons the sorry fellow has, and not a one more fit to rule than a mutton chop. It is enough to drive any decent soul daft."

"Had George seen fit to assign more duties to the Prince when he was younger," Dulcie said tartly, "he might have been spared some of his heir's excesses. You cannot expect a man to sit idly about waiting for a throne for nigh on fifty years!"

"Beg pardon, Mother. I was not aware your precious Prinny was dissatisfied with his current lot of fathering bastards, seducing maidens, and spending England's scant resources on such monstrosities as that pavilion of his."

"Just wait until you see the interior," the countess told Tatiana. "There is nothing like it in all Christendom."

"In hell, though, perhaps," Lucas put in.

"I directed an invitation to him at once, naturally, for the fourteenth," Dulcie went on, unperturbed. "Though since he will have only *just* arrived in town, it may be too much to hope he will attend."

"Too much to hope indeed," her son said with a scowl.

His mother turned on him. "As for you, if you cannot display more respect for your nation's rightful ruler, I would strongly suggest you absent yourself from the company that night!"

"What, and miss my cousin's first encounter with royalty? Not likely, Mother. I shall be here, wearing bells."

"And so you should," exclaimed the exasperated countess as he withdrew to his rooms with the *Post* and his brandy, "for you are an utter fool!"

There was a moment of silence after he had left them. Tatiana found herself embarrassed by their strong emotions, but her sympathies lay with the countess. Lucas's patent dislike of the Regent was recommendation enough for the man in her eyes. Still, much of what Lucas alleged of him was common knowledge. Prinny did have mistresses, and babies by them. His conduct toward his lawful wife, Princess Caroline of Brunswick, and their only offspring, Princess Charlotte, was by all accounts abominable—though the whispers among the ladies of Brighton were that Caroline's coarse conduct more than excused that fact. Tatiana was curious to view the man and form her own judgments. Worldly creature that she had become, she could not restrain a slight flutter of her heart at the prospect of being presented to a king—or the next best thing. Pietr, she thought wistfully, what would you make of this?

Common sense told her he'd be cowed, daunted. Pietr had been the finest catch in Mizhakovsk—but Mizhakovsk was a long way from English society.

For the first time since leaving Russia, she faced squarely

the fact that her present life—materially, socially, and intellectually—was infinitely richer than the one she had left behind. She had books now, and newspapers and gazettes and pamphlets—and she could read them. She'd seen great works of art; she spoke knowingly of political and religious and literary matters that two years past had been beyond her ken. She had a mind, and she had learned to use it. All the sweetness of Pietr's embraces could not stand against that.

The realization made her unbearably sad. *I have betrayed you, Pietr. I have betrayed our love.*

She would atone for leaving Pietr so far behind, though, if she paid Lucas back for what he'd caused at Mizhakovsk.

"Shall I ring for tea?" asked the countess.

Tatiana roused herself from her thoughts. "Not for me, thank you. I am going with Susannah and her family to the concert at Preston Park. Wouldn't you like to come?"

"Not I. I must go and make my peace with Lucas. There is a most exquisite Hepplewhite table at Mr. Griscombe's that would be perfect for the yellow salon."

"Costly?" Tatiana inquired, and laughed at the countess's nod. "Then you must make your peace indeed! I wish you luck."

"And I you," Dulcie said rather wistfully. "Oh, to be nineteen years old and so carefree again!"

The concert was a fine one, featuring a quartet of strings and the new Italian tenor who was all the rage among the ton, but the music was lost on Tatiana. She sat on her stiff wooden seat and brooded over how she might work her revenge. It had become vital to her that she punish only Lucas, and not the countess, who had shown her such kindness. Of course, she realized dimly, Dulcie was bound to suffer if her only son did. Unless . . .

Susannah had risen to her feet, and was eyeing her friend oddly. "Are you going to sit there all day, Tat?"

"Oh!" Glancing up, Tatiana realized the music had ended; even the appreciative applause hadn't pierced her gray fog.

"Mamma has a table reserved for us at Longchamp's for tea." Susannah untied her parasol and pushed it up. "I thought we would walk through the park, if you are not too warm."

"Not at all. It's a delightful day." Tatiana joined the mass of gentlemen and ladies exiting the concert shell. Mrs. Cuthbert and her younger daughter, Sarah, were in the lead. "And perhaps we will see Mr. Hyde Parker," she added slyly. "The countess has not yet received a response from him about the fourteenth."

"He is in London on some tiresome business or other," Susannah reported, crestfallen. "I doubt he will arrive back in time."

Tatiana put an arm through her friend's. "What is it, do you suppose, that men *do* when they go away on business?"

"Gamble and drink, I reckon. The same as when they are at play." Suddenly she clutched Tatiana's elbow. "Oh, merciful heavens! Will you look at that!"

Coming toward them along the path was the most amazing creature Tatiana ever had seen. She wore a gown and half-cape of cinnabar and gamboge stripes, with a shako hat as high as a tower perched atop a lavish cascade of gleaming red-brown ringlets. She led a brace of greyhounds at leash, and they had little coats made of the very same stripe. Two boys in mustard liveries were following behind her, carrying her train; the man walking beside her, tall and thin and gray-haired, held her parasol for her.

"She looks proud as a Royal, doesn't she?" Susannah murmured. Tatiana was covertly watching the woman from beneath lowered lashes. There was something about her that was vaguely familiar—though she'd have sworn on her life they'd never met before.

The apparition swept toward Susannah's mother, came abreast of her, and said in a low, cultured voice, "Mrs. Cuthbert, how do you do?"

Mrs. Cuthbert, head held high, stepped past without so much as a nod.

"Dear God," Susannah whispered, clutching Tatiana's arm. "What an unlikely thing! To cut her straight like that—and Mamma with the heart of a lamb! I've never in my *life* seen her be deliberately rude! Who *can* that have been?"

Tatiana, flouting politeness, had turned to stare at the small procession. That shining bronze hair . . .

The press of the crowd pushed them on. Mrs. Cuthbert had met Mrs. Bellestairs on the path; the two women were murmuring together. "She may go where she likes," Tatiana heard the latter matron declare with vigor, "but no decent household will receive her—especially not with Somerleigh in town!"

Tatiana's head whipped back toward the bronze-headed woman. Her tresses were exactly the shade of the big, blowsy blossoms on Lucas's most cosseted rosebush.

Gillian Innisford. It had to be.

Tatiana put a hand to her temples. "Is something wrong?" Susannah asked anxiously.

"Megrims," her friend lied—though she had gone so pale it was entirely believable.

"Take my salts," Susannah offered.

"I have some of my own. But I think I must get out of the sun."

"Mamma, wait! Tatiana feels ill!"

Mrs. Cuthbert rushed back solicitously, unfurling her fan. "It's this crowd, my dear. Presses always have the same effect on me. We'll walk home with you, shall we?"

"Oh, there's no need for you to miss your reservation at Longchamp's," Tatiana protested. "I know how difficult they are to procure."

Susannah's mother looked dubious. "I don't like for you to go off alone."

Tatiana laughed faintly. "But I am hardly alone in this throng! I'll simply go to the edge of the park and hail a hack."

"Let her go," Sarah urged callously. "I am simply dying for my tea."

Some of the color had crept back into Tatiana's cheeks. "No, really, Sarah's quite right. I feel stronger already."

"I'll come with you," Susannah offered loyally.

Tatiana, glancing over her shoulder, could barely see that imperial bronze-haired figure. "If you insist. But it truly isn't needed." She grabbed her friend's arm and started off at a trot.

"I'll take a hack myself to Longchamp's!" Susannah called to her mother as she tried to match Tatiana's brisk pace. "Heavens, Tat, you will make yourself more ill if you keep this up!"

"Susannah." Tatiana slowed a bit. "Can you keep a secret? There's a gentleman up ahead whom I would very much like to encounter. Encounter *alone*."

"Oh!" said Susannah, her gray gaze wide. "Who is it?"

"I don't like to say. Not until I know whether my interest is returned."

"You wretched thing! After I have poured out my heart about Hyde Parker to you!"

The shako bobbed toward the gates of the park. "Susannah, *please*!"

"But you can't encounter him without a chaperone! What will he think of you?"

"I'll say I lost my party in all this throng. He is certain to offer to accompany me home."

"Oh!" said Susannah again. Then she smiled. "How very daring! I wish I had such nerve."

Tatiana kissed her quickly. "Now, go back to your mamma and leave me to my machinations."

"And you'll tell me all about it afterward?"

"On my heart!" Tatiana called, already hurrying away.

The shako was nowhere in sight when she reached the gates. Tatiana paused, catching her breath. "Hack, miss?" a waiting driver called.

I wonder . . . Tatiana stepped toward him. "I have lost my . . . my aunt." She wasn't certain of Gillian Innisford's age, but that ought to suffice. "A bronze-haired lady with a pair of greyhounds. She was with a gentleman—"

The driver nodded knowingly. "Just missed 'em, ye did. Took off in Harry's rig, down toward the High Street."

"Do you suppose you could follow them?" Tatiana asked plaintively.

"Follow 'em?"

"Aye. I'd made other plans, but now I find—" She reached for her handkerchief, dabbed at her eyes. "Oh, Lord! That cad! That utter *cad*!"

The hack driver was a sympathetic soul. He stepped down to lift Tatiana in, and even patted her shoulder. "Don't you worry, miss. I'll get ye safe back to yer auntie all right."

He was as good as his word. Within three minutes he was able to assure Tatiana he had Harry's hack in sight; within ten he was just behind it as it pulled to a stop outside the Savoy, the most elegant hotel in Brighton. Tatiana thanked him effusively and added a large tip to the fare, all the time watching as the lady, her dogs, the boys, and the companion disembarked. "You have saved my life, sir," she said very humbly.

"Glad to be of service. Just don't let that rotter spoil ye

on all men!" He winked and tipped his hat, and Tatiana quickly went inside.

The lobby was cool and quiet after the rush in the streets. Tatiana glanced about, wondering what to do next. A smiling young fellow in livery approached her. "May I be of some assistance, miss?"

"Oh, yes, please. Just now on the street I saw an old friend of my mother's. I recognized her, but I cannot for the life of me recall her name. And I know Mamma would be ever so cross if she discovered I had missed the opportunity to pay my respects." Her lashes fluttered becomingly. "She came in here, so I know you must have seen her as well. A tall woman in a shako hat. She had two dogs on leashes, and—"

"That would be Lady Innisford, miss."

"Of course! Lady Gillian Innisford! How kind of you to refresh my memory. Is she in residence here?"

"Aye, miss. She just arrived this morn."

So Lucas would not yet know of her coming—though Tatiana had no doubt the gossips would not be long in bringing the tale to the countess. There was no time to lose. "I don't like to interrupt her when she has company," she said dubiously. "Perhaps . . . if I might send up a note?"

"Certainly, miss. You'll find pen and paper there in the desks." Tatiana thanked him with a shilling and a dazzling smile, then sat, wondering what on earth she would write. She had just decided on the barest of missives—her card and a request for an interview—and had dipped the quill when from the lobby a familiar voice at her back made her freeze.

"Tatiana!" Good God. It was the countess. Tatiana turned, and her pen clattered to the floor. "My dear, imagine finding you here!" Dulcie swept toward her with an expression of the utmost delight, and Tatiana saw—to her horror—that Lucas was at her side. She glanced down at the paper on which, thank heaven, she'd not yet written a word. "Such happy circumstance!" the countess burbled on. "Lucas has agreed to the table!"

"The . . . table?"

"At Griscombe's! The Hepplewhite. I told you about it."

"So you did." Tatiana recalled with a sinking heart that Griscombe's shop was not two hundred yards away.

"I've dragged him here to tea to celebrate. And now you can join us!"

"Tea? *Here?*" Tatiana's gaze darted toward the staircase.

"Does something about that prospect disturb you, Miss Grimaldi?" Lucas asked, his own eyes narrowed and glinting.

"No, no. Not at all. It is just . . . while I was at the concert, you see, I was taken with a fit of the megrims."

"And so you came across town to the Savoy to soothe them." *Damn his shrewd gaze!*

"The Savoy? Is that where I am?" Tatiana asked with a bewildered air—and then swooned on her feet.

"Good heavens, Lucas, catch her!"

He did, before she hit the floor. His arms were very strong, but she took no comfort in that. Eyes shut tight, she willed herself to go limp in his grasp, then smelled the vial the countess hurried to wave under her nose. "Put her there, Lucas," Dulcie commanded, and she felt herself dropped, none too gently, onto a chaise. "Lord, Lucas! Have a care!"

Tatiana moaned softly, eyelids fluttering. "I want to go home. . . ."

"So you shall, pet, once you—"

"I want to go home now!"

"Well, perhaps it's best," the countess agreed. "Lucas, help her out to the carriage." Once more those strong arms raised her up. She did not dare to look at him.

He carried her through the doors and signaled to Braunton, who drove up in the carriage, bells jingling. Once inside, Tatiana sank back onto the seat with a sigh of relief. The countess bustled in beside her, patting her hands, fanning her forehead. "I always say 'tis madness to attend those park concerts," she fretted, plying the hartshorn again. "All that crush of folk in the hot sun!"

Tatiana peeked between her lashes. So far, so good. Lucas was climbing in as well.

"Oh!" the countess cried suddenly, leaning toward her son. "We haven't any headache powders at home. Do be a pet, Lucas, and run into Fortunay's. It is just next door."

"I don't need any—" Tatiana began, and then nearly swooned in earnest as through the carriage window she saw a pair of handsome greyhounds prance out through the Savoy doors, followed by Lady Gillian Innisford in all her striped splendor. Lucas had stepped outside again and around the box. She could not see his face, but she could see the way he froze abruptly, and the sudden flush of red at his throat.

He stood rigid for the space of a moment. Then he moved with frightening speed, climbing into the coach and slamming shut the door. "The powders, Lucas!" the countess chastised.

"I don't need any powders," Tatiana said very quietly, sliding the window cover shut.

"Why in the world are you doing that?" Dulcie demanded. "It's stuffy as Hades in here. Fresh air, that's what you need."

Tatiana put a hand over hers. "I'm sorry, milady. But I've a dreadful chill."

"Dear Lord, you don't suppose you've caught the fever? That would be absolutely dreadful with the fourteenth so near! We must have Dr. Travis come posthaste. Home, Braunton!" she called, and the carriage clattered off.

Lucas's voice was a study in controlled ferocity as he said very calmly, "I believe, Mother, you'll find our cousin has no objection to your letting back the window cover now."

Tatiana had her eyes clenched again. She was afraid of his fury, truly afraid. Hadn't she heard what this man could do when aroused? Oh, why had she given in to her impulse to follow Lady Innisford? What would he do to her? Kill her? Or throw her out on the street—and what could she do then? She owed everything she had to him and to the countess; if their patronage were withdrawn, what would become of her? He was rich and powerful enough to spread any sort of tale he cared to about her—that she'd been an impostor, that she'd fallen into disgrace. And anything he said would be believed. She had never before realized how completely at his mercy she was. She sat across from him in abject silence. When they arrived, she watched as, without a word, he climbed the stairs to his rooms.

"I don't need the doctor," she insisted to Dulcie, who was fluttering over her. "I feel completely recovered."

"You don't look at *all* yourself, pet. You're so dreadfully pale!"

"No doctor," Tatiana said again. "I am going to lie down."

But she sat instead, curled on the chaise by her bedchamber window, looking out over the roofs of Brighton to the wide, spangled sea. Well, it has been a pretty interlude, she thought ruefully, this season of splendor, the routs and gowns and the adoring young men with their heady words and bouquets. At least she had not fallen in love. However Lucas chose to punish her, her heart would not be broken. He, of course, would be going back to Dorset to his roses. She'd given him the excuse he had been searching for to call off their charade.

A loud knock sounded at the door. "Who is it?" she asked in a small voice.

"Who the devil do you think?" Lucas Strathmere demanded, and strode into the room, slamming the door so hard it rocked the windowpanes.

He was in riding clothes, his storm-ringed eyes flashing lightning. Tatiana forced herself not to collapse on the chaise; she stood up to meet him instead. "I warned you about playing games with me, did I not, Tatiana?" She hesitated, then nodded. "Yet I find you have been trifling indeed. You knew Gillian was in Brighton." There was no point in denial. "What message, I wonder, were you about to send up to her there at the Savoy? Something about the two of you joining together to exact your revenge?" The stab was so close to what had been in Tatiana's heart that she could not help gasping. He took a step, swearing beneath his breath, and she thought he would strike her.

"I only learned she was in Brighton today!" she cried quickly. "I saw her in the park!"

He'd gained control of his temper. "What a pity you did not see fit to share such news with those it most concerned. Of course, that would have spoiled your chances for a tête-à-tête. I can understand anything you might care to do to me, but how you could see fit to conspire against my mother, who has shown you naught but kindness and goodness—"

"I did *not* conspire!" she said, blushing hot and red.

"No? Cozying up to every old gossip in town? Examining Turner for details of my past?"

"You have been spying on me!" She was genuinely shocked.

"It was my occupation once. Call it force of habit. Perhaps you'd care to tell me what you were so eager to discuss with Lady Innisford." She raised her chin, remained silent. "So," he said, long fingers curling on his crop. Tatiana's shoulders drew together, cringing at the prospect of the lash of the whip, untasted for so long. But bravely she unfastened her bodice hooks, reaching behind her back. "What on earth are you doing?" Lucas demanded, brows lifting as she pushed down her sleeves.

She turned, bare except for her chemise. "Go on, then. Beat me."

"*Beat* you—" He glanced down, saw his grip on the crop, and abruptly relaxed it. "God. What sort of man do you think I am?"

"I know what sort you are," she spat at him. "I saw what you wreaked at Mizhakovsk—or did you think I'd forgotten? The carnage, the smell of burning flesh—"

"Is that it, Tatiana? Is that why you hate me, what you blame me for?"

"Whom else should I blame?" she cried angrily. "If you had not come there, Pietr and the others would still be alive. There would still *be* a Mizhakovsk!"

"Pull your damned gown up," he said shortly, "and sit back down." She didn't move. "I said sit!" he roared at her, and she did then, sinking back against the cushions, putting her arms through her sleeves. "Now. If you want to know why I came to Mizhakovsk, why don't you ask?"

She sat tight-lipped. "Damn your willfulness!" he exploded. "Go on and nourish your grudge for the rest of your life. I'm off to where a man can have a spot of peace, without wenches bedeviling him at every turn."

To Dorset, and the roses. Let him go, then, and be damned!

She managed to let him get all the way to the threshold before she relented. "Very well, then. Why *did* you come there?"

"Ah, that's more like it. Since you inquire so nicely, I'd made a promise to a friend."

"What friend? *Dyed* Ivan?"

He looked at her, astonished. "You remember him?"

"Oh, yes. We had not many strangers in Mizhakovsk, you will recall."

"What was he like?"

"Short. Thick. Dark. He had a scar here—" She touched her chin. "And strong." She colored faintly, recalling the power of Lucas's arms. "I . . . he was kind to me. He never hit me. And he brought me sweets. I remember how I felt when he stopped coming."

The description fit Casimir. Lucas looked down at the crop again. "Georgi—your foster father. Did he beat you?"

"It was not so much," she lied. "But more once *Dyed* Ivan no longer came. Was he . . . my father?"

"I don't think so. Would you like for him to have been?" She nodded, and he saw in the depths of her eyes the specter of the conflagration of her village.

Then she straightened on the chaise. "So. He sent you to me. Why? To bring me sweets?"

"I don't know," Lucas said bluntly, and told her of the vow Casimir had sworn him to and the paper sealed until his death, with only those two words on it: *Mizhakovsk* and her name.

Her gaze grew ever wider. "And you came? All the way across the world to Russia—for that? Two words on a paper?"

"I'd made a promise," he said stiffly. "Casimir was not a man to ask such an outlandish favor for no reason. And what happened when I arrived—that only proved how right he was."

"Who were the men who burned the village?" she demanded.

"I don't know. They had no identification. They were trailing me, though. They were with me in the coach to Lipovsk. But I would have sworn on my life they had not followed me to you." He closed his eyes, remembering how he'd stopped and listened, staring behind him across the endless snow. . . .

"They were trailing *you*," she echoed pointedly.

"They were following me to you."

"Nonsense! What in God's name could they want with me?"

"I don't know. Casimir—*Dyed* Ivan—he never said anything to you about your parents?"

"I cannot recall it. But Georgi and Vera—they must have known."

"If they did, they did not let on to me. Was he a good liar, Georgi?"

Tatiana snorted. "Speak about unsubtle . . ."

"I thought as much. And if they did know, they can't tell us now."

A sea change was coming into her eyes, the clear green shading to cloudy. "But if you came because of me—if those men were after you on my account . . . oh, that is impossible. I am nothing, nobody! They *must* have been chasing you. You said yourself you were a spy."

"I had not been to Russia in five years. And I'd never been within a hundred—two hundred—miles of Lipovsk before. No. It was something about you, and Casimir."

She had drawn within herself, very small, on the chaise. "If it was because of me—then it must be my fault. All of it. The village. Georgi and Vera . . . Pietr . . ."

"I scarcely see how you can take responsibility when you knew naught about it."

"Still . . ." Her face showed her anguish at the realization. "You didn't come here to buy a hunter at all. You came because you think I may still be in danger."

"It's highly unlikely," Lucas said with a shrug. "Nothing happened once we returned to England, nor when Mother took you to the Cotswolds. Nonetheless, Casimir entrusted you to me."

"Oh, God! And all this time I have blamed you!"

"You were right to," he said then, intently. "I ought not to have gone there. I should have left you to your happiness."

She raised her tear-swept face. "You think . . . I would have been happy with Pietr?"

He hesitated, shook his head. "I don't know. It seems to me that you were meant for something more."

His candor exacted hers. She met his gaze. "I am happier now than I ever was in Mizhakovsk."

"Even with Pietr's arms around you?"

"Even with Pietr's arms around me." And at the confession she began to cry again—for her lost innocence, for the completed betrayal, for her relief that it should finally be so. "He was . . . a nice boy, Pietr." She sniffed, reaching for her handkerchief, taking the broad white one he offered instead.

"Like Freddy Whittles."

Against all odds, she nodded and laughed. "Very much like Freddy. Stalwart and strong and good—and an utter fool."

"Yet Georgi told me Pietr was the greatest catch in Mizhakovsk."

"You ought to have seen the others." Then her small face turned solemn. "Lady Innisford—forgive me. It is true, I had harbored some notion of . . ."

"Conspiracy?" he prompted, when she did not finish. "Not with that one. Take my word on it—she would eat you alive."

"I thought you were in love with her," Tatiana whispered.

"I was," he answered evenly.

She was on the point of asking more when the door burst open behind him. "Oh, Tatiana, dearest! I know you aren't well, but I am so distraught, and Marianne has just brought me the most *dreadful* news!" It was the countess, eyes red-rimmed, bodice heaving. "And just when Prinny writes his acceptance for the fourteenth! Oh, all is ruined! *She* is—" For the first time she saw her son, in his cloak and boots, standing beside the door. She glanced back at Tatiana uncertainly. "I . . . I do beg your pardon. Am I interrupting?"

"Not at all, Mother," Lucas assured her. "Do share this information that has sent you into such straits."

"This information . . . oh! Oh, it is nothing, really."

He leaned against the wall, enjoying her discomfort. "No? I should have said it has stood you on your head. And I do believe you've been weeping. I cannot bear to see you so upset. Tell us your news, I beg."

Dulcie proved her eyes could flash fire as readily as his. "You unnatural boy! Very well, here you are: Gillian Innisford has come to Brighton." Then she considered his clothing. "But I see you are already acquainted with the fact, since you are dressed to run cowering home to Dorset."

"In point of fact," Lucas said coolly, "I am on my way to a card party at Captain Rawleigh's. I expect it will be most diverting, as I just told our cousin. No women are allowed." He bowed to them, his gaze glinting. "Good night, ladies. Don't wait up for me."

Then he was gone. The countess stared after him, amazed. "A card party!" she exclaimed. "Why, he has not bestirred himself for such a thing in nigh on twelve years! And he *knows* she is in Brighton!" She shook her head in bewilderment.

Tatiana, filled to the brim with contrition—how *could* she have been so wrong about the man?—let out a sigh. "They do say wonders never cease."

Fourteen

TATIANA DRESSED WITH particular care for the countess's rout on the fourteenth of July. She wore a sheath of the silver-spangled celadon silk—cut across the bodice as low as decency allowed—and Dulcie's amethysts at her throat and ears. Her hair was in a braided chignon at the nape of her neck, caught in an argentine net scattered with sequins; the sea air of Brighton had more than vanquished any further attempts to have it take on curl. But Turner, come for a final inspection of Carruthers's handiwork, declared herself satisfied.

"Sleek," she decreed, grinning. "That's how you always look, miss. No more on you than there should be, anywhere. Not like some 'uns, who need to gild the lily." So the maid, Tatiana realized, had heard of Gillian Innisford's arrival in town. Everyone would have by now. Since that revealing conversation in her bedchamber, she'd found herself realizing more and more how daunting the force of gossip had to be to a man as private as Lucas Strathmere. What he'd told her about coming to Mizhakovsk had altered her opinion of him considerably. To have gone so far for nothing more than a promise to a dead man—he could not be so cold and distant as she'd always believed. She'd resolved to try to be more kind to him—if he would allow her to be.

But just now, her heart was pounding at the prospect of finally meeting Dulcie's beloved Prinny. "What is he like, Turner—the Regent, I mean?"

"Faith, how should I know? He pays no heed to the likes of *me*." Then she unbent a bit. "La, you'll do fine, miss. He's not so different from a duke or earl. He's nowhere near as rich as the young master, not with the way he spends. Anyway, what he likes best in this world is a pretty face and a fair tongue to go with it. And I reckon you've got that." She gave Tatiana a final, minute examination. "Go on downstairs, then, and see what use you can be to Her Ladyship."

"Yes, Turner." Tatiana dropped an admirable curtsy that made the maid reconsider.

"Here, now, I think we might just pull up that bodice a bit!"

But Tatiana was gone.

The salons on the first floor had been cleared of all extraneous furnishings to accommodate the expected crush, and the pocket doors to the parlors beyond had been opened as well. Card tables were arranged in the drawing rooms, and the billiards room, which she'd never seen Lucas use, had been made ready, the lamps lit, the baize napped, and the sideboard equipped with bottles of cognac and port.

It still lacked a half hour before even the most ill-mannered guests might be expected to arrive. Tatiana wandered through the empty rooms, straightening an occasional stem of rocket or larkspur in the countess's arrangements, fixing the sofa pillows at angles more pleasing to her eye. Having nudged a set of Sèvres vases further apart on the mantel in the blue salon, she left the room—and then, hearing stealthy footsteps behind her, turned to see Smithers undoing her well-intentioned aid.

"Does something displease you, Smithers, about my positioning of those vases?" she asked with infinite politeness. Caught in the act, he huffed and quickly left the room. Of course, thought Tatiana, there were some folk only too ready to remind her that she was overreaching herself. What if the Regent recognized her as an impostor? What if she made some dreadful error in etiquette and brought the household to shame? Lost in such dark thoughts, she stepped across the hallway—and smacked straight on into Lucas as she did.

He steadied her with a hand on her elbow. He was in evening dress, black, very formal; the clothes emphasized his height, so that he seemed to tower over her. *Kinder*, she reminded herself, and smiled up at him. "I beg your pardon, cousin."

He met the smile with a scowl, eyes raking over her, and she found herself wishing she'd listened to Turner's advice about her décolletage. "Are you waiting for a compliment, Miss Grimaldi? Very well, here is one. You look more than nineteen in that gown."

"I was not aware that for a lady, being thought older than her age was considered complimentary," Tatiana said coyly.

"No. But I thought it would please a mere child like you."

Her hackles rose. "Is that the way you think of me? As a child?"

"It is how I try to," he answered obliquely. "Mind your

backside when Prinny comes. He likes to pinch." And he brushed past her, whistling a bit of a waltz.

So much for kindness, Tatiana thought indignantly, just as the door knocker struck and Smithers bustled to answer it.

It was Susannah and her mother and sisters. "*Dreadfully* early, I know," Mrs. Cuthbert assured the countess, "but I did think you might require some assistance with the arrangements. So difficult to entertain, isn't it, in a house that isn't truly your own?" They went off to debate the position of a chaise and sofa, while Susannah led Tatiana aside.

"Have you heard?" she asked in a rushed whisper. "The most extraordinary news! Eliza Boothton is on the verge of engagement to Lord Mells! I know for a *fact* that she has had a tendresse for Captain Shillington ever since she came out last year."

"What could make her agree to marry Mugger Mells, then?"

"Oh, Tat!" Susannah shook with laughter. "Where *did* you ever hear that name? Not she. Her mother has agreed. He—Lord Mells—has got fifteen thousand a year."

Tatiana cocked her smooth blond head. "Does it ever seem odd to you, Susannah, that English mothers are so ready to sacrifice their daughters' happiness on the altar of Mammon?"

"Oh, when it comes to that—" Susannah waved a hand. "Hasn't Mamma told us often enough it is just as easy to fall in love with a rich man as a poor one—easier, even? What chills me is that he is so very *old*. Why, it would be like marrying your cousin Lucas!" She turned a neat pirouette on the carpet. "I'm just glad to have her spoken for. Clifford is coming tonight! He told Captain Rawleigh, who told William Shelton, who told his mother, who told Mamma! And she told me. Apparently, my own dearest friend never bothered to pass the word along."

Tatiana blushed guiltily. It was true; she had neglected to send Susannah the news of her beau's acceptance. Susannah only laughed, though, and rapped her with her fan. "Silly thing, I am teasing! It made no difference whatsoever, except to spare my nerves the waiting. Oh, and Madame had to rush *madly* to finish this gown. What do you think of it?"

They were interrupted by more arrivals: Freddy Whittles, who despite Lucas's discouragement of his suit was far from giving up hope, and Lady Bournemouth and her daughters ("The countess felt she had no choice," Tatiana whispered to Susannah's questioning look), and Captain Rawleigh, dapper in his regimentals, and Lady Shelton and her husband and son—and then the carriages began to stop at such a dizzying rate that Tatiana scarcely had time to catch her breath before they sat down to dinner, with full fifty guests. She'd been placed between Lord Shelton and an elderly earl she'd never met before, but Freddy Whittles sat across from her and sighed and made such eyes over the watercress bisque that she was hard put not to laugh.

Her humor faded, though, as she observed Lucas's behavior. The countess had set him beside Selma Bournemouth, no doubt intending that his churlish manners put the scotch to her mother's pretensions once and for all. If that was the hope, the result had to give Dulcie pause. He was applying himself to the plain, silly girl with more dedication than Tatiana had ever glimpsed in him outside the rose gardens. He leaned his silky black head close to her dull brown one to catch her conversation, helped her to dainties from the trays, and once, when she let her napkin slide from her lap, retrieved it with great gallantry. From the far end of the table, Lady Bournemouth beamed at them and said in very loud tones, "Miss Grimaldi informs me, you know, that on the Continent misses are not considered marriageable until at *least* the age of twenty-three!" Lucas glanced at Tatiana with something unreadable in his blue eyes.

The countess seemed taken aback by her son's attentions to his neighbor; more than once Tatiana saw her staring at the couple incredulously. Not until the third course had been laid did Tatiana realize she herself had been paying unusual heed to her cousin. Considering its target, his behavior could only be considered chivalrous to the extreme. Why, then, was it so galling to her? Watching him help Selma to an omelet, it dawned on her: *He has never been as publicly solicitous of me*.

But then, Lady Bournemouth's daughter boasted an impeccable bloodline. And I, thought Tatiana, am only a girl from Mizhakovsk. *What should I expect?*

She was glad when the ladies removed and she could distract herself with soothing Susannah, who was jealous over some flattery paid by Clifford Hyde Parker to her sister Sarah. "I'll scratch her eyes out," she swore in a hiss, "if she tries to steal him from me!" Lady Bournemouth was speaking in glowing terms to anyone who would listen of what she termed Selma's "capture" of the Earl of Somerleigh.

A rush of new arrivals invited for dancing and cards brought relief from Tatiana's disquieting reflections. She had no dearth of partners, but her "cousin" danced two sets with Selma Bournemouth—one number was a waltz—and then vanished into the card rooms. Pleading a need for air, Tatiana had Captain Rawleigh escort her in that direction and saw Lucas seated at a table across from Lady Bournemouth. She could not tell if the woman's triumphant expression was due to her piquet hand or to the conquest her daughter seemed to have made.

But what is it to me, Tatiana thought, reimmersing herself in the dancing, if he courts Selma? She had known from the first of the countess's devout hope that her son's reintroduction to society, of which Tatiana was only the engine, would result in his wedded bliss. Still—Selma Bournemouth! Why, that sprigged muslin was more suited to a schoolgirl. And as for that hair, Tatiana thought spitefully, she'd seen more flattering curls on the countess's spaniels. Not to mention that she danced as if she were putting out a fire with her shoes. . . .

There was some sort of commotion at the front doors. Dulcie rose from her chair, hearing Smithers answering the knock. Tatiana, who had given in to Freddy's persistent begging for a dance, watched over his shoulder as the countess signaled the musicians to break off. The room grew hushed as a tall man in a gold-embroidered waistcoat, a crimson coat, and astonishingly wide pantaloons strolled in, with a small band of companions in his wake.

"Please, please, no ceremony," the Prince Regent—for it had to be he—decreed grandly, waving a beringed hand. "Do go on as you are!" After a false start, the musicians found the beat and began playing again. The dancing recommenced, but no one in the room was unaware of the Royal in their midst.

Tatiana stared at him covertly as Freddy whirled her past. He was quite handsome, she decided, observing his fine head of fair, waving hair, his patrician nose, and his gorgeous attire. He was larger than she had expected—quite corpulent, really—but he bore it well; his splendid carriage made one overlook his size. And his manners were absolutely exquisite. He was far more natural, kissing Dulcie on both cheeks in greeting, than she'd ever seen the countess's own son be.

"Amazing coat he's got on," Freddy murmured enviously.

"Oh, he is the soul of elegance! Who are those gentlemen he's brought with him?"

"Some of the dukes, his brothers. Quite a coup for Dulcie to have drawn that bunch here; they're more apt to keep company with—" He caught himself, coughed. "I have a devil of a time keeping 'em straight. That must be Adolphus, Duke of Cambridge, in the checquered waistcoat.

I wonder what that cravat knot is called? And Frederick—he's a decent sort, Frederick, though as you can see quite hopeless in matters of fashion. A decent soldier, though. Thick as coal, they say. And that is Ernest, Duke of Cumberland. With the eye patch."

Tatiana considered this last, who was still in the doorway, contemplating the gathering with a haughty sneer. His hair, lighter than his brothers', curled backward from a forehead that was high and proud. "He looks quite intimidating," she murmured to Freddy.

"Who?" asked her devoted swain, who'd been contemplating her delectable earlobe.

"Cumberland. What happened to his eye?"

"Battle of Tournai," Freddy said briefly, not relishing her attention to another man. "He's the black sheep."

"Why? Does he pinch?" Tatiana asked, smiling.

"He kills," Freddy said matter-of-factly and, when she stared at him, confirmed it with a nod. "That is what everyone says, anyway. That he stabbed his valet to death."

"Why would he do such a thing?" she demanded, astonished.

Freddy's lips were tight. "It's not a fitting matter to discuss with you, cherub." Curious, Tatiana twisted to have another look—and found the Duke of Cumberland's one good eye trained straight on her. Quickly, she lowered her gaze and let Freddy spin her off. But when the waltz brought them back past the doorway, Cumberland was still staring. Tatiana felt an odd tingling at the nape of her neck.

"Freddy," she began, intending to ask him to take her for champagne.

"I see, I see. The countess is beckoning. Time for you to come face-to-face with Prinny." He frowned at her. "Promise you won't be swept away."

"Oh, Freddy, of course I won't!" But Tatiana was trembling as he led her toward Dulcie, who'd been trying for some time to catch her glance. I will be very calm, she told herself. *I will do the countess justice. I will—*

"Your Highness," Dulcie said to the Prince Regent, beaming a brilliant smile. "I have the great pleasure to present to you my cousin, Miss Grimaldi."

"I am honored, Your Highness," Tatiana said faintly, dropping a low, lovely curtsy—which she wished had not been quite so low when she peeked up to find the prince's pale eyes fixed on the swell of her breasts.

"Charmed, utterly charmed," he said in that deep, thrilling voice, taking her hand. "But why, my dear Countess, have I never chanced upon Miss Grimaldi before? For I know I surely would recall it if I had."

"Miss Grimaldi only just arrived from the Continent," Dulcie explained smoothly.

"Ah-hah! I thought I detected the trace of an accent. Italian?" he hazarded, and Tatiana nodded shyly. "Naturally. Italy lays claim to the most beauteous women in the world. Tell me, Miss Grimaldi, what think you of my England?"

He was still gripping her hand. "No one could have received a warmer welcome here than I, Your Highness," she replied.

"And no wonder. Why, she's as pretty a pigeon as ever I laid eyes on, Dulcibella!" The countess glowed, and Tatiana blushed becomingly. "You must favor us with a dance, my dear."

For some reason Lucas chose that moment to press forward through the crowd, shouldering Freddy aside to stand by Tatiana. Though disconcerted by his sudden appearance, Dulcie said graciously, "I'm sure, Your Highness, you recall my son, the Earl of Somerleigh."

The Regent let go Tatiana's hand then. "I'd heard you were in Brighton," he said to Lucas, "though I did not altogether credit the report. What, pray tell, impelled your sudden reimmersion into society?"

The dislike between the two men hovered in the air like smoke. Lucas smiled tautly. "Nothing more than my need to oversee my cousin's introduction to the same."

"Ah, doing the avuncular thing and all that. I daresay you have your hands full with such a lovely chit, eh? Plenty of bouquets on the mantel?"

"Enough to keep me occupied protecting her virtue." Was there a veiled threat in the words?

"Rather a novel posture for you, I imagine," the Regent said with infinite politeness.

"You think so?" Lucas asked, just as politely. "Perhaps we differ in our definitions of virtue." And the countess blanched.

Prinny drew his brows together. "Your Highness," Dulcie said swiftly, with a warning glance at her son, "I've been telling Miss Grimaldi of the marvels you have crafted at the pavilion—assuring her, in fact, there is nothing like it in her homeland or anywhere else in the world."

He relaxed his stance. "Ah, yes, my pavilion! You and Miss Grimaldi must visit us there one of these nights, eh, so she can see for herself? I do not flatter myself, I trust, in having heard quite reputable authorities account it more extravagant than the palace of the de Medicis." He trained his gracious smile on Tatiana. "I should be most interested in your opinion of the place."

"I am honored beyond words by your invitation," Tatiana said prettily, "though I fail to understand how my humble opinion could add to what has already claimed the whole world's renown." She had the dual satisfaction of seeing Dulcie sigh with relief and Lucas scowl at her.

And she had pleased the prince; his pale eyes glowed as he bent over her hand once more. "Fine words indeed, to hear from a native of the birthplace of beauty! You cannot tell me, though, that they speak in Italy of my little—"

"I beg your pardon," Lucas broke in, wresting Tatiana's hand into his. "My cousin has promised me this dance. I trust you will excuse us."

"Lucas, for heaven's sake!" his mother murmured, appalled.

"Come, Tatiana!" He tucked the hand through his arm.

She had time only to drop one more hurried curtsy in the Regent's direction and say defiantly over her shoulder, "I should very much enjoy visiting the pavilion, Your Highness!" Then Lucas, glowering, led her to a place in the line.

She stiffened as they began the gavotte, and he glanced at her. "Is something troubling you, cousin?"

"You were abominably rude to him."

"He's an ass."

"I found him the soul of politeness," she said archly, "which is more than anyone would ever think of you!"

He held her small, unyielding body at arm's length, staring down at her. "It is perhaps incomprehensible to a creature so willful as yourself that you might plunge in beyond your depth. But this is not Mizhakovsk, Miss Grimaldi. And he is not some peasant boy trying to grapple you beneath the pine trees."

It took enormous effort not to spit in his face. "Is that how you think I spent my time there—grappling boys beneath the pine trees?"

"I haven't any notion how you spent your time there. I only know it could not have prepared you for this." His stormy gaze swept over the elegant throng in the room.

"Your mother, though," said Tatiana, determined not to let him know how his words stung her, "has gone to great trouble to prepare me for just such occasions. Do enlighten me, pray. Is it her training or my ability to assimilate it that you mistrust most?"

His eyes came back to her. "Don't think I underestimate you. I am surely the one soul in England who will never make that mistake; I've seen you drive a wolfhound at sleigh."

Her own eyes burned with tears at this unwelcome reminder of their first encounter. She blinked them angrily away. How utterly like him to throw that in her face when she'd just held her own with the Regent of England! It was he who'd been uncouth, challenging Prinny with his posturing and threats.

His hand tightened on hers. "It's not you I mistrust, Tatiana. It's that worthless Regent and all his despicable siblings. If you might have known King George when he was still himself . . . there was not in all the world a more simple, noble man. And they—Prinny and his brothers and sisters—have thrown away all the goodwill and honor he earned." She looked up at him, surprised. Something had softened his harsh face—memory, or pity, or another emotion she could not name. "There is in you that which they could never hope to find in themselves. And I . . . do not care to see you swallowed up by them." He spoke, for once, without sarcasm or contempt. Those words, she might almost believe, had come from his heart—or what was left of it.

But the music had ended. He released her with a bow, the mask once more firmly in place. "You are not wont to heed my advice, cousin. But I will prevail on you in this one instance: Steer clear of the Royals."

Tatiana tossed her head, sending a sparkle of sequins up into the light. "And if I do not?"

"Then you will find me unalterably at your side." He laughed at her appalled expression. "Since there is nothing you could find less appealing, I am confident this once in your obedience."

"Won't your treasured Miss Bournemouth find your continued attendance on me curious?" she asked tartly.

"Who?" He recollected himself. "Oh, I trust not. Her mother has your assurance that on the Continent a girl is not considered marriageable until she is at *least* twenty-three."

His voice so closely approximated Lady Bournemouth's round tones that Tatiana nearly laughed herself. But there was nothing amusing in what he was proposing. "Am I to understand that if I accept His Highness's invitation to dance—"

"We will make an awkward threesome," Lucas confirmed.

"He is your mother's honored guest!" she hissed.

"I admire much about my mother. But not always her taste in companions."

"What would you know about companions, you . . . you misanthrope!"

He arched a brow. "Why, cousin. Considering how late you are come from foreign shores, your grasp of English never fails to astound me." Smithers, baleful as always, stood in the door to announce the late supper. Lucas once more proffered his arm. "Shall we go in and see those cherries Mother has been so frantic about?"

Tatiana looked around for a less objectionable escort. Where the devil had Freddy disappeared to now, when she needed him? Her gaze alighted on the Duke of Cumberland, who adjusted his eye patch and started toward her across the salon, a sense of purpose in his stride. She could not help but shiver. Something about that man made her flesh crawl.

Reluctantly she laid her hand on Lucas's. "If His Highness invites me to the pavilion," she said stoutly, "I *will* go."

"Understand this," he said pleasantly enough as he led her to the tables. "If you do, I will let drop to every busybody in Brighton exactly how and where I first met you."

She stopped in mid-step. "Bastard. You wouldn't dare."

He smiled. "Go ahead and try me."

Tatiana took a plate to hide how her hands were quaking. "Do as you please, cousin dear. Consider this, though. After you and your mother have lavished such attention on me, on whom is the resultant censure more likely to fall: a peasant girl from Russia, or a peer of the realm who has already been accused of shooting a man in the back?"

Surely that would shake him. But he merely scooped a ladle into the chafing dish of brandied cherries. "Never play dare," he told her, smiling complacently along the line at Lady Bournemouth, "with a man who has nothing to lose. Can I help you to some of these?"

Fifteen

DESPITE LUCAS'S LOATHSOME behavior, the aftermath of the countess's rout was all Tatiana could have hoped for—indeed, even more, for among the nosegays arriving the next morning was one of snow-white orchids, its card bearing the Regent's name. " 'Your devoted servant, George Augustus Frederick,' " she murmured, tracing the words with a disbelieving finger.

"And," Dulcie said complacently from the table, "here's an invitation to dinner at the pavilion. Soon, too—Thursday next." She smiled at Tatiana. "I am pleased, young lady. Most pleased indeed. It only goes to show that Lucas—"

"Yes?" demanded the gentleman in question, who'd come in to breakfast.

"Oh, that you are a fool. See what pretty posies Prinny has sent our cousin."

Lucas cast a glance. "God. Orchids. I can't abide them. They smell like human flesh."

"Thank you," said the countess, "for that disgusting observation." But Tatiana, taking a quick sniff, found that somehow they did. "You might at least congratulate her."

"On what? I'd be amazed if he didn't send her flowers. He has a standing order at Binchley's, you know. Twenty bouquets a day."

"Not all of them so costly as that," Dulcie said. "And not all of them accompanied by invitations to dine at the pavilion." She waved the vellum in his face.

"I trust I am included in the party?"

"It does not seem you are. Not surprising, considering your outlandish behavior last evening. Why, I quite expected you to borrow Captain Rawleigh's sword and suggest a duel."

"I would not be averse." Lucas carved the beef, then helped himself liberally to horseradish sauce. "But since I'm not included, she's not going."

"The devil I'm not!" Tatiana said hotly.

He finished his mouthful. "The devil is what I am trying to spare you from."

"Oh, really, Lucas." The countess frowned at him. "I realize you and he have had differences in the past. But I scarcely see how ruining Tatiana's prospects—"

"I see it as preserving her prospects—for any sort of reputable match."

"He is as good as the King of England!"

Lucas looked at her for a moment. "No," he said finally, definitively. "No, he is not."

Dulcie flushed. "That is not what I meant. I only thought . . . well, he *will* be king someday. And I fail to comprehend how Tatiana's reputation could be anything but enhanced by his favor."

"If you believe that, why do you no longer receive Mrs. Beavers?"

The flush deepened. "I am not suggesting she become his . . . his intimate!"

"Merely a very dear friend, such as you?" He lowered his knife at her. "Listen, Mother. You have become blind—or choose to be blind—to certain aspects of the Royals' behavior that our cousin might not so readily ignore."

"And why is that, pray tell?"

"Because," he said bluntly, "you are a widow of five-and-fifty—oh, a very well-preserved five-and-fifty—and she is nineteen."

The countess was so aghast at this unwonted revelation of her age that Tatiana thought she would burst into tears. Quickly she stepped in to speak for herself. "The only obvious conclusion to be drawn from Cousin Lucas's obstinacy on this matter is that he has no faith in me to govern my behavior—"

"With some reason," Lucas growled.

She ignored that, since from his point of view it was certainly true. "Or of the Regent to take interest in me for any other than the extremely sordid cause he has just revealed. I can only lay this down to some defect in character that makes him imagine in other folks' minds what occupies his own."

He reddened at that. "Cousin, if you imagine I have any such thought toward *you*—"

"Then you would not deny," she said brightly, "the possibility, however remote, that the Regent might find me an entertaining companion for conversation, or perhaps for dancing or cards—pastimes you and I, you'll recall, have occasionally enjoyed."

"You'll not flummox me with your too-clever tongue, chit. You and I are family."

"But we're not, of course. Not really. And yet you admit

yourself you have not the slightest inclination toward seducing me."

"Tatiana," the countess reproved.

She shrugged, settling the orchids in their vase. "No doubt His Lordship thinks himself above other mortals in his scrupulousness. I wonder what a certain lady currently in residence at the Savoy might say to that."

His jaw was tight as a vise. "Why, you—" he began.

But he was interrupted by his mother's laughter. "Come, come, Lucas! Give her her due. Do you honestly think poor Prinny stands a chance against her?"

The look in his eye was downright dangerous. "I would not underplay, Mother, the appeal of an intrigue with the Regent of England for a foreigner—one who is only too aware of what a complete revelation of her true circumstances could cause in such an event."

"God, Lucas!" the countess burst out. "You see shadows where there are none! No one but you or I could make such a revelation. And even if we did, by now it would not be believed."

Tatiana's green gaze had narrowed. "So you think I still hold Russia so much to heart."

"I know how I love England," he retorted, "even though it be governed by a fool. Who's to say your *dyed* did not send me to Russia for that reason—knowing I would bring you here, and set you up, and expose you to the Regent's crowd?"

"As to such intentions," she told him coldly, "I know nothing. It was you who made that promise to your friend."

Lucas felt a hint of shame. It was only her provoking words about Gillian that had put the thought in his mind. Whatever Casimir had intended, it could not be that. Nonetheless, "You will not go to the pavilion without my company," he decreed.

"I must confess," said Tatiana, running a hand back over

her smooth hair, "I am by now utterly perplexed as to your motives. Are you protecting me, milord, or the Regent you profess to despise, or England?"

Lucas was no longer certain himself. He sat in silence. She stared at him for a moment with evident contempt. "If you will excuse me," she said then, "I'll withdraw. I am going to my rooms. After I do a bit of 'broidery, I shall write to Napoleon and then to the Tsar on my efforts so far to foment a war between my homeland and England. There's not a moment to waste."

She was so angry by the time she climbed the stairs that she was close to tears. How *dare* he? she thought furiously. *Just because he himself is lacking in any sort of self-control or virtue! To imply that I am angling to become the Regent's mistress—and for such a reason! I will go to the pavilion, by God! At least I'll be assured of company with manners there!*

There was a tentative knock at the door. Lucas, Tatiana thought, lip curling. Come to apologize for his outrageous allegations.

But it was the countess, pleating her skirts in her hands—something she had warned Tatiana against from her first lesson in etiquette. "Leave us, Carruthers," she commanded. The maid went out, closing the door with unaccustomed care.

Dulcie paced to the window, stood for a moment, then paced back. "I cannot help but feel, Tatiana," she said at last, "that you are owed some explanation for my son's rudeness to you."

"No explanation is needed. He despises me."

"No, no, my dear! Whatever bizarre allegations he has made, it is his feelings for the Regent—but I must go back a step. I do not know what rumor or gossip you may have heard regarding my son—"

"I heard he shot a man in the back," Tatiana said tautly.

"Oh, dear. The trouble with *on-dit*, you know, is that it is so rarely true."

"He did not shoot him, then?"

"He did. More's the rue. But the circumstances . . ." She glanced back at the door. "These are matters, you must understand, that are known only at the highest level of government."

"I wonder, then, why you would entrust them to me."

The countess laughed. "You mean the accusation that you are a Russian agent? I honestly fear sometimes that Lucas is losing his mind. My late husband, the Admiral—he was always able to view matters from the proper perspective. But then, he was more of the world. Lucas has spent these last years in such solitude. . . . You spoke of Gillian Innisford. You ought not to have."

"He ought not to have said what he did about me."

"Quite true, quite true. I, of course, have sufficient faith in your gratitude for all we have done for you to trust you completely."

"All you have done *for* me," said Tatiana, "is in expiation of what your son did *to* me."

Distressed, the countess sank into a chair. "Do hear me out, Tatiana, and perhaps you will understand why Lucas is so opposed to your further intercourse with Prinny. Many years ago, when he was young and impressionable, Lucas took a fancy to a most unsuitable young woman. Unsuitable on every count—breeding, family, reputation, manners. Oh, it was not unexpected, I suppose. Every youth will have his fling. If it had remained that . . . but Lucas formed the intention of marrying this creature. This . . . this dealer in a gambling hell! The Admiral and I forbade it, of course. It was not to be borne! Lucas proved, however, steadfast in his devotion. He had some grand idea, I think, of reforming her, converting her. It took but ten minutes in her company to recognize *she* saw no need to reform. She was the most *brazen*—well, she still is. The upshot was, the Admiral swore to disinherit him if the marriage took place. Lucas was altogether willing. Gillian was not. Within days of the Admiral's pronouncement, she'd contracted herself to Lord Innisford. The ceremony took place, and the Admiral and I breathed a heavy—and all too premature—sigh of relief."

Tatiana, glowering, was considering she was not the first female to whom Lucas had played Pygmalion. "Your son has made it a habit, then, to elevate undeserving young women?"

Dulcie met her flashing gaze. "There is rather a vast difference between Gillian Innisford and you. She was a common fortune-hunter. Your plight was not of your own making. Anyway, as I say, we were too sure of ourselves. Gillian's marriage showed no sign of quelling Lucas's passion. To distract him, the Admiral engaged him in the Foreign Office. I urged that he be sent abroad immediately, but the Admiral's superiors thought he would prove more useful infiltrating the inner circles of discontent here. He went on playing the gay roué in London while identifying sympathizers with Bonaparte's cause. He was most adept at his work. A number of arrests were made—but who would suspect Lucas Strathmere, who whiled away his time with gambling and drinking? Then Lucas heard, somehow, that Lord Innisford was smuggling arms into England to support an invasion by France."

She spread her hands on her lap. "Lucas formed the intention of procuring evidence against him. I think he still harbored hopes of rescuing his beloved Gillian from a traitor's clutches. Unbeknownst to his superiors, or even to his father, he stood watch over the wharf at Lord Innisford's estate. After many nights, proof arrived in the form of a jolly boat rowing to the dock just at dawn. Lucas stood ready with his pistols. Lord Innisford came forth through the fog and mist. Money was exchanged; the cargo was about to be unloaded. Lucas stepped out to make the arrest. Just then, a gaggle of 'prentice boys came up along the riverbank. Heaven only knows what brought them there at that unhappy moment. But the men in the boat began to shoot at them. Lucas called to them to stop, but they ignored the warning. Lucas felt he had no choice but to fire. He called another warning, then he fired. And the next moment, Lord Innisford lay dead in the grass."

"So his actions were in the course of his duty as an agent of the Crown," Tatiana said thoughtfully. "Why, then, was an inquest held?"

"That, alas, is where Prinny comes in. By the time the servants ran down from the house, the jolly boat, the cargo, the 'prentices—all had vanished into the mist. There was only Lucas's word on what had happened. And Lord Innisford had been a particular intimate of the prince's. With King George's health so uncertain, Prinny could not afford the scandal of having it become known that one of his closest confidants had been aiding Napoleon's cause. He was so desperate to be named Regent, poor man. So he commanded that no mention of the true reason for Lucas's actions be made public."

"Which left your son branded a murderer."

"It was not so bald as that. Someone in the Foreign Office had the notion of laying all the trouble at Lady Innisford's feet. Considering her background, it was not preposterous to think it true—the Admiral certainly did! And since Lord Innisford's marriage was so recent, very little stigma would transfer to him. The Crown's case was prepared accordingly. It was *Lady* Innisford who had made arrangements for the delivery, *Lady* Innisford who came to the wharf that morning. Her husband's arrival on the scene was accidental and tragic. Lucas had fired at the men in the boat, and Lord Innisford threw himself by mishap into the bullet's path."

"Very neat," Tatiana commented.

"It was, wasn't it?" The countess sounded wistful. "If only Lucas had allowed it to go forward that way, he'd have been cleared on all accounts. But—"

"He would not testify against her," Tatiana said with sudden certainty.

Dulcie bowed her head. "No. He would not speak a word at the inquest, either to accuse her or in his own defense. Lord, but Prinny was furious! It is a tribute solely to the respect the Admiral commanded that our son wasn't held over on murder charges. His punishment instead was to be sent to St. Petersburg. To his father's surprise, he distinguished himself admirably there, until the alliance between the Tsar and Bonaparte extinguished all his hopes. Then he returned to Dorset. And there he languished, nursing his bitterness, until—well, until you came into his life."

"Well!" Tatiana said after a moment. "I can understand his violent dislike for the Regent. To have supposed that any gentleman would acquiesce to so gross a miscarriage of justice—"

"Oh, come, come! Men lie all the time, for all sorts of reasons. Even the best of men."

"Your son did not. I gather you urged him to?"

"We did what we thought proper," the countess insisted. "The immediate gain—the extinction of any possibility of Lady Innisford's ever returning Lucas's love—seemed more than worth the cost."

"She could hardly marry her husband's murderer," Tatiana agreed. "That would cause all manner of stir." She thought of the rosebush he'd named after Lady Innisford, and his pampering of it. "I do not think, though, that you managed to extinguish his love for her."

"I did not think so either, for the longest time. Now, however . . ." She shrugged, with a hint of her accustomed sunniness. "Here she is in Brighton. And he has not run away!"

"Perhaps he intends to renew their acquaintance."

The countess turned distinctly pale. "You don't honestly believe that! You haven't any . . . any *basis* for believing that?"

I thought you were in love with her.

I was.

Tatiana might have taken pity on her—if not for the fact that all her and her husband's plottings had been to prevent their son's marriage to an *unworthy* girl. "I hardly know," she said blithely. "You pointed out yourself, though—he is going to card parties, attending routs."

"Perhaps I should have left him to his roses in Dorset," the countess fretted. "I only thought . . . is it so horribly wrong for a mother to have hopes for her only child? I am getting on in years, dash it all. I yearn to see him settled. I begin to think I could abide Selma Bournemouth as a daughter if it meant his happiness."

Tatiana could have settled her mind on that count, but she chose not to. "I thank you, milady, for your frankness to me. But I am late to luncheon at the Cuthberts'. What answer do you intend to send the Regent regarding his invitation to us?"

"I scarcely know, with Lucas so set against it. He fails to see how vitally important such an opportunity is to you in your aspirations! An acquaintance with the Royals is the sole imprimatur you lack. And his objections are so utterly without foundation! If there is one thing you have proved in these past months, Tatiana, it is that you are a very *sensible* girl."

"I am glad to hear you say so," Tatiana murmured.

"And I mean it," the countess said with great warmth. "Lucas has warned me several times about trusting you too far. You may imagine my response to that!"

Tatiana, remembering her abortive inclinations toward conspiracy, put on her poke bonnet to hide her blush. "I may indeed."

"I'll get you to the pavilion, my dear," Dulcie vowed. "Never fear about that!"

Sixteen

LUNCHEON AT THE Cuthberts' was soothingly distracting; in that household of women, the talk was all of hairstyles and fashions and who would get bids for marriage before the summer was through. Susannah was still irked at Sarah for flirting with Mr. Hyde Parker, but a nosegay of dainty rosebuds from the gentleman in question had done much to restore her pride. Admiration of those flowers led Tatiana to mention her bouquet from the Regent, as well as her invitation to the pavilion. The girls oohed and aahed, but Mrs. Cuthbert showed uneasiness. "Many a girl of good repute has come away from there with her credit in tatters," she noted with a frown.

"Oh, Mamma, you are just jealous that it isn't Sarah or I," Susannah teased her gaily.

"Not at all. Remember poor Constance Beavers, if you please."

Tatiana would very much have liked to hear more about Mrs. Beavers, whom she'd heard mentioned more than once by Susannah's mother as a cautionary example. But the girls' quelled expressions warned that further pursuit of the topic would be in poor taste. She did broach it again when she and Susannah were walking on the promenade, with Carruthers trailing behind them. "Who is Mrs. Beavers," she asked in a whisper, "that your Mamma turns so grim at her mention?"

"Oh, you must have seen her here and about." Susannah reconsidered. "Or perhaps you haven't. She is a very nice young widow. She used to be ever so blithe and gay."

"Used to be? What changed her?"

Her friend shrugged. "I only know she no longer goes to the routs and suppers, not since last summer. Mamma still receives her, but only privately. And whenever Sarah or I admires some young man Mamma considers a here-and-thereian, she says, 'Remember poor Mrs. Beavers!' "

"It would be more to the point," Tatiana noted, "if you knew what to remember her *for*."

"It must be something the older set considers truly shocking," Susannah said, twirling her parasol as they approached a bunch of likely-looking soldiers.

"Aye, such as sipping from the finger bowl, or wearing stripes with plaid."

Susannah's merry laughter drew appreciative glances from the soldiers. "Honestly, Tat! Are they stopping?" She'd paused to adjust the ribbons of her bonnet.

"No. They must know we're too grand for the likes of them."

"Let's go to Regent's Park instead," Susannah declared, standing on tiptoe to stare up and down the strand. "I don't see Clifford anywhere here."

Her luck was better there. They'd no sooner turned in at the gates when Mr. Hyde Parker appeared in the distance, causing Susannah to blush and fidget with her reticule for several hundred yards. He greeted them with great delight, offering to accompany them on their stroll. "But you have already been along this walk," Susannah pointed out.

"I shall see it all anew with you beside me," Mr. Hyde Parker said gallantly.

For a time they talked of the countess's rout—the music, the oysters, the Regent's exquisite manners and dress. "Miss Grimaldi has got a nosegay from him," Susannah told her beau, who raised his brows.

"It is not so great a matter," Tatiana said, embarrassed. "My cousin tells me His Highness has a standing order every day for twenty bouquets."

Mr. Hyde Parker whistled. "That makes my paltry offering to you, Miss Cuthbert, look mean indeed."

"Better, surely," Tatiana noted, "to be alone among the recipients of such favor than one among many." She smiled slyly. "I do trust, Mr. Hyde Parker, that this morning you ordered a single bouquet?"

"You have found me out," the gentleman said gravely. "I am honor-bound to admit I gave direction for two."

"Two!" Susannah cried.

"Yes, indeed. One for the young lady with whom I had the pleasure of dancing last evening—and one for Lady Strathmere, who made it possible I should do so." Susannah beamed up at him, her face made lovely by bliss.

Providentially, they had just then arrived at a fork in the path. "My silly Carruthers has lagged behind," Tatiana said, turning to glance around. "Do go on ahead while I wait for her, or she may mistake our way." The couple made some protest, but Susannah's was halfhearted, and Tatiana was able to persuade them to do what they most wanted to anyway. They went along the right side of the lake, Susannah's chestnut curls tilted toward his fair head, so engrossed in conversation that Tatiana had no fear of quickly catching up to them.

As for Carruthers, she had likely been frightened by a dog, or a stick she thought was a snake. Tatiana stood in the shade of the trees, by no means averse to being by herself for a space. Now and again the constant press of town society made her recall with some wonder that in Mizhakovsk, to see the faces of more than a dozen souls in a day—or in the winters a month—had been reckoned a great deal. And London, she knew, was infinitely larger than Brighton. Still, there would be parks and copses and heaths there as well, where one could listen to the silence, see a stretch of green, and feel at peace.

Though it was beastly hot. What the devil could be keeping Carruthers? She stepped out from the shade to stare along the path. No one was in sight—and Susannah and her beau had long since disappeared around the bend of the lake.

For some reason, her unaccustomed solitude made her nervous. She wondered if she ought to hurry after Susannah or just turn back. Here is the result of the pampered life you are leading, she thought, smiling to herself. Five minutes alone in a woods and you are set on edge, where once you traipsed across miles of wilderness with no companions but the wolfhounds!

A twig snapped suddenly in the dark shadows behind her. She whirled about. "Carruthers?" she called hopefully. But the maid never would have ventured off the path.

Another snap, loud as a pistol. Tatiana just had time to think that even a badger was not that big when a man burst toward her out of the trees. She caught a glimpse of hood over his face, ragged clothes, and something shining in his hand as he sprang at her, swift as one of the hounds she would have given anything to have with her at that moment.

Instinctively she brought her knee up as he grabbed her, and thrust it as hard as she could right between his legs.

His breath went out in a *whoosh*, and he staggered. Tatiana did not stop to see what more might happen. She was running as fast as she could back toward the entrance to the park, dropping her parasol, hiking her skirts in her hands.

She'd been a fine runner once, but that had been unhampered by such yards of fabric, by her dainty strap sandals, by the poke bonnet whose flower-trimmed brim flipped up and down in her eyes. She tossed it from her head, threw it away, and kicked the sandals from her feet. She would have ripped her skirts off as well, but she needed her hands to hold them. God, this bloody corset! Her lungs could not seem to take in enough air. She glanced back and saw that her assailant was coming after her, though none too steadily. She should have put her parasol tip through his eye, she thought regretfully.

But she was in an English park at the height of afternoon promenade. Surely someone would appear to rescue her! She tried to scream, but the grip of her corset was too tight. Thinking that it was her purse he wanted, she flung it behind her as far as she could. He did not pause to pick it up. That was when she truly grew afraid.

Keep running, she told herself, silk-clad feet slapping on the path. Just ahead, it wound past a little pleasure pavilion and then into a clearing that gave onto the gardens. There would be help there—she prayed. *Please, God, let there be—*

She made the turn toward the pavilion and caught sight of a pair of elderly women, their mouths agape at the appearance she made. "Help!" she cried as loudly as she could. They turned their faces away. "Oh, please!" she tried to beg. Footsteps were pounding behind her. Her skin, which had felt so hot a moment before, suddenly went clammy. Christ,

I am going to faint, she thought, damning the corset with her last bit of breath. Blue sky and green trees went swirling in a whirlwind . . .

"Tatiana." Strong arms, sure arms, clasped her. The scent of horseflesh and leather, bracing as the first snowfall. . . .

"Lucas?"

"It's all right. I have got you now. Don't talk. Wait until you can breathe."

"There is . . . a man—"

"I know. I saw. He's gone back into the trees. You're all right. I have you."

"He . . . he . . . he . . ."

"Would you shut up?" he said brusquely.

She began to cry.

He slapped her sharply on the cheek. Shocked into silence, she stared at him with wide eyes like willow-leaves. "That's better. Here." He had a flask in his waistcoat. The harsh burn of brandy seared her throat, but it brought back her breath. "Can you tell me what happened?" he asked finally.

"Susannah and I were walking. We met Mr. Hyde Parker, and I thought to . . . to let them go on ahead. I said I'd wait for Carruthers. But she never came, though I waited and *waited*—"

"I know. She came back to the house in a tizzy. Seems she'd stopped to watch a man doing magic tricks and lost track of you. Didn't I warn you about hiring such an idiot?"

"It was not her fault! She could not have known about that man!"

"If she had an ounce of sense, she'd know these woods are favorite haunts for thieves."

"He wasn't a thief."

His arm around her tightened a bit. "Why do you say that?"

"Because I threw my purse back at him, and he never stopped to pick it up!"

"Threw it back at him? How did you ever get the jump on him at all?"

"I—" She could not bring herself to say it, so she showed him. "Thus. Just as he came at me. Hard as I could. Just as I did with the hounds."

Instead of looking scandalized, he laughed. "It is no laughing matter," she said reproachfully. "If he did not want my purse, then what *did* he want?"

"I cannot imagine," he said, and his expression now was very grim.

Leaning on him, Tatiana drew her skirts aside to examine her stockings. "Ruined," she noted. "And a brand-new pair."

"Where are your shoes?"

"Worried about the expense? Behind on the path somewhere, with my bonnet. You will want to fetch that back. It cost you fourteen pounds."

"Christ, do you think I give a damn about any of that, so long as you are—" He stopped. Coming toward them from the pleasure pavilion was a woman in a gown of diaphanous bronze silk. Her long red-brown curls were swept back beneath a cunning hat of pheasant feathers, and she had two greyhounds at leash. She had the arm of a tall, gray-haired gentleman in immaculate coat and breeches, who lifted his quizzing glass and peered through it at the couple below. "Good God, Gillian," he declared, his voice carrying easily on the air, "ain't that Strathmere there, and his little Italian cousin?"

For an instant Lucas's grip on Tatiana slackened. Then he looked back down into her frightened green eyes. "So long as you are safe," he finished, and astonished her by kissing her damp forehead.

Lady Innisford swept grandly toward them, and Tatiana

quickly looked away, aware of what a spectacle she must present—bonnetless, shoeless, her clothes all disheveled, skin glowing unbecomingly. But even that brief glance showed her something dreadfully harsh in the woman's olive-brown gaze. Suddenly self-conscious, she pulled free of Lucas. "Nonetheless, we must go and get it—and my shoes and purse. And find Susannah as well. She must be frantic by now."

He arched a thick black brow. "You are willing to go back into that woods again?"

Oddly, she was, so long as he was there. "I still have my knees about me, don't I?"

He laughed again, taking her arm with a dignity that much belied her tattered state. "So you do, Tatiana." And beneath Lady Innisford's hard stare, he led her down the path.

Seventeen

CARRUTHERS WAS BLUBBERING with fear by the time Tatiana climbed the stairs to her rooms. "Gone 'n' lost my post, I have," she mumbled miserably, helping her mistress out of her clothes.

"You silly thing, of course you haven't lost your post. Do fetch me up a bath."

"I have too lost my post," Carruthers said morosely. "Master told me so."

"Well, I am telling you otherwise. Anyone is entitled to a mistake. You'll know better next time, won't you?" The girl nodded tearfully. "Go on and fetch me that bath, or I might reconsider." Carruthers hurried off with unaccustomed speed.

The bath was wonderfully restorative. Tatiana took her time at it, soaking in the rose-scented water until she realized it must be nearly the supper hour; quickly she dried off and put on a dressing gown. Had they plans for that night? Surely Dulcie had said something about the theater. Tatiana winced. She did not feel up to making conversation with a bevy of suitors. Her feet and ribs still hurt her. Lord, what if Lucas hadn't come when he did? She shivered, remembering that masked face, the glint of the weapon, the stealth of the man's attack.

The countess surprised her by arriving at her door, trailed by Smithers with supper on a tray. "Lucas said there was a spot of trouble in the park," she explained. "He thought under the circumstances you should spend a quiet evening in your rooms. What happened, my dear?"

Tatiana glanced at Smithers, who undoubtedly would find some way of blaming her for what had gone on. She wished he'd withdraw, but he was removing the covers from the platters, his back to them both. "A thief, milady. He came at me from the bushes."

"Lord, imagine that! In Regent's Park, in the middle of the day! Did he hurt you, pet? Shall I send for Dr. Travis?"

"No. He frightened me is all."

"Well, if you are certain—I can offer your place in the box to Lady Hyde Parker. I know for a fact she is at loose ends this evening."

"Please do," Tatiana said warmly. "And if you can manage it, put in a good word or two for Susannah with her son."

Dulcie cocked her head. "Is that the way the wind blows? I shall, by all means. I find Susannah Cuthbert a most engaging young lady." She rubbed her hands together. "I do adore matchmaking, despite—or perhaps because of—the utter failure of all my efforts toward my own son. I do think he is coming 'round, though. He said something about another card party tonight somewhere. And I thought I saw on his desk this morning some correspondence from White's. It would be something if he took up his membership there again! It was one of the great sorrows of the Admiral's later years that Lucas let it lapse."

Tatiana was hard put to imagine Lucas seeking companionship at White's, whose membership list was crammed with the sorts of idle stuffed shirts he despised. Nonetheless, "It is certainly to be wished for," she agreed politely.

The countess came and kissed her cheek. "Do get a good night's sleep. We have an early appointment at Madame's tomorrow to have a new gown made for you for Prinny's supper."

Smithers cleared his throat and bowed. "Will there be anything more, miss?"

"Absolutely not," Tatiana told him. "I'll send Carruthers down with the tray."

He blinked. "I was under the impression Carruthers was no longer employed here."

"Your impression was wrong, then."

"Very good, miss," he said, in a tone clearly indicating that in his opinion it was *not*.

Tatiana dined well and peacefully on salmon and duchess potatoes and green salad and the half-bottle of Sauternes that Smithers—or perhaps Lucas—had thought to provide. Far from making her sleepy, the wine served to keep her awake. Toward midnight she finished the book she'd been reading—*Pride and Prejudice*, newly published and excellent, she thought, though enormously wordy—and, still quite alert, went down to the yellow salon in her robe and slippers to fetch another from the shelves.

The doors were open and the sconces lit against the countess's return. Tatiana took her time in surveying the volumes; reading did not come so easily to her that she was willing to waste her time on fluff. She rejected out of hand an earlier work by the anonymous author of *Pride and Prejudice*—it would take some time to work up to that—considered Milton, read two pages of the first part of Gibbon's *Decline and Fall of the Roman Empire* before clapping it shut, and finally settled on a thick, promising novel by Miss Edgeworth, whose *Castle Rackrent* she had previously—rather guiltily—enjoyed.

"And what, pray tell, have you decided on?"

The voice at her back made her start. She turned and saw Lucas Strathmere seated in a dim corner of the room, a chessboard before him, a bottle at his side. "You ought to have made yourself known!" she said, blushing at the length of time he'd been watching her, unnoticed.

"I did not want my presence to influence your choice of book."

"As if it would!" Tatiana said hotly, though she did tuck the novel behind her. "Your mother informed me you would be absent from the house this evening, playing cards."

He laughed, crooking a finger at her. "Come, come, don't try to change the subject. Let's see what's in your hand. I notice you rejected poor Mr. Gibbon."

"It would take me ten years to finish the thing," she admitted.

"That you contemplated starting it at all stands much to your credit. It is one of those works folk are far more apt to talk about than to have actually read. Is that one of Miss Edgeworth's? Which? Ah, *The Modern Griselda*. You will be disappointed if you liked *Castle Rackrent*. It is not nearly so naturally written. What thought you of the book you returned?"

"*Pride and Prejudice*? It was . . . very long. But I liked the argument. That Mr. Darcy and Miss Bennet should be kept apart so long by mistaken circumstances . . . and," she added bravely, "that in the end her embarrassed situation should make no difference to him."

"Well. It is a work of fiction. I daresay in true life no man worth fifteen thousand a year would offer for a girl whose family had been so thoroughly disgraced."

Tatiana flushed in the half-darkness. "Money means a great deal to you, doesn't it? With all the thousands you have, you still count your pennies."

"That is only because my mother constantly throws in my face the fact that I inherited my wealth rather than earned it. Consequently I feel a duty to conserve what I can."

"Your mother's disquiet," Tatiana said after a moment, "comes more from wishing you happiness than any other motive. She would see you wed."

"And do you feel, cousin, that marriage would serve to bring me happiness?"

"It could not hurt," she said bluntly.

He laughed so loudly that she glanced toward the doors, expecting Smithers to appear with his disapproving frown. "Am I so churlish as that?" he asked when his amusement abated.

"Most of the time." She hesitated, her sympathy aroused by finding him alone here with his bottle and board. There was in him something of Mr. Darcy, so proud and unyielding, so unwilling for his good works to be known to the world. "Your mother told me this morning about the killing of Lord Innisford," she said softly.

His eyes in the darkness were veiled. "Did she? And of her dear Prinny's part in it, I trust?" She nodded. "Then you must think me even more of a boor than you used to."

"On the contrary. I find your behavior in the affair the only aspect beyond reproach."

"I should have stood up and exposed the lot of them," he said bitterly.

"I don't see what good that would have done, besides landing you in jail. As it was, you managed to preserve Lady Innisford's reputation."

"I am not sure for what. All these years Mother has told me such stuff about her . . . but now I see for myself the companions she chooses."

"She would have done far better to prefer you to Lord Innisford."

He let out a sigh. "It soothed me to imagine she had chosen him because of love. Then at least I had the comfort of honoring her."

"Perhaps she did," Tatiana offered without conviction.

He smiled a twisted smile. "No. Given her choice between a young fool and an older idiot, she would have chosen me, for her vanity's sake. But when the Admiral said he'd disinherit me—" He stopped, refilling his glass. "Do you know what I thought when I first laid eyes on her again the other day after so many years? I thought: In all the time I spent with you, Gillian, I can never once remember laughing in your company. I remember longing, and desperation, and the itch you raised in my loins. But happiness? Contentment? I did not even wish for them then."

"You were so young," Tatiana murmured.

"Not so young as you. And yet your head has not been turned by the gaudy gentlemen you've met. What is it that you want, Tatiana, in a husband?"

'Someone whom I love . . . more than I loved Pietr."

"Do you think that possible, given the prospects you've encountered?"

She dropped her gaze. "I . . . hope for it, at least."

"Ah, there's the difference between us. For my part, I cannot imagine the sort of passion I once held for Gillian united with any sort of common sense." He winced. "Not, at least, for misses such as Selma Bournemouth."

"I am glad to hear you say it," Tatiana told him, feeling herself on more solid ground. "She would not suit for you. But there are other girls."

"Yes, yes. Each season an entire new crop of them. Yet

all, somehow, the same . . ." He frowned at the chess-board. "You never answered my question as to whether you play this infernal game, Miss Grimaldi. Do you?"

"Not with any skill."

"Nonetheless, perhaps you might give an eye to this white queen and her predicament."

Tatiana moved to his side, surveyed the pieces arrayed on their squares. "You've got her fairly boxed in there, haven't you?"

"I thought to defend her."

"What, by strength alone? No, no. You must use wit." She slid a white knight forward. "Give yourself an opening."

"I shall lose my pawn."

"Of what worth is a pawn?"

"There you have laid your finger on my trouble with chess—and, perhaps, with life. I find I can no longer bear to risk even so much as a pawn. Which explains my absence from Major Thornton's card party this evening. On reflection, I feared the stakes might prove too high."

"You went to much risk when you came to Russia in search of me."

"Aye—and see where that got me!"

She made a moue at him. "Not to mention coming to Brighton, knowing how tongues would wag."

"I expected far worse," he admitted frankly. "You were right in what you said to me once. Money and a title go a long way toward excusing anything in England these days."

"I imagine most folk think that simply by depriving yourself of society for so many years, you have made your penance."

"I'd wager Lord Innisford does not—or would not, were he still here." He looked down at the board. "You, on the other hand, have no fear of risk at all. Did you never harbor even the slightest doubt you would find yourself the season's sensation?"

Tatiana thought back to those long, long days with the lessons on grammar and cutlery and manners. "Nearly every minute."

"What made you press on, then?"

My hatred for you. . . . But she did not hate him now. She pitied him, instead, for the constraints his honor had laid on him. She at least had the consolation of hoping she might come across true love yet. Whereas he—what did he have to hope for? "I suppose," she said slowly, "I had nothing better to do."

He laughed again, more quietly. "There is something to be said for that. Therefore, since you advise it . . ." He advanced the black bishop, annihilating the victim pawn. "And what advantage does that gain me?"

"Now the rook, thus—"

"Lord, you leave her bare to the barbarians!"

"Not exactly. The king answers so—"

"And then?" He paused, suddenly smiled. "I see. The white knight again—"

"And check to the black king."

"All that for the loss of one pawn!" He looked at her in the darkness. "You have not been frank with me, cousin. You *do* know this game." He pushed out the chair across from him with his boot. "Come and play."

"I don't think—" She glanced nervously toward the doorway, imagining Smithers and the imminent return of the countess, and drew her robe together at the throat. "I am hardly dressed."

"What is life, cousin, without a little risk?" Still she hesitated. "Please?"

"Oh, very well. One game. But only if you turn up the lamps."

He did. They were still at it, well toward half-past two, when the countess came in. They did not notice her at first; their heads were drawn together over the board, black and white, dark and fair. Lucas was laughing at her attempt to withdraw a move that left her king in danger. "But you have removed your hand!" he cried, grasping it in proof.

"And when were you ever such a stickler for rules?" Tatiana demanded, just as Dulcie cleared her throat.

"I see, Tatiana, you are quite recovered from your harrowing ordeal this afternoon."

The two heads sprang apart mutually, abruptly. "From my—oh!" It had slipped her mind in the pleasure of competing with him. "Yes, indeed, milady. Quite."

"I thought some quiet diversion," Lucas began, a glower of resentment in his eyes.

"Still, you might have been more mindful of your cousin's condition. Have you any notion of the time?"

"None at all," he admitted. "But it cannot be so very advanced, since you are only just come home."

The countess's color heightened. "A late card party at the Hyde Parkers'. Very kindly arranged. But I see no need to explain my comings and goings to you."

"Nor I, I trust, my stayings to you."

Tatiana was profoundly uncomfortable sitting there in her robe, with her hair unbound. "I came downstairs for a book." She searched for it on the table—evidence. "And Cousin Lucas . . . but that does not matter. You are perfectly correct, of course. I ought not to have stayed."

"No, you ought not to have. But the fault lies rather with my son for encouraging you to."

Lucas rocked back in his chair, and Tatiana hurried to forestall the tempest she saw coming. "In truth, I lost track of the time," she said, and quickly feigned a yawn. "I must to bed straightaway."

"Finish the game," Lucas urged her.

"Nay, nay. I am exhausted."

"I'll leave the board," he said belligerently, "for another time."

Tatiana looked from one to the other—the man who'd saved her, the woman who'd sponsored her in the face of his scorn—and could not decide where her loyalty lay. She mumbled something noncommittal and fled away to bed. On the staircase she heard the doors click sharply shut in her wake, and then the countess's voice, and Lucas's, louder, angry. What they might find to quarrel about she could not imagine. It had only been a chess game! And if her dishabille were inappropriate, what did it matter, when they were family?

But family, she realized, only in the eyes of the world. Not in those of the countess. Not even after all this time. The insight tightened her throat, made tears spring to her eyes. As though, she thought, I have ever given *her* cause to doubt me. Only Lucas knew how close she'd come to betraying his and Dulcie's trust in her—and he seemed to take it in stride, almost as his due.

She had to find a husband, she thought wildly. That was the only way to free herself from this tangle. But whom could she marry? In all the men she'd met, talked to, danced with, flirted with since coming to England, not one seemed desirable. Not a single one—

Then she remembered Lucas's delighted laughter as she'd shown him how to save his queen, and his tentative confession: *I find I can no longer bear to risk even so much as a pawn.* A man such as he—willing to doom himself for his lady's honor, to chase across all Europe to maintain a promise no one alive even knew had been made—that was the sort of man she admired. Knowing no more than her name, he'd brought her into his home, into his life. Would even Freddy, with all his professed devotion, have done the same for a foundling from Mizhakovsk? The notion made her laugh. Freddy would have ridden past her in the snow that night without a sideward glance, the same way he skirted beggars on the street. Beneath his facade of uncaring stoniness,

Lucas Strathmere was more decent than all the lofty, mannered peacocks who flocked to the assembly balls. His experience had made him chary—but oh, if he ever did love again, that would be a love worth having indeed.

He would not love her, though. That would be too much of a risk, knowing as he did where she'd come from, having seen with his own eyes the hovel in Mizhakovsk, Georgi's sullen temper, and Pietr, vaunty Pietr, whose love she'd been so proud to claim. He might have been willing once, when he was young and defiant. He'd learned from his mistake, though, and would not repeat it again.

Yet there had been in his eyes that evening, across the chessboard, something warm and lively, something more than the claret alone was wont to put there. She'd seen admiration in their stormy depths, and amusement at their contest of wills, and intrigue at her boldness of play.

Oh, Tatiana, she thought despairingly. It would serve you right for all the sins of your past if you fell in love with him—the one man in England it is certain never could return your devotion! Find yourself some pliant swain with ten or twenty thousand a year and wed him quick as you can. You will be happy enough—and a bloody deal better off than, in your wildest dreams a few years past, you ever thought you could be.

It was hard, though, to think of marrying someone who would never know the truth about her. It was harder still to imagine that anyone who knew the truth would ever ask for her hand.

Impossible situation! She turned it over in her mind, this way and that, until at long last she slept, and dreamed of checks, black against white against black, across an endless board.

Eighteen

THE FOLLOWING AFTERNOON brought a visit to Madame Descoux's, with the usual interminable flutterings over sleeves and bodices and hemlines. Dulcie seemed determined to push on Tatiana the most expensive stuffs in the place, rejecting every suggestion of muslin or even damask in favor of rich brocade and sarcenet. Tatiana still had a headache, and was increasingly uncomfortable at the thought of spending so much of Lucas's money for the sake of her visit to the pavilion, of which he so thoroughly disapproved.

"How do you know, milady, that Cousin Lucas will even let me go there with you?" she asked in the midst of the pinnings. "I thought he made it quite plain—"

"Leave my son to me," the countess replied with a gleam in her eye.

So Tatiana stood miserably, temples pounding, as the two women concocted an outfit that left her feeling completely undressed. She had no standing to quarrel. She had displeased the countess—though she was not quite sure how—and this was to be her penance, apparently.

She was immensely relieved, then, when on the morning of the Regent's dinner party Dulcie did not come down to breakfast and sent word that she was unwell. When Tatiana visited her rooms, she found the countess still abed, looking pale and wan, with cloths wound around her head. "It was that wretched fish soup at Lady Maltingly's," Dulcie moaned. "She may crow about her cook as she likes, but I would not keep him under my roof!"

"I'm so dreadfully sorry," Tatiana told her. "I'll have some broth sent up, and I shall read to you. There is yet another installment of *Childe Harold* out. We'll have a peaceful, quiet day."

Lucas, who had followed her upstairs, raised an eyebrow. "Isn't this the night you were to visit the pavilion?"

"I've already sent our excuses," Dulcie said miserably.

"Never mind," Tatiana soothed her. "There will be another time."

All that day the countess kept to her bed, the draperies shut, the servants coming and going in whispers. At six o'clock Lucas stopped in again, to announce his intention to ride to Lord Rushford's for a look at a horse. No sooner had he left the house than the countess straightened up on her pillows. "Go on, child," she hissed. "Hurry and dress, or you'll be late to the pavilion!"

"To the—oh, milady! You cannot mean all of this was a trick!"

"Of course it was! Who does Lucas think he is, to try to dictate to me?"

Tatiana's insides fluttered. "If he finds out, he'll be dreadfully angry!"

"He won't," the countess said complacently. "Lord Rushford's house is all the way out to Richmond. And since there is rain approaching I have no doubt of his spending the night there. However, just in case, I shall remain here."

"Oh, no! I cannot go *alone*!"

"No, no, of course you can't. But I've made suitable arrangements. Lady Bournemouth has most generously agreed to attend in my stead."

"Lady Bournemouth?" Tatiana swallowed.

"Yes, indeed. She has long harbored a wish to see the inner fittings of the pavilion."

I'll wager she has, Tatiana thought. "But, milady, surely the substitution will be remarked on! She is not, after all, of the Regent's inner circle."

"I daresay the replacement of one matron for another will occasion no concern. After all," the countess purred, "it is you whom dear Prinny particularly wished to invite."

Thus it was that the countess's carriage stopped at Lady Bournemouth's house to fetch the chaperone in question, who was so giddy at the prospect of a private dinner with the Regent that her usual loquaciousness was quelled. In the course of the drive she confined herself to two comments— one on the weather, which did indeed seem pitching toward storm, and the other regarding her heartfelt sorrow that it was not Selma or Clotie she was accompanying.

Tatiana was glad for her silence. It gave her time to gather her own thoughts, which were whirling like the dust on the streets. She had to believe that the crux of this unlikely arrangement lay in the quarrel between Dulcie and her son the other evening after the chess game. What could their angry words have been about? She was certain of one thing: Lucas never would have allowed this plan to proceed.

Her qualms were overcome by sheer wonder as they were admitted to the pavilion. A servant led them through room after room decorated in the Oriental fashion, in nigh unimaginable luxury. The entrance hall was a startling, lizard-skin green, the corridors French blue, and everywhere were stacked porcelains and cloisonné and objets d'art. And the flowers! Blossoms hung heavy and ripe from vases perched in all available niches—roses, peonies, lilies, but mostly orchids, suffusing the close air with their peculiar perfume.

They were at last admitted to a spacious apartment done in brilliant lacquer red, with the furnishings all of bamboo. Some dozen or so guests were already drinking champagne and nibbling tidbits from the waiters' trays—all of them strangers to Tatiana. Lady Bournemouth recognized a few, though by appearance only. "There is Lord Grenville," she whispered, "and Lady Hertford, and Lady Campbell—oh, the countess was correct; it is unex*cep*tionable company! How I wish Selma were here to enjoy the acquaintance of the utmost tier of society!"

Tatiana, the new sapphirine gown clinging to her every curve, could not help but concur, so long as she herself had been spared. Something about the vastness of the place, the rich appointments—or perhaps it was her knowledge of Lucas's disapproval—had brought her headache back. She rejected the offer of a glass of champagne, but Lady Bournemouth dug an elbow into her side. "Go on, then! Who are we to decline the refreshments? Oh, do look, it is the Duchess of York! What splendid jewels she wears!"

No formal introductions were performed, for their host was not there to initiate them. Instead, the bold-eyed gentlemen approached her, one by one, and made themselves known first to Lady Bournemouth, who presented her. "Ah, so you are Dulcie's little cousin!" one man—she had not caught his name—murmured in admiration, putting his hand on her elbow. Tatiana was trying to decide how to escape from his grasp when a silk-robed servant brought a baton crashing against a bronze gong with so deafening a result that she jumped, thus accomplishing her end. "His

Majesty arrives," said the man beside her, and made a deep bow.

Tatiana peeked up from her curtsy to see the Regent enter in quite amazing attire: a sort of cloth-of-gold dressing gown over voluminous trousers of peacock-blue silk and a crimson shirt, with a spangled turban on his head. He seemed a bit unsteady in his gait, in a way that was oddly familiar. Not until he had started toward her did she realize he was walking just as her foster father had when he was in his cups.

His smile, though, was warm and genuine. "Miss Grimaldi! How splendid you were able to join us. And in that extremely becoming attire! Lady Strathmere." He bent to kiss her companion's hand. "It is always a pleasure."

Tatiana drew in her breath. Lady Bournemouth, flustered, stammered out, "I do beg your pardon, Your Majesty. I am Lady Bournemouth."

He straightened, eyes swimming slightly. "You are . . . who?"

"Lady Bournemouth," she repeated eagerly. "The countess found herself indisposed and asked me to do the honor of accompanying her cousin tonight."

The Prince Regent hiccuped. "Beg your pardon. Thought you *were* the countess. Who are you again?"

"Lady Anthea Bournemouth. My late husband, Lord Bournemouth, was—"

"Yes, yes. Well, our dinner is waiting! Shall we?" He looked at Tatiana once more, and she prayed he would not offer his arm. Fortunately, Lady Hertford stepped between them with a squelching glance, and Tatiana was spared.

Even the uncomfortable faux pas could not subdue Lady Bournemouth's spirits. "Did you remark how graciously he apologized?" she whispered as they followed the guests into the banqueting hall. "Such impeccable manners! Oh, I would not have missed this for the world!"

Tatiana, by that point, willingly would have. The meal went on forever. The Regent ate copiously, drank even more, and dominated the conversation completely, recounting jests so risque or else so old and worn that she was embarrassed for him. He gave an endless recitation of his heroic actions on the Continent in the war against Napoleon—all of it, she knew, wholly without foundation. Every soul at the table must have known as much, but they all listened and nodded their heads—though Lady Hertford had to restrain more than one yawn. The Duchess of York fed scraps to a spaniel sitting in her lap and murmured an occasional, "How very *brave* of you, Prin!"

Tatiana could only pick at the vast array of dainties, each elaborate presentation greeted by a chorus of praise. The wines and liqueurs offered with the courses kept her busy with her hand over her glass, and the gentleman beside whom she was seated noted with a sniff that she was "not much fun." Lady Bournemouth, however, was only too willing to partake of the largesse. By the time the pastry creations were wheeled out, on carts the size of beds, her eyes were as glazed as the sugary tower of profiteroles.

There would not be, Tatiana trusted, dancing, with the Regent's condition. When the meal was finished, the ladies made no move to withdraw. The men lit up pipes and cigars, port and sherry were dispensed at the table, and the Regent once more made her the object of his attentions. "My new violinist, Miss Grimaldi!" he called down to her. "What think you of him?"

She listened, through a clamor of conversation that did not abate, to a very fine performance of Mozart's *Il rè pastore*, complete with boy sopranos. The Regent smoked and drank and spoke of his tribulations against the mad Luddites, who were smashing looms throughout the north. "A reign of terror and insurrection unprecedented in our history," Lord Grenville noted soberly—or solemnly, rather, since he'd just spilled his fourth glass of port. .

In the midst of a passage by the violinist that Tatiana thought hauntingly lovely, the Regent suddenly sprang to his feet, knocking over his chair. "Everyone out to the lawn for fireworks!" he shouted with glee.

That part of the evening, at least, held Tatiana in thrall. Against the black sky over the ocean, a series of swirling, bursting rockets made a glorious show. Standing in the darkness, she could almost forgive Prinny for his excesses; she had never seen anything so wondrous as those long tails of red and gold and green fire sparkling over the sea.

A smattering of rain brought screams from the ladies, who ran for the doors to save their dresses and hair. Tatiana lingered, watching the last smoldering glow of those glorious artificial stars fading high in the air. When she turned to the pavilion again, she found herself alone. For a long moment she considered bolting, calling for her carriage and returning home. But the countess's lessons in manners were by now too deeply ingrained to permit such transgression. She must thank the Regent before parting, or her behavior would reflect on Dulcie unfavorably.

She hurried for the doors and was admitted by a liveried servant. Once inside, the odors of orchids and incense brought her headache to the fore; she stared uncertainly at the numerous exits from the room. "That way," the man said negligently, waving a hand toward one of the portals. Tatiana crossed to it, found it locked, and turned to find that he had vanished from sight.

"Oh, honestly," she said with impatience, and tried the next set of doors. When they, too, would not open, she decided manners could be damned; she'd go outside and bespeak her carriage at the main entrance. She rattled the handles of the passage to the strand, searched for a latch, in vain. It was no use. She had been locked in.

Of all the silly things—*why* had she lingered at the fireworks? She looked about for a bellpull, then, finding none obvious, pounded at a different set of doors with her fists. From beyond the gilded wood, she heard bright sounds of music. Perhaps if she tried louder . . . She took off her shoe and struck at the wood, then was appalled to see she was causing the gold leaf to flake off. Could she escape through a window? She'd just crossed to the nearest one and was trying its fittings when the music abruptly swelled. She whirled about and saw a heavyset figure in wide pantaloons silhouetted against a square of light.

"My dear Miss Grimaldi!" The Regent came toward her, smiling. "Whatever are you doing in here?"

Her relief at rescue was profound. "Oh, Your Majesty! I had stayed behind on the strand, and then the servant who let me in disappeared, and all the doors were locked—"

"Of course! My staff is understandably alert to my safety." He glanced at the shoe she held. "Have you broken your sandal?"

"No. I took it off to hit at the doors. No one could hear me on account of the music. I . . . I broke off a bit of gold there. I do apologize."

"What's a bit of gold to me?" the Regent said very kindly, moving closer.

Tatiana was suddenly aware of how her gown, damped with the rain, clung to her even more. She slipped the sandal back onto her foot. "I count myself unspeakably grateful that you happened this way. But we must not let my stupidity keep you from your other guests."

He loomed toward her in the gloom. She caught the smell of his breath: brandy and sweets and tobacco. "My other guests have departed."

"Oh, that is impossible! Lady Bournemouth is my chaperone."

"Is she? How odd. I sent her home in my own carriage—

with a promise of a future invitation for her daughters."
Tatiana's heart began to sink. So Lady Bournemouth had
abandoned her for the sake of a ride in a coach with the
royal arms and the prospect of introducing Selma and
Clothilda to *this*—

"What think you of my pavilion then, Miss Grimaldi? Is
it as fine as any doge's palace?"

"Finer," she assured him, certain that flattery could only
help.

"You are most discerning. Did I already mention how
extremely fetching I find your gown?" His thick fingers
alighted on her shoulder, trailed downward to her breast.
"So much in the Continental style."

"Don't you touch me!" Tatiana said sharply.

"Don't be coy, Miss Grimaldi. You were made for touching." She wrenched away from him, then gasped: He'd
caught his hand in her chignon and yanked her back with
unexpected force. Her first instinct was to knee him as she
had her assailant in the park. But he was prepared for the
move; as her leg came up, he thrust it away easily and
propelled her backward onto the chaise, flopping atop her
with all his considerable weight.

Her breath came out in a rush. She lay pinned beneath
him, hoping against hope that he had merely fallen, as
drunk as he was. The situation was more comical than anything else; she might have laughed if only she could breathe.

"My dear Miss Grimaldi, how unbecoming of you to resist the ardor of your adopted country's sovereign." He was
panting against her, his hot, fetid breath blowing in her
face. I must not faint, she told herself, no longer inclined to
mirth. He planted a wet kiss across her mouth that threatened to bring up what she'd managed to swallow of the
dinner. His fat fingers scrabbled at her bodice. "Ah, so
young and firm! Forgive the liberty—"

She did, for she had the folds of his cravat in her fists and meant to strangle him with them. Gasping for breath, she yanked as hard as she could. The linen loosened in her grip, sprang free. The Regent raised his head briefly. "I call it 'the Breakaway,' " he said, and giggled, falling on her again.

She felt the thrust of his thighs against her. Half her mind was certain no man in his condition could complete the act of rape. The other half was coolly considering that even if he could not, if the circumstances of this tryst ever became known, she would be ruined in the eyes of any man she could admire. And Lucas—God, with what he had professed her capable of before, how could she ever hope to make him believe this was against her will? Frightened, she raked her nails along the Regent's cheek, his ear. He laughed and pinned her arms back over her head with one hand. "I like a bit of spirit in a wench," he confided. "Only not, mind you, too much."

She spat at him. He looked at her for a moment, wiped the spittle from his chin, and raised his fist up. She heard the blow before she felt it—a jarring crash that seemed to rock the room, tilt the chandeliers at crazy angles. How could it be, then, that there was no pain?

Because Lucas Strathmere had hauled him off her into the air and proceeded to drop him in a heap to the floor.

"Christ!" the Regent gasped as his chin hit the carpet. He rolled over blearily, just in time to see Lucas swing at him.

Tatiana grabbed for his fist. "Don't," she begged. "Please—"

"By God, I'll beat the bloody hell out of him," he vowed.

Prinny had lumbered to his knees. "Lay a hand on me, Somerleigh, and I'll see you hanged—with, may I add, great pleasure."

"You miserable tub of—"

"Lucas!" Tatiana cried. "Stop! He is not worth it!"

That checked his fury. "You are right about that." He

pulled her up from the chaise, storm-cloud eyes taking in her skewed gown, the tangle of her hair.

"See here," the Regent put in, gaining his feet with great difficulty. "I had it on excellent authority the chit was altogether willing!"

Lucas's gaze narrowed dangerously. "You lying scum—"

"It's God's truth! Her own chaperone told me."

Tatiana stopped Lucas's fist again. "It might be true," she whispered.

"Of course it's true!" Prinny blustered. "She sidled up to me as we went out to the strand and told me you were wild for me! Then when I noticed you hadn't come back in with the others, and found you here, so prettily grateful to be 'rescued' . . ." He straightened his cuffs and turban. "Good God, man, I hope you don't believe I must resort to force to conquer hearts! Why, I can have any woman in the kingdom with a wave of my hand."

"Not this one," Tatiana said evenly.

He grinned, the unabashed grin of an aged roué. "Perhaps not yet, my dear. Give it time. My charms deepen upon further acquaintance. No hard feelings, eh? It was a simple mistake."

"Someday," Lucas said, glowering, "you will get yours. I hope to God I will be there to see it." He wrapped his cloak around Tatiana's shoulders. "Let's get the hell out of here."

"Do come back anytime, Miss Grimaldi!" the Regent called after her cheerily.

Lucas did not speak another word in all the time it took for her carriage to come from the stables. He handed her into it in silence, sat across from her, and stared stonily from the window. "I am sorry," she said finally, miserably. "I gave him no encouragement. I *swear*—" He grunted something unintelligible. "I cannot imagine what might have prompted Lady Bournemouth to say something so wicked!"

"Hoping for another Mrs. Beavers, I suppose," he told her shortly.

"What . . . precisely happened to Mrs. Beavers?"

"Very much what nearly happened to you this evening. Only Prinny left her with something to remember him by. The French pox."

"God in heaven!" She shuddered within his cloak. "But how would that avail Lady Bournemouth?"

"One less obstacle to getting her own daughters wed."

"No woman could be so coldhearted as that!"

The carriage rattled on, rain pounding the roof. "No? What about my mother, who sent you there tonight in—" He was interrupted by a sharp snap of thunder, very low and close, that made the windowpanes shake. Tatiana clapped her hands over her ears. The sound had spooked the horses; they balked, and something heavy thumped against the box above her head. Then a bulky shape fell past the window and splatted in the mud of the road.

Lucas sprang up in his seat. "Braunton!" he bellowed, pounding on the box. "Braunton!"

Only the rain, and silence. "Damn," he muttered, and shoved Tatiana onto the floor.

"What—" she began, starting up, seeing the flash of silver in his hand.

"Braunton's been shot, I think. Stay down." He kicked the door open.

"Shot!" She grabbed at him. "You're not going out there!"

"I'm damned well not going to wait for them to come in." The door slammed in his wake. There was another shot, then another. They sounded just like the fireworks. Ignoring Lucas's order, she pressed her face to the pane. She could see nothing but the dark, thrashing rain. Then Tatiana caught a glimpse of his face as he bent over a bundle in the road. The shots were still coming. He returned the fire, then hauled the bundle toward the coach. "Open up!" he shouted, and when she did, he shoved the coachman in.

"Is he dead?" Tatiana asked in horror.

"I don't know. I told you to stay down!" Lucas went back outside, moving toward the stamping, wild-eyed horses, trying to catch the reins. God, he couldn't shoot and drive too! Casting off his cape, she clambered over Braunton and slipped out through the coach door. He turned and saw her, his face white in a streak of lightning. "Get back, damn you!" he roared at her.

Instead, she clambered onto the box. "Throw me the reins and climb on!"

For an instant, she thought he meant to argue. Then a shot winged by that made him flinch and clap a hand to his neck. Tatiana leaned down herself, scrambling over the footboard to the shafts, groping blindly for the lines against the horses' rain-slicked backs. They had to be here somewhere—

There! She grabbed them in her fist, crawled backward onto the seat, and cried, "Get on, for God's sake! Get on!" He ran toward her, swung a leg up on the brace, and clung there. "*Yah!*" Tatiana screamed at the bays in a terrible voice. "Yah, you nags! Go on! Run!" She slapped the reins as hard as she could; the startled team leaped forward just as another burst of bullets riddled the night air.

Lucas fired back, getting off two rounds before he had to reload, one-handed, hanging from the box side. "Are you hit?" she called, hearing him grunt in pain.

"Just drive!"

"Where shall I drive to?"

"Anyplace where there will be people and lights."

That meant into town. Tatiana hauled at the lines, feeling the pull in her shoulders. God, she had grown soft. But she headed the team through the turn onto the promenade—which was, naturally, deserted in such dire weather—and toward the faint blur of gaslights in the distance. Lucas had drawn himself up onto the box beside her and was crouching on it backward, steadying his hand against the iron rack. "How many are there?" she asked breathlessly.

"I don't know. Can't see. But I got one of them, at least."

"Highwaymen?" she ventured.

He shook his head. "They knew the coach they were looking for." Hooves slapped the wet road behind them, and he fired again. A horse screamed in the darkness. The bays shied, sidestepped, faltered. "Drive 'em!" he shouted in her ear.

"I am *trying* to! Here, yah, get on!"

They careened around a bend, barely missing the embankment. The wind and rain had whipped her hair over her eyes, but she did not dare let loose her grip to push it back. The team was fresh and strong—and frightened out of its wits. Still, only a few hundred yards and they'd be to the palace pier. "Can you make that turn?" asked Lucas, glancing briefly ahead.

"I can." She did, too, straining with all her might to keep the bays in hand and barely slowing down. For a moment his eyes met hers, frank with approval.

"Easier than wolfhounds?"

"Well . . ." She bit her lip as they skittered on the wet stones. "Better trained, anyway. I hope that Braunton—"

"Don't think about him—not until I have got you safe." Another loud report; he ducked, pushing her down beneath him, then returned the fire. "Got the bastard—I think."

They'd reached the south gate and went galloping through onto Queen Street. "Can I let up now?" Tatiana asked in the glow of the streetlamps.

"Not yet. Go through to the Savoy. There will be hackneys there, and the doormen. They won't dare follow us so far."

"Who *are* they?" she started to say—then stopped, seeing the back of his collar pink in the lamplight. "God, Lucas! You are hit!"

"It only grazed me." In her fright, she'd let the reins go slack; he picked them up with his free hand. "Go on. Don't fail me now."

By the time they drew abreast of the Savoy, the street behind them was empty. The eyes of the hack drivers and doormen went wide at the sight they made, soaked through to the skin. "Stop for tea?" Lucas suggested, finally secure enough to turn around on the seat. He took the lines from her, gently prying them free of her clenched fists.

"Oh, Lucas. How can you jest about it? Poor Braunton—"

"If he lives, he'll have you to thank for it." His eyes were very dark. "You were . . . magnificent." She stared at him. He put his arm around her, pulling her close. "You must be freezing."

She leaned against him, actually very warm, and felt his mouth brush her drenched hair. She twisted her face toward his, wondering if she had imagined it. He grinned, and tucked her more firmly into his side.

Crescent Street was dark, but the upper windows glowed when they reached Number 10. Lucas dropped down from the coach as Smithers opened the doors. "Sir! We did not expect—"

"Shut up and see to Braunton. He's in the coach. He's been shot."

"Shot?" The butler stood frozen, and Tatiana had the satisfaction of watching Lucas do what she'd so often longed to—slap his supercilious face.

"Yes, shot, you idiot. Send someone for Dr. Travis. And have Jem rub the horses down and feed them well. They showed their mettle tonight." He turned back for Tatiana, lifted her, wet and dripping, and stood with his hands on her waist. "So did you." He lowered his mouth toward hers, just as the countess appeared in the vestibule.

"Lucas! Tatiana! Good Lord, child, what have you done to your gown?"

Lucas made her a bow, and Tatiana saw with shock that blood was flowing at the back of his neck, mingling with the rain streaming from his black hair. "You see before you, Mother, the happy result of your meddling." Then he staggered, making Tatiana grab for him. "I could use some claret," he admitted thickly.

"Jesus in heaven!" Dulcie screeched. "Is that *blood*?"

"He wants claret," Tatiana repeated, helping him over the threshold. "Which sofa do you least mind ruining?"

To the countess's credit, she did not hesitate. "Any one at all," she said, taking her son's other arm. "You—you haven't killed Prinny?"

"No. I only wish I had." And he collapsed onto the carpet at her feet.

Nineteen

DR. TRAVIS CAME with admirable promptness, and examined the two patients—Braunton first, at Lucas's insistence. The coachman had a ball in his shoulder. It was dug out, and his survival assured. Only then did Lucas allow the physician to tend his own wound. "A graze," the doctor confirmed, applying strips of gauze. "But he's lost a great deal of blood. Beef tea, and laudanum if he wants it—"

"I don't."

"You're a fortunate man," the doctor told him sternly. "Another inch closer and it would have severed your spine." The countess blanched. Dr. Travis paused, gathering his instruments. "Bullet wounds," he noted. "I shall have to report them to the constable. With some explanation."

"We were attacked by highwaymen," Tatiana offered.

"There are no highwaymen in Brighton," the doctor scoffed.

"There were tonight. Did you ask Braunton, the coachman?"

"He thought he'd been struck by lightning."

Lucas laughed from the sofa. "Perhaps we all were. Put that in your report."

Dr. Travis stiffened. "Your humor astonishes me, sir. So near as you have come to death, I should have thought to find you—"

"A good deal more grave?"

Tatiana could not help but giggle. The doctor frowned. "As for you, young lady, if I don't mistake it, you are bordering on an hysterical condition. I'll return in the morning. Perhaps by then there will be some sense in you both."

Tatiana, seeing Lucas about to retort, said hurriedly, "We will cooperate, of course."

"Hmph! I should hope so! Can't have folk firing pistols on the Brighton strand!"

When he'd gone, Tatiana refilled Lucas's cup with claret. "Don't you want to go and change, pet?" asked the countess, tucking a shawl around her shoulders.

"I imagine she'd rather know, Mother, what you had in mind by sending her off tonight with Lady Bournemouth as her chaperone."

"Let's talk of that in the morning, shall we? After you have rested."

"We'll talk of it *now*," Lucas said with surprising vehemence, considering his pallor.

She fluttered a hand. "I only thought—I *was* indisposed. Ask Turner! What . . . what did you think of the pavilion, dear girl?"

"The Regent tried to rape her," Lucas announced.

"Prinny?" she cried. "I don't believe it! I won't believe it!

He would never, *ever*—unless he had some reason to think—"

"Lady Bournemouth informed him your cousin was eager to become his bedmate."

Dulcie's mouth made a perfect O. "Anthea! That *bitch!* But, Lucas, you cannot think—you cannot imagine I suggested such a course to her!"

"No. I acknowledge that embellishment to be the product of her own febrile mind. But you did send our cousin into the lion's den, alone and unarmed."

Her eyes, so much like his, darted toward Tatiana and then away. "I only thought she might find some congenial company there. So many eligible men, such a display of manners . . . oh, dear. He did not hurt you, did he, pet?"

"If he didn't," her son growled, "it was only because I arrived when I did."

"How *did* you happen to come there?" Tatiana asked curiously.

"You may thank Carruthers; she sent a message to me at Lord Rushford's when she noted your discomfiture at having Anthea Bournemouth for a chaperone. I take back everything I ever said against that girl. She's a treasure to cherish. But all of that aside, Mother, you have not explained what inspired you to provide Lady Bournemouth as a companion." The countess, flushed, stood beside him in silence. "Let me guess. Was it . . . a hundred pounds?"

"Lucas! As though I would ever be so *venal*—"

"Two hundred?"

"I am shocked, *shocked,* at your insinuation."

"As much as five hundred?"

"Is it so outlandish to arrange an introduction for a favored friend," Dulcie said archly, "that you must insult me to the core of my marrow?"

"A thousand?" he said incredulously.

"And if I *were* tempted to such exigency, it would only be because you keep your purse strings so narrow!"

"Gambling debts," Lucas said to Tatiana, with a withering glance at the countess. "From the Hyde Parkers' party the other night."

Dulcie dropped her gaze. "These sorts of arrangements . . . why, it goes on all the time." She stretched out her hand to Tatiana. "You must believe, though, I had no idea she would try anything so abhorrent!"

"You have only Tatiana to thank that I didn't crack open his head," Lucas said. "I would like to crack yours. Does Prinny get a cut?"

"Honestly, Lucas!"

"Does he?"

"He has expenses, too!" she cried angrily. "All of us do!"

"You make Judas seem noble, between you," he said, repugnance in his eyes.

The countess gathered her skirts. "I don't need to stay and suffer these indignities from a man who's been engaged in a pistol fight along the Brighton strand!"

"No," Lucas agreed, shifting his weight on the sofa, testing whether he could stand. "You haven't the leisure. Not with so much packing to do."

"Packing?" his mother echoed uncertainly.

"Aye. You leave this cesspool tomorrow. *Early* tomorrow."

Dulcie's hand fluttered toward her heart. "Leave? But where would we go?"

"Somerleigh House, of course."

"But we cannot leave now—not at the height of the season!"

"Think of it as penance, Mother, for your greed."

She took another tack. "Punish me if you must," she said grandly, nobly, "but don't make Tatiana suffer. She has worked so hard for this success; you cannot mean to snatch it away. Why, if she goes back to Dorset she will lose an entire month—not to mention however long it takes us to prepare for London, mired in that hinterland."

"You may forget London, too, for this winter at least."

"Forget London!" Dulcie clutched her forehead. "All for one small lapse in judgment?"

"Someone tried to attack Tatiana in the park the other day. Someone tried it again tonight. I have no reason to suspect those men knew you were not in the carriage with her, Mother. On the contrary, they probably believed you were."

Tatiana followed his train of thought. "If you had not been there instead—"

"Then you and Mother—or Lady Bournemouth—would be lying in the rain on the strand, victims of 'highwaymen.'"

"You think there is a connection between the attacks?" Tatiana asked intently.

"Not to do so strains my imagination."

"But why would anyone want to harm Tatiana?" the countess cried in confusion.

"That is what I intend to discover. I never should have left Russia without learning more about what Casimir had entrusted to my care."

There was a pregnant pause. Then, "Russia?" the countess screeched. "You are going to Russia? Impossible! Just when I had such hopes of securing your happiness!" She sank onto a chair, shaking her head frantically, then brought her chin up abruptly, her eyes gone shrewd. "But what makes you think we will be safe at Somerleigh if you abandon us there?"

"I've given that some thought. You'll write tonight to Mrs. Cuthbert and Lady Hyde Parker and anyone else it might concern, informing them that you and Tatiana have been called to Italy by the sudden illness of one of her relatives. Tatiana, you'll send the same message to Susannah and Freddy and your friends." Tatiana, at least, nodded dutifully. "Timkins can procure the services of a dozen stout men to guard the house. They can always be put to use redigging the rose beds." He looked apologetically at Tatiana. "It will be worse than dull for you, I'm afraid. No visitors, no riding, no entertainment—"

"I could go with you," she offered, a catch in her voice.

"Dull for *her*?" Dulcie cried with growing resentment. "What about for me?"

"You forfeited any claim to consideration when you sold Tatiana to the devil tonight." She started to protest, then thought better of it, seeing the wrath in his eyes. They gentled, though, turning to Tatiana. "Thank you for the offer. But it would prove awkward. Alone, I can merely profess a wish to revisit old haunts, old friends."

It seemed entirely too much sacrifice on his part. "Or *I* could go away. Somewhere. America. India."

"Australia," the countess proposed tartly. "Really, Lucas! Haven't all our lives been upended enough on account of one—"

"Go and start packing, Mother. Or would you prefer I inform the ton you've been selling introductions to Prinny?"

"Oh, you . . . you *blackmailer*!" Dulcie snarled at him, and flounced off up the stairs.

Tatiana pulled the shawl tight, her emerald eyes downcast. "She is right," she said abjectly. "I am not worth it."

"So far, someone has thought you worth razing a village, risking a kidnapping—if not a murder—and engaging in a firefight within spitting distance of the Regent's pavilion." His harsh features relaxed into a teasing grin. "I, of course, value you even more highly than that."

"You must wish you never had met me."

"What, and forgo the chance to see you driving that team tonight? Not for all the world."

She did not, could not, smile. "We will miss you," she said in a whisper.

"Write to me. In care of the embassy at St. Petersburg."

"She will blame me for this. This loss."

He shook his head. "No. She is too honest a woman for that. She knows the fault is hers."

She felt she ought to make one last stab at dissuading him. "Milord—"

"Tonight you called me Lucas. I would like to hear you do so again."

"Lucas. Don't go."

"You might have it in your power to convince me."

"How?"

He looked down at her with his storm-ringed eyes, beckoned with a finger, then touched it to his mouth. Tatiana looked away. "What, you won't kiss me, when I am about to risk life and limb for your sake?"

"I would rather you sent me away."

"Sorry. I can't oblige. I take it as a personal affront when men fire pistols at me."

"What can you possibly expect to find out?" she demanded with quiet anguish. "It is a wild-grouse chase."

"Goose-chase, you goose. Come here."

She went to him, reluctantly, slowly, and raised herself on tiptoe to peck at his cheek. "There is your kiss. God go with you."

He caught her elbow. "You give warmer kisses to my dogs," he muttered. And, very deliberately, he put his tongue out and licked along her cheekbone. Tatiana shivered. He touched his mouth to hers with unbearable gentleness, like a whisper of wind that signals a coming storm. He tasted of rainwater and earth and blood and wine, like life itself distilled into a single savor, pungent and delectable and heady. His eyes were wide open, staring into hers, searching her soul. She stared back at him, knowing that whatever she did next would forever alter both their destinies.

"Lucas," she whispered haltingly. "Oh, Lucas—"

The storm broke in a sudden fury as he pulled her against him. Her shawl fluttered to the floor. He kissed her throat, her shoulders, her eyes, drenching her in kisses as surely as the rain had soaked them both. He caught his hands in her disheveled hair. "God, if you knew how long I have been wanting to do that!" he told her, laughing as the long blond curtain unfurled around them, and in his laughter was the wondrous, miraculous sound of a man set free from the bondage of the past. He raised her up in his arms, whirling her across the room in a mad waltz, crushing her so close that she could feel the hard bulge in his breeches and the pounding of his heart.

"Tatiana. What a lovely name," he murmured, lips teasing at her ear. He broke off dancing abruptly, held her at arm's length, contemplating her, smiling. His fingers edged toward her throat, trailed lower, over the swell of her breast beneath the rain-damp silk bodice. "What a lovely girl." His thumb brushed against her taut nipple, and she drew in her breath as the brief touch reverberated all through her body, made her quiver with desire. He cupped her breast in his palm and slowly lowered his mouth to it, tongue tracing circles against the silk.

"Oh!" she whispered. "Oh—"

"Oh, Tatiana. Yes." He lifted her up again, carrying her toward the sofa, already reaching to unfasten her ribbons as he laid her down.

At that moment, Tatiana heard footsteps coming on the stairs. She pushed free of his embrace, coloring furiously. Dulcie appeared in the doorway. Her eyebrows slowly arched as she saw where Tatiana lay, her son kneeling over her. "I . . . I felt faint of a sudden," Tatiana stammered. "And Lucas very kindly . . . " Her voice trailed away as she glanced toward him, saw regret—and yes, anger—in his winter-blue eyes. Now she had done it. He would think she did not love him—but what else could she say, with all she owed the countess?

There was a long moment of silence. Then Lucas stood up abruptly. "If you like, *cousin,* I can carry you to your rooms."

Tatiana shook her head. "No. No, thank you. I am feeling much stronger already. It won't be necessary." The hateful, conventional words . . . in their dull echo she could hear the last fading sparks of their passion sizzling into nothingness, fireworks drowned in the sea.

"In that case," said the countess, "I think it best you come and start your packing, Tatiana."

"Of course, milady." She stumbled up from the sofa, brushing past Lucas, trying hard not to remember the taste of his mouth, the touch of his hands. At the door she turned back. "I . . . I thank you for rescuing me tonight, Cousin Lucas."

"Don't mention it," he said, with a bitterness that tore her heart to shreds.

Twenty

SHE DID NOT expect to miss him the way she did, with a dull, constant aching, like the phantom pain of a severed limb. She sought to lose herself in continued lessons with the countess—they had begun on the pianoforte, and on crewelwork—but no distraction served to make her forget even for one moment that he was absent from her life.

The household was in an uproar. The sailors Timkins had hired to stand guard were a merry, carefree lot, given to laughter and raucous singing and harassing the maids. The countess despised them, despised her imposed isolation, and, Tatiana was convinced, despised *her*, for having caused her son to risk his life in the theater of the war.

They had occasional brief letters from him in St. Petersburg, reporting on his inquiries; their tone was brusque and businesslike, as though he were filing reports to the Foreign

Office again. Dulcie dictated responses to Tatiana that made her cringe to set them down on paper, complaining relentlessly of the lack of company, the dreary weather, the tedium of waiting, and the awful sailors who were making life at Somerleigh a hell on earth. Both their names were signed at the end of each long, grumbling epistle, and Tatiana dreaded to think he might believe she shared his mother's sentiments. That he had gone to Russia at all after the way she had spurned him, after she'd so cowardly denied the passion she felt toward him, left her riveted with guilt. He was too good for her. She had no doubt of that now.

September came and went; autumn brought the last late flush of roses. November seemed to drag on endlessly, and as the holidays approached, the countess's correspondence took on even more of an edge. How long, she asked again and again in the letters, did he intend to stay in Russia? How much more would he punish her—and, she always mentioned, punish Tatiana, who had no hopes whatsoever of procuring a husband in such circumstances—by stranding them here at the ends of the earth?

In mid-December Lucas wrote that he had been to Lipovsk and learned that the decimation of Mizhakovsk had officially been laid at the hands of marauding Cossacks—this despite the fact that everyone admitted no other such attacks had been made in the past two hundred years. Tatiana read the words and then closed her eyes, remembering her village in winter, the cold that tore through any amount of clothing, those endless white plains. And here she sat, comfortable by a roaring fire, a glass of sherry at her elbow, stitching a chair cover. She was consumed with shame.

Meanwhile the countess fretted and glowered, the sailors sang lustily, and Christmas passed in a dull haze of bad cheer. Dulcie was compelled by the utter absence of any other educated soul to take meals and spend her evenings with Tatiana. But her resentment showed; she blamed her protégée for this misery, and clearly regretted ever having made her acquaintance. More than once, Tatiana soberly considered the possibility of running away. Her disappearance would free the countess to return to the winter season in London—and, more, would liberate her son from this misguided adventure that could cost him his life.

Then, early in the new year, there came a letter from Lucas that changed everything. It was addressed to Tatiana, not to the countess, and she read it hurriedly while Dulcie was still abed:

St. Petersburg
7 January, 1814

My dear Tatiana:

A brief note only, alas, for I depart this afternoon for Orensburg in the wake of the Tsar. It has come to my attention that among his officers is a certain Platov, the hetman of the Don Cossacks; I hope he may shed some light on what occurred at M____. He is by all accounts a most monstrous savage, unschooled in any tongue but his own, with a magical white stallion that has carried him safely through constant campaigning. If I cannot pry open his mouth as to M____, I shall at least assay to buy that horse, regardless of the cost.

I did have a brief meeting with the Tsar whom you so adulate, and I must admit my opinion of him is completely altered. He truly has ennobled himself in these latest campaigns. It would not suit England ill to serve a spell beneath his rule. The hardships suffered by the populace here are beyond description. Were anything comparable to fall upon the English, the entire government—and not merely the ministers—would be overthrown. The Tsar holds this nation together by the strength of his convictions; I wish to God England had such a monarch. And that, I suppose, is in way of apology to you for any slights of the past.

Here is some hard news, not to be shared even with my mother. There is a plan of fight against Napoleon, supported by all the Allies, to be put into place very soon. It seems too much to hope at this late date that the Corsican's gains can be reversed, yet military history teaches, from Caesar on down, that the expansion of empire can only reach a certain point before crumbling inward. One wonders why tyrants never will be satisfied until that point is reached.

Do not imagine my removal from this city bears any relation to the end of the embassy's stores of claret, of which I wrote you earlier—though the prospect of the wines of France is a mighty draw. After I speak to Platov I will move on to Paris; I feel more and more that Casimir is at the heart of this mystery. Pray direct any further correspondence to the embassy there.

This much of the writing has been easy. Now I sit by a very small fire, pen in hand, and ponder what more I should add. Let me say this, on the chance that war or accident removes me forever from your sphere: In your last missive, you wished me the love of the season. I would to God I had your love for all seasons.

You may put that down to the vodka. It goes to my head—rather as you do—and there is nothing else to drink. I will post this now, before the light of day makes me regret it.

Yours,
Lucas Strathmere, Earl of Somerleigh

"Where is your letter from Lucas, Tatiana? I know you had one; Smithers told me."

Tatiana started so suddenly that she knocked over her cup of tea. The steaming liquid spilled onto the page, obliterating the words before she had even one more chance to read them, devour their sweetness again. "Oh," she cried, "it is ruined!" And she watched, her heart sinking, as the tea made puddles of her dreams.

"Did he say he is returning home?"

"He . . . he is removing to Orensburg, and then to Paris."

"God, such a deal of risk to so little purpose! If he truly fears for your safety, why not come home and keep an eye on you, rather than relying on these ruffians?" A sudden burst of song from the sailors belowstairs made her clap her hands over her ears. "I am within an *inch* of heading back to London. Why shouldn't I go, when he is so negligent of me? I might very well say I've left you in Italy with your ailing relation." The countess frowned. "Nonetheless, he did place you under my care. I shall stick it out. Never let it be said a lady of the house of Somerleigh was one to shirk her duty."

"You are too good," Tatiana murmured, with only a hint of despair.

"Let us to work on our reply. We shall write it jointly," decreed the countess, "and send it off straight in the morning. Pray God we can deter him from this madness of Paris! Is your pen ready? Take this down."

Somerleigh House, Dorset
21 January, 1814

Dear Lucas:

We send this posthaste to Orensburg in the devout wish it intercepts you there. If you go to Paris, be warned: We will not be content to bide our time here. The situation is too unnatural: the isolation, these dreadful sailors, the lack of commune with all for whom we care.

"New paragraph," Dulcie announced while Tatiana looked over the one she'd just written with cold foreboding.

The weather has been as intolerable as our circumstances. Nothing but drear and damp. We had a quiet Christmas, relieved only by the celebrations of the servants and sailors, making do with a roasted turkey, some quail Costner brought in, brussels sprouts from the garden, two cakes, and a trifle with potted cherries.

Tatiana thought of what Lucas had written of the suffering in Russia and bit her tongue.

"Here, you might put this in," the countess noted, handing her a sheaf of papers. "It's some sort of report from Billings, the overseer."

Billings wishes to inform you that the profits from the estates last year totaled as follows:
Corn—12,000 bushels sold at 4 shillings per
Oats—5,000 bushels sold at 2 shillings per
Sheep—5,000 head sold at 7 shillings per
Roses (bush)—2,000 sold at 2 shillings per

"Oh, Lord." The countess stifled a yawn. "You cannot put it all in; it will make the letter too heavy. Just give the summation, if you can find it."

Your mother begs me cut this short and give the total income for the estates for the year 1813, which is—

Tatiana gasped. "What? Is it so bad as that?" Dulcie asked in alarm.

—forty thousand pounds.

"Are you certain of that figure?" The countess's eyebrows were raised. Tatiana showed where she'd got it. "Forty thousand! It is double what the Admiral ever made, God rest his soul!" Dulcie rubbed her hands in anticipation. "Oh, when I only get to London! What can he possibly deny me now that I know of this?"

"Perhaps the increase is the result of his taking so great a hand in the management of the estates," Tatiana ventured.

"Oh, I daresay it is just the increased value of commodities, what with the war."

Forty thousand pounds. It was unimaginable, beyond a fortune. Tatiana was suddenly glad they weren't in London, where such news would have caused even more of a frenzy for the Earl of Somerleigh's hand. Yet he had said, in that last letter—

"Do close it, dear, somehow, and send it off. I must plan how I will spend all this wealth! Perhaps a new town house—or, better, two. One for us, and one for him when he marries. Oh, how I long to let word of this slip to Lady Shelton! He is beyond eligible now!"

Tatiana dawdled as long as she dared, pretending she was thinking, hoping Dulcie might leave so that she might put down what was in her heart. But the countess was not about to budge from her side. "What is keeping you? Go ahead— and tell him not to go to Paris. Oh, and mention that he cannot expect another such year if he goes on gallivanting around the Continent!"

> *Billings's impressive report has filled your mother with anticipation. She reminds you it is your presence here that has made the estates so profitable.*

"*I* said it was the war!"

"You want him to return, do you not?"

"Of course I do. But it's no earthly good to me if he comes back only to mire himself in the management of the estates! I want him to marry!"

And she trusts this income will impel you at last to the blessings of matrimony—

"With," the countess interjected tartly, "some acceptable young lady."

—with some acceptable young lady. We join in our pleas: Do not go to Paris. Return home, where you are so ardently needed.

" 'Ardently' seems the wrong word."

"Johnson says it means 'eagerly'. Have I misused it?"

"Not if that's what Johnson says. Here, I'll sign it." Dulcie put down, in her more flamboyant hand,

Very earnestly yours,
Dulcibella, Lady Strathmere
Miss Grimaldi

"Now give me the sealing wax. I'll take this down to Smithers myself. He can have Costner ride with it tonight. You've done a very pretty job, Tatiana. In fact, I think this letter quite the finest you have ever writ."

Orensburg
4 February, 1814

Dear Cousin:
    Your letter reached me in good time, and offered much food for thought. It is clear what you thought of my last missive. I apologize for any offense you may have taken at my jottings. I shall not venture to impose on you that way again.
    That said, this letter is brief enough. My attempts to engage the formidable Platov in conversation have come to naught. He has a war to fight, and nothing to say to foreign

diplomats. You would admire him. He is a man of action. I daresay he does not bury his head in his account books—if Cossacks even have account books. It warms my heart no end that Mother considers me more eligible thanks to my increase of income. I can picture her straining at the bit to share this news with her cronies in London. Do not burst her bubble, but know this for yourself: I am more sure than ever that I will not wed, with your letter in my hand.

I do go to Paris, on the morrow. I cannot consider further correspondence to be anything but a wretched chore on your part, but Mother might like to know she can reach me in charge of the embassy there. What I know of the progress of the Allies would not reassure her—though it would no doubt please you—and so I leave it unspoken, like so much else in my heart.

I hope to return soon and free you from the deplorable conditions I've subjected you to.

Yours very truly,
Lucas Strathmere, Earl of Somerleigh

"Damn it all!" Tatiana cried so vehemently that Bellerophon left the hearth rug to come nosing at her skirts in concern.

"What is it?" asked the countess, who was just passing her doors. "Bad news of Lucas?"

"No, no. Well, yes. He is gone to Paris after all."

"Against my express wishes? Oh, I cannot believe it. You must misunderstand him." Before Tatiana could react, Dulcie had come and snatched the letter out of her hand. She read it through once, and again. And then her eyes, more stormy than her son's, peered over the edge. "What sort of 'jottings' did he write you, pray tell, that he is now disclaiming?"

"I scarcely know, milady." But she felt a tear roll down her cheek, and buried her face against Bellerophon.

There followed a lengthy pause, during which she felt the countess's gaze bearing down on her. Then, "Has my son been making love to you?" Dulcie asked evenly.

"No." But how it tore at her to lie, not to proclaim it proudly!

"I have wondered at times whether his interest in you was not more than could be accounted for by his remorse at the destruction of your village," the countess mused. "That evening I came in so late and you were playing at chess—you seemed quite cozy together."

One of the happiest memories of all her life . . . "His behavior toward me has always been impeccable," Tatiana said with a hint of spirit.

"I was not thinking of *his* behavior. I was considering yours."

"Everything I know of propriety I learned from you, milady."

"But you had years before that to absorb quite different teachings, didn't you? Now that I contemplate, who is to say your latching onto him so conveniently back in Miz-whatever was not some sort of scheme from the start?"

"Convenient?" Tatiana cried, indignant. "To lose my home, my betrothed,—"

"Oh, you've not done so badly for yourself. Where would you prefer to be now—back there in wherever you came from, or here?" Tatiana did not, could not, answer. "I see," the countess said thoughtfully. "Do you know, I'm beginning to wish I'd left you the little, savage, unwashed creature you were. I ought to have paid more heed to the warnings Lucas gave me."

"What sorts of warnings?" Tatiana demanded.

"He mentioned blackmail at one point. Asked what was

to keep you, once married, from threatening to disclose your true past to your husband and hold it over our heads."

"It is fortunate, then, I did not accept the offers that were made me."

"Is it? Where is the good fortune in having a nameless foreign chit angling after my son?"

"I am not . . . I wasn't . . . I never have *angled*! Any professions he made—" Tatiana broke off abruptly, but the damage was done.

"So he made professions. And you made . . . responses?"

Tatiana met her gaze then. "You can read well enough from his letter how little I encouraged him. But had I to do it over, I would tell him what is in my heart."

"Oh! To think I have nourished such a viper at my breast!" The countess turned away, dramatic in despair. "Have I not treated you as my own daughter—nay, better than a daughter! When did I ever naysay you anything you wished?"

"Only now," Tatiana whispered. "Only in this."

Dulcie crumpled the letter in her fist. "He is as good as dead to me already, and has been these many years. All the hopes I cherished for him—"

"In all those hopes, was his happiness ever among them?"

"His happiness was my utmost desire!"

"I could make him happy," Tatiana said earnestly. "I know that I could."

Dulcie scarcely seemed to have heard. "This impossible propensity for the most *common* sorts of women—that is what has thwarted me at every turn!" She pitched the letter onto the fire. "I have had enough of this misery. I shall return to London on the morrow. *You* may bide here with the servants and sailors. You seem comfortable enough with them. It is your own true milieu."

Tatiana was pleating her skirts with her hands. "You must believe . . . I never had the least intention . . . I was not encouraging! His going to Russia was none of my doing!"

"Oh, that's true enough, I'll warrant. That must have thrown quite a hitch into your plans."

"How is that, milady?" she asked cautiously.

"Why, you must have been aghast at the prospect he might actually uncover the truth about your parentage—now that you've demonstrated the appalling baseness of your character." The countess stabbed at her with an elegant finger. "What news did you expect him to bring you—that you are a grand duchess?"

"Of course I didn't! It never mattered to me!"

"Ah, but it does to him! Why else would he have made such a dangerous journey?"

"I—" Tatiana swallowed. There was no doubting the countess's reasoning. Going to Russia had been Lucas's own scheme. "He has found nothing so far—"

"No, and you must be down on your knees every night thanking God he hasn't! Go on and dream your pleasant dreams, girl, but rest assured of this: If Lucas can't confirm that your parents were more than peasants, he won't be offering his hand. He's learned that lesson well enough. The most you might hope for is a carte blanche."

Tatiana's chin came up. "And who is to say I might not accept?"

"Of course you would," said the countess, her voice silkily insinuating. "What more could be expected from your sort?"

Tatiana found her strength of will, and managed to wait until Dulcie had swept out of the room before bursting into tears.

* * *

She cried for a long time, clinging to Bellerophon for comfort, while all around her rang the sounds of preparation for the countess's departure: servants scurrying, trunks being hauled from storage, Smithers directing all in a loud, satisfied voice. Compounding her misery was the fact that Dulcie had every right to be angry. She had been betrayed—and she was absolutely correct in her appraisal of the situation. Enticing as Lucas's letter had been, the fact of his departure showed plainly that who she was, where she came from, mattered inordinately to him. If he came home empty-handed in his search, how much more unbearable would her circumstances be! It was easy enough to say she loved the man, but altogether harder to imagine his affections remaining fixed on her—against the wishes of his mother, the manipulations of Lady Bournemouth and a thousand like her, but even more, against the innate nobility she had always seen in him.

He deserves better, she thought. *If I truly loved him I would want him settled honorably.*

Carte blanche, though—Dulcie had mentioned that. To become his mistress, take his money but not his name, give him pleasure in return . . . it was so much less than she longed for, but so much more than she deserved. No, she decided in an instant. If this journey did not prove she was worthy to become his wife, she would leave her love forever undeclared. He was such a solitary man. Having a paramour would make it all too easy for him to go on avoiding the life to which his birth and fortune called him. He warranted a wife, and the joy and fulfillment that could only come through lawfully begotten heirs, the acceptance of the world.

And if he honestly loved her? In time, with removal and distance, his affection would fade. Just as his passion for Gillian Innisford, and Tatiana's for Pietr, had.

She gave one last sob and then released the mastiff, went

to the desk, took a sheet of vellum, and uncovered the nib of her pen. Heart aching, she began to write.

Somerleigh House, Dorset
23 February, 1814

Dear Cousin:

I was dismayed to receive your letter, indicating as it did your intent to continue on to Paris. I cannot comprehend what possible use you can imagine your trouble might be put to. Perhaps in the cold of Russian winter, deprived of your accustomed sustenance, you fell prey to wild fancies regarding all sorts of things. I dearly hope there will be food and wine enough left in Paris to restore your senses. Some few lines you wrote make me fear you have misconstrued my feelings for you.

She wiped her tears away before they splattered the page.

While I shall always hold you in the highest regard, there is so great a difference between our temperaments, not to mention our ages, that my affections for you are altogether fixed as those most cordially reserved for an elder brother or, better, an uncle or cousin, as we have professed before the world to be. I am chagrined to think you may have interpreted my behavior or my letters in any other way. Since I can only assume you have, I ask your abject pardon. We were always wont to treat each other more freely than perhaps was wise.

The weather here has been intolerable, and the absence of company has left us so bereft that we are determined to go on to London. I do not think I can abide another day without dancing and the theater and all the other amusements I have come to love. Pray don't be offended. I'm sure you meant well in this undertaking, but our isolation has become such a burden that we cannot prolong it on any account.

And do not trouble for my safety. I daresay I will find young men enough to look after me once we return to civilization. The more I reflect, the more absurd it seems that the two incidents that led to your departure were in any way related or in any way directed personally against me. To imagine anything else presumes two suppositions that my soul leans opposed to: that I am someone of reckoning, and that anyone could care what becomes of me.

No, that was wrong. Tatiana crossed it out, back to *reckoning*, and then went on:

—and that anyone besides you, knowing my true background, could be convinced of that fact. You have been misled, I fear, by your role as my savior and protector. As soon as I am able, I intend to transfer those responsibilities to a husband and relieve you of them once and for all.

I must go now; there is packing to be done. Thanking you for all your endeavors on my behalf, I am,

Your devoted—

No. She crossed that out, too.

Your dutiful cousin,
Tatiana Grimaldi

That task accomplished, she made the seal and took the letter down to the hallway console. On her way back to her room she passed Smithers, who brushed by with his accustomed chill. "Smithers!" she called. "Would you see if one of Costner's boys has a shirt and some breeches he can spare?"

"To what purpose, miss?"

"For me to wear," Tatiana said shortly. "I intend to work again with the horses and dogs."

For the first time in all their acquaintance, the butler genuinely smiled at her. "Very good, miss. I'll see to it directly."

At least *someone*, she reflected, wearily mounting the stairs, was at peace tonight at Somerleigh House.

Twenty-One

TATIANA FILLED THE days that followed with exercising
the mastiffs and the horses, once more taking her place
beside Costner and his boys in mucking out the stalls, fetching oats and water and hay. The servants of Somerleigh
House were not at all sure what to make of her abrupt fall
from grace. It was no more than what they'd all wished on
her, having observed her meteoric rise above her proper
station. Yet now that she had her comeuppance, they could
not quite bring themselves to treat her with complete scorn.
She detected, in fact, a certain sympathy in their manner,
and the compassion galled her more than their former disdain ever had.

Only Timkins was unchanged in his regard for her—and,
by extension, so were his sailors. She had consigned her
finery to the depths of Somerleigh's wardrobes, but they

remembered how she'd looked in sarcenet and jewels—or, in Timkins's case, had always thought leather breeches suited her as well.

She'd changed her spacious apartments for a small room in the attic. Carruthers was hard-pressed to deal with her mistress's changed circumstances. She remained at Somerleigh, though Tatiana urged her to go to London and find new employment. But the maid was nothing if not stubborn. Master had told her to protect Tatiana, and she would do so until he relieved her of her duties, she said. It did not hurt that she was free now to idle her hours away in the company of the sailors. By the time March gave on to April, she was betrothed to one of them—a wiry little man called Thomas, quite adept at the hornpipe and with no end of other accomplishments to recommend him to a young girl of Carruthers's temperament.

Spring was everywhere—bursting forth in the hedgerows, smothering the crab trees in blossoms, pushing fat green shoots out of the flower beds. Only in Tatiana's heart was it still midwinter, the cold, endless winter of Russia. She worked as hard as she could, so that when she took to her pallet at night she would be too exhausted to remember the past.

In the first week of April, something odd occurred. Cook was at market, and a stranger accosted her to inquire what she knew of Miss Grimaldi's whereabouts. For an instant, as Cook later told it, she nearly forgot that they'd all been sworn to secrecy. But then she recollected herself and responded as she'd been taught, that Miss Grimaldi was in Italy with a relative. What relative? the man had demanded. Cook disclaimed any further information. Something about the fellow, she told the servants gathered at the kitchen table for supper, did not seem quite right.

That night as Tatiana was undressing, she heard the clump of boots beyond her door, peeked out, and saw the gardener settling onto a stool with a musket beside him. "Timkins! Whatever are you doing?"

"Master bid us watch o'er ye," the old sailor said stolidly, " 'n' so I shall."

"Oh, do go on to your bed," she told him, heartily embarrassed. "There's no need for such precautions."

"I'll be the judge o' that," he said, and reported Cook's tale.

"No doubt it was just a friend, Timkins. Freddy Whittles or someone, in the neighborhood on business." But nothing she could say—not even pointing out that Bellerophon slept in her room—could change his mind. She fell asleep to the soft sound of the sea chanteys he sang beneath his breath and the scent of his tobacco—and did so, despite all her pleadings, for the next fortnight, while he refused to abandon his post.

By that time she'd grown accustomed to his presence, and had leisure to muse over the extent of his devotion to Lucas. "I do hope, Timkins," she said one evening as he took his place, "that when the master weds, you will serve Her Ladyship so well as you do me."

The sailor knocked out his pipe and fixed her with his good eye. "That'll depend, I reckon, on what woman he picks."

She had trouble falling asleep that night, though she had Gibbon—she was on to the third volume now—to aid her. She was bedeviled with worries about the future. If Lucas did wed, it could hardly be expected his wife would welcome her presence on the estates. She had burned her bridges with regard to the countess; Dulcie would not be sponsoring her at London or Brighton again. If a new Lady Strathmere turned her out, what would become of her? Freddy Whittles, she thought, cringing at the prospect. But even he wasn't likely to want her now that the countess had disowned her. Not even worthy of Freddy, she reflected in misery, the covers up around her head. She was nobody, nothing—back to exactly where she'd been three years before.

She sat up, though, at a sound from below of hoofbeats against cinders. Costner, returning home from his night out—but no. That had been yester evening. Who else could it be? She went to her small window, but could not see the front drive. Nervous despite herself, she pulled on a robe. Bellerophon had his ears pricked and was moving restlessly between the window and the door. She followed him, knocked, and hissed, "Timkins? Are you awake?"

No answer—and his snores, which she'd grown so used to, were missing. She raised the latch and opened up, just a crack—then jumped in surprise as the mastiff suddenly thrust his way through. Timkins's stool and pipe were in place, but he was nowhere in sight. Bellerophon bounded off along the corridor to the staircase. She trailed after him and down the first flight.

"Bellerophon?" she called softly at the landing. It was very late; no muffled laughter drifted up from the kitchens. The house was dark and still. Where in the world was Timkins? She crept down another set of stairs—and stopped dead at the sound of a shrill female scream.

Where had it come from? The west wing, where her old rooms were situated. Only Carruthers slept there now, in the chamber beside the one that had been her own. Where in God's name was Bellerophon? If there was an intruder, why hadn't he raised a ruckus? Tatiana stood alone in the darkness, hearing her heartbeat drum. But Carruthers was in danger—she must go to her. She rounded a corner, reached the landing, and gasped as her bare foot encountered a bulk—a form. Human flesh. She forced herself to reach down, feel across the rough jacket to the neck, up to the face. Curly beard, hooked nose . . . it stirred at her touch.

"Timkins?" she whispered, and was rewarded by a groan. "Someone . . . heard him comin' . . . "

Another scream split the air. "Carruthers!" Tatiana cried.

"Stay away, miss. Go back to bed. He'll never find ye."

"I cannot leave Carruthers to be terrified!"

"He's come for ye, milady!"

Tatiana was equally sure of it, but who had come she had no idea. "Did he hurt you?"

"Nah, nah. 'Twas that damned dog. Pushed me down the stairs. Came through like the house was a-fire 'n' knocked me straight over."

"Where are your sailors?"

"I thought I saw . . . a late frost comin'. I sent 'em out to cover the bushes." Tatiana felt him thrust something toward her: his musket. "Can ye shoot, milady?"

"I can if I must." She tucked it under her arm. "Are you coming?"

"If I ain't mistaken, my leg be broke."

There was the sound of wild blubbering now from the west wing. Tatiana stood up, moved toward the hall. "Don't!" Timkins cried. "Go back to yer bed!"

She ignored him, stepping steadily through the dark toward Carruthers's room.

The crying had abruptly subsided. Tatiana felt with her hand that the door was shut; no speck of light showed from within. There was a rectangle of glow, however, around the door to her old apartments. Tatiana tiptoed toward it cautiously. The musket weighed on her shoulder. She had lied to Timkins; she hadn't the least notion how to use it, but having it made her feel more brave. She hesitated on the threshold, ear to the door, and heard a slow, heavy breathing. Bellerophon? But no—he must be dead, or he'd be barking like a banshee. She grasped the knob, turned it soundlessly.

The door swung open. Blinking in the onslaught of light, she saw her armoire, her desk, her bed—and something vast and dark splayed across it. Too big to be Carruthers. Too big to be anything human. It had too many limbs—God in heaven, it had two heads! "What *are* you?" she whispered in dismay, and nearly fainted as one heavy head rose from the white coverlet and turned toward her, huge mouth agape, tongue lolling, showing great pointed teeth. Then it let out a whimper, and she started in recognition: "Bellerophon!"

The mastiff whined again, and snuffled at the motionless form beneath him. Tatiana took a step closer, saw the thick, waving black hair, the broad shoulders, the Hessians crusted in mire. And she saw, too, the slowly spreading pool of red, stark against the coverlet where he was lying.

"Lucas!" she screamed, dropping the musket where she stood and running to the bed.

Twenty-Two

HE LAY FACEDOWN in his own blood, insensate, cold to her touch, and Tatiana was engulfed in terror that he was dead. She tried to roll him over and found she could not budge him. Frantically, she pushed his cuffs back, tore the stained cravat from his neck, felt for the throb of a pulse. When she could not find one, she cried in anguish, "Dear God, no! No!" Bellerophon howled with her, pausing between yowls to nose at his inert master, lap at him with his tongue, nip him gently in an animal urge to bring him back to life. "Help me, boy," Tatiana ordered. "We've got to push him over." The dog seemed to understand, and he thrust his head and shoulders under Lucas's ribs. Together they managed to turn him onto his back.

There was something bound around his chest, soiled and bloody—his handkerchief. Tatiana touched it fearfully. "Lucas!" she said loudly. "Lucas, can you hear me?" His eyes opened slowly. They were horribly vacant, the storm in them vanished, given way to a blank, empty blue. But at least he was alive. She fought off an urge to slap him, to try to bring some spark to that listless gaze. Bellerophon was crouching silently, his big head moving between her face and his. Tatiana steeled herself and peeled the handkerchief away. Beneath it lay a wound, ugly and open and gaping, right where his heart must be.

She had to stop the bleeding. She took the lacy coverlet and held it to the wound, pressing to stanch the slow crimson flow. He cringed, murmuring something unintelligible. He'd been cold before, but he was hot now to her hand, his flesh burning like fire. She left the bedside for Carruthers's room, found a pitcher on the nightstand, and returned to mop at his forehead, using an embroidered pillow for a sponge. The cool seemed to calm him; he fell back, his breathing wildly uneven. He needed a doctor, Tatiana realized. He needed a doctor *now*.

From the corridor, she heard a clamor of voices and the rush of footsteps. Carruthers hurried into the room, with Smithers and his wife in her wake. "There he is! Didn't I say so?"

"Good God," said Smithers, stopping in mid-step. Mrs. Smithers pushed past him impatiently.

"Is he dead, then?" she cried. "Is it true what she told us?"

"He isn't dead yet." Tatiana held tight to his hand. "But the blood—he needs a doctor."

"I'll get Costner to ride for Dr. Swartley," Smithers said, backing out of the room.

"How far away is he?" Tatiana demanded.

"A half hour's ride, no more," Mrs. Smithers assured her.

A half hour there, another half hour back—what if he wasn't at home? Smithers was still standing there, looking green. "Carruthers!" Tatiana cried impatiently. "Tell Costner to go—and, please God, have him hurry!" The maid took a step into the hall and let out a yelp.

"God 'n' Mary preserve us!"

"Move aside, lass," Timkins said curtly. He was crawling along the floor, dragging his injured leg. He had crawled all the way from the landing, Tatiana recognized dimly; he was ghost-pale with pain, but he clearly intended to take charge. He hauled himself to the bed. "Here, now, let's see what we've got." Tatiana helped to pull him up beside his master, watching as he pushed the pillow away. "Knife wound," he pronounced succinctly. "Old—a week old, I'd say. Putrefying." His gaze swiveled toward the housekeeper. "Bring boiled water 'n' fresh bandages, 'n' heat up an iron—a clean one—in the fire. Then, for the poultice, mustard seed 'n' vinegar 'n' herb Robert. Have ye got those?" She nodded dumbly. " 'N' somewhat for the pain."

"Laudanum?" Mrs. Smithers ventured.

"If that's the strongest ye got. In wine—good red wine. None o' yer weak-willy stuff." She hadn't moved. "Go on, woman, unless ye want his death on yer conscience!" She bustled off, brushing past her husband.

"Smithers," Timkins said briskly, "I'll need ye to hold him when I put on the iron."

"I?" the butler gasped. "Oh, I think not. I really think not."

"Dammit all—" The gardener turned to Tatiana. "Go and fetch Big Jon." That was one of his sailors. "He'll do the job right enough."

"I can do it," she offered.

"Nah. It won't be a pretty sight—'n' the smell will likely make ye faint."

"I won't faint."

"Well—p'raps ye wouldn't. But I need a more brawny set o' arms than yers."

"I'll go and bring him, shall I?" Smithers escaped eagerly into the hallway.

"Useless idiot," Timkins muttered, turning back to the task at hand.

"Do you think you can save him?" Tatiana asked, eyes brimming with tears.

"Faith, I've seen worse wounds in my day." He stole a glance at her frightened face. "If I do, will the two o' ye put off yer shilly-shallying 'n' do what's plain as day ye have been achin' to these past three years?"

"And what is that?" Tatiana demanded.

"Ye tell me, why don't ye?" Timkins trained his attention on the patient again.

Carruthers came rushing back a few minutes later to report that Costner was on his way to fetch the doctor. Hard on her heels came Big Jon, his placid calm a solace to Tatiana's fears. "Ye may as well go," Timkins told her by way of dismissal.

"I am not going anywhere." She thought she glimpsed approval in his gaze before he began explaining what he needed to Big Jon.

Carruthers tiptoed up beside them. "Scared me more'n half to death, he did," she reported of the master. "Heard a noise in here, didn't I? Got up from bed to see what it might be. Opened the door, 'n' he came lungin' at me, all covered in blood 'n' blatherin' nonsense, clawin' at me—here, ye can see the prints o' his hands." She held her nightdress out. "I screamed again, 'n' he backed toward the bed, 'n' the door busted open, 'n' who should it be but that blasted dog? Must o' had the scent o' his master. He leaped at him 'n' sent him sprawling onto the bed, 'n' then leaped up atop him. Near out o' my mind I was by then, crying 'n' blubbering—but I knew right enough I must fetch Smithers straightaway."

"Smithers?" Big Jon chortled. "La, might as soon send for a newborn babe!"

"My instructions," Carruthers said with a touch of hauteur, "are to always inform the butler when anything is amiss in the household."

"Never mind," Tatiana soothed her. "I can only imagine how startled you were."

Mrs. Smithers trotted in with a tray. "Got all ye asked, sir, I do believe—"

"Put it there," Timkins directed. "Is the iron hot?"

"Hot enough to curl hair." She wet her finger to prove it.

"Hold him down, Jon. Ladies, ye'll want to be leavin'." Mrs. Smithers and Carruthers quickly backed away. Tatiana stayed where she was, and watched the gardener blot the wound, then press the iron to it. Lucas's whole body tensed, and he let out a low, agonized moan. "No curin' without some hurtin'," Timkins said complacently, the iron searing against flesh. A sickening scent, like the worst sort of charred meat, filled the room. Tatiana put her fist to her mouth. Carruthers moved for the windows, throwing them open to the clean night air.

"The poultice now. Miss, hold those bandages, would ye?" Glad for something to do, Tatiana spread them out while Timkins smeared them with the physics and bound them on. "Now the wine. Hold his head up, Jon. Aye, that's right." Tatiana saw Lucas's throat bulge with the medicine and then contract. She squeezed his hand and, surprised, felt his fingers clench on hers.

"Hold him up, Jon!" the gardener ordered. "Got to get more o' this down his gullet—that's the way. That's the way. Forget the pain, aye." His voice had turned low and soothing. "Sleep, now. That's the best thing for it. Ye must sleep now."

Lucas seemed to rouse, pushed himself up on his elbows. Jon abruptly thrust him back. "Sleep!" he barked. "Didn't ye hear the doctor?"

"Sleep," Tatiana added in a whisper. "Go on to sleep, my love."

The fingers gripping hers relaxed. Bellerophon, still puzzled but accepting, lapped his master's face and settled down with him, curled against his side. Timkins slid off the bed with a thump.

"Good Lord," said Tatiana, coming to her senses. "We must see about your leg!"

The old sailor groped toward the tray. "If there be any o' that laudanum left, it would not taste amiss," he murmured, just before he pitched headfirst onto the floor.

By the time they heard horses pounding up the drive, Big Jon had settled Timkins on Carruthers's pallet and, with Tatiana's help, poured laudanum and wine into him as well. Dr. Swartley, short and brisk and bespectacled, looked at Lucas first, approved the cauterizing, asked what was on the bandage, and allowed it could do no harm and might even do good. He had a tincture of opium that was stronger than the laudanum. "Will he live, doctor?" Tatiana asked fearfully.

"Chose the fastest way he could have not to." The doctor pushed his spectacles up on his nose. "A wound such as that, so close to the heart—the man who fetched me said he'd ridden his way here. From where?"

"The last we heard, he was in Paris."

The doctor barked a laugh. "He didn't come from Paris with a hole that deep in his chest, or I'd be making out his death writ." Tatiana shuddered. "Keep him quiet and absolutely calm. I'll stay the night in case I'm needed. Now, let's see this other patient you've got."

After a thorough probing of Timkins's left foot, Dr. Swartley declared the ankle was indeed broken. "Must have been excruciating. How did it happen?"

"The mastiff knocked him down the stairs."

"I'll have to set it. Where'd that huge fellow get to? You, there!" he called to Big Jon through the doorway. "Come and hold him for me while I turn this leg."

"Lift 'em up, hold 'em down," Big Jon grumbled, coming to his summons. "That's all anyone ever bids me do. Like I ain't got a brain in my head."

Tatiana helped where she could, cutting the bandages as the doctor directed, smoothing down the edges as he held them. When he'd finished, he looked at her. "You're pale as sheets. Take some wine yourself and get off to bed."

"I wouldn't mind the wine. But I'd prefer to stay. In case one of them needs me."

He shrugged. "Suit yourself. I'll go see if your housekeeper can provide a bit of sustenance. You'll want to inform His Lordship's mother immediately, of course. I believe she is in London?" Tatiana nodded, hoping her face did not show her dismay. Dulcie coming here, just when Lucas had returned . . .

"Naturally. I'll send a letter off tonight."

"Good, good. Now, let's see about that supper! God, I've a hunger on!"

Tatiana went back to Lucas's bedside. His breathing had steadied, she noted, watching the rise and fall of his chest. Bellerophon was hunkered down beside him, snoring comfortably. Tatiana sipped her wine and sat and watched them, counting herself blessed. He was here. He'd come back. She could stare for as long as she liked at the way his hair curled back from his forehead, his long, strong hands against the bed sheets, the feather of his lashes laid down in perfect black half-moons.

Later she would fret about the countess. Tomorrow she would worry about what the future held. For now, she was content to remain here and watch him, drink her fill of the proud, stern face she loved more than anything on earth.

Twenty-Three

THE DAYS THAT followed were a blur of busy chores and anxious worrying and far too little rest for Tatiana. Dr. Swartley visited each evening and declared himself satisfied with Lord Strathmere's progress—which was to say, no fever arose, no further putrefication ensued, and the patient did not die. But Tatiana could not share his confidence. Though Timkins was up and about by the third day, moving with the aid of crutches Big Jon fashioned for him, Lucas went on sleeping. It began to seem impossible that he ever would awake.

He did, though, on the morn of the fifth day, just as Tatiana was changing the dressing on his wound. He stirred beneath her hands; his eyes blinked, blinked again, opened, and then shut quickly, as if to block the unfamiliar sunlight falling across the bed.

"Lucas," she whispered.

He shook his head, his dry lips parting. She wet them quickly with a cloth. "Won't . . . won't look again."

"Won't look at what?"

"You. Not really . . . there."

"Of course I am here." She laid her hand on his cheek.

"Dream," he said succinctly.

His mind was so clouded with opium still. . . . Tentatively Tatiana bent down and pressed her mouth to his. God, how long had she been aching to do that? She drew away, and his hand groped for hers, pulling her back. Eyes still pressed tight, he returned the kiss slowly, then paused, murmuring against her lips, "Now I know . . . just dreaming."

"I am here," she whispered fiercely.

His eyes opened just a bit, then gradually went wider, until he looked straight at her. His pupils were still wide and swimming, but the blue sky held hints of storm again. "Where am I?"

"Home," she told him, loving the way it sounded, loving him beyond all reason.

"Home," he echoed. His eyelids drooped closed. "I like this dream," he mumbled. "Can I go on dreaming?"

"If you like."

After that, his recovery went more quickly. Tatiana spent every moment she could in his rooms, but she was careful, now that he was sentient, to keep her behavior absolutely proper—at least while he was awake. When he slept, she held his hand or smoothed his forehead or let her fingers wander through the black waves of his hair. In another two days, he could sit up. After three, he was eating—broth and milk toast, which he utterly disdained, and then custard and soup, also fit for naught but toothless old men, he declared mutinously.

"Dr. Swartley says," Tatiana began.

"Damn that nitwit sawbones. Bring me a chop of veal and roasted potatoes and some decent bread. And some claret, while you're at it."

"Not a chance," she said sweetly. "But if you finish all this lovely custard, I might have Cook make you some nice hot porridge."

"You're a hell of a jailer."

"You're a hell of a patient."

"Kiss me," he said, his eyes dark, "and I might try that custard."

How much did he remember of the opium dreams? "Oh, no, milord," she said lightly, teasingly, "you'll not get around me so easily as that."

Slowly, between sips of soup and bites of sop, he told her what had happened. He'd reached Paris just after the fall of the city to the Allied forces, and had immediately called on a Lord Willoughby at the embassy there. "Tried to be helpful, I suppose, but he had his hands full with prisoners of war and much more weighty matters. Suggested I check in at the Russian embassy," Lucas explained. "I was on my way there when some bastard came out of nowhere and stuck a knife right in my ribs."

"How terrible!" Tatiana held out the spoon. "Did you see him?"

"I'm ashamed to say not. He sneaked up from behind. I really have lost my touch."

"Who could it have been?"

"Lord, anyone—a thief, a hungry peasant, a lunatic. The whole city was a madhouse. Between the looters and the fanatics and the poor bewildered citizenry, folk were getting stabbed and shot at right and left."

"Did you go to hospital?"

"The hospitals were full of soldiers. No. I went back to my hotel—where I had the misfortune to be recognized by one of the Admiral's old cronies." He glanced at her sidelong. "This next part's not awfully noble. Right in front of him, on the stairs, I fainted dead away. He bundled me onto a ship bound for Dover before I could come to."

"He likely saved your life, you fool."

His eyes, the storm fully returned now, considered her closely. "I'm not at all sure I wanted him to."

"No more nonsense like that," she said cheerily, holding out the last bite of custard. "Once you are mended and feeling your old self—"

"Aye?" he broke in. "What then?"

"Then I am sure you'll be as glad as I am that your life was spared."

He swallowed the custard. "So long as *you* are glad . . ."

She stood up, turning to put the spoon and cup on the tray. "Of course I am. You know how fond I am of you, cousin."

"Bah," he said balefully.

"I'll send Big Jon in to bathe you."

"You might do it yourself."

She had done it, before his consciousness returned. She'd wiped with a cool sponge all along his arms and chest, down his belly, over his groin and legs—suddenly flushed, she managed a passable laugh. "Cousin! What sort of girl do you think me?"

"I think that you kissed me."

"Opium dreams," she said indulgently, and grabbed up the tray, escaping for the stairs.

She stayed away from him all the rest of that day and into the evening. Mrs. Smithers sent her up a bath, and she lounged in it gratefully, letting the smells and grime of the sickroom float away. That had been a close call—she was not at all certain he was convinced he had been dreaming when she gave him that kiss. But it would not matter much longer. The countess was sure to arrive at any time.

The water had turned chill, just like her heart at the

prospect. She climbed from the tub, dried herself, and was just teasing the last tangles out of her hair when she heard frantic footsteps in the corridor. "Miss?" It was Carruthers's voice, high and nervous. "Miss, the master's askin' for ye. He says he wants to play chess."

"Inform Lord Strathmere that you found me asleep," Tatiana said after a moment.

"Smithers already tried that, miss. The master said to wake ye up."

Sighing, Tatiana went to the door. "Tell him I'm not decent, then."

"Mrs. Smithers tried that," the maid said plaintively. "Told him ye was bathin'. 'Well, which is it—sleepin' or bathin'?' he roared at them. La, but he's in a temper. Timkins says if someone don't—doesn't—calm him, he's like to burst his dressin's. I really think it best ye come."

If Timkins was concerned, the situation was serious. Tatiana reached for her robe, tied it 'round her, and pulled her damp hair out from the collar, handing the brush to the maid. "I will, then, straightaway."

She hadn't turned the first landing when she heard Lucas bellowing, and Bellerophon joining in with frantic barks. On the second stair she came upon Mrs. Smithers, who had a bottle of claret and a cup on a tray. "Thank God," the housekeeper said fervently. "He's like a madman, miss! Nothin' 'n' no one can quiet him!"

"Did you try the opium?"

"He won't take it. Keeps shoutin' out for claret instead. Shall I send for Dr. Swartley?"

From Tatiana's old rooms came the sound of Lucas shouting in fury: "Take your bloody hands off me, Timkins, or so help me God, I'll put your other eye out!"

"Not yet," Tatiana told her. "Here, give me the tray."

When she reached the doorway she saw Timkins, crutches under his arms, struggling to push Lucas back onto the bed from which he'd raised himself. The old sailor was talking in soothing tones, Bellerophon was howling, and Lucas was cursing roundly. "Lord Strathmere!" Tatiana said in a tone of shock. The cacophony abruptly subsided. Timkins stepped away, Lucas stood on his two feet, and Bellerophon leaped to her side. "I've brought your wine," she went on calmly, "and I will pour it for you—*if* you get back into your bed."

"Fuck my bed."

"Listen here," Timkins said sharply, "there's no cause to use such language to her!"

Lucas made a fairly credible bow. He was in a loose shirt and trousers, his hair wild and unbound, a fortnight's beard shadowing his face. He looked, Tatiana thought, more like his own stable-hand than an earl—and as handsome as she'd ever seen him. "I beg your pardon—*cousin*," he said with a sneer. "But I've had my fill of playing invalid. I am well enough to do as I please."

"And is what you please terrorizing your entire household, which has worked so hard to make you well?"

"Fuck my—"

"Here, now!" Timkins cried, with a mortified glance at Tatiana.

"Never mind, Timkins. It's not anything I've not heard before from Costner—though I did think His Lordship had a greater vocabulary range." She had the satisfaction of seeing Lucas flush. This is more like it, she thought; we are back to being adversaries. She knew well enough how to deal with him when he was in this mood. "I've brought the wine," she repeated, "and I understand from Carruthers that you have a fancy for chess. Let's have at it, by all means. You are in such a lather, I daresay I'll stymie you in a dozen moves."

"I'll wager you won't," he growled.

"Your wager is taken." She set the tray beside the bed.

"Timkins, will you fetch up the board for us? It is in the kitchens, where Jon and I used it last."

Lucas scowled. "I don't like to leave ye with him," Timkins said hesitantly, "when he is—"

"Lord Strathmere would not harm a member of his own family. Besides, if he tries anything I shall have Mrs. Smithers send for Dr. Swartley. No doubt he'll have some tincture to recommend for His Lordship's distempered state."

"Fuck Dr.—"

"Yes, yes, I know, fuck them all. Go get the chessboard, Timkins." Both men were staring at her in amazement. She settled onto a chair beside the bed, fluffed out her robe, and pointed to the mattress. "In bed, milord. Or I will not play."

Lucas crossed defiantly to the tray and poured himself a brimming cup of wine. "Want some?" he asked in a belated attack of something resembling manners.

"No, thank you. You go on. It will make it all the easier for me to win."

He shot her a furious glance and gulped the cup down, then stood glaring at her silently.

How Timkins, hobbled by the crutches, could have returned so quickly with the board and pieces Tatiana could not fathom. He bore them in awkwardly, balanced across the armrests. "Thank you, Timkins," Tatiana said, moving to meet him. "And now you may go."

He looked at her uncertainly, but she nodded resolutely, and he pivoted for the door. Just before he reached it, Tatiana asked Lucas, "Has anyone told you how Timkins came to be on crutches?"

"No one tells me bloody anything," he snarled.

"Bellerophon knocked him down the stairs. Timkins was following your orders to defend me. He'd heard you on the drive and thought you were an intruder. He'd been camped outside the door to my room for a fortnight, sleeping on a stool, a musket at his side."

That took the bluster out of Lucas. He looked at Timkins, then at Tatiana, then back at the sailor. "I say," he began, in quite a different tone. "I say, I *am* sorry. I hadn't any idea. F—" He glanced at Tatiana again. "Damn you, too, Bellerophon."

Timkins grinned at him, reassured. "My sentiments precisely, m'lord."

When he'd gone, Tatiana busied herself setting up the pieces. Lucas poured himself more wine, then grabbed for a chair. "I said in bed," she told him evenly.

"I'll sit where I please."

Tatiana shrugged. "Suit yourself. But considering your pallor, I would venture to alter our wager. Shall we say six moves?"

He hesitated, then sat down heavily on the mattress. Tatiana tried without success to hide her smile. "What is it?" he demanded sharply.

"Just . . . something your mother told me. About how your nanny got you to bed when you were four years old. By telling you your parents wanted nothing more than for you to stay up all night."

He snorted. "White or black?"

"I'll be white, naturally."

"The White Lady," he murmured.

She glanced up. "What's that?"

"What we diplomats in St. Petersburg used to call your country in winter."

She considered it briefly, pushing back her long, loose hair. "I've heard worse. Draw to begin?" She hid two pawns in her palms, then presented her closed fists to him. He chose the white. "My opening," she said brightly, and moved pawn to king four.

He countered with the same move, sipping the wine, not gulping. Tatiana advanced her king's knight to king's bishop three. He responded with his queen's knight to queen's bishop three. Tatiana looked at him from beneath her lashes, surprised. He was playing with unaccustomed license. "Whatever became of not bearing to lose a pawn?" she asked curiously.

"I find I am no longer so afraid of risk."

"Evidently not." She pushed her king's bishop to queen's bishop four. Without hesitating, he moved his piece in mirror.

"Pawn to queen's bishop three," Tatiana murmured.

"King's knight to king's bishop three." The play continued intensely for several more minutes, until Lucas unexpectedly sacrificed his rook to her queen.

Tatiana had to stop and think—but did not for long, lest he sense her sudden uncertainty. The game was moving in a direction she was no longer familiar with. "Pawn to queen four."

"Pawn takes pawn," said Lucas, capturing his victim.

"And pawn takes pawn," she responded, making the obvious move.

He nudged his king's bishop forward. "Check," he said in a low voice.

Astounded, she stared at the board. Her fingers fluttered toward her own knight, pulled back, alighted on her queen's bishop, hurriedly withdrew.

"You touched it," Lucas declared. "You have to move it."

She raised her eyes, dismayed. "Oh, come, milord! A friendly game—"

"Move it," he repeated.

Reluctantly, unwilling to beg for mercy, she did.

"Mate," said Lucas, with satisfaction in his voice.

Tatiana folded her hands in her lap. "You have been practicing."

"I had little enough to occupy me in Russia. Did you imagine me dancing with the ladies of the Tsar's court? Now, for our little wager."

"I wagered only that I would win."

"Correct—but since I am the victor, I will name the stakes. I will ask you one question, Tatiana, one question only. And when you answer, you will tell me the truth."

One question only . . . She steeled herself, prepared to lie. "Go on," she said sedately.

"Why did you write that last letter to me?"

It wasn't what she'd expected. She'd thought he would query her about the kiss, or why he'd found her here at Somerleigh when she'd written she was going to London. "Because," she began, since she had to—and then had no notion where to go. A dozen plausible falsehoods flashed through her mind. The trouble was, she could not settle on which. "Because—"

"The truth, Tatiana."

Might as well, she decided, give the one most likely to be believed. "Because your mother . . . formed a suspicion about me."

"What sort of suspicion?"

"That I was . . . angling after you."

"I see. Was her suspicion justified?"

"You said one question only!"

"We can play again, if you like."

"No!" she cried with sudden heatedness. "I told her I had never done any such thing. But she called me . . . horrible names. And said such vile stuff about me—then she went back to London and told me to stay here with the stable-hands. In my 'true milieu.'"

"And that was why you wrote as you did."

"I understood then, in light of what you'd written me . . . words I did not dare let her see . . ." She lifted her green gaze, shamefaced. He reached for the pieces to move them back to their starting places. "Don't bother," she said curtly. "It was wrong. Because you are who you are, and I am . . . what I am."

He looked away toward the open window, beyond which the branches of a willow, new-green, were swaying in the light of a rising half-moon. "Why did you bow to her will?"

"Because she told me—she said—" And then the words came out headlong. "She said you'd gone to Russia because you cared about my provenance, because you never would marry me if you could not determine my parentage. She said the most I could hope for in such circumstances was a carte blanche."

"And that would not have suited you?" he asked very gravely.

She hesitated. He pushed his king's pawn forward, though, and she shook her head, incapable of thinking of chess. "I should have been very happy for that. More than happy."

"Then why write such a letter?"

"Because it would not suit for you," she said with more determination. "You deserve better than that. You should have a proper home, a wife, children worthy to carry on your—" The words tangled in a sob; she could not go on.

"Tatiana. Look at me." She wouldn't, so he reached across the board to tilt her chin up with his fingertips. "*That* is why I went to Russia. Not for me. But because I was afraid you would not love me for just such specious reasons."

"They aren't specious! The difference in our stations—"

"Do you think yourself less worthy a human being than Selma Bournemouth?"

"That isn't—"

"Or, for that matter, my mother?"

"The ton—"

"I'm not asking the ton's opinion. I am asking yours." She did not answer, her small face crumpled in misery, and he sighed. "There, you see? You will not be convinced."

"It was only the vodka talking. You said so yourself," she told him stubbornly.

He set his wine cup down abruptly. "I offer you carte blanche, then. Become my mistress." She stared, her eyes green as the new leaves. "Do you accept?"

"With all my heart," she whispered, and looked down at the board bashfully.

"Well, I don't. I want you for my wife, Tatiana."

"No."

His fist slammed onto the bed, making Bellerophon jump. "You impossible girl! You know well enough I don't give a fig what the world thinks."

"Don't you? Why did you sequester yourself away here for so long?"

"What the world thinks of *you*," he amended. "And let me remind you, they all believe you an extremely well-off heiress. My grandmother's sister's daughter's—"

"But I'm not," she said wretchedly. "I am only—"

He put his hand across her mouth. Her lips parted, and he moaned in frustration. "Am I to understand you will become my paramour—"

"Gladly," she whispered.

"But will not marry me?"

"I cannot aspire to such a position. It would not be right." She swallowed a sob. "I would not make you happy."

"Christ! Would you stop thinking of *me*?" He broke off, seeing her tears start to flow. "I'm sorry," he said more gently, brushing them away. "But you may as well know this. I have some scraps of honor in me, too. Indeed, you bring them out in me in ways . . . Marry me, Tatiana."

"I can't."

His gaze was stormy enough now. "Then I take back my offer of carte blanche. You'll be my wife, or you'll remain my cousin."

She stood up and curtsied. "As you wish, milord."

"Dammit all!" he shouted at her. "Don't you care that I love you?"

More than life itself . . . But she shook her head resolutely. "Your mother is expected any day now. No doubt she'll make you see reason. I'll send Timkins in to change your dressing. I am tired. I'm in need of sleep."

"Tatiana!" He reached for her across the board, caught the cloth of her robe, held on fast.

"Milord, please!"

He kicked the table aside, sending the pieces flying through the room. Bellerophon howled, roused from sleep. The board had been the last barrier between them. He pulled her to him, kissed her, frantic with his need. He was aching, burning for her, his mouth like a brand. "You said it was a dream that you called me your love," he murmured.

This was all she had ever dreamed of. But she'd sworn that he deserved better. "God, Lucas. No. Don't—"

He had pushed back the robe and was kissing her bared shoulders, her throat. "I want you—as I have never wanted anything, anyone." He put his mouth to hers. At his hungry touch, she felt her resistance melting like snow beneath a midday sun.

"Milord." Against all odds she found the strength to fight him off. "Milord, I beg you. Do not force me—"

He let her go, so suddenly that she staggered back against the door. "Force you? Oh, Tatiana. Tell me honestly that you don't love me, and I'll never touch you again."

"I—" Where were the words? Where was her will? "I—"

He came toward her, smiling. "Didn't I warn you once never to play dare with a man who has nothing to lose?"

Bellerophon, alarmed, had leaped from the bed and thrust himself between them. Lucas grabbed him by the collar, slinging him out the door and shutting it again. Then he took her into his arms, and his mouth closed over hers once more.

"Oh, Christ," he murmured against her throat, hands

caught in her hair. "If you knew how I have longed for
this—"

"And I, too," she answered shyly, returning his urgent
embrace, giving way to all the love for him she had con-
cealed so long, kept so carefully hidden. With the confession came her tears, now of joy, and he kissed them away,
raising her up in his arms, carrying her toward the bed. He
kicked the covers back so ferociously that she dissolved into
giggles—then sobered abruptly as he lowered her down atop
the soft loft of feathers. In the candlelight she saw the lump
of bandage under his shirt. "Are you certain you are up to
this?" she asked dubiously.

For answer he took her hand and pressed it to the bulge
in his breeches. "I am up *for* this," he said, and untied her
robe, slipping her arms from the sleeves. The nightdress
beneath was a sheer scrim of dimity, dainty with ruffles and
lace, that plainly showed the rosy buds of her nipples. With
infinite patience he unfastened the tiny bone buttons, eyes
gazing straight into hers. Then he lowered his head and put
his mouth to her breast.

"Oh," Tatiana whispered as a whirl of sensation filled
her, more heady than champagne. He sucked at her eagerly,
tongue teasing those taut pink buds, first one and then the
other, until she thought she would swoon with pleasure.
"Oh, my dear heart—"

"You taste the way roses smell."

"It is Mrs. Smithers's soap," she felt honor-bound to tell
him.

"This goes beyond soap." He brought his hands up,
kneading the soft mounds of her flesh, fingertips plucking at
her nipples while his lips pressed against hers with frightening intensity. His tongue pushed inside her mouth, savoring,
devouring, thrusting, and then drawing back, mimicking
the movements of his hips. She surrendered to the rush of
heat, clinging to him, hands at the small of his back, draw-

ing him tighter to her, no longer caring who she was, who he was. *You were meant for something more,* he had told her once. She was meant for this. She was meant for him.

He groped for the hem of the nightdress, drew it over her head, then knelt, staring at her naked splendor for so long that she grew embarrassed and tried to cover herself with the sheets. He pulled them away, let his fingertips graze along the smooth white line of her calf, her thigh, moving ever higher, until his palm cupped the thatch of pure blond hair that capped her mound of Venus. "Curls," he whispered, his hand tracing circles against her.

"The sole ones I have."

"I love curls—here." He bent his head, licked them. Tatiana drew back, suddenly shy again. He let his palms slide around to her buttocks, lifting her upward, hard against his face. His tongue was darting at her, pushing, insistent. "Milord," she said in a strangled voice.

He raised his head briefly. "Don't ever call me that again."

"Lucas. You have rather the advantage of me." His brows drew together questioningly. "I mean . . . your clothes."

"Oh!" He tore them off eagerly. "There! Better?"

She wasn't certain. His rod was standing straight out at her, rigid and long and thick. Tentatively she touched her thumb to its smooth, round head, felt his whole body convulse. "Did I hurt you?" she asked anxiously.

"Jesus. Hurt me again."

Reassured, she closed her hand over his manhood. He shuddered, precisely the way Bellerophon did when she scratched the fold of his ear. The notion made her laugh. He frowned at her. "What is it?"

"Men—and dogs."

"Beasts. We are all the same." He was doing *something* with his fingers that was driving her mad: stroking her curls, reaching lower, finding warmth and wetness and a soft, sweet spot—

"Lucas! Oh, love—"

His touch quickened; he brought his mouth down onto hers once more. Now she could feel that hard rod pushing against her, pressing at her thighs. He shifted so that his hands were on her breasts, pulling at their tips, while he kissed her cheek, her ear, her eyes. He arched back, high above her. She looked up at him, saw the faint hint of question in his expression. *He would stop, even now, if I asked him to,* she thought—and the realization only made her want him more. She parted her knees, staring into his stormy eyes.

"Oh, love. Oh, love—" The rod thrust inside her, making her gasp. He felt so huge, so potent, like a god. He pulled back, hesitating, and she grabbed at him, desperate with yearning, wanting to hold him there within her, wanting to merge with him, melt into him, become his for all time. "Oh . . . my . . . love." He'd pushed into her again, his loins setting a rhythm, even and slow. Into her, out of her, back into her again—she bent beneath him, lithe as a willow, drawing him further in.

"Oh, Tatiana!" She glanced up, saw his face set, his teeth on edge, bared. "Jesus help me, I cannot hold back!"

She did not want him to. Whatever this mad dance was, she meant to see it to the finish, his finish. He thrust inside her, deeper, deeper, that long rod slicking against her while she held him tight . . . and then, eyes widening abruptly, she clung even more closely as the pull and thrust of his manhood evoked an imperative response, as the tide of longing within her swelled to a flood. "Lucas!" she gasped, knowing her nails were raking at his back, but far beyond caring. "Lucas, what is it?"

He stopped only for an instant, pride in his gaze as he looked down at her. "Love. This is love." Then he fell on her with a vengeance, that smooth rhythm tightening, quickening, turning fierce and wild. "Love," he grunted again, just as her soul shattered into a million gleaming pieces that went soaring into the sky, higher and brighter than even the Regent's fireworks. Stars, she thought, seeing them explode against her eyelids. *The most beautiful, wondrous stars . . .*

And when they dropped to earth, together, it was in a dazzling, splendid conflagration, hot as the sun, sure as truth, as pure-white as Russia's snow.

Tatiana lay still for a long time, a lifetime, hearing his heavy breathing at her ear, feeling his welcome weight atop her. At last she grew a little frightened. "Lucas?" Why didn't he move? Lord, she'd known this was too much for him! What had she been thinking of?

He groaned, reinforcing her fears. "Lucas?" she whispered again. "Shall I fetch you claret?"

He burst out laughing. "Shall you fetch me claret? Jesus! What can I fetch you? Would you like the crown jewels?"

Reassured, she let her fingers trail over that scratch of new beard. "I thought perhaps I'd killed you."

"Oh, you did. You did. But I'll recover, never fear." He rolled over heavily, falling back onto the pillows.

"Still, I think some claret—" She reached for it, caught the cup, and was pulling it toward her when his hand, groping for her cheek, knocked it away. It spilled, spreading across the white linen in a growing stain.

Tatiana knelt on the bed, grabbing for her nightdress to sop it up. "How clumsy of me!"

"There's nothing clumsy about you."

"Of course there is. I've spoiled your bed."

"Made it, rather." But he roused himself, swinging his legs aside, sitting up. Tatiana mopped at the wine, then paused, seeing another red stain.

"That's not the claret," she whispered.

He looked where she was pointing, and a slow, highly satisfied smile spread across his face. "No. That would be your maidenhead."

"My—" She blushed furiously. "Of course it is that." Then she glanced at him sidelong. "You seem surprised to see it."

He cupped her chin in his hand. "Not surprised, love. Pleased. You *were* betrothed to him, after all."

"Grappling boys beneath the pine trees," she said hotly. Then her anger faded. "You might have asked."

"It made no difference to me."

"Liar."

"It made no difference," he repeated firmly. "I wanted—want—you, anyway I can have you." His hand trailed toward her breasts. "So long as I can have you forever."

She relented. It was true; he never had asked. "Again and again?" she whispered.

"Again and again. Until you do kill me with loving." He smiled, put his mouth to hers. "Can you think of any finer way to go?"

"Absolutely not."

Bellerophon howled morosely from behind the closed door. "Poor old thing," Lucas murmured, kissing her ear, letting his tongue rim its shell-like curves. "I ought to get him a mate."

"Perhaps one of your mother's spaniels."

"Oh, no. Like to like." He felt her stiffen. "Lord, Tatiana. After what we have shared, how can you—" Another frantic burst of howling. "Damn that dog! Where's Smithers, that he doesn't put him out?"

"I'll do it," Tatiana offered, reaching for her robe.

"You stay here. I'll do it. He's still my dog—much as you would like to think otherwise." She made a face at him as he got up from the bed, his manhood once more engorged. Tatiana lay naked, her arms twined behind her head, contemplating the fine line of his back leading into his buttocks. He was right. There was nothing more to fear after what they had shared.

He pulled the door open. Bellerophon bounded in, licking him ecstatically, leaping up onto the bed. Tatiana giggled—then clutched for her cast-off robe, seeing a shadow in the hall.

"I have the honor to announce the arrival of Her Ladyship, the Dowager Countess," Smithers intoned in a voice of the utmost complaisance. "Would it be more convenient for you, milord, to see her at another time?"

Twenty-Four

"Jesus!" Lucas swore, pushing back his hair with both hands and lunging for his robe.

"Lucas, darling!" The countess, not waiting for his answer to Smithers, elbowed her way past the butler. "I came the instant I heard. Never in my life have I been so frightened! My poor dear boy, I was so certain I would find you dead!"

"Mother, please!" Lucas tried to push her away. In her rush to embrace him, Dulcie had not yet seen that he was not alone. A blessing, Tatiana thought, since it gave her time to yank on *her* robe. Perhaps by some miracle she could slip past the two of them and hide in the wardrobe.

"A knife wound! You!" Dulcie was clinging to him, alternately crying and beaming. "Oh, Lucas, didn't I warn you nothing but trouble would come from chasing all over Europe? And all for the sake of that common little—"

"Mother!" he said in a tone that silenced even the countess. She stepped back a pace and looked past him to the bed, from which Tatiana arose hurriedly, her knees shaking. Those cold blue eyes took in her hastily knotted robe, the flowing cascade of her hair, the blush on the heights of her cheekbones. "Have you no greeting," Lucas said evenly, "for our cousin, who has tended me so faithfully?"

"I see how she has been . . . tending to you," the countess said frostily.

"You couldn't see your nose," her son told her, "if nature hadn't fixed it to your face."

"Well!" she huffed. "I came to offer you aid and comfort. If you think I am about to stay only to be insulted—"

"Sit down and shut up," said Lucas, thrusting her toward a chair. "And as for you, Smithers, you damned voyeur, take that damned dog outside and shut the bloody door or I'll toss you downstairs."

"Certainly," the butler replied, unruffled. "I only stayed to inquire if there was anything milady might be needing."

"Milady could use a hiding. Would you care to administer it, you simpering—sit down!" Dulcie, outraged, had risen from the chair. She sank back with a glance at Tatiana that spoke daggers. "But there's no cause to forget courtesy, I suppose. *Would* you like something, Mother?"

"I don't intend to stay."

"I intend that you shall. Bring her orgeat, Smithers."

"Pah. Bring me brandy."

Lucas raised his brows. "Strong drink for you, Mother."

"I have need of it." She pulled off her gloves. "We had the devil's own journey, hurried as we were—though I can see now there was no need for my inconvenience. You seem well enough recovered, despite the shocking report that I had. *More* than well enough. Am I to understand from this cozily domestic tableau that your mission met with success? Do tell all, Lucas. Who is the mystery maid? Napoleon's unacknowledged daughter?"

"By God, I should have had Smithers bring a bullwhip," Lucas growled. Tatiana shot him a beseeching glance. "But since you ask so nicely, no. My inquiries—" There was a knock. "What is it now?" he roared.

"Smithers, milord. With the brandy."

"Bring it in and be gone!"

The butler opened the door, took the snifter to the countess, and bent to whisper, "If you would like me, milady, to summon the authorities, I would be only too—" The sentence finished in a gurgle as Lucas shoved him out again, slamming the door in his wake.

He then calmly went to pour more claret and looked at Tatiana. "Care for a drink?"

"Very much," she murmured.

"You take the glass." He kept the bottle, and swigged from it liberally. "Where was I? Oh, yes. My inquiries were curtailed by this blasted wound."

"How very opportune," Dulcie said with a sneer. "See how the whole world conspires to aid this hussy in her plottings."

"Which plottings would those be?" Lucas demanded in a dangerous voice.

"To have you, one way or another. Dr. Swartley wrote he was administering opiates. If there has been a marriage, you ought to know that vows made in a narcotic state are not considered—"

"It's a wonder I don't strangle you, Mother."

The countess pulled aside the admirable ruff of Cluny lace at her slim throat. "Go on. Nothing could cut me more than a *mésalliance* such as this."

"For your information, Mother, I did make Miss Grimaldi an offer of marriage."

Dulcie swooned back in her chair. "Oh, my worst fears are confirmed! We are ruined!"

"She refused me."

There was a very brief moment of silence. Then the countess sat up. Her well-kept face contracted, brows knitting, mouth pursing, eyes crinkling into slits. She turned to Tatiana. "You refused him?" Her voice rose incredulously. "*You* refused *my son*? On what grounds?"

Lucas burst out laughing. And even Tatiana, cowed as she was, could not restrain a smile. To see the countess go so swiftly from horror to indignation . . .

"On the grounds," Lucas finally answered, having caught his breath, "that she is not good enough for me."

"Absolutely proper," Dulcie decreed, nodding in approval. "I take back all I have said or thought about you, my dear girl. You clearly know your place."

"That offer," Lucas continued, "followed fast on the heels of another I made her—that she become my mistress."

The countess paled. "Oh. And she refused that, no doubt hoping—"

"No, no, Mother. To that she agreed."

"She agreed to become your mistress and naysayed your offer of marriage?" Dulcie was losing control of her voice again; she quickly downed some brandy. "I must say, I find myself perplexed. Why on earth would you even present the second proposal, Lucas, when she'd accepted the first?"

He moved to the bed, put his arm around Tatiana's trembling shoulders. "Because I love her—totally, utterly, now and forever. Because I want her for my wife."

"I must say . . . I must say . . ." But whatever it was, the countess didn't. Her mouth opened and closed several more times, like a parrot's, before she thought of something to do with it and raised the snifter again.

"It would please me," Lucas acknowledged, more gently, "to have you welcome her into the family. But I do not require your approval. I will have her, one way or another." His fingers stroked Tatiana's cheek.

"But you say she has refused you!" the countess offered brightly, with the air of one grasping frantically at straws.

"Because she fears offending you."

"And so it certainly would! Oh, my dear boy, look at reason!" She twisted her hands. "How I wish the Admiral were here to assist me! He managed to keep you from the clutches of that Innisford creature!"

"Thank God he did. My destiny was . . . this." He bent and kissed Tatiana, long and hard, full on the mouth, then drew away regretfully, tracing the tears that had sprung to her eyes. He looked at Dulcie, his gaze defiant. "Will you give us your blessing?"

The countess turned plaintively to Tatiana. "You do understand, child, it is nothing personal I hold against you. Until all this arose, no one could have been more proud of you than I. You helped to bring my son back into the world. For that, I always will be grateful—"

"Grateful enough," Lucas interjected, "to provide that blessing?"

"It is simply not what I always expected—always dreamed for you, Lucas."

"Which part of it? That I should fall in love? Be happy?"

"That it should prove to be with someone—"

Tatiana felt the need, at last, to intervene. "I am completely in agreement with your sentiments, milady, and have told Lord Strathmere so."

"Tatiana. For God's sake." Lucas's voice was strained.

"Did you imagine I might think otherwise? The inequalities between us lie beyond her powers of erasing. They are in our blood, our marrow—and they cannot be changed."

"Yet you would wed some idiot like Freddy Whittles?"

She smiled slightly. "Perhaps. Because to smirch his family's tree would not prove of much consequence. Whereas yours . . . Do you know what I thought once, dancing with him? That had it been he that night in Mizhakovsk, he never would have stopped for me."

"Do you know what I wish?" Lucas said suddenly, intently. "I wish I were Pietr—or Costner, or even poor damned Freddy, if it meant that you would marry me."

The countess had been silent all this time, contemplating her brandy. Now she swallowed the last of it and rose from her seat. "You must wrangle all this out yourselves. I'm exhausted by my journey. I am not thinking clearly, not at all."

"I trust you've made your sentiments plain," Lucas said bitterly.

"I fear, actually, that I haven't. My conception of the . . . the progress of this affair has been skewed by my prejudice. I assumed from the start, Lucas, that you were the pursued—the victim, as was obviously the case with Gillian Innisford. Now I am not so sure. Tatiana is not after your money, or she would have accepted your offer of marriage. Yet she is willing to become your mistress. Such scruples are rare indeed."

"I hardly see," said Tatiana, blushing as she clutched the robe at her throat, "how one could consider moral laxness a scruple."

The countess's eyes, no longer stormy, considered her curiously. "Don't you? Under the circumstances, there's no conclusion to be drawn but that you love him desperately."

"Do you, Tatiana?" Lucas demanded. She hung her head, not daring to answer. "Do you?" he said more urgently. "Because if you do, no force in this world could be enough to part us, since I love you that same way."

The countess looked at the two of them for a long moment. Then abruptly, she smiled. "Since that is so, I find my former objections without foundation. If she'll have you, Lucas, you blazing idiot, I think you should take her. You're not likely ever to find a love so pure again."

Tatiana raised her clear green gaze, disbelieving. "Do you mean—"

"Aye, aye. You have my blessing, for what little that is worth." She stood up, gathering her gloves. "Now at least I shall have something to *do*! A wedding to plan!"

"The lady has not yet accepted my proposal," Lucas said, his eyes burning.

There was a knock at the door. "Damn," Dulcie muttered. "Who is it?"

"Smithers, milady. With Dr. Swartley. Come to sedate the patient."

"I'll murder him," Lucas swore. "I'll murder *both* of them."

Tatiana laughed, spring melt tumbling down a mountain. "I'll see to them," said the countess, and left them alone.

He put his hand to her cheek. "Tatiana. Will you?"

"I do not deserve—"

"No! I do not deserve! Dammit all, I'll not take no for an answer!" He lunged for the chessboard, began gathering the scattered pieces. "Here. We'll play for it. White or black?"

"White," she answered softly.

The game was over in ten moves. She let him cheat.

"That's that," he said with satisfaction. "It's official. We're betrothed."

Tatiana, hands shaking, reset the board, nigh overwhelmed with emotion. Lucas leaned back in his chair, arms folded over his chest. "You know," he said thoughtfully, "a betrothed woman is permitted certain liberties that an unattached maiden is not."

She nodded. "The countess has acquainted me with them. She may ride with her fiancé in an open carriage. She may be seen dining alone with him in public. She may refuse to dance with other gentlemen at assemblies and balls without fear of offense."

"I should certainly take offense if you did not refuse. But I had other liberties in mind."

"There are more?" she asked innocently.

"Oh, yes. Did Mother not teach you that a betrothed woman may sit upon the lap of her husband-to-be in his bedchamber?"

"I'm quite sure she did *not*."

"It is true, though. I swear it. Ask Lady Shelton if you do not believe me."

Tatiana giggled at the thought. "I'll send a letter to her directly. Are there any other liberties I should inquire about?"

He crooked a finger at her, smiling lazily. "Absolutely. Come and sit in my lap, and I will tell you about them."

She crossed to him slowly. "You ought to be in bed—"

"I was getting to that one." He drew her down on his knees, his arms encircling her, caught in the long, soft sheen of her hair. "Mm. Roses. It is permitted that her fiancé kiss her."

"Briefly," Tatiana amended, "and chastely. The countess mentioned that."

"Brief and chaste, then." He pecked a kiss. She pulled prudently away. "Or not." His mouth captured hers once more, with such passionate intensity that she was left breathless.

"Oh, milord—"

"And," he added, "she is to address him by his first name only—never by honorifics, and certainly not as 'cousin.'"

"I shall strive to remember that."

"See that you do," he murmured, just before he kissed her again. She returned the ardent pressure of his mouth. Lucas sighed with pleasure, shifting in his chair, gathering her closer, tongue probing her parted lips, tasting her gently before venturing inside. His tongue flicked in, out, in again. Tatiana, savoring the sensation, wrapped her arms around his neck, held him tight, enveloped by a rush of new heat and longing, until she thought if he stopped, broke off, she would surely die.

He did stop, though, holding her hard against him, his breathing deep and rough. Resentful, Tatiana echoed his motions with her own tongue, thrusting it into him. "Ahh," he murmured, surprised but pleased. He leaned back, and she followed, moving higher on his knees, aware of the taut pressure of his manhood just beneath her thigh. The realization of her power over him was heady; she shifted again, settling in, and was rewarded with a heartfelt moan. "Christ, love! What are you doing?"

"Kissing you as you kissed me." She put her hands to his hair and pulled him down to her, fingertips exploring those thick black brows, the curve of his cheekbones, the prickly brush of new beard along his dark skin. "Is that not permitted a betrothed woman?"

"Ask Lady Shelton." He turned her cheek, capturing her ear, letting his tongue ride over its shell-like curves. Tatiana liked that too, especially the way it intensified his harsh, jagged breaths. He'd moved his hands to the front of her robe and was pulling at the sash, hauling at the knot. There was a swift rip of fraying silk.

"Lucas!"

"Sorry. No, I'm not." He pressed his lips to her throat, and she shivered with delight. His big hands tugged the robe open, inch by inch, and all the time his mouth was following, teasing, tracing slow circles against the rising curves of her breasts. His fingers brushed her nipples.

"I'm quite sure Lady Shelton . . ." she began.

"Ask her," he said shortly, then took one taut bud in his mouth. "God, you taste sweet." His tongue teased each rosy areola in turn, making her wild with desire.

She found the buttons on his shirt and laid it open. His chest hair was pitch-black and wiry; she wrapped her fists in it, tugging, and he raised his head from her breast. "Is it permitted I return that as well?" she asked breathlessly.

"It isn't . . . customary."

"Why not?" Pushing him back in the chair, she planted kisses down his throat and chest until she reached his nipple.

"Tatiana," he said, his voice strangled.

She ignored it, sucking at him eagerly, loving the harsh brush of his hair on her cheek, the feel of that bud, so round and hard, on her tongue. She shifted again, straddling him now with her legs clasped around his waist. He let his hands slide down her back, peeling the robe down to her waist in a bundle, then traveling up the bared expanse of her flesh to her shoulders, raising and releasing the white waterfall of her hair. He pushed her from his chest and sat staring at her—the glow of her flesh in the moonlight, those high white breasts crowned with proud pink tips, her narrow arms and waist. "God, you are beautiful," he said hoarsely. "The most beautiful woman I ever have known."

"You are beautiful, too."

"Men can't be beautiful. Certainly not old men like me."

"Decrepit," she agreed, and snuggled down so that his manhood pushed through the robe. "Past the age of arousal . . ."

He groaned, hands pinning her to him. "Far past," he agreed, that hungry bulge proving it a lie. "I may as well pleasure you, though, pert young thing that you are." He put his mouth to her breast once more.

Tatiana arched back beneath his caresses, hands on his shoulders, hair trailing all the way to the floor. His kisses drove her wild, made her writhe atop him. She moaned, pressing against his hard, stiff manhood. "Oh, Lucas. Oh, love—"

"Tatiana," he said urgently, lips at her ear. "Tatiana. Wait."

"I cannot wait!" She grabbed for him, but he thrust her eager hands away.

"Don't. God, don't tempt me so."

"I? You are provoking me!" She dived for him again. To her chagrin, he raised her up bodily and settled her less seductively onto his knee. The fire drained from her blood and bone. "I was too forward," she whispered, shamed. "I have offended you—"

"Offended?" He laughed, as well as he was able with his entire body rigid with desire. "Oh, my dear heart, no. It is just that . . . unlike chess, some games cannot be prolonged without a certain ending to them."

"I desire an ending!"

"As do I." He kissed her tenderly, softly. Even that was enough to arouse in him again the ferocity of longing that had made him pull back. He tucked the robe up over her breasts. "But you must agree, you need not write Lady Shelton to determine the impropriety of some liberties."

"I don't understand," she whispered, feeling confused, forlorn.

"Pietr must have been after you often enough to let you make love to him. But you didn't, did you?"

"No! I never would outside of marriage!" Her blush deepened as she realized what she'd said.

"You agree, then, that a betrothal is not the same as a marriage."

She dropped her eyes. "You think less of me for what went on before. That I was so . . ."

"Passionate? No. That was what made me sure I could not live without you for my wife." He smiled crookedly, made a nod to his bulging manhood. "The state you see me in now is the same state I have been in nearly from the day I met you. Do you remember when you waltzed with me first, in the room downstairs, and how abruptly I left? You awakened desires I hadn't experienced in twelve long years."

"Not since Gillian," she said with resentment.

"Gillian," he told her, his voice suddenly fierce, "isn't worthy to wipe your boots. If I honestly believed you could be jealous of her—" Some odd nuance of emotion flickered over her face. "You aren't, are you?"

"I uprooted her," she whispered.

"You *what?*"

"I pulled her out of the ground. Timkins had to help. Her roots went very deep."

He stared at her for a moment. Then he threw back his head and laughed—the laugh she loved so, rich and full and free. "Bully for you! I should have done so years ago. What did you do with her then?"

"Threw her onto the compost pile." She scrunched up her face. "Would you believe even that did not kill her? So I hacked her into pieces—little pieces—and burned them." Her eyes were wide and contrite. "Forgive me. I know you treasured the bush."

He was grinning, broad as church doors. "I only wish I had been there to see it. What did Timkins say about your sudden urge to violence?"

"Oh, it was his idea. I never would have had the nerve on my own."

He laughed again, uproariously. "The two of you conspiring—Christ! I think I'll double his wages. Nay, triple them. What the hell—I shall make him my heir." Then he tweaked her nipple through the robe. "For the nonce, at least."

"You truly aren't angry?"

He kissed her doubtful mouth. "How could I ever be angry with you?"

"Prevaricator. You rarely have been anything else."

"We never will be bored together." He slipped his hand

along her thigh to her waist, caressed her belly, and then resolutely pulled it away. "Alas, I've made my mind up. I'll not give in again to my baser instincts until our marriage is completed."

"Why not?" she asked wistfully, fingers playing in the hair on his chest.

He slapped them away. "Because that is what you deserve."

"It is not what I want."

"You flatter me," he said wryly.

"No," she replied in utter honesty. He heard the hitch in her voice and gathered her against him, smoothing her hair with his hand.

"Love, listen to me. You have been sequestered away all these months, no visitors, no social company. All those young men you dazzled in Brighton—"

"I never wanted any of them. I only wanted you."

"If that is so—"

"*If?*" she cried indignantly.

"Then your passion will abide the length of our betrothal." His mouth brushed hers. "I'd have the children I plant in you be legitimate."

She drew away from the kiss. "How long is considered a proper length for a betrothal?"

"In general, two to four years."

"Two to four *years?*" she wailed, with such complete hopelessness that he burst out laughing.

"God, I must be good."

"You are," she said, and let her hand trail down to his manhood once more.

"Of course," he added, breath quickening, "all that is really required is three postings of the banns."

"How long does that take?"

"Three weeks."

She sighed, her fingers tightening around him. "Three weeks—it is an eternity."

"We could," he grunted out, "procure a special license."

Her fist slid along his rod. "How long for that?"

"Oh, love. Only a matter of days."

She thought it over, shook her head reluctantly. "Your mother—after all that we have put her through, it does not seem right to deny her even three weeks for the planning of the wedding."

"She will not think three weeks enough," he warned.

Tatiana dug deep within her heart for forbearance. "Six months?" she allowed, but not happily.

"Oh, I daresay she'll find six months as inadequate as three weeks. No need to humor her too far."

She smiled. "I defer to your mastery of her temperament." And she dipped her head—

"Though I *could* ride to London to secure the license even sooner than that."

"What, let you go off again when I have only just got you back? I think not." Her tongue flicked against the smooth, round knob of his manhood. "And in the meantime—"

"Quite so. There always are those liberties."

Twenty-Five

TATIANA'S FINGERS HOVERED over the tableful of shimmering swatches—rich silks and velvets and laces as sheeny as the petals of a rose. "I can't decide," she finally admitted.

Dulcie was dancing with impatience at her elbow. "You must make up your mind *today*. Otherwise Madame will not guarantee delivery by the first of June." Tatiana lifted a square of soft charmeuse satin. "I think that one very handsome," the countess said hopefully.

"I don't think Lucas would care for the color. If only I could ask his opinion—"

Dulcie and Turner rolled their eyes in unison. "He isn't supposed to see—" the maid began.

"The gown. I understand that. But just the swatches—"

"Sure to bring bad luck," Turner said darkly.

"Pietr bought the cloth for my wedding gown himself, in Nadvollsk. There's no such superstition in Russia."

"Perhaps there should be," Dulcie said tartly, "considering what became of him. Do try to concentrate! Besides the bridal gown, we've all the ball dresses and morning suits and cloaks and lingerie to decide on yet. Not to mention the linens and such."

Tatiana sighed. "We aren't going on a honeymoon, so I don't need a trousseau. We are staying right here. Lord knows I've enough outfits for a country life."

"That is what you say now," the countess sniffed, undeterred. "I daresay in a month or so, once the novelty of marriage has worn off, you will be *begging* Lucas to bring you to London."

I daresay I won't, Tatiana thought, but held her tongue. The wedding she and Lucas had decided on—right here at St. Aidan's—was so abhorrent to Dulcie that when they broke the news she had burst into tears. "I thought St. Paul's," she'd gasped between sobs, "and the reception at the house in London!"

"St. Paul's isn't likely to be available on such short notice," Lucas had informed her.

"How short?" Dulcie demanded in horror.

"Three weeks. Just time enough to publish the banns."

"Impossible," the countess said in derision. "That isn't time enough to have the invitations engraved."

"We'd hoped you'd write the invitations out for us yourself," Tatiana said soothingly. "You have such an elegant hand."

Dulcie refused to be flattered. "Even if I did, I should have to order vellum. And how are we to post them? If it takes me a week to write them out and another to deliver them, that would be only one week's notice—and many of the guests have that long a drive to come!"

"Really?" Lucas cocked a brow. "No one on our list need travel more than fifteen miles."

"Then your list is hopelessly inadequate," she snapped. "What about Lady Shelton? What about Lord and Lady Barton, and the Hyde Parkers, and the Duchess of Portsmouth—not to mention Prinny, whom I must invite, though he doubtless will not come. And yet he might. The dear regard in which he holds me—"

"If you think, Mother, I intend to entertain that fat, predatory bastard at my—"

"Lucas," Tatiana broke in warningly.

"I don't care a cat's whisker for any of those folk you mention, nor they for me. Why should I put them up and feed them?"

"Oh, I might have known," the countess sneered. "It all comes down to parting with your pennies. Forty thousand pounds you made last year, and you would think the poorhouse just around the corner!"

Seeing the discussion was deteriorating, Tatiana intervened. "I only thought, milady, since Lucas is still so weak from his wound—"

"Weak!" She laughed. "I saw him from my window yesterday, digging up those blasted rose beds. And he does not seem too weak to stay up all hours of the night, playing chess with you. Don't speak to me of weak!"

"Mother." Lucas had that dangerous edge to his voice. "If anything about our plans fails to meet with your approval, I would strongly suggest you hie yourself—agh!" Tatiana had ground her heel into his instep.

"I might have known," the countess whimpered pathetically. "They say a mother loses her son's affections the instant that he falls in love. I wish you would not marry if this is a taste of how I shall be treated once you are wed!"

Lucas was too dumbfounded for a moment to speak.

When he did, it was in a bellow: "As if you've done any-thing for the past ten years but natter at me *to* marry!"

"Milady," Tatiana interjected firmly, "the truth is, in all the lessons you have been so kind as to teach me, we never touched on this. I've not the least notion how to plan a wedding, much less one so hasty. If you don't come to my aid, I am very much afraid I will disgrace your house. No one, I know, could triumph under such constrained circum-stances as we present you—"

"Hmph! I daresay no one could!" But the countess showed some hints of softening. "The haste *is* most unfortu-nate. Still, I recall when Adelaide Winthrop became en-gaged to Lord Tifleton—he was Captain Tifleton then, of course—just before his regiment was ordered off to Spain, and her mother put on quite an admirable wedding. Small, but in the height of taste." Her mouth curled. "Even so, as I remember, she had *four* weeks."

"That is precisely my point. Why, given time enough, any ordinary soul can make a memorable wedding. But to do so hampered by these obstacles would take a genius! Lucas, don't you agree?"

He was looking at her, his brows raised in disbelief. She stepped on him again. "Oh! Oh, yes, by all means!"

The countess gave a lofty wave. "Taste, of course, I can vouch for. But to speed things along, I should have to be assured of an open purse. And four weeks. No less."

"And you shall have them," Tatiana said warmly, "so long as you will help us. Won't she, Lucas? Lucas?"

"Certainly." He grated the word out.

"Well, in that case . . ." Dulcie fluttered off, trailing scattered driblets of plans. "Send at *once* to Madame Descoux for samples. . . . Get those invitations off. . . . Something for myself to wear, of course. And tell Mrs. Smithers—a most *thorough* housecleaning . . ."

"You frighten me," Lucas said when Dulcie was gone. "I

think at times I am marrying the feminine equivalent of Napoleon."

Tatiana stood on both his boots to kiss him. "Don't fret. In four weeks, how much can she spend?"

"I don't begrudge the money. It's the added time." He reached for her bodice, traced the swell of her breasts. She spun away from him, laughing.

"I must go to her now. Otherwise she really might invite Prinny. And for your information, I know you are lying. You *do* care about the money."

He looked down at his boots. "You've spoiled the polish."

"That will teach you discretion." She blew him a kiss, and hurried off in the countess's wake.

It was easy to be strong when he was beside her. But now, closeted with Turner and the countess in their fifth consideration of the swatches, Tatiana's head ached, and the fabrics all seemed to blur. "This?" she said tentatively, touching a luxe velvet the color of Lucas's eyes.

"Makes you go sallow," Turner observed. "Besides, you'd faint dead away, wearing velvet in June."

"Then what of this muslin?" She held up one patterned in roses.

"We can discount muslin entirely," the countess said crisply. "The women of Somerleigh are not wont to be wedded in cotton, like some serving girl."

"Then why did Madame send it?"

"For a day gown, I presume." Sighing, the countess glanced at the clock. "Time we were dressing for dinner. You really *must* make your mind up."

"I'll sleep on it," Tatiana promised. "Leave them out, Turner, if you please. I'll come and have another look after supper."

"If 'twere up to me," the maid put in, "I'd say the oyster satin."

"*I* was married in oyster satin," said Dulcie. "And pearls on the bodice . . . I still have that gown somewhere at the house in London. Madame could no doubt make it over to fit."

Oyster, Tatiana knew, truly *did* make her go sallow. "I wouldn't dream of wearing your wedding gown," she murmured. "I simply am not worthy."

"Pish," said the countess, but looked secretly pleased.

"Hush!" Tatiana said as Lucas, trailing after her in the darkness, bumped into a table and cursed. "This is a serious matter."

"You don't believe that."

"Would you keep your voice down? No, as it happens, I don't. But your mother and Turner do. They swear if you so much as glimpse the fabric, our marriage is doomed." Tiptoeing, she led him to the room where the swatches were still on display, just across the corridor from the countess's bedchamber.

"This is probably," Lucas drawled, "the most absurd expedition I have ever been on."

"Shh!" She turned the doorknob and yanked him inside. "More absurd than running off to Russia on account of two words on a paper?"

"There was nothing absurd at all about that," he said, backing her against the wall.

She wriggled free. "Time enough for that once you have made your choice. Take off your coat."

"Gladly. And my breeches too?"

"The coat will suffice." She bent down to stuff it into the crack beneath the door.

"For someone who doesn't believe in this superstition, you are going to a great deal of trouble," he observed.

"I respect the beliefs of others. Particularly your mother."

"You've been amazingly patient with her so far."

"Someone has to be," she said pointedly, and lit a candle. "There. Go on and pick one."

Lucas moved toward the table. "As I understand it, you've had them for three days and still cannot decide."

"That's why I brought you," she hissed. "You have two minutes."

He scanned the swatches, then plucked up a square of slate-gray satin. "This."

"*Will* you be serious? A woman married in gray is certain to prove barren. It's common knowledge in Mizhakovsk."

"Ah! So there are superstitions you value!"

"Lucas," she said with such despair that he relented, searching with more attention.

"What about this?" It was a pale rose-pink gossamer silk.

"Fine—but you will have to choose another to line it. One can see straight through it."

"That's what I like about it." He leered at her. "Could you have a nightdress made of it?"

"It's twenty pounds the yard!"

"There are some things for which I don't mind paying."

"Fine. I'll have a negligée of it—five or six of them. But what about the wedding gown?"

"Bring the candle closer." He perused the swatches, seized another. "This. I like this."

It was the rose-patterned muslin. "I liked that, too," she whispered. "But your mother said it wasn't suitable. No Strathmere wife, she said, ever has been married in muslin."

"But it has roses on it. It reminds me of how you looked—how you smelled—that night . . ." His hand caressed the line of her lips. "You said you like it. You must have it."

She shook her head, dubious. "I don't know . . ."

"Tatiana." His eyes were grave in the glow of the candle. "You needn't give in to her on every point, you know. It will only prove an execrable precedent. What about the children?"

"What children?"

"Ours. The ones I long to give you." He crushed her to him, smoothing back her hair. "Legitimately. Though I doubt a difference of a few weeks ever would be noticed."

"It was your notion—"

"Don't remind me," he groaned, her breasts taut against him, his manhood hard between his legs. "Damned stupid one. What say we throw it over, decide it with a game of chess?"

"You have gotten too good," she confessed, feeling the pounding of his heart, his blood.

"No," he said with sudden certainty. "I haven't done many things right in my life, but I intend to do this. What's another—how many more days?"

"Twenty," she said regretfully. "What could happen in twenty days?"

"That reminds me. I haven't sent a notice to the London gazettes."

"Your mother has. It was the first thing she did."

"So everyone in London knows it."

"And a thousand hearts are broke on your account."

"Nonsense. No one suffers over me. But you—I have stolen away the sensation of the season before she ever got to cross the hallowed threshold of Almack's. Resentment will run deep."

"Anything I ever was was only the result of your attention."

He bowed his forehead to hers. "You would have shone like the diamond you are in any setting. My White Lady." His mouth closed on hers.

"We are forgetting our task," she murmured breathlessly.

"I made my choice."

"But there never has been a lady of Somerleigh wed in—"

"Roses. Tatiana, love. Gainsay her. Who cares? There has never been a lady of Somerleigh to equal you."

A heaviness lay on her heart, come from God knew where, like the weight of summer air before a storm. She clung to him, trying to lose the sensation in his wild kisses, but it was not so easy to throw off. Superstition, she reminded herself. Another nation's fantasies, not even her own . . . "The muslin, then. If you will have it so." Twenty days. Her own words mocked her: *What could happen in twenty days?*

"I love you," Lucas said, and snuffed the candle. "Now let me see you to your rooms, before I forget my blasted nobility."

Twenty-Six

"I DETEST SAYING THIS, Tatiana, but I believe you chose well."

Unable to believe her ears, Tatiana spun from the image in the pier glass of her wedding gown—pleated squared-off bodice, leg-of-mutton sleeves, wide skirts flounced in front into a froth of cascades trimmed with pointe de Venise lace and ribbons, all in muslin sprigged with full-blown roses. "You don't mind that it isn't silk or satin?"

The countess shook her head, smiling. "No. Muslin suits you. And I don't mean that the way it sounds. You look young and fresh and lovely—all the things you are. Now, for the jewels. Open the box, Turner, please. The pearls first, I think." Tatiana held perfectly still while the maid clasped the countess's neckpiece around her throat. Dulcie considered a moment, then shook her head. "Too heavy. Try the emeralds." But neither did those satisfy her. "The topazes? No, altogether the wrong color. I know—the amethysts! Those always have become you."

Tatiana watched as Turner fastened them. "I love the amethysts," she said uncertainly.

"But they hang down too far for that bodice. What else is in there, Turner? The rubies? Perhaps if we had them reset in something lighter, a filagree . . . But there isn't time for that, is there?" She sounded faintly accusing. "We have only three more days."

"I am sorry," Tatiana murmured.

"Not so sorry as I am." Then Dulcie snapped her fingers. "Where are those diamonds, Turner, that the Admiral gave me for our tenth anniversary?"

"In the safe in London," the maid said dourly.

"Damn, damn, damn! I am certain what that gown wants is diamonds. Do you suppose, if we sent someone now—" Both Turner and Tatiana rolled their eyes. "No, I don't suppose so. Well, try something else. Try the opals."

"Opals are bad luck," Tatiana said faintly. "At least in Mizhakovsk."

"They are in Dorsetshire, too," Turner confirmed.

"I suppose if both nations are agreed, we shouldn't take the chance. The cameo?"

"Nowhere to pin it," Turner noted.

"On a ribbon? A rose-colored one, perhaps?" It was dutifully assayed. "Hideous," said the countess. "Tourmalines? Beryls?" They were put on, dismissed.

"Perhaps," Tatiana ventured, "a simple gold chain?"

"I'll not have you going altogether shepherdess on us. Who do you think you are—Marie Antoinette? Isn't there a collar of seed pearls, Turner?"

Unexpectedly, Tatiana put her foot down. "No seed pearls." She wanted no reminders on their wedding day, for herself or for Lucas, of Pietr.

"You're quite right," the countess said. "They wouldn't suit the gown at all."

"I do like the amethysts," Tatiana said again, rather hopelessly.

There was a knock at the door. "Go away!" Dulcie snapped.

Smithers's voice, deferential: "Begging your pardon, milady, but the master is returned from London. You asked to be informed."

"Oh, God, he'll be coming up here straightaway. We've got to get you out of that gown! Hold him off, Smithers, as best you can. Unbutton her, Turner!" But before the maid had even eased the sleeves off, they heard voices in the corridor: Smithers vainly trying to distract Lucas, and Lucas not about to be distracted:

"Oh, go polish a chandelier or something, man. I want to see my lady."

The countess ran to throw herself against the door just as Lucas knocked. "You can't come in!" she cried, gesturing frantically at Turner to hurry.

"Why the devil not?"

"Because she isn't dressed!"

There was a pause. "All the better," Lucas said then, with an undercurrent of laughter.

"Lucas!" said his mother, outraged.

"Sorry. I'll wait." He did, for a good thirty seconds. "Now?"

"Don't be ridiculous. Go have a drink or something."

"I don't want a drink."

"Have one anyway. Have two or three." Turner had finally got the bodice loose and was tugging the skirts up over Tatiana's head.

"I am coming in."

The countess grasped the knob in both hands, shoulder

braced against the door. "The devil you are! To accost a lady in her own dressing chamber—"

"In three days, that lady will be my wife." The satisfaction in his tone made Tatiana blush.

"Hallo, darling," she called to him.

"Hallo, my love. What are they doing to you in there?"

"Making me decent."

"Pity."

"How was London?"

"Miserable as ever."

"I don't suppose," said Dulcie, "you bothered paying any of the calls I asked you to."

"Of course not."

"Then what were you doing?"

"Business," he said tersely.

"What sort of business?"

"My own." Tatiana suppressed a giggle, standing in her lacy underskirts. Turner was desperately shaking out the flounces of the wedding gown. "I am coming in," Lucas declared again. "Move aside, Mother, or I'll flatten you against the wall."

Turner, breathing hard, bundled the wedding gown and tossed it in the wardrobe, slamming that door shut just as the other burst open. Lucas stood on the threshold, grinning as he considered Tatiana. "I like that. I like it very much indeed. Madame has done you proud."

"You insufferable idiot," his mother sputtered, "those are her underskirts!"

"More goes over that?" He clucked his tongue. "What a shame."

"Do stop tormenting your mother and wait for me downstairs like a good boy," Tatiana said calmly.

"In a moment." He crossed to her and wrapped her in his arms, kissing her with an abandon that made Turner glance away. The countess did, too—though not without a wistful little sigh. "In the rose garden," he whispered, tongue flicking against Tatiana's ear. "Five minutes."

"Ten."

"Five." She nodded, and he went out, whistling cheerfully.

It was closer to a quarter hour, though, before she came through the arbor and saw him kneeling at the foot of the stone bench. "What are you doing, crushing aphids?" she teased.

"It's that new bush I wrote you of—the one that did not bloom last spring. It has budded at last."

"Yes, I know. Timkins has been pampering it terribly. What do you expect the blossoms to look like?"

"Damned if I know. It's a volunteer. Parentage unknown—though judging by the foliage, I'd guess there is *chinensis* in it, and damask and Alba. It could be anything: glorious, or as rank as a weed."

The late-May sun, so bright a moment before, had been swallowed by a cloud. Tatiana shivered. He noticed and shrugged off his coat, pulling it over her shoulders. But the chill had come from her heart. *Parentage unknown* . . . He guessed her thoughts, reached for her hand, and kissed it. "Oh, Tatiana. If there is one thing my experience with roses has taught me, it is that nothing matters except the flower. And you are the most glorious flower in the world, regardless whence you came."

She wanted so much to believe him. "Ask Timkins if you don't trust me," he murmured, holding her tightly. "He is there behind the arbor, watching us—but being very discreet. No, don't look! There, you've frightened him off." Sure enough, she saw the gardener stumping away, still on one crutch, but with a decided lilt to his step.

"He has been so kind to me . . . from the start," she said falteringly.

"That's because he knows you can't judge the worth of

anything by its heritage." His tongue traced the smooth line of her throat. "And if you ever wonder why he is so solicitous of that bush, only ask him its name."

"He told me you never name a bush before it blooms," she protested.

"I never have before. But I christened this one more than three years past—when I saw how thorny its branches were. It is called 'Lady Strathmere.' "

"For your mother." She laughed.

"Lady Tatiana Strathmere."

She drew back from him, wide-eyed. "No. You couldn't have. Not all that time ago! I was still a hoyden in leather breeches!"

"The most devastating hoyden I have ever seen."

"He would lie for you," she said. "Even if I did ask him."

"The others would. Never Timkins."

She knew in her heart it was true. Awed, she stared down at the bush. "I don't see how you could be so sure."

He shrugged, pulling her to the bench, setting her on his knees. "There are some things a man just knows. Here, now, what's there on that branch, just at the top there?"

"Dewdrops," she said, seeing the sparkle. "Odd they should hold on so late in the day. Don't they look just like—"

"Diamonds." Smiling, he reached into the bristle of thorns. "Dewdrops always do." His fist came away draped in dazzling brilliance.

Tatiana gasped. "Oh, Lucas!"

The necklace was a gossamer web of silver studded with crystalline dew. He fastened it around her throat. "Like it?"

She put her hand to it, unbelieving. "It is lovely—exquisite! But you shouldn't have. The cost—"

"No more than one would spend on a hunter," he lied.

"Alexander's own war-horse!"

"Perhaps," he allowed. "The most curious thing: I find I

am beginning to enjoy spending money, so long as it is on you." And he kissed her again, smoothing back her thick blond hair.

Still holding the diamonds, she looked beyond his shoulder to the seedling rosebush. "What color do you think it will prove?"

"White. My White Lady. And with a fragrance"—his hands reached beneath the coat for her breasts, tracing their sweet buds through the silk of her gown—"beyond imagining. God, three more days!"

"I can't wait."

"Nor can I."

"No, Lucas, I mean it. I honestly can't."

He raised his head from her breast. "If I'd known diamonds were the trick, I'd have showered you with them ages ago." He slid her skirts up over her knees. "Three days. Well within the margin of error for an heir to Somerleigh." The bulge in his breeches strained against her.

"Timkins," she whispered.

"Is no doubt on guard with his shovel and shears against all interlopers."

The diamonds lay heavy on her throat. Close to the bench she saw the vacant spot where Lady Innisford had once stood. "Was the necklace . . . the sole reason you went to London?"

"Oh, no." He reached negligently into the thorns again. "There were the eardrops, too." Very carefully, he put them on her, then plucked one last spark of brilliance from the topmost branch and slid it onto her finger. "And this. You never inquired about a betrothal ring, but I thought you ought to have one anyway. Does it fit?"

"Perfectly," she said, and bit her lip to hold back her tears. "You are too good to me!"

He laid her down on the bench beneath him. "Just wait,"

he promised, his voice hoarse with passion, "and see how good I can be."

"M'lord!"

It was Timkins, sounding oddly distraught. Lucas waved a vague hand toward the arbor. "Not now, man! Not now!"

"M'lord, there is a courier come—"

"Well, send him off again!" Lucas called impatiently as Tatiana pulled him down to her.

"M'lord, I cannot send him—"

"Lucas Strathmere? Earl of Somerleigh?"

The unfamiliar voice brought Lucas up short, just as he was lowering his head to Tatiana's breast. Cursing beneath his breath, he glanced up. "Aye? What of it?"

"I've a letter for you, m'lord, from His Majesty."

"From King George?" Astonished, Lucas drew Tatiana's skirts down and raised her to sit beside him.

"Nay, m'lord. From His Majesty the Prince Regent."

"Bah," Lucas said with derision. "Go away."

The messenger, in the royal colors, took a step into the garden. "I've orders to put it into your own hand."

Lucas hesitated, then thrust his fist out. "Go on and do so, then."

"Very good, m'lord." The man stepped forward briskly, proffering the sheet of vellum, rolled and tied. Lucas crushed it in his palm and tossed it into the shrubs. "And to wait, m'lord, until I have your answer."

"My *answer?*" Seething with impatience, Lucas snapped his fingers. "Go on. Retrieve it, then." The courier dug it out of the thorns, muttering as they tore at his gloves. "Forgive me, love," Lucas murmured. He unrolled the sheet and perused it briefly. Then he laughed, and hurled it back into the garden. "Inform His Majesty that I refuse his invitation. I am not at freedom to come to London. I am being married in three days."

The messenger stood squared off against him. "My understanding, m'lord, is that His Majesty's request is not an invitation, but a summons."

"How he couches it matters not to me. I am not at liberty."

"Lucas, what is it?" Tatiana asked curiously.

He looked at her, and she saw hesitation in his storm-ringed eyes. "Some silly whim of Prinny's."

"What whim?" Her intuition hadn't failed her; he did not want her to know what was in the note. She went to pick it up, then stopped. "Do you forbid me to read it?"

"I—yes. No. Tatiana—"

But she'd smoothed out the page, scanned it, caught her breath. "Tsar Alexander . . . coming to London! His Majesty requests your expertise in translation . . . Lord! Not just the Tsar, but his sister, the Grand Duchess of Oldenburg. And Platov! The Cossack hetman, Platov!"

"Tatiana," he said urgently. "Three days. Nothing anyone, not God himself, could possibly do to change—"

"You said yourself, if you could speak to Platov—"

"I tried. He would not meet with me."

"Because he was at war! Because there was no time! But now that he is coming to England—"

"Do you want to marry me or no?" he demanded. "Toss the bloody thing back into the shrubberies. Look at the date Prinny's put! He wants me there by the first—our wedding day! I should have to leave tonight to make London in three days."

"We should," she corrected him softly.

The muscles around his mouth tightened. "Not a chance."

"But, Lucas—" From the corner of her eye she saw the messenger standing, avidly following their discussion. "Timkins! Show this fellow to a meal and somewhat to drink."

"My instructions were," the courier began.

"You can wait in the kitchens, not eavesdropping on your betters!" Her tone was so imperious that he went without a further protest.

Lucas arched a brow at her. "That was worthy of a countess."

She was astounded at herself. "I've never in my life pulled rank on anyone!"

"It suits you. Perhaps you're having second thoughts now, and considering holding out for a prince." His voice was teasing, but those blue eyes were dark. "How else to explain your willingness to rush off to London, abandoning our wedding?"

"Lucas. My own dear love." She took his hands in hers, held them tight. "*Dyed* Ivan—your friend—he was well-regarded by the government in St. Petersburg, was he not?"

"Exceptionally so."

"And you trusted him, you found him worthy of reliance?"

"He saved my life. I saved his. I—he was like a brother."

She nodded thoughtfully. "No doubt others would have trusted him, too."

"This is nothing I've not already considered. What would you have me say? If a lady of the court found herself in difficulty—yes, she might turn to Casimir. And yes, I find it hard to believe anything short of some such connection could have resulted in the destruction of your village—not to mention the attacks in Brighton. What the devil do you think I went back to Russia for?" He straightened on the bench. "I have some skills in diplomacy, Tatiana. And I asked. I asked anyone who could conceivably have known of such a scandal, from the Tsarina's own ladies-in-waiting to the milking girls."

"It is not so impossible they would withhold the truth from you—a man, and a foreigner." She toed the grass at her feet. "A woman might do better."

"A woman might get herself killed trying. And that I will *not* allow."

"It's just as well we are not yet married, then," she said, and rose from the bench.

"Why is that?" he asked suspiciously.

"If we were, you might forbid me to go to London—and I should have to obey."

He stood as well, towering over her, glowering. "Dammit, what does it matter? Who gives a damn who you are? I love *you*, not your bloody mother or father!"

She turned in a circle, considering their surroundings—the garden, the park beyond, the crenelations of Somerleigh House rising against the sky. "It is easy for *you* to say what does not matter, when you know, have always known, who you are, where you came from!" She turned back to him, her lower lip trembling. "And it *doesn't* matter who they were. It is only the not knowing I can't stand."

"If you think I will stand idly by while you risk your life plunging back into that sewer—"

"Lucas, have reason! If someone wants me dead, I'm no safer here, married to you. They will come for me, in time. They *will* come."

The words were a perfect echo of Casimir Molitzyn's eight years before. And Casimir was dead. Lucas stared down at her, fear coiling his bowels like springs. He gathered her in his arms, felt her slight, pliant weight, the fragility of her blood and bone. "I can keep you safe," he promised, a hitch in his voice.

She pressed her cheek to his. "From war, from fire, from pestilence and accident—yes. But how can you protect me from the past? The only safety for me, ever, will be in knowing. Then at least I will understand what I have to fear."

He wanted to deny it. He tried to deny it, but he knew she spoke the truth. What else had sent him back to Russia and then on to Paris but this same certainty? He made one last stab at sanity. "Let us be married first, then. Go to London after."

"No," she whispered.

"Why the devil not?"

"Because . . . if the worst should happen, it will be easier for you this way."

Against all odds, Lucas felt the unfamiliar sting of tears in his eyes. "If I lost you, Tatiana, I would—"

She put her finger to his mouth. "Hush, my darling. Hush." He bowed his head against her forehead. When she looked up at him, her smile blazed through her own tears. "Look at all we have come through already, just to be here, together. Surely fate is on our side. Don't be afraid."

He brushed his eyes brusquely with the back of his hand. "Why shouldn't I be? Aren't you?"

"Only of breaking the news to your mother."

He laughed unsteadily. "I daresay she'll take it in stride. We can always hold out hope for the ceremony she wanted at St. Paul's."

"Oh, that would never suit. Not in a muslin dress."

He raised his head, took a deep, ragged breath, and pushed back his hair with his hands. "We are going to miss the roses again."

"For the last June ever," she promised, and kissed him with infinite tenderness.

"You are the bravest girl in all the world."

"The luckiest, rather."

I hope so, Lucas thought as he held her, tighter than forever. *I hope to God so.*

Twenty-Seven

"How are you holding up, love?" Lucas murmured to Tatiana as they stood among the notables on the dais at Carlton House.

"Better than those poor souls in the pit. Why does he invite more people than his house can hold?"

"My mother would say it is out of his benign good nature." Tatiana snorted. "I'd say it soothes his monstrous vanity to see so many here." His hand tightened on hers. "You were superb when I presented you again, by the way. Not a hint of repugnance on your part."

"Nor on his," she reflected. "He truly is without shame. He did pinch me, you know."

"You hid it admirably."

"I feared if I didn't, you might take a dagger to him."

"I might yet." Lucas straightened, seeing the curtains

behind them part. "Here come the Russians. There, that's your beloved Tsar."

"Oh! He is very grand," Tatiana breathed, admiring the tall blond man in his exquisitely fitted uniform of light green.

"He looks better to me all the time. And that is his sister, the Grand Duchess."

"She is lovely. Don't you think she is lovely?"

"She is lively, I'll grant you. She danced until dawn last night at the embassy."

"With you?"

He glanced down at her, amused. "No. Not with the lowly translator. With her husband and some of the Continental princes. She hasn't even danced with Prinny."

"Good for her." Tatiana considered her again. She had wheat-blond hair and an enviable complexion, very pale, very smooth; she was slight of figure, dressed in a gown of deep purple satin, with a neckpiece and tiara of pearls and amethysts. "Who are those men behind her?"

"The Prussian princes, Augustus and Frederick. Then Leopold of Saxe-Coburg and Prince Paul of Wurttemberg."

"Such a company of princes!"

"And all of them," Lucas said reflectively, "eminently eligible. Look at Princess Charlotte and her betrothed." Tatiana glanced at Prinny's only legitimate heir—fat, sloppy Charlotte, who was openly staring at the range of handsome foreign luminaries. Beside her, dwarfed by her bountiful bosom, stood her fiancé, small, sickly William of Orange. "I wonder," Lucas mused, "why the Grand Duchess should have brought with her so many gallant young men."

"You think she aims to make mischief? How can she? Your mother says Princess Charlotte's trousseau is already on order."

"So was yours," he said, with a mock frown. "No Grand Duchess would be deterred by that from attempting to ally

Britain's heir with someone more sympathetic to Russia than Orange."

"You see conspiracy everywhere," she scoffed—but the avid admiration on Princess Charlotte's round face as she surveyed the foreigners did give Tatiana pause.

"And wouldn't that tweak Prinny," Lucas murmured to himself.

"Don't you *dare* interfere! Where is Platov?"

"There, behind General Blûcher." She had to crane to see him—a short, swart man, broad-shouldered, heavy-chested, with a permanent grimace on his face.

"He looks like *Dyed* Ivan—Casimir," she said in surprise.

"Casimir was a Cossack."

"Was he? I did not know."

The Regent, with Tsar Alexander sitting stiffly beside him, signaled abruptly for Lucas. "Pardon me, love. Duty calls." He hurried to the Tsar's side, listened a moment, then bent to murmur in Prinny's ear, with a glance at Tatiana that seemed to say, *I may be a long time. . . .* The Grand Duchess, seated by her brother, was staring at the Regent with palpable disgust.

Tatiana sighed and scanned the crowd in a leisurely manner, searching for Susannah Cuthbert. She'd not called on her friend in the three days since her arrival in London, though she'd read in the *Post* that Susannah's younger sister Sarah was engaged to Lord Derring. She was anxious to learn what progress Susannah had made in her pursuit of Clifford Hyde Parker, and hoped she was not too much upset at Sarah's upstaging of her.

As she searched the room, her gaze alighted on Lady Anthea Bournemouth, who looked back at her with an expression of bitter resentment. Hurriedly, Tatiana glanced away—and straight into the hard olive eyes of Lady Gillian Innisford, whose red-brown curls tumbled fetchingly over her low-cut gown of matte bronze silk. She'll have read of

Lucas's betrothal, Tatiana realized, though she could not see what difference it should make to her. And yet apparently it did; those eyes shone with something very much like hatred. Tatiana shivered in her bare-shouldered gown. For someone who had only just arrived in London, she thought ruefully, she was well-supplied with enemies.

Just then she caught a glimpse of Susannah's chestnut head among the throng. She started to inch her way back along the platform, then froze as the curtains parted to reveal the tall, eye-patched figure of the Duke of Cumberland. Tatiana ducked her head low, praying he would not take notice of her. She had not forgotten the way he'd stared at her at Dulcie's rout in Brighton. Immensely relieved, she saw him push forward to Prinny's side without a sideward glance. More anxious than ever to escape from the dais, she slipped behind the row of princes to the curtains. Just as she reached out to part them, someone touched her elbow. She tried ignoring the hand, but it tightened, demanding her attention. Steeling herself, she spun around with a stiff smile of welcome, ready for whatever role she was required to play.

But none of her mental preparations could keep her from starting as she met the stony gaze of the hetman of the Don Cossacks. Matvei Platov released her arm and made a small bow. "I beg your pardon," he said in Russian. "Have we been introduced?"

"*Nyet*," Tatiana said reflexively—and then bit her tongue.

"But you are Russian, surely."

"Italian, actually." Tatiana blushed. "I am Miss Tatiana Grimaldi."

He clicked his heels. "Matvei Platov, at your service. You speak excellent Russian."

"My nursemaid came from your country. And my . . . the man to whom I am betrothed—" She waved a hand toward Lucas. "He has encouraged my interest in your tongue."

Platov looked at Lucas with his heavy-lidded eyes, then back to her. "I have heard," Tatiana said, searching wildly for conversational matter, "that you have a most remarkable horse."

Abruptly he smiled, teeth making a crease of white in his sun-darkened face. "Your nurse was from the province of Ologda."

"How could you tell that?"

"By your accent, lady." He bowed again. "Forgive me for imposing on your time." He withdrew, leaving Tatiana shaking. *She had to be more cautious until she knew her enemies.*

Prinny, bored with diplomatic conversation, had stood up to dance. He offered his hand to the Grand Duchess, who after the merest pause shook her head. Lucas was called on to provide translation. Whatever it was he said, Prinny did not seem pleased. The Grand Duchess stood in a rustle of satin and vanished through the curtains, trailed by her ladies and the princes. The Tsar lingered only a few more moments before he, too, withdrew. There arose an audible sigh from the assembled guests, who had hoped for more time in which to gawk at the foreigners. Princess Charlotte had swiveled in her seat to follow the departure of the princes with her wide, pale eyes. Her father yanked her back around with a furious glare and led her onto the floor. William of Orange sat miserably in his seat, staring at his hands.

Lucas made his way back to Tatiana with a speculative gleam in his eye. "I daresay if he had his choice, Prinny would exile the Tsar to Elba along with the Corsican."

"What did the duchess say to him?" she whispered.

"Merely that she was too tired to dance. But it was rebuke enough. Mark my words, there is trouble ahead." He smiled down at her. "Would you like to dance?"

"I'd just as soon go home."

"I was hoping you'd say that. Let's be gone. There will be no further need for my services tonight."

He edged close to her in their coach. "Well, you have seen your Tsar now. What think you of him?" His fingertips caressed her cheek.

"He seems a most admirable man."

"So he is. He has no patience for Prinny's airs and artifices. They are fire and water."

They are Russia and England, Tatiana thought, and swallowed.

"I thought I saw you speaking with Platov, more's the wonder," Lucas went on. "I don't think he's said five words to anyone since he's been here."

She hesitated, not wanting him to learn how indiscreet she'd been. "I had some notion of conversing with him," she said finally. "But you were right—he does not speak English."

Lucas tucked his arm around her. "Just as well. Still, the ladies of the court seem to find him tremendously intriguing. What is there to attract, pray tell, in such a fierce, scowling man?"

"I've always harbored a soft spot for that same type."

He laughed and kissed her ear. "God, I was mad to let you talk me into this postponement." He traced the swell of her breasts beneath the celadon silk. "On the other hand, I'd not have missed seeing Prinny so put out for any other purpose in the world."

"Lucas," she began, intending, really intending, to tell him how she'd accidentally lapsed into speaking Russian with Platov.

He found her mouth with his, pulling her into his lap. "Have I told you lately how I love you?"

There was such a little distance until home. Tatiana succumbed to his embrace, parted her lips beneath the force of his. He would only be angry if he learned she'd spoken Russian publicly. That Platov had approached her was intriguing, but it would not mean a thing unless he pursued the acquaintance. Time enough to tell Lucas then . . .

He pulled back from her, tracing the bow of her mouth. "Why have I got the feeling your thoughts are a thousand miles away?"

"I am sorry," she apologized. But in fact, they were—on the windswept plain where Mizhakovsk had once stood, where as a child she had run and played . . .

He nodded understanding. "You must be exhausted. All that long journey from Dorset, and the crush of people tonight—when we arrive home, you must go straight off to bed."

Had they remained in Dorset, they'd be married by now. They would be sharing that bed. "Gillian was there tonight," she said suddenly.

"I saw her. It would be hard not to remark her in that gown."

What did he mean by that? Had he thought her seductive, or outré? God, if she should begin to doubt him—she threw her arms around his neck. "I love you, Lucas," she whispered.

The carriage rolled to a stop. Gently he disengaged her arms, lifted her from his lap. "I love you too, little one. Now, upstairs." He handed her to Braunton, giving her bottom a swift pat.

"Aren't you tired as well?" she asked, seeing him turn toward his study as they entered the house.

"I have some reading to do."

"I could bring you brandy—keep you company."

He blew her a kiss. "It is only some reports from the Foreign Office that I have to go over. Go and get your rest. There is the reception at the embassy tomorrow, and then Dulcie's dinner party. You will need your strength!"

She started up the stairs, and heard at her back the obsequious voice of Smithers: "A satisfying evening, milord, I trust?"

"Bring me a brandy." Lucas said shortly. A satisfying evening—no. It had not been that.

He went into his study, lit a single candle, and waited until the butler had withdrawn before smoothing out the letter that had been pushed into his hand at Carlton House. He'd crushed the thing the moment he'd recognized Gillian's spidery penmanship in the salute—and then had held on to it, impelled by curiosity. What could have driven her to write him after so many years? He read the words over slowly, sipping the brandy, thinking how he would have given his soul for such a letter not so long ago.

My dearest Lucas:

It was with a full heart that I read the recent news of your betrothal. I am a fond, foolish woman, if you will, but through all these years I had clung to the hope that despite the difficulties of the past, you still harbored some regard for me. I have never told you how greatly I appreciated your refusal at the inquest to bend to the Crown's attempted lies concerning me. That took courage. But I always knew you had courage—witness how you flaunted your family's wishes in your courtship of me.

Nor have I explained why I chose to accept Lord Innisford's proposal of marriage over your own. Suffice to say, I was not then so courageous as you. The opposition of the Admiral and the Countess terrified me, and I was unwilling to be the instrument of your certain rupture with them. I realize now I made a dreadful mistake. You are so much better a man than was my despicable husband, who proved traitor to everything you stood for. If the past could be dissolved . . . yet I know that it can't.

To see you now returned to public honor, standing at the

Regent's side, fills me with such gladness. And I am overjoyed
at the prospect of your marriage. I cannot say I am acquainted with the fortunate young lady, but I have seen her,
and she appears the epitome of perfection you so richly deserve. I wish you every happiness together, from the depths of
my heart.

No doubt you find this letter a surprise after such long
silence. Yet know how very often I have rebuked myself for
never acknowledging the enormous debt I owe to you. If there
is in your honorable soul any trace of fondness for an old,
worn-out lady, I beg this last request—that you call on me
and let me tell you face to face of my gratitude and eternal
admiration. I shall be at home tomorrow afternoon from one
to five o'clock. I impose, I know, on your valuable time. If
you choose not to call, I will understand. And I remain
forever,

Your devoted admirer,
Gillian, Lady Innisford

What was she after? That was his first thought, but his
glass of brandy brought him no closer to answering the
question. The whole tone of the letter—the self-denigra-
tion, the apologetic air—was thoroughly unlike the Gillian
he had known. Then he thought of Tatiana, and the way
she'd uprooted the rosebush of her rival, hacked it into
pieces. Women! He smiled, feeling indulgent. Who could
account for their jealous whims?

That Gillian *was* jealous showed in those lines about
Tatiana. He'd never, in their heady season of love, heard her
speak one complimentary word about another female. To
the contrary, she'd been as ruthless as sin. And here she was,
actually calling herself old! *Oh, Gillian, I have gotten your
goat at last, haven't I, by daring to be happy?* He laughed out
loud.

But some parts of the letter were troubling. That she should explain now, belatedly, why she had chosen Innisford—he could well understand how cowed she must have been by his parents' reaction to their proposed marriage. Why, she must have felt very much the way Tatiana had—that she wasn't worthy of him. And he had been so young, so callow. He hadn't known how to soothe her qualms, assure her that love would conquer all. He was grateful, of course, that he hadn't. Yet he sympathized with Gillian's sense of rejection in a way he could not have then.

Fourteen years . . . God, it seemed a lifetime. And she had never remarried, despite her vast fortune. Surely that bespoke some decency on her part. He remembered, briefly, that once she had been as fresh and young as Tatiana. He saw again the curve of her arm across the baize of the faro table, her bronze curls tumbling over the lush swell of her breasts. . . .

Bemused, he shook his head and poured another brandy. Tatiana would never forgive him if he accepted this invitation. But why must women be so silly? Nothing, no one, could alter his affection for her. What could be the harm in one last meeting, when the future blazed so bright?

For a moment, he allowed himself to imagine his reception. Gillian would be wearing some preposterous creation—in bronze, of course, and cut below decency. She would be languid, draped in a chaise. She might even try to seduce him. He did not doubt his ability to withstand that. But, God, he had suffered for her sake. For so many years he had yearned for her, tortured himself with her memory. And now, finally, he was strong enough to stand against her wiles. Suddenly, as he took another swallow of brandy, it became monstrously important that he should. If he didn't, could he ever be certain he had moved beyond her, that the image—white arms, white breasts, red-brown hair—that had tormented him for more than a decade had been laid to rest?

One o'clock to five o'clock. Clasping the snifter, he began to think of ways. Between the reception at the embassy and Dulcie's dinner, he should have an hour free. He would have to make excuses to Tatiana. She had spoken of visiting the Cuthberts, he recalled.

Make excuses? Call it what it was: He would have to lie.

But it had been her choice to postpone their wedding, come here to London to settle her past. Was it so wrong for him to want to lay to rest his own? If he'd had his way, he would be lying beside her now—or, more likely, atop her—instead of cloistering himself away with brandy, trying vainly to keep his wayward lust for her under control.

One final visit . . . He pondered it, and then he downed the last of his brandy before tramping upstairs to his solitary bed.

Twenty-Eight

"Good morning, love! Wait until you hear this letter I have—" Lucas stopped on the threshold of Tatiana's bedroom, surprised by how swiftly she had moved to thrust something *she* was reading beneath her pillow. Why, she had overturned the pot of chocolate on her tray.

"Lord, Lucas, see what you have made me do! Hand me that towel before I am scalded to death!" He flung it to her, and she sopped up the steaming liquid, kneeling atop the bed in her sheer nightdress. The morning sun through the open shutters pricked out each curve of her body beneath the pale dimity—her small waist, the glorious swell of her breasts, the smooth, graceful line of her thighs. "It is customary to knock before entering a bedchamber," she said curtly.

"Ah, but if I had knocked, you would have covered over

that negligée." He slid onto the bed beside her, hands gliding over those beguiling curves.

"All these sheets—and the coverlet! Mrs. Smithers will be furious."

Disappointed at the reception of his overtures, he drew back with a frown. "Who cares if she is? Toss them onto the fire. I'll buy her more sheets."

"You may very well have to. Chocolate sets a stain." She went on dabbing with the towel. "You are sitting in it, Lucas! You will ruin your breeches!"

"They are very near the color of chocolate," he said with a grin.

"I'd best ring straight for Clarrie," she went on as if she had not heard him. "If we soak them in cold water and bleaching powder—"

"Will you stop fussing like some city housewife?"

She straightened her slim shoulders. "I was only trying to save you the expense of replacing the linens."

"I don't mind spending money on you," he said more gently, and looked at her. Her cheeks were flushed, and her eyes did not meet his, but stayed fixed on the stain she was attacking with such determination. "Is something wrong, Tatiana?"

"You have spoiled my breakfast, you have spoiled my bed, and—" She sighed, seeing the splotch on the negligee's hem. "You have spoiled my new nightdress."

"I am sorry for that," he said gravely. "Especially since you look so fetching in it." He nuzzled her again.

She spun out of reach, bare feet hitting the floor. "If you would be so kind as to move, I may still spare the featherbed damage."

"Leave that for Clarrie."

"I hope I am not grown so lofty I cannot strip my own bed!"

Lucas, bedeviled by the sight of her in the sunlight,

grabbed her by the waist. "I like it when you play the serving wench. Shall I be the cruel master, or the stable-hand?"

"Lucas, please!" She'd gone rigid at his touch, all her muscles tensed. He released her abruptly, irked. He'd thought they'd moved beyond that stage.

"I do beg your pardon," he said, just to show her he could stiffen, too. "I'll return when you do not find my presence so distasteful. You can send one of the servants to inform me when that might be."

She turned to him slowly, the bedclothes gathered to her breasts, the clear green of her eyes gone cloudy. "It is just that I cannot stand to be startled that way! And your mother says that even in the best marriages, there must be respect for privacy."

It was not a well-chosen tack. "Oh, Mother says so, does she? Why don't you tell her—"

The door flew open, pushed by Carruthers's businesslike shoulder. "Brought that jam ye wanted, miss, 'n'—" She broke off, seeing the chaos of linens. "What has gone on here?"

"His Lordship spilled my chocolate," Tatiana said briefly. "Take these down to be laundered, please."

Carruthers took the sheets. Tatiana looked at Lucas. "If you'll excuse me, I'd best get out of this and see it laundered as well."

He was staring after the maid, his stormy eyes thoughtful. "What were you reading so intently?"

"A letter."

He waited. She did not offer more. "Might I inquire from whom?"

"It's none of your affair."

"Susannah?" he asked. Tatiana said nothing; she'd slipped behind the japanned screen in the corner. "Or perhaps Freddy Whittles? I'd heard he is in town. You might remind him in your response that we are engaged."

"Freddy is aware of that fact."

"So it *was* from Freddy! Does that fop dare still pursue you? By God, I'll meet him with pistols on Blackheath. No, with slingshots in Piccadilly Square."

She came back from around the screen, curves well-hidden by a brocade robe. "Don't be absurd."

"I mean it utterly. I'll teach him to trifle with my intended."

"It was not from Freddy," she said slowly, reluctantly.

"Then who was it from?"

"You claim your privileges, Lucas. I will hold to mine. I do not ask to see your private correspondence."

He flushed, wondering if she might know about the letter from Gillian. No, that wasn't possible. "It was merely a jest. You needn't be so haughty, love."

"And you need not presume so much! I'll thank you to knock the next time you enter my rooms—at least until we are wed!"

Carruthers had come back, and was standing edgily in the doorway. "I-I think I hear Mrs. Smithers callin'," she said nervously. "I'll just go 'n' see—"

"His Lordship was just leaving—weren't you, Lucas?"

If she had relented even then, he might have done what he'd meant to do when he entered the room: told her of Gillian's proposal, laughed with her over its preposterousness and had it done. But the letter was from that damned fool Freddy—he was sure she was lying. And that provoked him. If she clung to her confidences, so could he.

"I was, as it happens. I only wanted to tell you I won't be able to see you home from the embassy after the reception. Something has come up."

"In that case, I'll not go to the embassy at all. I'll go straight to Susannah's instead."

Lucas felt a nagging of guilt. "See here, Tatiana. I am sorry I barged in. It was only—well, I would have hated for you to put on that robe before I glimpsed the negligée." He smiled crookedly, winningly. She did not seem to notice; her green eyes were distant. Shrugging, he bent to kiss her. "But we are firm for dinner here with Mother. Whom has she invited, do you know? Not Lady Bournemouth, I trust."

She hadn't heard him; she was lost in thought. It was not a good enough riposte to repeat, so he saved his breath. "I'll see you at seven, then."

"Mm? Oh, yes. At seven." She seemed to rally herself, smiled up at him. "Enjoy the reception. Mind you don't muddy the waters as you translate. Watch those irregular verbs."

He left her, oddly disquieted. Carruthers closed the door in his wake. He lingered in the corridor, wondering if he should go back and apologize again. It couldn't hurt, he decided, and reached for the latch.

The door was locked. So much for apology, he thought, and stalked downstairs to his breakfast. It would serve her right if he *did* go visit Gillian.

At four o'clock precisely, Lucas arrived at the Pultenay Hotel and had his card sent up to Lady Innisford's rooms. A few moments later, a liveried boy appeared on the staircase to show him the way. From behind the door came a flurry of barking—the greyhounds. Then he was ushered in to a tasteful sitting room done up in velvet and chintz. A fire was guttering on the hearth, though the day was more than fair. Lucas pulled at his neckcloth. The air was close, and redolent of a perfume he had not forgotten: Gillian's scent, heavy and musky, civet or ambergris. A long row of nosegays adorned the mantel, with their cards still attached. Curious, he went to examine them. *To my darling, Always, Tommy. From your bad, bad boy, B.L. Yours, my precious, Bugsy. Your slave, dearest Gillian, J. Willoughby.* Just like fourteen years past, he thought ruefully—though something about that last name nagged his memory. Before he had time to place it, the pocket doors slid open at his back.

"Lucas." She came toward him in a rustle of silk—black, he was surprised to see, not bronze, and not décolleté by even the most Puritan standards. "I'd nearly given up hope for you." She offered him her hand.

"Gillian." After a moment's hesitation, he bent and kissed her fingers. To his relief, the spell she'd cast on him once was worn off; he noted only that her hand was white, and fair, and soft enough. "Forgive me. I was detained at the embassy. When the foreigners are not on show, there is a mountain of work to be done."

"It must be very gratifying for you to take part in such momentous events." She waved him to a chair. He waited until she was seated, then sat himself, studying her in the half-light. She is still lovely, he thought, remembering how he'd worshiped her beyond all reason.

"My share in the proceedings is small enough."

She smiled, ringing a little glass bell. The boy came in with a tray. "I thought tea," she said tentatively, "though there is brandy or claret if you would prefer."

He would have killed for a drink. But since they were being so damned civilized . . . "Tea would be delightful. No—"

"I know. No sugar, just lemon. Did you think I would forget?" She poured, her slender arms in their web of black net as graceful as ever. "So, Lucas. How have you been?"

"Very well, thank you. And you?"

"I have no cause to complain—thanks to you. I meant what I wrote you. It was unconscionable of me to let so much time pass without extending my gratitude for your generous behavior."

"Considering I'd murdered your husband," Lucas managed to say, "I can't imagine what you might be grateful to me for."

She passed him the cup. "Poor Harry. That was his own fault, wasn't it, for dabbling in matters so far above his head. But we have no secrets from each other, Lucas. I knew what Prinny and his counselors planned to do—make me his scapegoat. That I am able to hold my head up at all in society today is wholly due to you."

Lucas thought of his mother, and colored. "I ought to have done more for you."

She trilled a laugh. "What more could you have done, considering how they packed you off to—where was it? India?"

"Russia."

"Of course it was. Russia. That is why you are in London now. The Regent's honored guests . . . but tell me of your fiancée! I recall so clearly a day last summer, in the park at Brighton, when I saw you with her. It was evident even then that you were meant for each other. My heart rejoices in your happiness."

He glanced at the flowers on the mantel. "What about you, Gillian? Will you never remarry? You have a multitude of admirers; that is plain enough."

Lady Innisford stirred cream into her tea, black slowly swallowing the white. "I think not. Having failed to realize my chance for contentment long ago, I find I cannot entirely trust my heart. I suppose you thought me greedy to have married Harry."

"No, no," he protested. But he had, and she knew he had.

"To be a woman can be a rather lonely thing," she reflected, tilting her head so that those radiant curls spilled over the black net. "One is so utterly dependent for one's stature, one's position, on the opposite sex."

"I did not mean to abandon you, Gillian. I would have wed you even after—"

"Oh, let's not speak of the past!" she interrupted gaily. "You must look to the future now. I rather thought from the wording of the *Post*'s announcement that by this time you would be wed to Miss Grimley."

"Grimaldi."

"Of course. Just like the clown—no offense meant! She is from Austria, I understand?"

"Italy, actually. But she has Austrian blood as well."

"A true Continental. A cousin on your mother's side, I gather?" He nodded, and she smiled knowingly. "Then to this connection, at least, the countess can make no objection!"

"One would think not," Lucas allowed. "And yet she raised a few. I begin to realize how very daunting she must have appeared to you when—"

"She was well within her rights," Gillian said crisply. "I know now—no one better!—how vital it is to do what one must to protect one's offspring." She reached for the bell again, let it tinkle softly. From beyond the doors, there appeared a shadow. "No doubt, Lucas, you are wondering what impelled me to renew our acquaintance after so many years. I have the honor to present to you my daughter. Araminta, won't you come in?"

The shadow hesitated. Lucas rose to his feet. "I didn't know you and Lord Innisford had children."

"Just the one. Come, Araminta! Don't be shy. She has been away at convent school," she explained as the girl took a few steps forward. "Come, my pet! You must not be afraid. This gentleman is a very old and dear friend of your mamma's. Do make your curtsy to him."

The child—she might have been thirteen or fourteen—bobbed and whispered, "I am pleased, milord, to make your acquaintance."

"And I yours, Araminta."

She sought her mother's gaze. "Shall I go now?"

"As you wish. Are you working your 'broidery?"

"Yes, Mamma."

"Go on back to it, then."

"Yes, Mamma. Good-bye, milord." She bobbed again and withdrew.

"A very pretty little miss," Lucas said, watching her red-brown head vanish through the doors. "She has your hair."

"And your eyes."

Lucas sent his teacup crashing into its saucer. "I beg your pardon?"

Gillian smiled again, with a hint of sadness. "Forgive me, Lucas. There likely was a more deft way of presenting you with this, but for the life of me I could not think of one."

Lucas felt he'd stumbled into a dream. "Are you telling me . . . she is *my* daughter?"

Lady Innisford stared into the swirls of her tea. "She is. Did you never think it odd I should betroth myself to Harry Innisford so soon after your parents threatened to disown you if we married?"

"I thought—"

"You thought what the world thought." Her mouth curved bitterly. "That I took that old man for his fortune. The truth was, there were no other men of my acquaintance willing to offer marriage when I carried another man's child beneath my skirts."

"You mean Innisford *knew?*"

"Of course he knew. How could you believe I'd keep such a secret from him?"

"You bloody well kept it from me!"

She set her spoon aside. "Had I told you, you would have insisted on marrying me despite your parents' opposition."

"Of course I would have!"

"They'd have made good their threat, Lucas. Disinherited you. It would have ruined your life. Who was I, that you should sacrifice so much for me?"

He glanced wildly back toward the doors through which the child had disappeared. His child. His daughter . . . "Bring her back," he begged, still stunned by the revelation. "Let me see her again."

"No, Lucas. Never. She knows nothing about you. And by God's grace, she never will."

"How can you be so cruel?"

She laughed a little. "Cruel? I? Think, Lucas, dear. If I had mentioned in the course of the very thorough examination made me by the Crown's prosecutors at the inquest that I had borne your child, what coroner on earth would have delivered a verdict of accident in Harry's death?"

Lucas buried his face in his hands, took a deep breath, pushed back his hair. "God, Gillian! To spring this on me now, from the blue—"

"I should have kept my secret."

"No, no! But if you'd only told me—and to think I killed him! He knew I was the father?" She nodded. "Christ! That noble man . . . Gillian, how can you even bear to look at me? How can you not hate me?"

"I have always loved you, Lucas," she said slowly, softly. "So much that I could not bear to see you lose your reputation and your fortune. Not even for *her* sake."

He felt numbed, dazed, oppressed by the hot scented air. "And yet you tell me now—"

"I . . . since you are marrying, I thought it best. . . ." She turned, hiding her eyes. "I thought you loved me still, fool that I am. Despite all that has passed between us. It is *not* that I wish to spoil your joy. I only thought you should know."

"I could acknowledge her now," he said desperately.

"No. It would only confuse her. She believes herself Harry's daughter. It is best that way."

"Gillian—"

She rose from her chair. "Thank you for coming, Lucas. I know how busy your schedule must be." He looked at her more closely. He was not mistaken; tears were rolling down her cheeks.

"God, how I have wronged you!"

She shrugged a little. "The past can't be changed."

He took out his wallet. "Let me give you money. I have—" It was not enough. "I shall write you a bank draft."

She had stiffened. "I never asked for your money. I don't want it now."

"Gillian, Gillian!" His own daughter. Flesh of his flesh. "Let me make amends!"

She raised her tear-stained face proudly. "She wants for nothing. I have seen to that—though in ways your mother no doubt would not approve."

The girl appeared again in the doorway, a hoop and linen in her hands. "Forgive me, Mamma," she said very softly, "but I've tangled my silks. Will you help me undo them?"

"Of course, my love." Lucas had started forward, but Gillian stopped him with a warning shake of her head. "Lord Strathmere was just leaving."

"Gillian. *Something*," he whispered. "A trust fund. An annuity . . ."

"I've tried and tried," the girl said plaintively, "but the threads just go awry."

"Life is like that, Araminta. Say farewell to Lord Strathmere, won't you?"

"Farewell, sir. God be with you." Her eyes, blue ringed with stormy black, met his.

God. "And with you, Araminta. Gillian—"

"Don't make a fool of yourself, Lucas, or I'll wish I hadn't told you."

"Told him what, Mamma?"

"Nothing, darling. Let me have that needle. You will

need to open the drapes; my poor old eyes cannot see in this light."

"Gillian!" His voice was desperate, pleading.

"Good day, Lucas. It was so very kind of you to call on me. Congratulations again on your betrothal."

He left them. What else could he do but leave them, when she would allow no more?

Twenty-Nine

HE WAS LATE COMING down to the countess's supper party that evening. Tatiana, who'd had all day to regret how badly she'd behaved that morning, kept watching the salon doors. She meant to make amends, be charming and enticing; she'd worn the celadon silk gown he liked so much, and his diamonds were at her throat and ears.

And still he kept her waiting, kept the whole company waiting for so long that Dulcie, raising a puzzled brow at Tatiana, whispered something to Smithers that sent him trotting upstairs. He returned to the salon promptly, gave his mistress a small confirming nod, and bustled off into the dining room. A few moments later Lucas himself appeared, his black evening clothes impeccable but something wayward to the waves of his hair, as though he had forgotten to brush it or even to glance in a mirror. Tatiana hurried to him and stood on tiptoe to kiss him, a little more than briefly and chastely. "I missed you, darling," she whispered. "Where on earth have you been?"

There was brandy on his breath. "Meetings," he told her, nodding at the guests. "I got back about five, and fell sound asleep. Good evening, Lady Barton, Lord Barton. Forgive my tardy arrival."

"Quite all right," the lady said, patting his arm. "We all know what hard work you are doing in these negotiations."

"How does Europe look to be shaping up?" her round, elderly husband inquired.

"Too soon to say."

"But all, I hope, is friendliness for the Regent's grand reception tomorrow evening?" the old diplomat pressed.

"I trust so. Will you excuse me, please?" He was headed to the sideboard for brandy, but Tatiana tugged him firmly toward Susannah's mother. "Mrs. Cuthbert, how delightful to see you. My congratulations on Miss Cuthbert's betrothal. Sterling fellow, Derring."

"And mine to you on yours," Marianne Cuthbert said warmly, beaming at Tatiana.

"Mrs. Cuthbert has another announcement to make," Tatiana told Lucas.

Susannah came forward on Clifford Hyde Parker's arm, shy and blushing. Tatiana nudged Lucas, who started. "Oh, I say! Is it to be two daughters in one season, Mrs. Cuthbert?"

"I am gratified, milord, to answer you yes."

"Best wishes, Hyde Parker. And to you, Susannah."

"Thank you, milord." Susannah curtsied prettily, clinging to her catch.

"I see my mother is signaling us to dinner. I have kept you all waiting long enough. Shall we go in?" He offered Tatiana his arm. She took it, vaguely disappointed. Not one compliment—and what could he be thinking of, not to have combed his hair? She tried to reach up and smooth it down for him, and he jerked away from her hand. "What are you doing?"

"You still look half asleep," she whispered. "Your hair—"

He pushed it back absently. "Better?"

"Worse, rather. Never mind. You must be famished." She sat as he pulled out her chair.

It was a convivial table, as Dulcie's could be counted on to be. There was much talk of Napoleon's exile to Elba, of the foreigners, of the chances that Princess Charlotte's betrothal to William of Orange would withstand the combined assault of the princes in the Tsar's entourage. But most of all, the guests gossiped about the ball the Regent planned on the morrow. Rumors were running rampant: that Prinny had planned a fireworks display the likes of which had never been seen, that he intended to flood the gardens to present a Venetian spectacle, that he'd imported ten thousand white doves from Spain to be released among the guests. Tatiana joined eagerly in the conversation, and noticed only toward the end of the second course that Lucas was saying little. Of course, he was not at his best in such surroundings. Still, somehow she'd hoped their betrothal might make him more sociable. He was not eating much, either, she noted, yet he gestured to Smithers to refill his wineglass more times than she could count.

"Lucas," she whispered as he reached again for claret, "you had best go easy."

He shot her a stormy glance. "Afraid I will disgrace myself? Don't worry. I won't."

She nibbled her lip and turned to Mr. Hyde Parker, who at least could be counted on not to jump down her throat.

The third course—crimped cod, calf's fry, mushroom fritters, pastries, and pies—came and was removed, with Lucas having abandoned eating altogether. Tatiana felt the need to smooth things over before they got out of hand.

Beneath the table she caressed his thigh. "Love. I am sorry I was rude to you today. Pray forgive me."

He turned to her, nonplussed. "Rude? When?"

"You know. The chocolate—in my rooms."

"The chocolate . . ." He seemed to gather his thoughts with an effort. "God. What does that signify?"

"You are not angry with me?" He hadn't heard; he was staring into his wineglass.

At the far end of the table, Dulcie rose with a gracious smile. "Ladies, shall we leave them to it?"

"Lucas," she began again.

But Susannah tugged her from her chair, dancing with excitement. "I need to talk trousseaux with you, Tat!"

She cast one last glance at Lucas. He was reaching for the decanter before Smithers even set it down.

It was hard to follow Susannah's giddy chatter of gowns and shoes and bonnets; Tatiana's gaze kept straying toward the dining-room doors. She had been wrong, she knew, to conceal the letter from him. But until she could decide what response to make, she wanted no interference, not even from Lucas. He would have his opinions, yes, but she wanted time to form her own. And surely one small fit of temper on her part did not warrant his behavior this evening! But perhaps he was simply working too hard. We ought not to have come here, she thought; he was right. Then she remembered her letter, and she realized: No. The bird has been started out of the bush. It is too late to turn back.

"The most *darling* ecru taffeta," Susannah was saying, "all trimmed in beadwork. Mamma thought it was all wrong, but I was certain you would not."

Tatiana wrested her attention back to her friend. "So what did you decide?"

"Why, for once in my life I did as you always advise me. I

put my foot down. 'Mamma,' I said, 'I *will* have it!' Now, just wait until I tell you about my veil!"

There was dancing after supper, but Lucas had withdrawn to the card room. Tatiana swallowed her sense of rejection dutifully when he failed to ask her for a single set. She had partners enough, and only Mr. Hyde Parker was bold enough to inquire whether she did not feel Lord Strathmere was neglecting her. "For if you do," he added manfully, "I can drop the hint—"

"Oh, no," she assured him as they went down the line of the mazurka. "I do not begrudge him his little leisure at cards. He has been so burdened with the Crown's business of late."

"I am pleased to see him involved in government again," Susannah's beau noted. "I have always thought he would serve well in the Cabinet."

"Lucas?" she asked, pleased but surprised.

"Oh, yes. I can't think of a man I know with more integrity. The nation could use his influence in countering the Regent's sometimes . . . unfortunate excesses. Do you plan to make your home in London?"

Tatiana hesitated. She had never before considered that Lucas might better serve the nation he loved in active duty than in cultivating roses. "I cannot say. Lucas must decide."

"It is good to have him back, in any case," Hyde Parker said warmly, before the parting of the lines separated them.

When the dance ended, she declined an offer for the next set and made her way into the card room, thinking to tell Lucas of Hyde Parker's compliment. She found him seated in a hand of hazard against Lord Barton, and stood beside him, her hand resting lightly on his shoulder. Watching him play, she thought at first he was deliberately allowing his opponent to best him. But she soon recognized he was playing senselessly—not recklessly, but with no attention at all. "The nine, I think," she ventured, as he tugged out a queen for discard.

"What's that?"

She tapped the card in his hand. "That one. Lord Barton has three queens laid."

"Has he?" He took a swig from his glass. "So he has. You go on, then, and finish for me. I am all done in."

"Lucas . . ."

He looked at her, his eyes hazy. "What?"

"Nothing," she murmured, holding her head high beneath Lord Barton's curious gaze. "Go on to bed. We cannot have you nodding off in the midst of Prinny's fireworks tomorrow night." He stood up from his chair, kissed the air beside her ear, and disappeared.

The rest of the evening was sheer misery for her. The countess was in a froth over Lucas's desertion, and said so bluntly when the last of the guests were gone. "This was supposed to be a party to celebrate your betrothal! That he should not ask you to dance even *once*—"

Tatiana hushed her with a quick glance at Smithers, who had come up behind Dulcie like a black-coated vulture. "I merely wished to inquire, milady, if there will be anything more," he intoned somberly.

"Yes. No. Oh, I am all out of sorts. I believe I'll go give my son a piece of my mind."

"I wish you would not," Tatiana said quietly. "The fault is mine. I . . . I quarreled with him this morning."

"You two do nothing but quarrel! What was it this time? Politics? Religion?" Tatiana shook her head. Smithers was still hovering, and looking smug. The countess considered her curiously. "Well, every love affair will have its ups and downs. Did you apologize?"

"Oh, yes. As soon as I saw him this evening."

"Don't fret about it, then. He isn't one to hold a grudge." She paused. "Actually, he is. But not with you, I'm sure. No, you have done your part. And regardless of what went on between you, he might have been more sensible of *my* feelings! Let him stew in his juices."

Smithers cleared his throat discreetly. "I was told in the kitchens, milady, he has had two bottles of claret sent up since he retired."

Tatiana glared at him. Bloody tattletale! "Well! That settles it!" Dulcie declared. "I'm not about to go to him if he's in *that* sort of mood! If this is what coming to London means, I wish he'd stayed in Dorset!"

So do I, Tatiana thought regretfully. She decided then and there to make a clean breast of the letter. She ought to have done so this morning; that she hadn't was the cause of this unhappiness. "If you'll excuse me, milady, I am much fatigued."

"I shouldn't wonder at it. Never fear—he will come around by morning. The Admiral always did. What, Smithers, are you still here? See that the back parlor is well-aired; there were cigars in there."

"Very good, milady." He headed off to the kitchens. Tatiana climbed the staircase, paused to make sure the butler wasn't following her, then made the turn toward Lucas's rooms.

No light showed beneath his door, and she was about to turn back when in the silence she heard the chink of glass against glass and a muttered curse. She knocked timidly, mindful of how she'd chided him for breaking in on her. "Go away," came his voice, slurred with wine.

"It is I, Lucas."

Another chink of glass, another burst of cursing. "Go away," he said again.

"I want to apologize to you, Lucas. There is something I must tell you—"

He started laughing. "Something you must tell *me*? Oh, that's rich."

"Won't you let me come in?"

"No," he said bluntly. "I don't want to see you."

The words brought tears to her eyes. "Please, Lucas. As you love me—" He was laughing again. Well! My offense was not so grave as *that*, she thought furiously, spinning away from the door. Then she heard him catch his breath in what might have been a sob. Frightened now instead of angry, she grabbed for the knob. It turned in her grip, and the door swung open to show him sitting by the window in a patch of pale moonlight, the bottle and glass in his hands.

He raised his head. "Dammit all. Thought I'd locked that."

She went to him, arms outstretched. "Darling, forgive me. I was wrong to keep a secret from you. But I was so surprised—and I feared you would not let me do as the letter said."

He stared at her as she stood swathed in moonlight. Then he lowered his gaze. "Go away," he mumbled. "Leave me be. Leave me be!"

She knelt beside him, clasping his wrist. "Don't be angry, love! I cannot bear it!"

"Me? Angry with you?" Now his laughter sounded broken, hollow. "What right would I have?"

"You have every right! I was keeping a secret!"

He moved his fist, and she sprang away, startled. "Don't talk to me of secrets."

"But, Lucas, we always have been honest with each other."

"Have we?" he asked, so coldly that she flinched from him.

"Of course! You have always known the truth about me. You were the only one who did."

"And you know . . . the truth about me as well. Christ, I did not know the truth myself!" He yanked her to him by her hands. "Come and sit in my lap, why don't you, and prattle about what a hero I am. Tell me again how no other man in England—nay, in all the world!—would have saved you at Mizhakovsk."

His grasp was so tight it was frightening. "That is true," she whispered, and shivered a little in his arms. His intensity was so odd, so strange. . . . He put his mouth to hers, kissing her with furious passion, tugging back her head by the hair. "Lucas, have mercy!" She fought to keep her voice light; he was tearing at her gown with his fist, ripping it from her breasts.

"I . . . want . . . you . . . as I have never wanted anything on earth."

"And you may have me, Lucas!" Her bewilderment subsided. He lusted for her. Of course. And she had spurned him that morning. . . . "You may have me," she repeated. "Now, my love. Now. It never was my wish to wait."

"Take you—" He put his head to her breast, caught its tip, pulling so hard that she gasped. He wrenched at her skirts, trying to draw them up above her waist. They caught beneath her knees; he tore them free with a violent oath. Tatiana began to tremble. This was beyond passion. She had never seen him this way.

"Lucas, go easy—"

His motions were frantic and clumsy, hands made awkward by wine and brandy. She tensed as he ripped her drawers away, deluged by qualms. Was this the price he meant to make her pay? He stood, thrusting her into the chair, then yanked his breeches down. She saw his manhood, long and throbbing, and raised her gaze to his face as he came at her. The moon had caught his eyes; they were thunderous, blue subsumed completely by the black clouds. She could not help herself. She let out a small, fearful cry, and pushed him away.

He fell back with a thud, straight to the floor, and sat there, dazed. "God. God, what have I done!"

She scrambled down beside him, instantly contrite. "It is all right, Lucas. Forgive me."

"Forgive *you?*" He started laughing once more, but there was no mistaking the pain in the sound. "Oh, Tatiana. If only . . ."

"What?" she whispered.

"The past," he ground out. "The past. Poor Tatiana—"

"Is it something you have learned about me?" she asked in rising horror.

He shook his heavy head. "Something I have learned . . . about myself." He straightened then, with drunken dignity. "I must ask you to release me from our betrothal."

It was the last thing in the world she expected. She stared at him, aghast. "Lucas! Why?" He said nothing, only averted his eyes, the storm gone from them now. "Don't you love me?" she asked faintly, disbelieving.

"I—" She saw him hesitate. That was enough, though. She stood up, the tattered gown gathered around her, blinded by her tears.

"I see! It is well, then, that we came to London, since it has clarified your feelings for me." She meant to maintain her arrogant posture, but a sob betrayed her. "I am good enough to hanker after in Dorset, I suppose, or even for a tumble here in London, but not good enough to take the precious Strathmere name!"

"Tatiana, it isn't you!"

"Evidently not," she agreed, recovering her composure with sheer strength of will. "I won't ask who it is. I'm sure she is infinitely my better. I wish you all the happiness you deserve—you bastard!"

"Tatiana!" he cried, the name a hopeless sigh.

But she had had enough of the whims of the lofty. She went to her own rooms, and locked the door behind her very steadily.

Thirty

THE COUNTESS'S EXTREME perturbation with her son could brook only so much delay in its airing. She gave him until after breakfast to make an appearance, and when he failed to show she marched up to his rooms in a flurry of righteous anger, intending to make him answer for his unspeakable behavior at her party the night before. She found Larkin, his valet, polishing boots in the anteroom, and she brushed past him. "M'lady," the fellow hissed at her.

She whipped her head around. "What?"

"I wouldn't go in there if I was ye."

Dulcie raised her chin. "*There's* an absurd notion," she declared, and threw the door open with a bang.

Lucas lay sprawled across his bed, still in his evening clothes. Dulcie went and yanked back the curtains, letting in a flood of midmorning light. He didn't flinch. Her gaze took in the bottles lining the window seat, the sticky glass on the table. "Good God," she said with distaste.

Larkin had followed her so far as the doorway. "Told ye, didn't I? Drunk as a lord he was last night."

"What else *would* he be drunk as? Bring coffee," she commanded. When he'd gone, she took the water pitcher and poured it over her son's head.

He moaned, raising himself on his elbows, opening his eyes a crack. "I'd have a word with you," Dulcie said in a voice that would cut diamonds.

"Christ, go away."

"I will not! Not until you explain what prompted that abominable display of rudeness last night—to me, to your guests, but most of all to Tatiana!" He mumbled something, rolling over, trying to find a dry spot on which to put his head. "Look at you!" the countess raged.

"If you leave, you won't have to." He was tentatively exploring his muscles, finding he could move his fingers and toes, though not without pain. And the light was going to kill him. "Close the drapes."

"Aren't you due at Carlton House at noon? It is nearly that now!"

"Not going," he muttered, burrowing into the bed-clothes.

"Why the devil not?"

He'd dug past the physical pain now, into the much greater agony of his soul. "No reason to."

"No reason?" Dulcie fought for control. "You postpone your wedding, drag us all back here at the drop of a hat, and now you say there's no *reason*?"

"I'm not marrying her." That much he remembered telling Tatiana very clearly. What he needed to block out, even more than the light, was the terrible shame that had flooded her small face. Eyes clenched shut, he saw again the slight girl standing in the shadows with her needlework. . . . *I've tried and tried, but the threads just go awry.* Gillian's hair. His eyes. He could not help himself; he let out a cry of such desolation that Dulcie, startled, stretched a hand toward him.

"Lucas?"

"God, go away. Leave me in—" Peace. But peace was gone for him forever. *Don't you love me?* Tatiana had asked. "Dammit, dammit, dammit!" he cried to himself, to Gillian, to life, battering the pillows, twisting to tear the bed curtains straight off their hooks in his impotent rage.

Dulcie's heart went out to him; suddenly he reminded her of the tantruming child he'd been so many years before. Once upon a time, she thought, I could soothe any hurt with a kiss and a hug. *What can I do for you now, my beloved son?* She moved to the bedside. "Lucas. Nothing is permanent. Whatever has made this breach between you—"

He turned on her so suddenly that she fell back, frightened by the wild look in his eyes. "You are wrong," he spat. "Blood and bone—these things last. There are errors that can never be put right."

"What . . . what have you done?" she whispered in alarm.

Ruined his life. Ruined hers, and Gillian's, and Lord Innisford's—and Tatiana's. Against his will he saw in his memory the blood of her maidenhead staining his sheets. He bowed his head, fists clenching the covers so tightly that his knuckles were white. Dulcie waited for as long as she could stand it; then she whirled to Larkin, who was cowering in the anteroom. "Get coffee in him," she said briskly, and hurried off to Tatiana's rooms.

There was a trunk open in front of the wardrobe there. Carruthers was singing to herself, wrapping gowns in tissue and laying them within it. Her song broke off abruptly when she saw the countess. "What are you doing?" Dulcie demanded.

"Packin' up, milady." The edge to Lady Strathmere's voice did not escape the maid; she quickly pulled the last gown off the pile. "On m'lady's orders. Have I done wrong?"

"Where is your lady?"

"Havin' breakfast with ye. Ain't—isn't she?"

Dulcie spun on her heel and strode down to the dining room, where Smithers was overseeing the clearing of the table. "Has Miss Grimaldi been down?" she queried the butler.

"No, milady. Shall I hold the platters for her?"

"I don't think so." She hurried back to Lucas's rooms. Too much up and down and back and forth had smothered her maternal instincts; she paused to catch her breath, feeling her age. He was still sprawled on the bed. She hurled an empty claret bottle at him; it glanced off his shoulder. "I don't know what you said or did to that poor girl," she said frostily, "to drive her away—"

That pierced his fog; he sat up, clutching his head. "Oh, God . . ."

"The coffee, Larkin!" Dulcie snapped. He sprang forward with the cup. Lucas took it and downed it, shuddering. When he looked up, his eyes were slightly less glazed.

"Driven her away? What do you mean?"

"She's gone. No sign of her in the house. Carruthers is packing her trunk, and was told she was coming down to breakfast. But Smithers hasn't seen her, and—"

"Jesus!" Lucas thrust the cup back at Larkin. "Another." He swallowed that, too, then turned his back on the countess and vomited into the chamber pot.

"For heaven's sake, Lucas!" She averted her gaze.

"Don't you understand, Mother? She is out there somewhere, without any protection!"

"Oh, I daresay she is gone to cry on Susannah's shoulder about what a bastard you are."

He flinched. She *had* called him that. "You think so?"

"It's what I would have done."

"Larkin. Go 'round to the Cuthberts' at once and see if Miss Grimaldi is there."

"Very good, m'lord."

Lucas went to pour water into the wash basin, saw the empty pitcher on the floor, and instead mopped his face with the damp sheets. Dulcie watched with a growing sense of horror. "Lucas. You can't be thinking—you must change your dress!"

"Who gives a bloody damn? I've got to talk to the servants. Someone must have seen her go, hailed her a hack." He tried to tie his soaked cravat, failed, and yanked it off, tossing it aside. Dulcie rummaged in his dresser and found him a clean one. "Forget it," he said with annoyance.

"If you expect to be answered like a lord, you ought to look like one."

He tied it, amazed at how his hands were trembling. "Would you go and assemble the staff, please, Mother?" She thought of saying more, then went.

There were forty men and women waiting for him in the drawing room when he came down. Lucas surveyed their familiar faces and squared his aching shoulders. "Miss Grimaldi—" he said, and had to pause to swallow.

Beside him, the countess's voice rang out clearly. "Miss Grimaldi left the house this morning sometime before nine o'clock. His Lordship is concerned for her safety. If any of you saw her leave or know aught about her whereabouts, say so now and there will be no repercussions. If His Lordship discovers you have been untruthful, though, whoever you are, you will lose your place."

The faces stared back at her. Lucas contemplated each in turn, summoning his will. Once he had had a sixth sense about such things . . . Smithers. His wife. Clarrie. Cook. Carruthers . . . His gaze moved past Tatiana's maid, abruptly returned. "Carruthers?"

"I'm sure I don't know, m'lord," she began, frightened. "She said nothing to me—"

"But you heard something. You know something."

"No! I ain't—*haven't* got any idea!" He stared at her, his blue eyes so stormy that she finally added haltingly, "Not unless it might be about the letter."

"What letter?" he demanded.

"The letter what came yesterday morn."

Vaguely, through layers of brandy-sotted brain, Lucas recalled that there *had* been a letter. She'd been reading it. . . . He pictured her, thrusting it into the pillows, sending the chocolate pot spilling. She'd gathered up the linens— what had happened then? She'd given them to Carruthers. "Who was the letter from?" he barked.

"I don't know, I'm sure! But I heard it crackle in the bedclothes when I took them down to laundry, so I pulled it out."

Larkin burst in through the back door. "No sign o' her at the Cuthberts', m'lord."

The letter. What had she said when she'd come in last night? *I was wrong to keep a secret from you* . . . "Where is the letter now?" he asked Carruthers, with sudden gentleness.

"I don't know, m'lord! I gave it to Mr. Smithers. That's what I was taught to do, wasn't I, when anything in the household seemed amiss?"

"Smithers?" Lucas turned to him.

The butler gave a little laugh. "Forgive me, milord, but I burned it."

"Burned it?"

"Aye, milord. Seeing that Miss Grimaldi had bundled it up with the soiled sheets, I saw no purpose in returning it."

Mrs. Smithers, standing at his side, was looking most uncomfortable, folding her apron in her hands. The butler was nattering on about linens and the fact that the paper had been crumpled and smeared with chocolate. Dulcie nodded her head in approval. "He's quite right, Lucas," she murmured. "Since Tatiana had discarded it—"

Lucas could not tear his gaze from the housekeeper's nervous hands. "Did you burn it before or after you read it, Smithers?" he asked the butler.

Smithers drew himself up, highly offended. "Milord! Such an insinuation—"

"Just answer the question, you insufferable prig."

"See here, Lucas," the countess said indignantly.

"Be still, Mother. Did you read it?"

"Of course not!" Smithers declared with all the haughtiness he was capable of.

"Liar," Lucas snarled. "You're dismissed. Permanently. Without references."

"M'lord!" Mrs. Smithers burst out, ignoring her husband's elbow digging into her side. "M'lord, he couldn't have read it!"

"And why not?" Lucas asked, a dangerous edge to his tone.

"Because it was in some heathen tongue!"

The last glimmer of hope for Tatiana's safety withered in Lucas's soul. "Oh, God. Oh, Jesus." He staggered against the wall.

"He saw the signature, though."

Lucas raised his head at this unexpected addendum. "What was it? Who signed it?" Smithers didn't answer. Lucas leapt for his throat, sending the servants scurrying away. "Tell me, by God, or I'll choke it out of you!"

"The Cossack!" Smithers gasped, as Lucas's huge hands curled around his neck. "The one with the white horse! Platov—Hetman Platov!"

Platov. Lucas released him so abruptly that the butler fell to the floor. "If any harm has come to her, I swear on my soul, I'll kill you!"

The countess looked genuinely alarmed. "Oh, Lucas. You must go and find her. If that wild monster has her—"

The door knocker sounded three times in quick succession. Everyone in the room stood frozen, immobile. It rang out again. Lucas grabbed Smithers up, thrust him toward the front of the house. "Go and answer it, damn you." The butler, slightly wild-eyed, straightened his livery and went. He returned a few moments later bearing a card on his tray. Lucas stared at it in disbelief, then rushed for the doorway.

Dulcie plucked the card up and gave an audible gasp. *Hetman Matvei Platov*, it read.

The leader of the Don Cossacks was standing in the vestibule, clad in an earth-brown tunic and wide breeches tucked into sueded boots, with pistols and a long, curving saber in his belt. Behind him in the street Lucas saw two of his soldiers on horseback—armed with spears, for God's sake—one holding the reins to the fabled white stallion. They shared their leader's swart skin and glossy black hair. God knows what the neighbors will make of this, Lucas thought as Hetman Platov snapped his heels together. "I do not speak English," he told Lucas in Russian.

"I know your language." Lucas was wishing he was armed as thoroughly as his opponent. There was a pistol—unloaded, alas—in the desk drawer in his study. "Won't you come this way?" The Cossack followed him, pausing only to mutter something Lucas did not catch to the soldiers in the street.

In his study, Lucas offered Platov a chair. The hetman preferred to stand. So Lucas stood as well, behind his desk, and suggested refreshment—wine or ale, perhaps? Platov declined, for which Lucas was grateful; hospitality would have decreed that he drink, too, a prospect he felt far from up to. The Cossack's eyes, a brown so dark they glittered like coal, scanned the book-lined walls. "Do you read a great deal, Hetman Platov?" Lucas asked icily.

He snorted. "Not at all. I know, however, you do. And you raise flowers. Roses, no?"

Lucas let his hand edge toward the drawer-pull. "You surprise me, sir. I cannot imagine how you would have become acquainted with that fact."

"I know other things besides that." The Russian soldier's hand, scarred and weatherworn, ran across the smooth leather back of a chair. "I know, for instance, that a few years past, you took a trip to my country. To take possession of something that had been . . . entrusted to your care."

Lucas stared back at him steadily, but in his mind's eye he was picturing the interior of the drawer, the placement of the gun and bullets. How long would it take him? Six, seven seconds. By which time he'd be dead. Platov did not have the air of a man who would suffer fools gladly. "You are well-informed indeed," he said softly.

"I consider it a necessity. As you did when you served your country as a . . . diplomat."

Lucas made a deprecating motion. "All that was a long time ago."

Platov nodded. "But the skills from such a career never really desert one." Lucas shrugged noncommittally. He was trying to gather his instinct, his senses, and inwardly cursing the bacchanal he'd engaged in the night before. Tatiana's life hung on the answers he made to this menacing foreigner, who contemplated his creased coat and damp shirt with those glittering eyes. "I have not been long in England, Lord Strathmere, and am not fully versed in your customs. But unless I am mistaken, those are evening clothes."

Damn the pistol, Lucas thought; I'll go for his throat. "I haven't been to bed," he said bluntly. He was tempted to add that he knew of the Cossack's letter to Tatiana, but held off, with an effort. Knowledge is power, he reminded himself.

Platov brought a hand up to his short, thick mustache. "I hope nothing is . . . amiss?"

You know damned well what's amiss, you bloody swaggering bastard. But Platov wasn't swaggering, exactly. Lucas had the sense he was being judged, his measure being taken by the Cossack's hard, quick mind. He returned the man's gaze without flinching. He would prevail. By Christ, he *would* prevail. Platov had given him an opening, about the roses and his trip to Russia. The rules required that he offer one in return. "I have lost something," he admitted.

"Was this something . . . precious?"

"Very," Lucas grated out.

"So that is how it is." Platov turned his back on Lucas, going to the window and pulling aside the draperies to look down at the street. Lucas made his move for the drawer, and had the pistol in his hand when he heard the Cossack sigh. The sound was so unexpected that he missed the bullets he'd been groping for. "Lord Strathmere. I have not been honest with you. I have been assured you are a man of honor. Let us begin again, on that footing. You knew Casimir Molitzyn."

"I knew him well," Lucas said proudly. "I counted him a friend."

"As did I," the Cossack said, to Lucas's surprise. "He was my cousin. Our mothers were sisters. We were raised in the same village."

Lucas reached back over the years. "My God. He spoke of a cousin. Mat, he called him." For Matvei.

"He spoke of you to me," Platov went on, coming toward Lucas again, "whenever I saw him. And with great respect. In fact, the last time I visited him before his posting to Paris, he told me that he intended to pass on to you for safekeeping a *tovarka*—a treasure—in the event of his death."

"Did he tell you the nature of this . . . treasure?"

Platov shook his head. "But I think I spoke to her a few evenings past, on the dais at Carlton House. Am I wrong, Lord Strathmere?"

Casimir's own cousin . . . "No." Lucas slid the drawer shut with the bullets inside.

"My cousin was a young man when he died," Platov noted, that weathered hand curling on a chair back.

"I know. A terrible tragedy. Dysentery—"

"I went home to our village for the funeral," Platov said, speaking right through him. "I helped prepare his body for the burial. And I saw on it signs that he had been tortured. Subtle things, not likely to be noticed—unless one was acquainted with the latest techniques."

"My God," Lucas said softly, slowly.

"I asked myself, Why should anyone torture Casimir?" Lucas was astonished at his calm, even tone; only those glittering eyes betrayed the emotion his stolid manner hid. "Then I remembered his *tovarka* that he had hidden away."

"Someone had tried to kill him once before," Lucas interjected.

"I know. You saved him. He told me that was thugs, waterfront smugglers. To track him so far as Paris, though, hunt him down, do to him what was done—" For a moment those eyes blinked. "This was not the work of amateurs, Lord Strathmere."

Lucas went toward the sideboard. "Let me pour you some wine."

But Platov shook him off. "I have vodka." He pulled out a flask. "May I offer you some?"

"Christ, no!"

The Cossack smiled for the first time. It made him look a good deal less demonic. "A taste one must be born to, perhaps." He took a healthy swig and wiped his mustache. "So. Lord Strathmere returns to Russia for a very brief visit on the heels of my cousin's murder. A village in Ologda province burns to the ground—a tragedy laid, most unjustly, upon my people. Lord Strathmere resurfaces in Brighton, accompanied by a very fair cousin with a Russian name."

"Italian," Lucas corrected him. "Grimaldi is Italian. How did you learn these things?"

"I have my contacts in England, just as you have in Russia."

"I tried to speak to you once, in Russia. Last winter," Lucas pointed out with a hint of anger. "You refused to see me."

"I had a war to fight," Hetman Platov said simply. "My nation's honor was at stake." There was no apology in his tone, and Lucas liked him all the more for that. "Now I find myself here with leisure to pursue what is, after all, a personal affair. But I *was* curious to meet you, Lord Strathmere. Very curious indeed. I was hoping you could tell me—why did Casimir choose you?"

"I've wondered that myself." *Only ten thousand times . . .*

"He tried to hide his treasure in Russia. He feared, clearly, his protection might fail her. In case it did, he made arrangements for her retrieval with an Englishman. What does this suggest?"

"An English connection," Lucas said thoughtfully.

"Precisely. One assumes, therefore, that the French had no reason to torture Casimir to learn her whereabouts. Only the Russians or the English would."

"But that Casimir himself was entrusted with this treasure argues Russian parentage."

"It takes two to procreate," the Cossack said, smiling slightly. "Regardless of nationality."

"Her mother must be Russian."

"Of course."

"And her father—English? God! It never occurred to me. . . . Who is the mother?"

"I have no idea."

Lucas believed him. "Twice last summer, someone tried to kill her." He swallowed. "Now she is missing. She left my house early this morning. I am . . . greatly concerned."

"As am I. I sent a letter to her yesterday, asking her to meet me this morning at nine at my hotel. She never appeared."

"Why did you write her?"

"Because," said Matvei Platov, coal eyes burning, "I intend to find who killed my cousin and repay his death."

Lucas bit his lip. "I hardly think it likely Casimir's death can be linked to Tatiana. In his work for the Tsar, he must have made enemies. Any one of them might have—"

"Perhaps. All of this has crossed my mind as well. Yet . . ." He paused, seeming ill at ease for the first time since he'd entered the study. "When I saw her—Miss Grimaldi—at the reception two nights past . . . Lord Strathmere, I am not, believe me, a fanciful man. Yet there is something about that girl that makes me think she is at the root of his murder. She puts me in mind of something, someone . . ." He shook his head, as though to clear it of such frivolous thoughts.

"Tatiana knows nothing about her true parents," Lucas protested.

The Cossack bowed a little. "I trust your judgment on that. But when she did not appear at my hotel, I had my doubts. I must admit, I prevaricated in my letter. I told her I had information as to who her parents were. I assumed she would come if she did not know their identity. Thus, when she failed to arrive . . ."

"You came here." Lucas nodded in understanding. "But your—instinct, shall we call it?—is wrong this time. Tatiana's disappearance is certainly unconnected with the death of your cousin. You see, we quarrelled last night."

"Yet you do not know where she is gone."

"Up until five minutes past, I thought you had abducted her," Lucas said with grim humor. "Now I am more inclined to believe she is hidden in Susannah Cuthbert's wardrobe."

"I hope that you are right." The Cossack still sounded dubious. "But I must not intrude on your time any more than I have. Will you inform me when you find Miss Grimaldi?"

"I will bring her to you, if you like. She has fond memories of Casimir. I'm sure she will enjoy visiting with you."

Platov brought his heels together once more, making a small bow. "Thank you for receiving me, Lord Strathmere."

"My pleasure, Hetman Platov."

The Cossack was almost to the door when he turned suddenly. "Lord Strathmere. I wonder if I might ask one more favor of you."

"Certainly, certainly," Lucas said quickly, anxious to be rid of him so that he could track Tatiana down. All his fears suddenly seemed absurd. If Hetman Platov hadn't abducted her, who else would have?

"I have a list here"—he reached into his coat—"of English agents who were once in Russian pay, but who cut themselves off from our service once the Tsar ended his alliance with the Corsican. It occurred to me that one of them might be behind Casimir's death."

"I know several gentlemen in the Foreign Office who would give their eyeteeth for that list," Lucas said with a laugh. "The English Bonapartists have been a constant thorn in our side."

"I'll be happy to show it to you—if you will tell me what you know of the whereabouts of each at the time of Casimir's death."

"I don't know how much help I can be . . ." Lucas took

the paper, scanned the brief column of names. "Tre-lawney—he left for America nine years past; you can safely discount him. Michael Cartwright—aye, we've known of him for a dog's age, but he's tight as new boots with the Regent; can't lay a finger on him. John Buskirk—God, was he working for Napoleon? There's one I never suspected. And we were together at Oxford. He's a possibility, perhaps. Willoughby—who the devil's Willoughby?"

"Attaché to your embassy in—"

"Paris." Lucas had placed the name—and the man. Tall, thin, gray-haired, long mustache. The official whom he'd visited at the embassy in Paris last spring just before he'd had a knife stuck into his ribs on the Boulevard de l'Hôpital. The man to whom he'd posed questions about Casimir's death . . . and, he suddenly realized, the same man he'd seen coming out of the gazebo in Regent's Park in Brighton with Gillian Innisford on his arm, the afternoon that Tatiana was attacked. He pictured Gillian just the afternoon before, pouring him tea in her demure black gown. *Poor Harry. That was his own fault, wasn't it, for dabbling in matters so far above his head.* The flowers on her mantel—the card, signed by Willoughby. *Your slave* . . .

Willoughby and Gillian. Gillian and Willoughby. The knife in his flesh. The flash of his gun on the bank of the Thames so many years ago . . .

"Does the name Gillian Innisford mean anything to you, Platov?" he asked abruptly.

The Cossack laughed. "I've not made the acquaintance of the . . . lady." His pause was meaningful. "But she is staying at the Pultenay, as am I."

Lucas's mind was ratcheting from thought to thought with rattling quickness. Willoughby was an agent of the French. He was evidently intimate with Gillian. And they'd both been there in Regent's Park that day. The Pultenay Hotel. Tatiana's appointment with Platov—she would not have missed that rendezvous for anything, not after what had passed between them last night. He knew with sudden certainty that she'd gone to the hotel in answer to the Cossack's invitation. What had become of her since, he could not even guess.

"Come on," he said, and tugged Platov toward the door.

"Where are we going?" the Cossack asked in surprise.

"To your hotel. To call on Lady Innisford about Lord Willoughby."

"I have not been introduced to her," the Cossack protested. "We have no acquaintance."

"I have," Lucas told him shortly. "To my eternal regret, I have."

Thirty-One

*L*UCAS MEANT TO send 'round to the mews for his bay, but Matvei Platov did not intend for him to wait. He ordered one of his henchmen down in brusque military language and left him, with his spear and all, to stand guard over the house. Lucas didn't argue; he raised himself into the vacated saddle, then started as the horse, a big-boned black, snorted and promptly reared. Platov, from atop his magical white stallion, looked at Lucas with a ghost of a smile. "He likes a firm hand," he warned. "All Cossack horses do."

Lucas tugged at the reins, digging in his heels, and finally got the bloody beast to more or less settle. Platov set off at a blistering pace, oblivious to the traffic—carts, couriers, ladies out to stroll—along the narrow street. Lucas followed as best he could; the black made a mockery of the common equine description *spirited*. Fortunately, Platov had already sent all bystanders scurrying out of the way.

Firm hand . . . Christ, the horse's mouth was brass; no amount of yanking at the bit had any effect. Near Burlington Street he took offense at a pigeon rising up from the road and spun in a full circle, hooves stamping like a Spanish dancer's feet. As Lucas grappled for control, he caught sight of the spearman trailing after him, who was rolling his eyes. "Fucking bloody beast," Lucas muttered, and then shouted its equivalent in Russian. To his astonishment, the black broke into a relatively placid canter. He glanced back at the spearman, who nodded, broad face split in a grin.

"That's the way!" he called approvingly. "You must talk to horses as you talk to women!"

Lucas winced at this evidence of the female Cossack's lot. But verbal abuse did seem the trick to controlling the black. He clattered through the turn onto Piccadilly only moments after Platov, and drew up beside the Cossack at the hotel before he could dismount. "You like the horse?" Platov asked, tossing his reins to the stableboy.

"I—" Lucas realized he did, very much. It had been entirely satisfying to ride through the most fashionable thoroughfares of London screaming Russian curses. "Yes. Very spirited."

Platov laughed, his even teeth showing white against his dark skin. "He is yours."

"Oh, no. I couldn't possibly—"

"In memory of the regard in which my cousin held you."

Put that way, how could Lucas not accept the gift? He bowed. "I am in your debt."

"Pay it," the Cossack said as they entered the Pultenay, "by helping me avenge his death."

We must make an odd pair, Lucas thought, glancing at the servant who came hurrying toward them, brows slightly raised. "Forgive me, sir," he told Lucas, "but we do not permit gentlemen in our hotel unless they are properly attired." Platov snarled something at him in Russian, and he backed nervously away.

"Don't you know who I am, man?" Lucas demanded in pure, rolling *ton* accent. The perplexed servant shook his head. "Then you don't deserve a post at the Pultenay." With Platov matching him stride for stride despite the difference in their heights, he ran up the curving staircase all the way to the third floor. Platov had cocked his pistol. Lucas shot him a glance. "I trust we won't be needing that."

"You did not see Casimir's body," the Cossack said briefly.

They paused outside the door to Gillian's suite. Platov moved to kick in the door, but Lucas waved him back. "Let me go in alone," he mouthed.

The Cossack hesitated, then nodded. "If you are not out in three minutes—"

"Ten," Lucas told him. "This is England, dammit. You must allow time for niceties." He pushed his companion out of sight as he knocked at the door.

It was opened by one of the liveried boys. "Lord Strathmere, to call on Lady Innisford," Lucas said in his best bland, bored aristocrat's tone.

"M'lady is not at home, m'lord," the boy replied, and went to close the door.

Lucas wedged his boot between it and the jamb. "Then would you be so kind as to announce me to Miss Innisford?"

"Miss Innisford?" The boy cast a glance behind him.

"Aye, Miss Araminta Innisford."

"Who is it, Derward?" a voice, as bland and bored as Lucas's, asked from the shadows within. A male voice, unfamiliar.

"Forgive me, m'lord," the boy piped to Lucas, half-closing the portal and scurrying off. Platov was inching forward in the hallway; Lucas had to glare at him to keep him back. There was a flurry of whispers. Then the door opened again.

"Lord Hastings, sir," said the smooth, blond man, younger than Lucas and nattily dressed, with a short, curling beard. He ushered him in. "May I be of service?"

Lucas, scenting Platov about to rush in with his pistol, kicked the door shut behind him, wondering from what point the Cossack might begin to count. He bowed to Hastings, who was unknown to him except by reputation—an intimate of Prinny's, a here-and-thereian, reputedly the best vingt-et-un player in England. And not, he noted mentally, on Platov's list.

"I came to call on Lady Innisford," Lucas said easily, sprawling into a chair that had not been offered. "Since she's not at home, I thought to visit with her charming daughter instead."

"Miss Innisford is too young to receive male callers in her mother's absence," Lord Hastings said with just the right air of deprecation.

"A most delightful little miss," Lucas noted approvingly. "She was having trouble with her needlework when last I saw her. I only thought to inquire how her 'broidery fared."

"I'll certainly inform her of your kind interest in her progress." Hastings smiled.

Lucas cleared his throat. "The dust on these London streets is abominable, isn't it? A drop of claret would drive it from my gullet, though."

Perfectly coolly, Hastings signaled to the boy. "Claret for Lord Strathby."

A nice touch, getting my name wrong, Lucas thought, all his senses alert. "Perhaps I might make free to remain here until Lady Innisford's return?"

Hastings laughed. "You'd have a tedious time of it. I do not anticipate her arrival until after the conclusion of the Regent's ball this evening. There was a *major* revision to be made to the gown she planned to wear, and the mantua-maker could not fit her in until noon. Lady Innisford anticipated going directly to the reception from there."

The boy had brought the wine. Lucas pretended to sip from it while inwardly counting. Four minutes. He had six left—*if* Platov was reckoning from when he'd shut the door. "Miss Araminta is too young to receive gentlemen callers," he said above the rim of his cup. "But not too young to be left here alone with you?"

Hastings laughed and wagged a finger. "Oh, I know what you are thinking! She is worth a great deal, that little one, to the fortunate fellow who becomes her husband. But I am far removed from the fray, and my presence here is perfectly proper. Lady Innisford and I are engaged."

"Are you? I had no idea!" Genially Lucas stood and crossed to him to pump his hand. "My heartfelt felicitations! She is a most remarkable woman. Do you know, she and I came very close to being married once upon a time. But you would not recall it. You must have still been in short pants then."

Hastings stiffened abruptly, with something in his manner that reminded Lucas achingly of his own blind passion for Gillian so many years before. "If that is meant to be some sort of disparaging comment about the lady's age—"

"No, no. Not at all." *Four minutes left, at most. Please God, Cossack, be patient.* "She is the embodiment of youth, and whimsy, and recklessness. I applaud you, milord, for succeeding where I failed. If you perceive any disgruntlement on my part, put it down to the ravages of jealousy. So you are to be little Araminta's stepfather! It's a role to which you seem well-suited, protective as you are. Yet I daresay, since you are here in milady's absence, it would not be improper for me to pay Miss Innisford my respects."

Hastings reached for his wineglass, sipped. Buying

time . . . Then he shrugged and smiled, and snapped his fingers again. "Derward. Show Miss Innisford in."

Two minutes. The boy scampered off. "Are you attending the Regent's gala, Lord Hastings?" Lucas asked pleasantly.

"I shall meet my fiancée there."

Lucas nodded knowingly. "Women and their wardrobes. My own intended—my cousin, Miss Grimaldi—has vanished into thin air, no doubt on some equally vital errand of apparel." He glanced toward the doorway as the timid girl from the afternoon before presented herself there. "Miss Innisford! How splendid to see you again. You have your embroidery silks unlooped by now, I trust?"

"I—" Her gaze, storm-blue ringed with black, glanced off his to Lord Hastings, returned. "Lord Strathmere, ai—isn't it?"

"You have a fine memory, my dear." *One minute.* Lucas stooped suddenly to pluck something up from the dark-patterned carpet. "But here's a bit of thread that has escaped your needle." He handed her the hank that had caught his eye the moment he entered the room—white-blond, as long as his arm.

She stared at it, perplexed. "That ai—isn't—silk, milord. That's a bit of—"

"Get back to your 'broidery," Lord Hastings interrupted, "lest your mamma find you—"

That was when Platov, pistol lowered, burst the door in.

Lucas had to hand it to him. He made a terrifying show: the saber clenched in his teeth, his dark face smoldering, black eyes glittering, the gun aimed straight at Hastings's heart. Araminta let out a scream. "What's your name?" Lucas barked at her while she was still open-mouthed, trembling.

"Araminta Innis—"

"What is your name?"

Platov whipped the barrel of the gun toward her. "Becca Sinkler!" she screeched, and covered her head with her hands. "Just please don't let him kill me!"

"Where are you from, Becca Sinkler?"

"Smithfield, m'lord! Jesus, don't let him—"

"Put the gun down, Matvei," Lucas said in Russian. The Cossack trained it on Hastings instead. "Smithfield Market? Lady Innisford found you there?"

"Aye, m'lord! 'N' said she'd pay me five pounds—"

"Shut up, you stupid wench!" Lord Hastings snarled.

"Is he Willoughby?" Platov demanded of Lucas. "Did he kill my cousin?"

"No. But he knows where Willoughby is."

"May I?" the Cossack asked, advancing.

"As you please. Mind, though, we are in a public hotel. Nothing too loud, if you please."

Hastings had been looking from one to the other as they spoke in Russian, his pretty face no longer bland nor bored. "Milord," he cried to Lucas, "I beg you, as one Englishman to another—" Platov sliced the saber right between his legs, so deftly that his breeches split along the inseam, straight as a tailor's cut. "Jesus!" He backed so far into his chair that it flipped over, sending him sprawling. "Get him away from me! For Christ's sake, Derward, fetch the management!"

"Don't move, Derward," Lucas told the boy, who did not seem much inclined to. His gaze, dark as Platov's, was fixed on the saber; he had his legs crossed tight. "Unless you want the next stroke to catch flesh, Lord Hastings, I'd strongly suggest you tell us Miss Grimaldi's whereabouts."

"I don't know what you're—" Platov kicked the toppled chair aside and hooked the tip of the saber into the cowering man's handsomely cascading cravat.

"Just the knot, Matvei," Lucas said in Russian.

With a minute motion of his wrist, the Cossack sliced it

free—then nicked off both ends for good measure. "You're bloody madmen!" Hastings gasped.

"Can you do the buttons, Matvei?"

"Shirt or breeches?"

"Breeches, I think." Lucas grinned at the frantic young man. "I wouldn't move just now if I were you," he said to Hastings.

One after another, the silver buttons whipped into the air. Hastings had gone pale as paste. "If I knew anything, don't you think I'd tell you?" he pleaded, hands shielding his privates.

"I'm not sure. We've only just met. But if you knew my friend better, you would."

Platov's black eyes glittered. "He needs a shave, Lord Strathmere, don't you think?"

"Call me Lucas. Please. Take half off," he suggested. The blade snickered forward. Hastings screamed as a little snow of downy blond curls feathered across the rug. "Would you care to reexamine your memory, Lord Hastings, before my colleague digs deeper?"

The young lord was beaten, and he knew it. "They took her to Mrs. Cuttleby's," he said sullenly, reaching for his tattered cravat. "Now, call him off me!"

Platov had turned to Lucas, black brows raised in question. "What does he say?"

"By God, give *me* that blade." Platov handed it over. Lucas raised it above his head, took a breath, then another, as Hastings quivered at his feet. Then he lowered it slowly. "Derward."

"Aye, m'lord?" The boy leapt to attention.

"Can you tie a knot?"

"I am very good with ropes, m'lord." His teeth gleamed.

"Tie up this bit of trash."

Platov knelt to gag Hastings with the sliced-off cravat.

The boy paused a moment, surveying the room, then yanked the pulls from the draperies and used them to secure Lord Hastings's feet and hands. Platov tested the ties, then ruffled the boy's hair. "Fine work," he announced. The approval in his tone made Derward beam.

Lucas turned to Araminta—Becca, rather—who was standing like a statue, eyes wide as plates. "Go home to Smithfield, young lady. And next time easy money beckons, remember it is always more wise to be honest."

She dropped a grateful curtsy. "I never meant no harm, m'lord, indeed I didn't! She—Lady Innisford said it would be like a play!"

"Well, the show is over." She skittered to the door. "Wait," he said. "Were you paid?"

"M'lady said . . . on the morrow."

Trust Gilllian to put it off as long as she could. He took out a five-pound note and gave it to her. "Thank ye, m'lord," she murmured, and escaped.

Platov rose from his squat with muscular ease. "Leave him here, do you think, or put him in a wardrobe?" he asked, while Hastings's eyes above the gag lolled in terror.

Lucas turned to the boy. "Is there a large closet in the suite?"

"Aye, m'lord, in m'lady's rooms. This way." Lucas went to help, but Platov had already hoisted Hastings over his shoulder. They locked him in the wardrobe, gave Derward the key and ten pounds not to use it, and left the hotel.

The spearman was standing ready with their horses. A small crowd had gathered, drawn by the white stallion and the Cossack's reputation. Platov ignored the curious onlookers as he asked, "Where to, my friend?"

"We are going to visit a brothel, Matvei. I hope you will not be offended."

The Cossack shrugged. "One must see the sights, I suppose, when in foreign lands." But his dark eyes glittered dangerously as he spurred the white stallion straight into the crowd, sending them screaming, scattering out of his way.

Thirty-Two

THE BOY IN THE stable yard of Mrs. Cuttleby's establishment sat up on the stone wall, all agog, as the white and black stallions raced neck and neck through the gates, the black's rider screaming at the top of his lungs in some outlandish tongue. The two men vaulted from their saddles, and Lucas shouted to Platov, "You beat me, you bastard!"

"You must learn more Russian obscenities. Even a horse tires of hearing the same thing time and again."

Lucas switched to English, snapping his fingers at the boy. "Does your mistress pay you to lolligag about all day? Come and see to your work!"

"Y-yes, sir." He scrambled down from the wall, straightening his livery and brushing smudged fingers through his tow-colored hair.

"Water 'em well," Lucas said more gently, "and hold

them at ready. We won't be long." He tossed him a shilling. "Matvei, come on."

The butler who opened the door to them gave a little sniff before saying, with a hauteur worthy of Smithers, "Very sorry, sir, but proper attire is—"

"Stow it, Henthrop," Lucas growled, "and let us past."

Henthrop bestowed on him a longer glance. "Why— Lord Strathmere, isn't it? I scarcely knew you, milord, after all these years. Welcome, milord, welcome! I'll just go and tell the mistress that you're here."

"No need for that," Lucas said shortly. "We'll show ourselves in."

He pushed past the butler, followed by Platov, who had observed their exchange with knitted brows. "Are you a frequent visitor here?" he inquired politely.

"I was. A long time ago. What of it? Have you never been in a brothel?"

The Cossack's teeth glinted as he drew his saber and tested it against the horny nail of his thumb. "Often enough. But I never have paid."

Lucas laughed. "I'll wager you haven't. Do try and keep your bloodthirstiness under control. Ah, Mrs. Cuttleby!" Lucas bowed at the short, matronly woman in rustling silk who had paused at the foot of the staircase.

She hesitated only for a moment before stretching out her hands. "My *dear* Lord Strathmere! What a pleasure to have you with us again after so long a time!" Her gaze, faintly anxious, glanced off Platov's scowling face. "And who, pray tell, is your . . . companion?"

"Hetman Matvei Platov. Confidant and adviser to His Excellency, Tsar Alexander of Russia." Platov, hearing his name, scabbarded his saber and snapped his heels.

Mrs. Cuttleby bobbed a nervous curtsy in return. "Charmed, I'm sure. How may I be of service to you, Lord Strathmere?"

"Hetman Platov is desirous of feminine company."

Mrs. Cuttleby's apprehensive eyes surveyed the Cossack again; he bestowed on her a ghastly leer. She drew Lucas aside with a hand on his coat-sleeve. "Dear Lord Strathmere, I *don't* mean to be inhospitable, not by any means. But my girls are accustomed to a *civilized* clientele."

Lucas stepped back with a show of affront. "Hetman Platov is a great hero of the war against the Corsican. Would you deny General Blûcher admission?"

"General Blûcher wears a cravat!"

"Oh, if that's the only trouble—here, Matvei." Lucas pulled off his own neckcloth and put it on the Cossack, fashioning a more than passable *trône d'amour* in record time. "There you are, my good man."

"I'm afraid, Lord Strathmere, I haven't made myself plain. The fact is, none of my girls would even consider accommodating your friend."

"Is that so?" Lucas turned to Platov. "She says none of the young ladies will accommodate you, Matvei. What do you suggest?"

Platov put a hand to his saber hilt. "Cossacks are not known to stand on accommodation."

"My thoughts exactly. On three. One, two, three!" Drawing their weapons with a flourish, they rushed past their hostess and hurtled up the stairs.

"Secure the doors, Henthrop!" Mrs. Cuttleby shrieked in most unladylike tones. Henthrop made a halfhearted effort to follow, but Lucas had already kicked them in. They flew open on the gaming room, only half filled at this hour with gentlemen and the house's exquisitely attired dealers, all of whom screamed at the sight of Lucas and his pistol and Platov with his saber a-twirl. A glance told Lucas Tatiana was not among them. That was as he'd expected.

"This way," he told Platov, striding among the tables toward the doors at the rear of the salon. Mrs. Cuttleby could be heard from below, bellowing for Henthrop to send for the watch. Lucas paused to stare at the butler. "Do, and you're a dead man." And Platov, cocking his pistol, shot out a mirror above the quivering fellow's head. "Matvei, Matvei. What did I say about restraining yourself?" Lucas murmured, just before he smashed the back doors in.

The echo of the shot had brought a bevy of disheveled heads in a full range of colors—blond, auburn, brown, black—to the thresholds of the small private rooms lining each side of the corridor within. They ducked back inside in a hurry when they saw the two men advancing; there was a flurry of keys thrust into keyholes, and many screams. Lucas nodded to Platov, and each taking a side, they went down the row, kicking any doors that would not open. It was an educational experience for the Cossack, whose eyebrows inched higher at each glimpse of English intimate behavior. "Do all of you use whips?" he inquired, halfway down the hall.

"I don't," Lucas assured him.

"You must prefer those little wooden boards, then. What are they called?"

"Paddles. Can't say I favor them, either." The next door flew open at the shove of his boot to reveal a familiar face peeking up in horror over the bedclothes. "Why, if it isn't Lord Barton! Good to see you, sir! And how is Lady Barton?"

"Strathmere!" The startled baron gasped. "If you speak one word of this to Agatha—"

"You have my assurance of discretion. Go on with it—if, that is, you still can."

Platov had reached the end of his side. "No sign of her, my friend."

"Try the last one over here," Lucas suggested. He didn't think Hastings had lied. But someone might have moved Tatiana from the gaming house. With grim purposefulness he kicked open the penultimate portal on a man and his dark-haired companion, both of whom were so engrossed in pleasure that they hadn't taken heed of the shot. "Beg pardon," Lucas murmured, leaving them to it. A few steps down the hall, Platov was frowning at the last door, which refused to budge. "Getting winded?" Lucas asked him, and together they rushed at the wood. It gave way with a splintering crash—bolted, he realized from the sound of the iron plate popping off the lintel. Bolted from inside . . .

Platov swore softly in the dim light within the room, and lowered his pistol. Tatiana, sitting cross-legged on the bed, did not lower hers. She was in her underclothes, and she was shaking so badly that even if she'd fired the gun she surely would have missed. "Put it down, Tatiana," Lucas said, moving toward her. "It's all right. You needn't be afraid."

Her green eyes were wide with horror. He had, very carefully, to pry the pistol from her clenched fingers. "Where did you get this?" he asked gently, tucking it into his belt.

She glanced across the bed to the floor, still trembling. He put his arms around her, held her tight to his heart. "Lucas," Platov said in an odd voice as he leaned down. When he rose, Platov held a limp body, the face horribly contorted, tongue thrust out, eyes bulging. Lucas did not recognize it at first. When he did—

"My God. It's Willoughby."

"I warned him," Tatiana whispered. "I told him . . . if he tried to touch me, I'd kill him. But he only laughed."

"Strangled," the Cossack confirmed, letting the body fall. "With his own cravat. Couldn't have done a better job of it myself."

Tatiana hid her face against Lucas's sleeve. "I *tried* to tell him—"

"Hush, love. Hush, my poor sweet love. I'm so sorry.

. . . That's Casimir's murderer, Matvei. I'd stake my life on
it. How long have you been . . . here, with him like that?"
he asked Tatiana gently.

"A long time. Hours." Her voice caught on a sob. "I did
not know what to do! I didn't dare leave. I thought . . . I'd
never killed a man before." She raised her green eyes, falter-
ing. "I did not think you would come."

Platov cleared his throat. "Forgive me, my friend, but
someone is bound to have summoned the watch. The
sooner we are gone—"

"Quite right." Lucas scooped Tatiana off the bed, lifting
her easily, then reached for the coverlet to drape it around
her.

"Lucas, no! I cannot venture out all undressed!" He
paused long enough to kiss her on the mouth, his shoulders
quaking with laughter. "What? What is it?" she demanded.

"Your scruples." He bowed his head against hers. "You
never fail to amaze me, Tatiana."

"Where are we going?"

"To Mother's house, of course." Following Platov, he
carried her down the back stairs.

"She won't be pleased," Tatiana fretted, drawing the coverlet closer.

"On the contrary, she will be ecstatic. Among other
things, you've killed the man who had me knifed in Paris."

The horses were waiting, snorting, in the stable yard.
The boy tipped his cap to them, grinning. They thundered
off just as the whistles of the city watch began to sound from
a few streets away.

Thirty-Three

TO TATIANA'S ASTONISHMENT, Dulcie had not one word of reproach for her outlandish apparel; as Lucas bore her in, the countess was all smiles and solicitude. "My dear girl, where on *earth* have you been?"

"Never mind that, Mother," Lucas said brusquely, brushing past Smithers, whose affronted air more than made up for the countess's sangfroid. "What do you want most, love? Brandy? Vodka? Something to eat?"

"I think . . . a bath," she murmured, leaning on his shoulder. "The way he touched me—"

"Have water sent up at once," Lucas ordered the bug-eyed butler. "Make it good and hot." Starting up the stairs, he noticed Platov lingering in the doorway behind him. "Mother. Would you be so kind as to entertain Hetman Platov while I see Tatiana settled?"

"I should be honored," Dulcie declared, not missing a beat. "If you'll come this way, sir?"

"Go with her, Matvei," Lucas said over his shoulder in Russian. "She'll feed you, if you like."

Platov was considering his handsome hostess, smoothing down his mustache. "Your father, my friend—is he also in residence?"

"Dead these past five years."

The Cossack's coal eyes gleamed. "Does she speak Russian, your mother?"

"Not a word. But I daresay you'll make yourself understood."

Lucas was chuckling as he crossed the threshold of Tatiana's room. He sobered, though, as he unwound her from the coverlet and saw she still was trembling. "All of this is my fault," he said quietly, his hand cupping her face.

"Willoughby told me of your daughter," Tatiana whispered, her eyes averted. "He said you would have to marry Gillian. Of course I understood then . . . why you behaved as you did last night. And he said . . . since you would not come to help me, I might as well—" Her small face crumpled. "But I wouldn't. I couldn't."

"Brave, brave Tatiana." He kissed her tear-wet cheek. "Gillian duped me. The child's none of mine, nor even of hers. She dug her up at Smithfield Market, and promised her five pounds to put on a show for me."

Her sea-colored eyes found his, with a flicker of hope. "Oh, Lucas. Are you certain?"

"Positive. The girl admitted as much, once Platov treated Hastings to a show of his saber in her presence."

Her mouth curved in a slip of a smile. "I can imagine. Hetman Platov cuts a most imposing swath. I was frightened to death when he burst open the door. But then I saw you."

Two servants brought the tub in then. Carruthers followed in their wake, bearing steaming jugs of water. When she saw Tatiana she fell to her knees, kissing her mistress's hands. "Oh, miss, we was so frightened for you! All of us was! But here you are, safe at home. Clarrie 'n' Mrs. Smithers are bringin' up the rest of the water. La, here they are now. Let me just help ye out o' those things—"

"For now, Carruthers, you may go," Tatiana said quietly.

The maid stared for only an instant before bobbing a curtsy. "As you wish, miss."

When the servants had gone, Lucas kissed Tatiana's forehead gently. "You'll want to be alone. I'll send up some wine and cheese and biscuits, shall I?"

Her clear green eyes stared into his. "I was counting on you to help me bathe. If you are willing, that is."

"Willing?" The word came out strangled.

She reached to stroke his face. "I don't want to let you out of my sight ever again."

"Nor I you." He tested the water. "Smithers took me at my word for once. It is still too hot. Let me help you undress, and you can tell me how you fell into Willoughby's clutches."

She turned so he could reach her tapes. "I had gone to the Pultenay. Platov sent me a letter—you know about that?" He nodded, teasing out the knots with his long, strong hands. "Does he truly know who my parents were?"

"I'm afraid not. He is Casimir's cousin, though, out for revenge." Briefly he explained what the Cossack had told him about his friend's death.

"*Tovarka?*" Tatiana echoed, wondering. "*Dyed* Ivan called me that?"

He nuzzled her bare shoulder. "And you were only a child when he did. What would he have called you had he seen what you have grown into?" She had flinched, just a little, at his touch. He lifted her over the edge of the tub. "Let me wash every trace of that bastard from you."

He did, his fingers infinitely gentle as he lathered her

back and arms and hair. "Lift your leg, please." She did, the water sluicing from its pale curves. Lucas bit his lip, fought to keep his voice steady. "And at the hotel?"

Tatiana had closed her eyes, relinquishing herself to his ministrations. "I was *hours* early in coming. I was so distraught. I could not think what would become of me now that you did not love me."

"I never stopped loving you." He planted a kiss on her wet knee. "But while I believed what Gillian told me was true—that she had borne my child, that Lord Innisford knew of it, married her anyway, and then I had killed him—" He paused, gathered his breath. "Willoughby was wrong. I would not have married her. But neither could I have married you. How could I ask you to forgive such a transgression?"

Those green eyes opened again, rested on him as he laved her foot. "It never was a matter of that, was it, Lucas? The question was how you could forgive yourself. She knew that. Such a deal of trouble for her to go to just to spoil your happiness! Why does she hate you so?"

"I did murder her husband."

"No. I think it is because she did not take you when she might have had you. Because you would have saved her, Lucas, just as you saved me. You offered her salvation, and she turned it down. I could see it in the way she spoke of you, so jesting and bitter."

"I'll see her dead," he vowed quietly, "for what she's done to you. But finish your tale."

"Oh! She was coming down the staircase with her greyhounds as I arrived. When she saw me standing there, she invited me up to her rooms. Fool that I am, I went. I had some notion of—"

"Conspiracy?" he interjected, remembering.

"No, no. But I was so curious about her! I always have been. Knowing how she had held your devotion for so long a time . . . I thought there must be more to her than I'd glimpsed."

"You overestimate me. It was fourteen years ago. I was a stripling, an idiot. I fell in love with her breasts and her hair. I never gave a damn what her soul was like."

"She does have lovely hair."

"Lovely like Medusa's. Other leg, please. So you went up to her rooms?"

"Aye. And we had a cup of chocolate, and I thought it tasted odd, but she said it was a Moroccan blend. The next I knew I was on my knees on the floor, and she was standing over me, laughing. I was so dizzy, but I kept trying to stand, and falling over, falling over."

"She drugged you," Lucas said with a grimace.

"I suppose she did. Then, while I was scrambling about on the floor, two men came in. A young one, and also Willoughby. The room was going 'round and 'round—" She clenched her eyes shut again at the memory. Lucas kissed her toes, soothed her with his hands. "The young one was bad enough—Hastings, his name was—but Willoughby was horrid. He kept pawing at me, touching me, until finally Gillian said, 'If you must, not here, James. Lucas could visit at any time.' That was the last I heard; I must have fainted completely. When I awoke I was . . . in that place where you found me. I thought at first I'd been rescued. I was dizzy still, but I got up and tried the door. I was locked in. I tried to climb out the window, but it was so high, and I kept going weak. Then Willoughby came in. He must have passed the time drinking; I could smell it on his breath. He came at me, and he said those things—that you were going to marry Gillian, that you had a daughter. That I might as well—but I wouldn't. I told him so, but he wouldn't listen! And so I—I—"

"Don't think about it," Lucas urged her.

"How can I *not* think about it? I killed a man!"

"Would you rather he'd had you?"

"God, no!" she declared, and shuddered.

He moved along the tub to her side. "Then you must put it out of your mind, move past it. He was a spy, an enemy of England. He has been for a very long time, Platov says. I am certain it was he who killed Casimir, and gave the order to have me killed in Paris when I turned up asking questions about it. What I don't know is why." He paused, fingers tangled in her hair. "I'll lay you any odds you name, though, that Gillian does."

"She wasn't at her hotel?"

"No. Hastings said she was going straight from her mantua-maker's to the Regent's reception."

"If that's so," Tatiana mused, "she won't have heard that I escaped. Or about Willoughby. We should have the element of surprise on our side."

"We?" He looked at her, arching his brow. "You mean Platov and I."

"I am going, too."

"Not a chance, Tatiana."

"And why not?"

"Why *not*? Look at all you have been through this day!"

"You said you never wanted to leave my side again!" she said accusingly.

"After this last exception."

She was silent for a moment. Then she knelt up in the tub, nodding down at her breasts. "You have not washed me here."

"No. I haven't." His voice caught a bit. He smoothed soap over the round, heavy swells of her flesh, lingering at her nipples as they stiffened to his touch.

"Nor here." She stood in a flurry of splashes, indicating her backside. Biting his lip, Lucas lathered her there.

"Nor here," she whispered, turning to face him, fingers

trailing over her mound of Venus. Her wet skin glowed in the slanting late-day sun.

He swallowed. "Christ, Tat. A man can stand only so much."

"Wash me," she coaxed him, and he rubbed the soap against his hand. "Here." She took his wrist, guiding him. "Here." Her legs parted slightly as he stroked her. "Ahh. Yes. A little lower." His breath was wildly uneven. He let his hand glide between her legs once more, withdrew it hurriedly. "Again," she whispered at his ear.

"Oh, God," he groaned, lost in the silken sensation of her soft white skin.

"Again."

He hesitated, consumed by love and need. "Tatiana. Don't." For answer she strained against his fingers, pressing herself to him. "You are only doing this because you think I will let you have your way."

"And will you?" she whispered, her small palm cupped on the hard bulge in the front of his breeches.

"No," he said hoarsely. "It's too dangerous. I cannot protect you properly when I am at the Regent's beck and call."

"Platov—"

"He has his duties as well."

"I did a fairly creditable job this afternoon of looking after myself." Her fingers were caressing him, provoking him.

"All the more reason for you to stay safely here. I'll not press your luck or—dammit, will you stop that? I cannot think while you are touching me so!"

"I would do exactly what you told me to. I would be very careful."

"For God's sake, Tatiana!" With a surge of will, he held her off at arm's length. "This only goes to prove how unsettled you are by what happened with Willoughby. What do you imagine could possibly convince me after all this to let you show your face at court again?"

Seemingly chastened, she ducked down into the tub to rinse. Heartened that at last she'd seen reason, Lucas reached to help her out—then gasped as she pulled him down to her, right into the water. "Jesus!" he sputtered, hauling himself out, dripping wet.

She smiled coyly, stepping from the tub in a cascade of sunlight. "Let me help you off with those clothes."

"Tatiana—"

"I promise, on my love for you, I will not show my face at court this evening."

Mollified, he let her undo his buttons. "That's better. Obedience suits you far better than willful—oh, God." She'd taken his manhood in her hands. "Don't you think we ought to dry ourselves off?"

"I don't see why," she said.

"Whatever happened to waiting until the wedding?"

"That was never any of my idea." She ran the tip of his rod along her slick, gleaming belly. "We can, though, if you like."

"No," he told her. "Not now we can't."

He made love to her there on the Aubusson carpet in a glorious tangle of wet skin and hair, arching above her, driving into her with desperate force. She sighed and clung to him as tightly as she could, needing his passion to cleanse her more than she had the bath. The storm of emotions she had passed through that day—fear, isolation, anger, lonely terror—all gave way before the pure sensation of his thick, swollen rod thrusting deep inside her. She had been so sure she would never hold him this way again. . . . The realization made her start to cry. He paused, staring down at her, his eyes dark with love and longing. "Shall I stop?"

"No, love," she whispered. "Never. Never stop, ever!" She wound her legs around his, pulling him close, and he sank into her, wildly eager. The floor seemed to rock beneath them, the furniture, the windows, tub, screens, bed revolving in dizzying orbits around them, as though their union were the nexus of the universe, drawing all things in. And at their center, where they were joined, there blazed a star brighter and hotter than fifty suns, consuming flesh and feeling into one ecstatic, molten core. When he erupted, when the flow of his seed burst out deep within her, the force was volcanic; she felt her soul rising, lifting. She called his name, and he answered with a long, shuddering, wordless cry. Then he lay atop her, drained, spent, shaken.

"Oh, God," he murmured, his mouth against her throat.

"Was that love?" she whispered, fingers twining in his hair.

"That was the *best* love any man has ever known." With a supremely satisifed groan, he rolled from atop her into the puddle they had made of the floor. "Vixen. *Will* you look at this carpet."

She pushed herself up on one elbow, the long, damp strands of her pale hair molded against her breasts. "I'd rather look at you. Now, and for all time."

"Time—Christ! I am going to be late to Carlton House!" He scrambled to his feet, reaching for his clothes, tossing her a towel. "Cover yourself, if you please." Dutifully she stood and used the thick terry to dry her shoulders and then her legs, very thoroughly. Lucas hadn't realized how intently he was watching until she glanced up at him, green eyes sparking with mischief. "You little minx! Try to tempt me again, will you? I am not so soft as that."

"I would not say you are soft at all," she noted with a pointed look at his manhood.

He started to laugh, then pulled his face straight. "I'll send Carruthers in to dress you."

She made a pretty pout. "I was hoping you would do that, too."

"I don't trust myself around you. Who knows what you might wheedle out of me?"

She held the towel out to him. "Very well. But before you go, could you just dry my back?"

He moved to take it from her. She turned, flipping her wet hair into a thick coil that hung to her buttocks, which were white and smooth and curved in the most delicious way. . . .

He snapped the towel at them instead, and when she gasped, staring back at him, all offended innocence, hurled it at her head. "Why, Lucas!"

" 'Why Lucas' yourself, you she-devil," he growled, and made his escape before reason and devotion to duty failed him utterly.

When he finally descended to the salon, washed and brushed and in fresh evening clothes, he was gratified to find Dulcie had ordered a light supper. "I *do* love Prinny's routs," she explained, "but one never can be sure of getting enough to eat." Platov was still there, though he'd changed into unusually elegant attire. "Your father's clothes," the countess explained to her son's questioning look. "I am not altogether certain I entirely understood Hetman Platov's account of today's events, hampered as we were by the language barrier. But I gather it best he appear as inconspicuous as possible this evening. We had more than enough time to have Turner take the breeches up, while you were . . . changing."

"You think of everything, Mother," Lucas said, and attacked the cold ham ravenously.

"Your betrothed does not join us this evening?" Platov asked in Russian.

Lucas politely translated the question for his mother,

then replied with a shake of his head. "No. I thought it best she rest quietly in her rooms."

Platov raised his brows. "And she was content with that, the little hellion?"

Lucas choked on his meat. "I was able to . . . persuade her to reason."

"To persuade that one against her will . . . you have depths to you, my friend, of which I was not aware."

"What makes you so certain it was against her will?"

The Cossack shrugged. "We have a saying in Russia: The thing left undone was better never started."

"I'll finish this one for her—with your help."

"You may rely on me completely," Platov told him, his coal eyes agleam.

Dulcie was nibbling at a salad of radishes and lettuce. Lucas started to summarize the conversation for her, but she waved her hand. "No need. As I used to tell your father, it's much simpler if I don't know what is going on. Makes for less lying all around."

"You've been splendid through all this, Mother," he said suddenly, gravely.

"Oh, pish," said the countess. "Would you ask Hetman Platov if he prefers coffee or tea?"

They were ready to leave the house at a quarter to eight—a miracle, considering Dulcie's usual inattention to punctuality. Lucas had spent a half hour sequestered with Platov over cigars and brandy, plotting how to deal with Gillian, and he felt very chipper as he handed the countess into her wrap. "Oh, and you'll need these," she said, reaching for two bundles of black silk lying atop the hallway console. Lucas shook them out, puzzled. Dominoes . . . The countess was fastening a dainty veil of blue tulle banded with sequins onto her headdress, so that it hid her face.

"What are these for?" he demanded.

"Oh, hadn't you heard?" Dulcie led the way toward the doors. "Prinny decided just yesterday to make tonight's fête a masque."

Lucas, about to explain to the Cossack what the black hoods were for, stopped abruptly, a horrible suspicion in his mind. "Tatiana!" he roared, turning to the staircase. She appeared at the top, dazzling in white peau de soie, her own delicately beaded half-mask already in place. "You *promised*," he began angrily.

"I promised," she interposed, calmly descending, "not to show my face at the reception this evening. As you can see, I intend to keep my word."

"Sweet blood of Christ, I ought to take you over my knee."

"You may if you like," she told him, her skirts sweeping the staircase. "But let me remind you, that was my own first choice of tactic earlier today. You didn't prove exactly . . . resistant." Dulcie suppressed a titter, and Platov snickered into his sleeve, all too aware of the conversation's gist.

"No!" Lucas said explosively. "Absolutely, positively, most emphatically—"

"We have a saying in Russian," she went on in that language, "don't we, Hetman Platov? The thing left—"

"To hell with bloody Russia!" Lucas bellowed furiously.

Tatiana squared off against him. "You may try what you please, Lucas. You can lock me in my room; you can swallow the key. You can bind me in chains, but I swear to you, I will find a way. I mean to see this thing through."

"Tatiana." His voice broke. She looked so ethereal, so frail, as though a breeze could break her. Yet she'd proved today she was not; there was steel beneath that pale, soft skin, and a will as hard as the diamonds sparkling at the swell of her breasts. He caught his breath; tears had sprung to his eyes. "If anything should happen to you—"

"Allow me to suggest she take this," the countess stepped

in soothingly, plucking from her reticule a small pearl-handled pistol.

Lucas stared at her. "Mother! How long have you been carrying that about?"

"Close on thirty-five years. It was the Admiral's notion. I've never once had to use it, thank heaven. But he was perfectly aware of the hazards of his business. He did not intend for me to be taken by surprise."

"I'll be damned." Lucas watched as Tatiana took the weapon. "But she doesn't know how to use it."

"Yes I do. Big Jon taught me." She cocked the gun, taking aim. "The bit of panel there by the door to the salon—the piece that's scratched." She fired, bringing Smithers at a dead run. Dulcie had clapped her hands over her ears.

Lucas went to look at the wall. "You were wide. By six inches."

"Close enough," Tatiana told Lucas grimly, "to have stopped a man. Or a woman."

"Reload it," he ordered. Dulcie fished out bullets, and Tatiana did, quickly and efficiently. "I'll be damned," Lucas said again.

"I *do* beg your pardon, milady," Smithers began, sniffing the air, flabbergasted, "but the staff is quite unnerved. Has a gun been—"

"There's a hole in the wainscot," the countess observed, "there by the salon door. See it's plugged up, Smithers. And now we really must be going. Lucas?"

He hesitated. Tatiana smiled beneath the satin curve of her mask, extending her hand. "Milord?"

Still he did not move. Platov clicked his heels together. "If you will permit me, Miss Grimaldi—"

"Oh, butt off, Matvei," Lucas snapped, elbowing him aside. He glowered down at Tatiana. "I'll have more to say to you about this at a later date."

"I trust you will." She tucked the pistol into the reticule dangling from her small wrist. "But I did keep my promise."

Lucas growled in his throat and led her to the carriage outside.

Thirty-Four

THE LINE OF coaches already stretched so far as the top of St. James's by half-past eight; they crawled toward the gates of Carlton House between rows of curious onlookers. Platov sat contentedly inside the carriage, having stabled the great white stallion at the countess's; its presence would instantly have betrayed his identity. Lucas, though, was jumpy, fiddling with his hood and tapping his feet until Dulcie finally snapped, "For heaven's sake, sit still! One would think you were five years old!"

"We'd get there quicker on foot," he mumbled.

"Why don't we walk, then?" Tatiana asked reasonably.

The countess rolled her eyes. "Arrive on foot? It is simply not done!" But Lucas had already rapped on the box. Dulcie let out a groan. "Lord, Tatiana, now see what you've done."

"We're getting out here," Lucas called to the driver of

the hired hack—his own coach, emblazoned with his arms, would have been as conspicuous as Platov's horse. He handed Tatiana down, waited while the Cossack alighted, then turned back for the countess. "Coming, Mother?"

"Certainly not!"

Tatiana shook out her skirts to a chorus of admiring hoots from the throngs lining the street. "That's the way, m'lady!" a fat man shouted at her. "Travel like us common folk!"

"You may proceed with Lady Strathmere to the gates," Lucas instructed the driver. But Dulcie surprised him by climbing daintily down, to be greeted by another outburst of wolf whistles. "Can't stand by and watch another woman garner all the attention?" Lucas murmured, taking her arm.

"Don't be absurd," she snapped. "I simply can't abide the thought of you three fools heading off by yourselves."

They strolled along the row of carriages nearly to the gates. Then Lucas turned, surveying the blazons on the coaches. He moved to one, beckoning to his companions, and rapped at the door. "Lord Barton, isn't it?" he said pleasantly to the astounded gentleman within. "And Lady Barton! How lovely you are looking this evening. Would you mind terribly if we came into your coach, just through the gates?"

"See here, young man," the affronted lord sputtered, "I don't know who you are, but—"

Lucas obligingly raised the edge of his domino. "Lucas Strathmere, sir. I was just trying to recall to my mother where I had seen you last. Was it at White's? No, that's not it—yet I distinctly remember it was a club of *some* kind."

"Why, you—"

"Or not a club, precisely . . ."

"Move over, Agatha," Lord Barton said with resignation. "Lord Strathmere's party is joining us."

"You're very kind," Lucas told him humbly, handing in the countess.

It was a tight squeeze, but there were only another hundred yards or so to stand it. Then the door was opened by the Regent's liveried footman, and they all discharged onto the drive. "Thanks again, old man," Lucas told Lord Barton, clapping his shoulder.

"You'll get yours one of these days," the lord hissed at him before turning to his wife. "Agatha, my pet. Shall we?"

"By all means. So nice to see you again, Dulcibella. I hope you and your son and his charming fiancée will come to dinner some evening."

"Over my dead body," growled Lord Barton.

"I won't even *ask*," said Dulcie to her son.

"Good. Better you don't." He switched to Russian. "Matvei. You'll stay with Tatiana?"

"Like the skin to a goat." The Cossack tucked Tatiana's hand tightly into his arm.

Lucas paused, then kissed her quickly. "You behave. Do as you're told. I mean it."

"You act as though you don't trust me," she retorted, smiling.

"That's because I don't."

They joined the sea of masked revelers meandering beneath the portico to the Blue Velvet Room and the maze of suites beyond. Lucas paused every few steps to check that Platov and Tatiana were still close behind him. The press was as intense as always at Prinny's receptions. Dulcie exclaimed in dismay at being tugged past her friends, the thronged tables of sweetmeats and wines, and the Rose Satin Drawing Room, where card tables were set up. But Lucas was headed for the Throne Room, where the Regent would be found. He kept his gaze sharp, searching for Gillian. She'd be masked, but he knew enough of her vanity to be certain she would not have hidden her bright Titian hair.

Twice he paused, thinking he had found her, then realizing he was wrong. So he went on looking, pushing his way through the multitudes.

They reached the Throne Room just as the little clocks were chiming ten. "For heaven's sake, Lucas, I am dying of thirst!" Dulcie said in despair. "Do let me search out some wine."

He turned to her in the crowd. "Go on, then. But, Mother—be aware. Gillian is out to harm me. She went after Tatiana. She could go after you, too."

"I'm not afraid of that hussy."

"Aren't you? I am." He bent and kissed her cheek. "Keep your mask on. Be careful."

"Why, Lucas, you sentimental—" But the rest of her words were lost as she was spun off into the flow.

Platov was eyeing the dais, where the Regent sat comfortably sipping wine and smiling benignly down on his guests in his elaborate costume of Jupiter, king of the gods. "The Tsar is not here," he observed.

"No, thank God. I need not make my presence known as yet. Did you see Gillian, love?"

Tatiana shook her head. "No."

"Nor I either. I think we—" He was interrupted by a flourish of trumpets. "Damn. Here they come. I'll have to go up there. Matvei, bring Tatiana along. I'll meet you by the curtains once I've told Prinny I'm here." He pushed through the crowd with sudden purposefulness. "Pardon me. I am required by the Regent. Excuse me. I must get past."

Platov followed in his wake, his grip on Tatiana's elbow so tight she feared he would leave bruises. "Hetman Platov—"

"Matvei," he corrected her.

"Matvei. I appreciate your zealousness. But you are breaking my arm."

He let his hand loosen slightly. "Forgive me. But I would

not care to be blamed by your betrothed should any harm—" He broke off, staring beyond her shoulder into the crowd. Tatiana started to turn, and he shook his head. "No! No, don't look. There is Lady Innisford, by the doorway. You may look now. She is staring at the dais."

Cautiously Tatiana turned and caught a glimpse of white breasts bulging above bronze taffeta, a peacock mask and headdress over tumbling red-brown curls. "What do we do now?"

"You go on as Lucas intended, and let him know I have found her. I shall stay on her tail, as they say." His hand tightened on her elbow again. "Listen to me, *tovarka*. Straight to the dais. No stopping. No speaking to anyone. Not to the Tsar himself."

"I'm not stupid," she said tartly.

"You are Russian. How could you be stupid? But you may be too brave." He patted her backside with clumsy solicitude. Tatiana had a sudden memory of *Dyed* Ivan making that exact motion when she was a child. She caught her breath.

"Matvei. What will you do to her if you find she helped kill your cousin?" He made a quick motion across his throat with his finger. Tatiana shivered. But it was no more than Gillian deserved.

He vanished into the throng. Left to herself, Tatiana discovered it was harder to force her way through the crowd than when Lucas had been in the lead. Standing on tiptoe, she saw that Princess Charlotte had joined her father and the Tsar on the dais. Her intended, Prince William of Orange, was conspicuously absent, replaced by dashing Leopold of Saxe-Coburg. Prinny, Tatiana noted, was looking decidedly out of sorts.

A burst of music from the gallery made every head swivel. "Good God," she heard a stout matron mutter, "surely he can't intend *dancing*!" But evidently Prinny did;

he stood up and waved his arms to clear a space, then beckoned to his mistress, Lady Hertford, to join him on the floor. Tatiana pressed on toward the dais, where Lucas was still tête-à-tête with the Tsar. He glanced up once, scanning the room, and their eyes met; he smiled in relief. Tatiana detoured around the disgruntled matron as she and her husband made way for the dancers, and he was lost to her sight.

Lucas had been trying for some minutes to disengage himself from Tsar Alexander, who had inconveniently chosen this moment to ask for a clarification of the Regent's position on the allocation of Alsace and Lorraine. Lucas had seen, as Platov had, that bronze head appear in the doorway, and witnessed the Cossack's desertion of Tatiana to follow their quarry. So long as Tatiana came straight to meet him, no harm could befall her—especially with Gillian otherwise occupied. So with one eye on the back curtain, waiting for Tatiana, he laid out for the Tsar the Whig and Tory opinions on the new France's boundaries. When she appeared, he felt a flush of relief out of all proportion. After all, he told himself, making abrupt excuses to the Tsar, they were in the Regent's own house. Still, he would not be satisfied until she was safely in his arms again.

He threaded through the packet of Russian-allied princes, noting that Leopold seemed to hold the upper hand in the battle for Princess Charlotte's affections, and advanced on Tatiana as she stood by the curtains with her back to him. She was conversing animatedly with one of the Grand Duchess's ladies-in-waiting—speaking Russian, he realized, coming closer. It must be a pleasure for her to have the opportunity. Her thick blond hair was caught up in a cunning chignon; the white dress clung to the curves of her slim waist and lovely hips, setting his loins on fire. Diamonds—his diamonds—sparkled at her ears and the nape of her neck. She was born to this, he thought proudly; she is regal as a princess. He slowed his pace as he approached, enjoying the view. Finally, however, longing overcame him; he let his arm settle familiarly around her waist and whispered into her ear, "You are so beautiful, *lyubov*."

She stiffened at his touch and whirled around to face him. The eyes that met his through the slits of her white satin mask were green as grass, and flashing fire. "How dare you!" she spat at him in Russian, and he stared at the woman before him. "Were we only in Russia, my brother would have your head for this affront!"

Confused beyond imagining, he managed a small bow. "I beg your pardon. I seem to have mistaken—"

The lady-in-waiting clucked her tongue. "God, these indecent English! Come away, Your Grace. Come away." Your Grace. Christ! It was the Grand Duchess of Oldenburg— and she *was* Tatiana. Why had he never remarked the resemblance before? It was uncanny; she had even gone taut in the exact same way when he laid his hand on her.

"Come, Your Grace," the Grand Duchess's companion murmured again, glancing back at Lucas with distaste. But something in Lucas's startled manner had arrested her mistress's attention; she turned to him slowly.

"Are we acquainted, monsieur?"

He raised the domino so she could see his face. "Lord Strathmere, Your Grace. Translator to—"

"That pig, the Regent."

"Quite," said Lucas.

After a moment, she laughed. It was Tatiana's laugh. "And what, pray tell, makes the pig's translator feel free to put his hand on the waist of a Grand Duchess?"

"I took you for your daughter," Lucas said, staring into those clear green eyes.

"I . . . have no daughters," she said falteringly.

"Haven't you? I must have been misinformed." But the

green eyes bore a wary look, like a cat that feared cornering. "Perhaps Your Grace would care to dance with me."

"I don't see why I should."

Lucas moved in close, so that the maid would not hear. "For Casimir Molitzyn's sake."

Her spine went rigid. For a moment she stood without speaking. Then she turned to her lady. "Sophia. Inform His Excellency that I have accepted Lord Strathmere's invitation to dance."

"But, Your Grace—"

"Do as I say!" the Grand Duchess snapped, and Lucas saw mirrored in her imperiousness the same regal air Tatiana had used in his rose garden to quell the Regent's courier. His heart was pounding. He was close to the truth at last, very close. The Tsar's own sister—Christ! No wonder mouths in St. Petersburg had closed so tight to his inquiries.

She let him lead her to their places in the line. It was a minuet, he was pleased to find; there would be time for talking. Fingers barely touching his, the Grand Duchess circled him, green eyes narrowed through the mask. "And now, monsieur, you will explain what you meant by speaking of Molitzyn."

He bowed as the dance required, stepped back and forward again. "Two decades past, a grave wrong was done to you, Your Grace."

"There have been many wrongs committed against my house," she said loftily, keeping her distance.

"This one touched you more closely than most." The music swept them together once more, and he took her down the line. "It offended your honor in the most . . . intimate way." She said nothing, but her bearing was taut as stretched wire. Lucas wondered if his hazard was wrong. But she hadn't contradicted him. . . . He took a deep breath. "And there were . . . consequences." A slow flush crawled toward her masked face above the cool white gown. Boldly,

Lucas plunged on. "Perhaps you thought the consequences had been disposed of."

That brought her head swiveling toward him, her eyes flashing fire. "We Russians are not monsters," she hissed at him.

He nodded, staring straight ahead. "Of course. That is why you put the consequences into Casimir's care."

She arched her delicate foot, bending it, withdrawing it, following the music. "I fail to comprehend, monsieur, what any of this has to do with you."

"Casimir was murdered in Paris." She nearly stumbled, and he held her upright, nodding politely at Lady Bournemouth, who had come opposite them on the floor. "The consequences then passed into my hands."

"Impossible," the Grand Duchess whispered. "An Englishman? He never would have!"

"He feared for their safety in Russia. He was right to. On the night I located the . . . consequences, following his instructions to me, a village in Ologda burned to the ground. All its inhabitants perished—"

She faltered, misstepped. "God in heaven!"

"Except one. The one I had come to find."

Those green eyes slanted toward him. "You . . . saved her?" He nodded. She breathed something in Russian— something like a prayer. Then her mouth beneath the mask made a moue of distaste. "And you brought her . . . here."

"I had no notion then of what had been entrusted to me."

The Grand Duchess had recovered her composure. "This is all most intriguing, Lord Strathmere. But you are talking in mysteries. What do you want of me?"

"Since our return to England, there have been three more attempts on her life. I thought perhaps you were behind them."

"I?" she echoed, taken aback. "Why should I—if I had—

I already told you! We are not monsters. Not like you English."

The dance was close to ending. He was running out of time. "If not you," he said softly, "then perhaps . . . the father?"

Her spine like iron . . . the veins on the curve of her pale wrist showing stark. "I tell you again, milord, I fail to see—"

"I love her," Lucas said desperately. "I want to wed her. You may not think me worthy of the House of Romanov, but I pledge you this, on my life: I mean to make her happy. If you care for her, if any part of you still cares—"

"Mysteries," she whispered hoarsely. "Nothing but mysteries."

"He is English, is he not? That is why you hate us—why you and your brother contrive to overset the Regent's affairs?"

"My brother knows nothing of this!" she said vehemently. "And if you have any notion of carrying tales, he will not believe you. You can prove nothing. You said yourself, Casimir is dead."

Only a few bars more . . . "She favors you," Lucas told her. "She honors you. She would not ask, I know, that you acknowledge her. But only to meet her—"

"Impossible."

"Then will you not tell me who the father is?" Implacably she curtsied to him as the music ended. "For God's sake!" The couples around them turned, surprised by his violent tone. Lucas no longer cared. "Someone is trying to murder the woman I love!"

"We have been speaking in mysteries," she repeated, those green eyes veiled, and withdrew her hand.

"*Damn* you!" Lucas swore as she started away.

For an instant she turned back. "Another of your countrymen has already assured that," she spat at him, her hatred crackling in the close air.

"Lucas!" Reluctantly he turned and saw his mother standing on tiptoe, waving at him from the edge of the crowd. He pushed his way through to her, oblivious to the outraged murmurs of those he shoved aside.

"Have you seen Tatiana?" he demanded.

"You don't mean you've lost track of her!" Dulcie cried in horror. Then her features relaxed. "Why, there she is, my dear. There on the dais, right by the Tsar."

Lucas glanced at the woman in white, shook his head. "That's the Grand Duchess of Oldenburg."

"You must be jesting. Why, I could have sworn—" She broke off abruptly. "Jesus in heaven. Lucas, is Tatiana—"

"Keep your mouth shut," he said curtly, "and help me find her. I've wasted too much time as it is."

"What has happened to Hetman Platov?" Dulcie asked, bewildered.

"He is following Gillian. At least—I hope to God he is." Lucas scanned the crowd for a glimpse of Tatiana. The music had started up again—a waltz. It was making his head pound. He felt helpless, defeated. If the Grand Duchess would not confess her secret, what hope did he have of learning who Tatiana's father was?

"There!" Dulcie said suddenly, pointing. "There, you see? She is dancing." Lucas followed her finger, saw the couple whirling past. "But who is that she is with?"

Lucas, flooded with relief, glimpsed the eye patch Tatiana's black-clad partner was sporting. "The Duke of Cumberland."

"My, my, the Regent's own brother! You had best watch out, Lucas, or you will manage to lose that girl yet." She watched them for a moment, then shook her head. "Nay, I take that back. You may lose her, but not to him."

"What's that, Mother?" Lucas asked vaguely, already starting off after Platov.

Dulcie laughed. "Only see how stiff she is in his arms! It puts me in mind of that first time she danced with you, dear, back at Somerleigh House. Do you recall it?"

Lucas paused in mid-step, remembering: hatred blazing in her gaze, consuming her soul, her whole body rigid, abandoned by her accustomed self-control. But why should she behave so with Cumberland? Slowly he turned, glanced back at that other White Lady, still poised on the dais beside the Tsar. She, too, was watching the dancers—was watching, particularly, the Duke of Cumberland and his partner. Her spine was once more inflexible as steel, and through the holes pierced in her pale mask those Eastern, slanting eyes were so incandescent with loathing that they glowed like the maws of hell.

Cumberland. Christ. "Tatiana!" Lucas shouted, rushing for the dance floor, bowling over everyone in his way. *"Tatiana!"* The name was whisked from the air in a sudden clamor of feminine shrieks. Every light in the room had instantaneously been extinguished, plunging the company into pitch darkness. Above the ensuing chaos, Lucas heard the Regent's hearty laugh. Then a brilliant flash of sulfur-yellow from over the dais shocked the crowd into silence. "Everyone out to the lawns!" Prinny cried gaily, reveling in his grand surprise while the glittering flares illuminated his rotund figure. "Everyone out to the lawns for the fireworks!"

What followed was a stampede. Lucas strove to move against the tide, fight his way to where he'd last seen Tatiana, but the wave of humanity was too strong; it swept past him, around him, then tugged him along despite his efforts to hold his ground. His only consolation was knowing Cumberland could no more withstand such a crush than could he. The duke would be out there somewhere, he and

Tatiana. His hand curled on the hilt of the pistol he'd hidden in his belt.

Moving with the throng through the nearest set of French doors, he searched the portico for some sight of her among the masses. A distant crash of thunder made the assembly breathe "Ooh!" all as one. Above the darkened gardens a rocket of light shot into the sky and erupted in a hail of stars. As they fell to earth, echoed in the long, black reflecting pool, he caught a quick glimpse of Gillian Innisford backed against a pillar close to the balustrade, with Matvei Platov planted before her like a squat, stout tree.

The stars sputtered out; Gillian and the Cossack disappeared. Lucas lunged in their direction; they could not have been more than ten paces away. "Matvei!" he shouted. Another burst of fireworks, fiery cascades of blue and white and yellow tails, illuminated the night. In their unnatural incandescence he saw Gillian smiling, saw her reaching into the sleeve of her gown, saw the sparkle of silver in her hand. The crowd had grown hushed, admiring the sparkling waterfall above the gardens. "Matvei!" Lucas called, plunging through the knot of men and ladies blocking his path. "She's got a—"

Boom!

"*Ooh!*" rose the chorus of admiration. And only Lucas caught the infinitely smaller explosion, very close at hand, that followed on its heels. The sky shattered into particles of light, arcing, cresting, falling—and Platov was falling too, collapsing onto his knees. "Damn!" Lucas cried, closing the gap, hurrying to catch him.

"Damn you, too!" screeched an outraged lady whose train he had ripped apart.

Lucas clasped the Cossack in his arms. As the stars died away, their effervescence lingered for one brief instant on a cascade of red-brown curls vanishing into the night. "Stop her!" Platov croaked at him.

Lucas lunged and caught the curls in his fist, hanging on like a bulldog. Gillian screamed, trying to wrench away, but he reeled her in, hand over hand, until his fingers closed on her throat. She fought to raise the pistol; he smacked it away, sending it sailing down into the garden below. "How badly are you hurt?" he demanded of the Cossack.

"Flesh wound. Shoulder. Nothing more."

Gillian fell on her knees, breasts straining against her gown, and attemped coquetry. "Lucas, thank heaven you've come! This foreign *beast* had the audacity to—" He took advantage of the momentary darkness to slap her, hard.

"Who killed Casimir Molitzyn?" When she did not answer, he yanked her head back with such force that her jaw snapped.

"Lucas! You are hurting—"

"Was it Willoughby, Gillian?"

"How the devil should I know?"

He found his gun, held it to her cheek. "Don't think I won't kill you. Not after what you let him do to Tatiana."

"I don't know what on earth you're talking about," she said coolly, her musky fragrance mingling with the sour sulfur in the night air.

Platov had raised himself upright. "Where is your saber, Matvei?"

"Here."

Lucas held out the hanks of Titian curls he was holding. "Cut 'em."

"Lucas! No! Not my—" She let out an agonized wail as the blade sliced through. He grabbed another handful, held it out to the Cossack. "You bastard!" The saber snickered, sang. Gillian was sobbing, the ringlets settling around her feet.

"He can shave you to the scalp if you like."

"Lucas! In God's name! For all the love we had once for

one another . . ." She simpered, played her trump. "For the sake of our daughter—"

"Are you referring to Miss Becca Sinkler, late of Smithfield Market?"

Another burst of fireworks. She stared at him in silence for a moment. And then she laughed. "You think you are so clever, so holy and clever." Her eyes narrowed in the afterglow. "Thought you could save me, didn't you, Lucas? Well, you'd best save your own soul. How will you like living, I wonder, with this? You shot the wrong member of the family that morning on the banks of the Thames. You killed an innocent man."

"Innisford," Lucas said in shock.

"That's right, my pet. Harry thought that skiff was unloading Scotch whiskey. *I* sent him down to the river at dawn. I knew that you were waiting there—did you think I wasn't aware what you were doing? That's why I sent Harry there. I even arranged for the timely appearance of those poor little 'prentices. Do you know what I'd promised them, Lucas?" Her rouged mouth was a hollow, gaping hole. "A tumble in my bed. And I made good my promise, too, just as soon as you'd conveniently murdered my husband for me." He felt the skin of her throat tighten with her smile. "They were better than you ever were, darling. They were jolly good fun."

His fingers clenched on her throat. She laughed once more, defiantly. "For God's sake, Gillian," he managed to whisper. "Why would you do that? *Why?*"

"Because he hadn't proved any more pliant than you were. He would not support the cause."

"Bonaparte?" he asked in disbelief. "Christ! What is Bonaparte to you?"

"A Corsican nobody. A tradesman's son," she said with relish, "who will rule the world."

"He is defeated, for God's sake! He is exiled to Elba! Your cause is dead."

"Is it?" The fireworks ignited the fervor in her eyes. "Just wait. You cannot stop us. None of you bluebloods can stop us. Just you wait and see."

Platov had grown impatient. "What is she saying? She is wasting our time!"

He spoke truth. Lucas caught his fists in the remaining tufts of hair above Gillian's mask. "Is Cumberland one of you?"

Stars split in the darkness. She smiled at him, and struck with the knife she'd had hidden in her skirts. Only the lightning flash of Platov's saber stopped the blade from driving home. Lucas gasped as it sliced into her breast.

"Forgive me, my friend." Platov pulled the blade free and wiped it. "I did not think that you were willing to kill her."

"I . . ." Lucas shivered, seeing the blood seeping out from the wound.

"There is Tatiana to think of," the Cossack said evenly. "Where is she?"

Jesus. "Cumberland. Cumberland has got her."

From the portico floor, Gillian was laughing, bloody bubbles rising from her reddened lips. "She should be safe enough," she managed to tell him, as the light faded from the skies, from her eyes. "In her . . ."

"In her what?" Lucas leaned close to hear her.

Laughter rattled in her throat. "In her dear daddy's arms."

He stood bolt upright, hands on the rail, staring down into the gardens. She had the gun, Dulcie's gun, he remembered, fear shrinking his bowels. If she used it against Cumberland, nothing could save her; murdering the Regent's brother was a sentence of death no excuse could allay.

The fireworks had reached their climax, a burst of ascending flares shooting into the sky, climbing higher and higher, then exploding into a fine mist like fairy dust that sprinkled onto the trees. His eyes caught a glimpse, a breath, of white gown and white-blond hair along the path past the reflecting pool. "There, Matvei!" he cried, and pointed. "There, by the willows!"

He launched himself over the balustrade into the yawning darkness thirty feet below.

Thirty-Five

He LANDED WITH a thud in a thicket of boxwood, drawing disdainful stares from the clustered bystanders. "Drunken idiot," he heard someone mutter. Then a woman screamed as a second figure came hurtling through the air.

"Matvei!" Lucas thrust out a hand to pull him from the bushes. "You are hurt. You ought not to have come."

"I won't slow you down," the Cossack vowed, and proceeded to prove it, matching him stride for stride as they ran toward the willow trees. "Who was the man with her?"

"The Duke of Cumberland. He's her father. And the Duchess of Oldenburg her mother."

"*Jesu,*" Platov swore. "So high as that. Didn't I say she seemed familiar?"

"You did."

They rushed into the willow grove, then paused, uncertain where to go next. Lucas caught a breath of a feminine giggle from behind the swaying branches, reached in, and caught hold of a sleeve, dragging forth a startled young gentleman. "A girl in a white dress," he barked. "White mask. Came this way. Did you see her?"

"Now, see here," the interrupted lover began, "you can't just—"

"*Did you see her?*"

"It's none of my business who—"

Platov stepped up with his saber. "Good God, Gilbert!" cried a lady in the shadows. "Tell him what he wants!"

"I will not! He's got no bloody right to—"

"Tell me or I'll rip your tongue out," Lucas said with deadly grimness.

"She went that way!" The lady came out from the tree, indicating a path. "She was going that way! Just don't hurt him!"

"Was there a man with her?"

"Aye. He was pulling her along. I *told* you, Gilbert, that you ought to help her!"

"Come on, Matvei," Lucas said in Russian, releasing the sleeve.

They followed the path to a fork. Lucas stopped, brought up short, and Platov ran up beside him. They stood still, listening, hearing only distant music and the hollow night wind. Platov struck a match and bent to examine the earth at their feet. "This way." He nodded to the right. "See how someone has crushed the ash from the fireworks? A man. And his stride—he was running, though not very fast."

Then they were running again. A hundred yards along, Platov was proved right by a crumpled white satin mask bearing a footprint. Platov lit another match. "See how they struggled." He pointed out the stirred-up dirt. "She is fighting him still."

"You're good at this," said Lucas.

"I'm even better in snow." The Cossack sounded winded. Lucas wasn't surprised; he'd seen the spread of blood against his white shirt.

"You should go back to the house. Have that wound seen to."

"Time for that later," Platov responded, and set out with a sudden spring.

Lucas expected at any moment to overtake their quarry. Cumberland wasn't a young man, and Tatiana seemed to be doing her best to slow him down. But they turned a bend around a stand of rhododendron, and there was the bulky outline of Carlton House not fifty yards ahead. "You, there!" Lucas's cry startled a boy who was sweeping up ash from the flagstones. "A girl in white and a man all in black—did they come this way?"

"Nah, sir."

"Would you have noticed if they had?"

The boy leaned on his broom. "Is she pretty?"

"Very," Lucas said, a catch in his throat.

"I'd have noticed 'er, then."

Lucas turned and started back up the path. "We must have missed something, somewhere." His eyes, sharp with fear, scanned the trees and bushes. "They couldn't just disappear!" The last word was swallowed by the sudden, sharp report of a gunshot. Lucas went pale just as Platov touched his arm.

"There. Between those trees." It was the garden wall, and in it, showing faintly in the light of a thin crescent moon that had risen, was the outline of a low, arched door. Lucas ran to it and flung it open, terrified by what he might find. It led onto an expanse of lawn enclosed on the far side by another high wall. There was an iron gate in the wall, still hanging agape. And just before the gate, a small spot of silver on the dew-damp grass—Lucas crossed to it, snatched it up. His mother's pistol, the barrel still hot. *Oh, God, Tatiana. What have you done?*

Platov pounded past him through the gate. Beyond it, the earth sloped downward in a gentle hill, leading onto a street. What street? Lucas tried to think as he ran. Cockspur, which gave onto Whitehall. They would not have headed left; that would bring Cumberland straight into the mass of carriages. He'd have gone right, toward the river, away from the crush. He reached the street and scanned it anxiously. *A sign, Tatiana. Send me a sign. . . .*

"Lucas! Look out!" Platov bellowed behind him.

More than a sign, it was a curricle, light and fleet, hurtling straight at him, driven by a man in black who'd whipped his pair to a froth. Lucas reached for his pistol, leveled it at the driver—then lowered it abruptly as he saw Tatiana, eyes wide with terror, clutched tightly to her captor's chest. "Don't shoot, Matvei!" he shouted—then fell to the cinders as a bullet winged past his head. "Dammit, I told you—"

"I could take him out still. I could take out a horse—"

"And kill her as well? They are moving too fast!" He stumbled to his feet, scanning the road. A carriage was meandering down from Carlton House. Lucas ran to it, stood blocking the road. "His Majesty's business!" he called to the driver. "We need your horses!"

The man reined in, perplexed. "Need my—"

"Here, now, what's going on?" A white head appeared in the window. Lucas nearly laughed, recognizing it.

"Lord Barton! Sir! It is Lucas Strathmere. Ever so sorry, but I need your horses. His Majesty's business." Platov, meanwhile, was using his saber to slice the handsome bays free.

"Dammit, Strathmere, you can't simply—"

"How is your lovely wife, sir? Do you know, it finally came to me where I saw you last. It was upstairs in Mrs.—"

"Why, you insolent—"

"I've got them!" Platov cried in triumph, with a final swish of steel through leather.

"Here, now," the muddled driver called, "ye can't ride them horses; they're carriage-bred! Not to mention ye ain't got no—" Platov vaulted onto a bay, wrapped his fists in its mane, and thundered off with a savage shout. "Saddles," the man finished weakly.

Lucas, not to be outdone, clambered onto its mate. "Get on, you bloody nag!" he screamed in its ear, and it took off like a shot, nearly sending him sprawling. "Spirited," he noted with satisfaction. "Matvei, wait for me!"

He caught up with the Cossack just at the turn onto Whitehall. "Can you ride?" he demanded, eyeing the spreading patch of red on Platov's chest.

"With a horse beneath me, I can go forever," Platov said briefly. They galloped into the night, the curricle still in sight, only a quarter mile or so ahead. "We're gaining," the Cossack noted, bent low against his horse.

"Not fast enough." Lucas could not shake the memory of Tatiana's terrified face. What was to stop Cumberland from hurling her out of the curricle, or simply throttling her? "Go, go, go," he whispered to the bay. "Go like the wind."

Cumberland was standing in his seat, lashing his team like a madman. Lucas knew he had to draw abreast to force the duke to stop. He nudged the bay with his bootheels. "Come on, girl! Is that the best you can do?" They were pounding along the edge of the Thames, following the embankment past Parliament Square and Westminster Abbey toward Millbank. There was a desolate stretch ahead leading to Lambeth Bridge. If he could only beat Cumberland there—

He glanced down at the bay. Lord Barton was not especially known for his taste in horseflesh. Still . . .

"Matvei!" he shouted. "You stay on the road! I am going to cut across the rough to the bridge."

Platov, too, looked at Lucas's bay. "Can she jump, do you think?"

"We'll find out," Lucas said grimly. "Hiah! Go, girl!" He tugged the bay's mane, sending her plunging off the road into the underbrush.

Somewhere in the horse's provenance must have been hunting blood, for she took to open land like a champion, gathering her legs beneath her, galloping for all she was worth. Lucas was just congratulating himself on his instincts when a hedge, a tall one, loomed up before him. The bay's gait faltered slightly; she turned to the side, beginning to shy. "You can do it!" Lucas urged her, low on her neck. "A little hedge like that—why, you could clear it sleeping! Come on, girl. Come on." He eased up, settling her into a long, loose rhythm. Ten lengths. Seven. Five. Three— "Now, girl!" He dug in his heels, and she sailed up, clearing the line of hedge easily, landing with perfect aplomb on the other side. Lucas wasn't sure which of them was more surprised. "That wasn't so bad, was it? Let's catch the bastard, shall we?" He looked to his right. The curricle was just starting to round the bend to the bridge. Platov was a scant fifty yards behind it. With a little luck—and his luck had held so far—he would beat Cumberland.

On he charged, up a knoll of grass and down the other side. The bay whinnied as her hooves struck shale, unsteady and shifting. "Damn!" Lucas swore. But she struggled for footing, found it, plunged ahead. "That's my good girl! Barton doesn't deserve you. Get me to the bridge before Cumberland, and I'll buy you, retire you to Somerleigh. Nothing to do for the rest of your life but eat oats and crop grass." They were very close now, with only one obstacle in their path: a low stone wall, not even hock-high. "This will be easy," he assured the bay, who approached it eagerly, never slowing down. Cumberland had cleared the turn, he saw with a glance, and was flying toward the bridge. "Ready—set—now!" he told the bay.

She stopped as though the hand of God had grabbed her by the heels. Lucas, hunched over her neck, grabbed wildly for her mane, felt the long strands slip through his fingers. He hurtled forward, tumbling headlong, soaring, scrabbling to bring his knees up, to shield his head with his arms. But he was moving too fast. He hit the road dead center, splayed like a frog, the wind socked from his chest.

There was thunder in his ears as he lay there. Cumberland's curricle, driving straight at him—he raised himself on his elbows, saw a forest of churning hooves, and heard Tatiana scream, "Lucas!"

He just had time to stretch himself longways and roll onto his side before the team was on him. Their heads passed above him, one to the left, one to the right. Their forelegs barely missed his groin. Beyond their foaming flanks he caught a glimpse of Cumberland's face, contorted in a smile of triumph, and of Tatiana, struggling desperately for the reins. She must have wrenched them out of the duke's grasp, for just as the staves and steps flashed above him, he saw the strip of leather fall free. He lunged up for that narrow band of hope, caught it with one finger, curled the finger, clasped it with both hands. The momentum of the horses dragged him, flat on his back, along the road beneath the curricle. The force was jolting. He refused to let go.

Cumberland, infuriated, was screaming at his team, laying on with the whip. But Lucas could feel the pull of the bits in his hands. He braced his feet against the crossbar connecting the rear wheel, to gain some leverage, and gave a sudden yank.

The horses shied, slowed, disconcerted by the opposing messages of the reins and the whip. Lucas yanked again, harder.

The carriage rolled to a stop halfway across Lambeth Bridge.

In the sudden silence, Lucas heard Platov bellowing in Russian, coming up from the rear. "Lucas?" Tatiana cried, her voice trembling with fear. She started down from the seat, then cried out again, this time in pain. "Let me go, you bastard!"

"Call off your man, Strathmere," Cumberland warned, cool as ice. "And let go the reins."

"Lucas, don't—"

"Do it or she dies!"

"Matvei!" Lucas shouted in Russian. "Stop! Don't shoot him!" Looking between his legs, he saw the Cossack slow his horse unwillingly.

Cumberland grunted in satisfaction. "Now, Strathmere, the reins."

Hidden beneath the carriage by the box, Lucas inched forward until his head was just below the staves. "I am letting them go now."

"Toss them to me. Nice and easy."

"Nice and easy," Lucas repeated, staring up at the staves. Cumberland would have to lean down over the box. . . . He curled his legs against the front axle, hooked his fingers around the edge of the step on each side. "Ready?"

"Just do it, damn you!"

Lucas flung the leather strip upward, just out of the duke's reach. "Higher, you idiot!" Cumberland snapped— just as Lucas shot forward from under the steps and let the reins fly again, this time settling them around the duke's neck. Tatiana, bless her, was quick. She caught the narrow band as it fell, pulling the ends across one another and then sharply upward. Lucas, looking skyward, had the distinct pleasure of seeing Cumberland's good eye bulge from its socket. He clawed at the reins, gasping for air. Lucas crawled out from under the curricle and waved Platov forward.

"Come, Matvei, and see. Tatiana's caught a big fish."

"You—you!" Cumberland's complexion had progressed through red to purple.

"Don't kill him," Lucas warned Tatiana, still in Russian.

"Why shouldn't I?" she demanded, giving the reins a tug.

"You know why," he said quietly.

She hesitated. Cumberland's eye had rolled back in his head. Platov stepped forward and took the duke's pistol from the floor of the curricle. "Let him go, *tovarka*."

Reluctantly, she did. The duke fell against the step, chest heaving. When he could speak, he mumbled plaintively, "Christ! What sort of chit would murder her own father?"

"The sort whose father tried to murder her," she said evenly.

Cumberland rubbed his striped throat. "There's been some misunderstanding."

"On the contrary," Lucas told him. "Everything has at last become clear. You've been dallying with Bonapartists, haven't you, Your Grace? For a good many years."

"You must be daft, Strathmere."

"Am I? How did Gillian Innisford know you were Tatiana's father?"

Cumberland laughed. "That whore would say anything to save her skin."

"She's dead," Lucas announced bluntly.

The duke only smiled. "Is she? What a pity for you. The dead can't talk."

"But the living can. The Grand Duchess of Oldenburg is very much alive."

"She'll never speak a word," the duke sneered. "Her shame would be too great."

"And you," Tatiana cried furiously, "have you no shame? To so abuse the sister of your host in a strange land—"

He shrugged. "She has her version of the story, I'm sure. Here's mine. She was only too willing."

Tatiana flushed in the moonlight. "Liar."

"What did he say?" Platov demanded, hand on his saber.

"That the Grand Duchess welcomed his advances," Lucas translated for him.

The saber flashed, and a silver button close to Cumberland's throat clattered onto the road. "I'll make him eat those words! Ask him how he knew where Tatiana was, that you had gone to find her."

Lucas posed the question. Cumberland was busy straightening his cravat. "A little bird told me," he said blithely.

"A bird named Willoughby?" Lucas demanded.

"It might have been."

Platov, hearing the name, lunged at him. Lucas had to pull him off. "Matvei, you cannot kill him! He is the Regent's brother!"

"He killed Casimir! I demand blood for blood!"

"He killed Pietr and the others," Tatiana said slowly. "It is true. He must die."

"What are they saying?" Cumberland asked, shaking out his lace cuffs.

"They want to kill you," Lucas told him.

The duke smiled. "But you won't let them, will you, Strathmere? Love of country and all that."

Lucas smiled back. "No. I won't let them." Then he leaned forward and yanked the duke from the curricle. "I'll kill you myself instead."

"You wouldn't dare!" Cumberland cried as Lucas dragged him toward the wall of the bridge. "You'd hang for it!"

"I might," Lucas said thoughtfully, seizing the shoulders of the duke's coat and hoisting him over the wall. "The thing is, Your Grace, there's no reason it should look like murder. A man like you, with such a checkered past—is it so inconceivable that one dark night, alone on a bridge, you might be overwhelmed by regret?"

The duke's good eye blinked, contemplating the churning waters of the Thames below. "Me? A suicide? No one would believe it."

"No? Your family is not, you know, especially famed for mental competency."

"Make him tell about Casimir," Platov urged, coming closer.

Lucas hung the duke farther over the edge. "Tell me about Casimir Molitzyn."

Cumberland clamped his mouth shut. Lucas let his grip slacken—then tightened it again as the duke gasped. "What do you want to know?"

"How did you learn of Tatiana's existence?"

"Put me down and I'll tell you." Lucas let the duke's feet rest on the wall, but did not leave go his coat. "There were . . . rumors. A Russian diplomat approached me through my valet back in 1810 in an attempt at blackmail. I killed the valet. The diplomat promptly returned to his homeland. But his ship, alas, was lost at sea." He smiled a little. "Tragic accident."

"And Molitzyn?" Lucas pressed.

"There were only a half dozen men the Grand Duchess would have turned to. It took some time to narrow it down. By then, Molitzyn was in Paris. I sent Willoughby there. I had high hopes of laying the matter to rest once I located the girl. But Willoughby was . . . overzealous."

Lucas grimaced, imagining how his friend must have suffered before he died. But he could not afford such regrets. "What difference did it make to you if Tatiana lived out the rest of her life in Mizhakovsk?" he demanded. "Why should you hunt her down?"

"You *are* stupid, Strathmere. What was to keep the Grand Duchess from fetching her back, acknowledging her anytime it served her purpose in policy with England? You know my brother. Faced with international rebuke for my beastly behavior, he'd have caved in to any demand the

Russians might make. And our father would disown me if he learned of it! She could have named her terms."

"You overestimate the Grand Duchess's greed," Lucas told him softly.

Cumberland's good eye narrowed. "Do I? She wants to marry Princess Charlotte to that puppet of hers. Leopold."

"Instead of to your puppet, William of Orange?" The duke simply smiled. "How did you learn Tatiana was in Mizhakovsk?"

"Through you, of course. After five years of coddling roses, you embark for Russia a week after Molitzyn's death? It did not take a genius to recognize the danger there." He paused, fingering his mustache. "And Willoughby did tell me Molitzyn's blood flowed more freely every time he mentioned your name."

"Bastard," Lucas grunted, holding him out over the river again.

"What is it?" Platov demanded of Tatiana. She translated for him. "Drop him, Lucas," he snarled. Lucas started to do so. The duke stretched out his gloved hands to Tatiana.

"My dear girl. My child. Surely you will not suffer your father to be treated this way?"

"Drop him," Tatiana said coldly.

Lucas, fists wrapped in the duke's coat, vied with his emotions. Cumberland was royalty, a sovereign of the nation he loved and served. If Lucas murdered him, he would be no better than the duke himself. And Tatiana—despite her bleak, bitter hatred of this man, being party to his death would tarnish her bright soul for the rest of her days.

"This is what we want of you," he ground out, staring the duke in the eye. "Tatiana is to live in peace. She will make no claims on you, will not reveal the truth to your brother or father—so long as there are no more attempts on her life. If there are, however—"

"You wouldn't dare drop me," the duke said with disdain.

"By God, don't tempt me. If any harm should befall her, I will go to the king and the Regent. I'll tell them, not only about the Grand Duchess, but about your machinations on Bonaparte's behalf."

"You've no proof, Strathmere. And my brother hates your guts."

"That is why he'll believe it," Tatiana said suddenly, proudly. "Because he knows Lucas is a man of honor. You know that he would."

Cumberland started to bluster, stopped. "But it doesn't really matter what your brother believes," Lucas told him tautly. "Because if she dies, you die. You have my oath on that."

Tatiana was interpreting for Platov, in a whisper. The Cossack stepped up, flourishing his saber. "The same goes for me," he said, very close to the duke, needing no translation. "I will be watching you. I will be everywhere."

Cumberland spat in his face. Quick as mercury, Platov slashed with his saber and sliced through a shoulder of the coat, so that the duke hung from Lucas's one hand. Cumberland blanched at the sudden shifting of his weight. The elegant superfine strained.

"One thread at a time, Matvei," Lucas said evenly.

The Cossack brought the saber up again, stuck its point through the opposite shoulder. There was a thin little *snick* as the first thread parted—then another, and another.

"Very well!" Cumberland cried suddenly, flailing above the black water. "I swear to you, I'll not try to harm her again. Just let me go, dammit all!"

Lucas moved to swing him back onto the wall. "It is not enough," Tatiana announced abruptly. "There must be reparations. For my foster parents. For Pietr."

Lucas considered it. His arm was growing weary. "Fifty thousand pounds," he decided. "For Russian relief."

"Fifty thousand—" Cumberland gasped as Platov severed one more thread. "I'll see it is arranged!"

"Not from public funds," Tatiana added thoughtfully. "From his own private income."

Cumberland gawked at her. "Do you think I am made of money, chit?"

"I think you are made of the devil," she said very evenly. "From your own income."

The duke paused. Platov smiled, his teeth white in the darkness, and sliced. The coat began to tear. "From my income!" Cumberland acquiesced hurriedly. Lucas jerked him back onto the wall of the bridge. He stumbled onto the roadway, straightening his tattered coat. Then suddenly he rose up and lurched toward Tatiana. "But if I am made of the devil, my girl, what does that makes you?"

She stared back at him. He laughed and headed jauntily toward the curricle. "Oh, I think not, Your Grace," Lucas intervened. "We'll need that to see your daughter home. Surely you would not leave a lady in distress?"

"Damn you all," said the duke, reaching for the reins.

Platov tapped his shoulder. Cumberland turned, and the Cossack met him with a blow to the chest from the blunt edge of his saber that made an audible snap. The duke clutched himself, crumpling. "Christ! That bastard's broken my rib!"

Platov was plainly itching to finish him off. "Matvei," Lucas interjected, realizing he was aching all over. "Would you drive us home, please? At a civilized pace?"

"He has eleven more," the Cossack said sullenly. "He could spare a couple."

Lucas lifted Tatiana into the curricle. "Matvei. Home."

Still Platov hesitated. "I need you," Lucas said in Russian, "to hold him to his word."

"Matvei," Tatiana pleaded. "Fifty thousand pounds—"

Abruptly he scabbarded the saber. "As you wish. But not

for the money, *tovarka*. For you, and for the Grand Duchess's honor. As Lucas says, he'll need help to keep this lying scum honest."

Cumberland watched, aghast, as the Cossack climbed in and whistled, starting the team around. "How the devil am I to get home?" he shouted angrily.

"There's a bay belongs to Lord Barton grazing there by the water," Lucas informed him. "No saddle, but she's steady enough if you don't take any—" He broke off; Tatiana had put her finger to his mouth.

"No need to advertise that, is there?" she asked, green eyes gleaming.

"You're absolutely right. Don't feel you must stick to the road. She is splendid in open ground!" Lucas called as the grays trotted off willingly under Platov's expert hand.

"She loves to jump!" Tatiana added encouragingly.

Lucas looked at her in the moonlight. "You're a bloodthirsty little thing, aren't you?"

"I still wish you had dropped him."

"No. You don't."

"Oh, yes, Lucas. I do."

"Such a lack of familial affection might make a man hesitate to wed you."

"So might such a father." Her face was downcast. On her cheek lay the pearl of a tear.

Lucas stared a moment. Then he threw back his head and laughed. "Oh, no, Tat. No, you don't! None of that!"

"It is true!" she said stubbornly.

He put his arm around her, leaning back against the smooth leather seat. "You cannot have it both ways, love. You can't refuse to wed me because you fear you are a peasant, then refuse again once you discover you are royalty!" He flinched suddenly, leaning away from the seat. "Christ! Do you know, I've got cinders planted all down my back!"

Thirty-Six

"N<small>EXT TO THE</small> last," Tatiana promised, leaning over Lucas's bared shoulders with a pair of pincers.

"That's what you said before," he grumbled, stretched atop his bed.

"This one is deep," she warned. "Carruthers, bring him more wine." The maid held a cup to Lucas's mouth. He took a swallow, then shook his head as she offered it again.

"I still don't comprehend," Dulcie said plaintively from the window seat, "how you could have got road cinders embedded in your skin."

"He was rescuing me," Tatiana said calmly, spreading the pincers and then making a swift, clean grasp. "Got it!"

"Agh!" Lucas clutched the pillow under his head. "Are you sure there is only one more?"

"Only one more on your shoulders," she clarified.

He raised himself on his elbow, eyeing her with trepidation. "Where are the rest?"

"In your—" She giggled, patting the shredded cloth covered his buttocks.

His storm eyes glinted. "Really? That should be interesting, don't you think?"

"*I* think," said the countess, "we should have the doctor 'round. What about gangrene?"

"Always a possibility," Lucas agreed, face muffled by the pillow. "But I presume Tatiana will apply some sort of poultice or salve."

"Several, I imagine," she answered gravely.

"Mm. Let's have at it, by all means."

"He is getting drunk," Dulcie pronounced. "He really needs a physician."

"*Are* you getting drunk?" Tatiana murmured.

"Take down my breeches and see just how sober I am."

She smiled and plucked another cinder from his skin. He barely winced.

"You are both extremely giddy," the countess sniffed, "considering, from what I gather—*not* that you've been exactly forthcoming—there was another attempt on Tatiana's life tonight."

"The last," Lucas said with satisfaction. "Let's drink to it, Tat." Carruthers brought the cup, and they each took a long swallow.

Dulcie shuddered. "I should think you'd want a steady hand, Tatiana!"

"She's a rock," Lucas declared. "My rock. My bright diamond."

Dulcie rolled her eyes. "I'm sending for the doctor."

"M'lady," Carruthers interrupted mildly, "d'ye suppose ye might come to the kitchens with me to see the poultices is—are—properly prepared?"

"Cook can look to that. What I want to know is, what makes you so certain this attempt will be the last?"

"Beggin' yer pardon, m'lady, but 'tis nigh on three o'clock. Cook's been abed for hours."

"Wake her up, then!"

"Ooh, m'lady, I don't want to do that. Not with company comin' tomorrow for dinner. Ye know how she crosses the sauces when she's short on sleep."

Dulcie hesitated. It was indubitably true. "Oh, very well," she said irritably. "Which did you want, Tatiana? Mustard and heal-all? Herb Robert and tansy? Vinegar and peony seed?"

"Some of each," said Tatiana.

"Not the vinegar," Lucas begged with a shudder.

"It only stings for a moment," she promised, leaning down to his ear. "And it takes *forever* to boil up properly."

"Oh, well, in that case—*lots* of the vinegar, Mother."

Dulcie frowned. Then she rose from the window seat. "I am not so dense as to be unable to tell I'm not wanted. Come along, Carruthers."

"That maid is a pearl beyond reckoning," Lucas said as the door closed behind them. "Go and lock that, love."

Tatiana obeyed, then came back to the bedside. "Time to hike down those breeches."

"Past time." He rolled onto his back, catching her by the wrists, pulling her onto the bed.

"I really ought to have those cinders out," she protested—weakly.

"We'll work 'em out," he said, grinning.

"Don't they hurt?"

"Not so much as this." He nodded at his bulging manhood.

"Oh, I see. Now that I am royalty, I am good enough to sin with," Tatiana said archly.

"Now that you are royalty, I am very much afraid you will not be contented with me."

She relented, stretching out beside him, smiling down at him. "Whom else would I reach for? One of the princes? They are mine own uncles."

"Don't flaunt your breeding. I knew you when you were only a ragtag girl from Mizhakovsk."

For a moment, her smooth white brow furrowed. "It seems a lifetime ago."

"So it should. It was."

"What if you had not come to get me, Lucas? What if you'd crumpled Casimir's note and thrown it out? Or lost it?" *What if you had not been the man that you are?*

"Those are questions best left to God, love." Rather, he thought, like why the offspring of so unwanted a coupling should prove as wonderful as you.

She nestled close to him. "Tell me again what she said when you told her about me."

He was so tempted to lie, soften it. *That she loved you. That she was sorry . . .* "That the Russians are not monsters," he said finally, knowing truth was the best.

And, surprisingly, sufficient. "She had no choice," Tatiana whispered. "I cannot blame her. And you honestly mistook her for me? Put your arm around her?"

"You should have seen *her* stiffen."

"I can imagine. She is very, very grand."

He kissed her. "So are you."

The kiss was warm and winning. Tatiana sighed, curled within his arms, feeling safer than she ever had before in her life. "I always dreamed—" She stopped.

"What?"

"Oh, just . . . when I was a child. That I had a princess for my mother. That she would come and rescue me someday."

"Dreams come true," he said fiercely, kissing her again. "I

know that mine have." He stroked her breast beneath its sheath of peau de soie. "Or will have, if you'll only stop talking and let me make love to you."

"Whatever happened to waiting until we are married?" she said teasingly.

"Tatiana, for all I know a company of Cossacks will burst through that door at any moment, demanding you return to Russia to become their sovereign."

"Nonsense," she scoffed. "There's no Cossack in me."

"Or my mother will arrive with the poultices."

"That's more likely," she allowed—then shivered with delight as he unfastened her tapes.

"My White Lady," he murmured, and put his mouth to the tip of her breast. She sighed with happiness, fingers caught in the thick black waves of his hair. His hands moved over the curves of her hips with tantalizing slowness, reached lower, hiking up the edge of her skirts.

A sudden thunder of hoofbeats on the street outside made them both bolt upright. "Jesus Holy Christ," Lucas swore, springing from the bed. "Didn't I tell you? What now?"

"Lucas!" cried a familiar voice from the darkness below. "I have come to serenade your most beauteous mother!" The voice was speaking Russian. A jangling chord from a balalaika echoed through the air.

Lucas strode to the window. "Go home, Matvei, or I'll wrap that bloody thing around your neck."

"I have written an ode to her, my friend! It has thirty-seven verses!"

Tatiana was limp with laughter. "Thirty-seven verses! She will be honored indeed!"

"Good night, Matvei!" Lucas pulled the shutters to, hooked them, and slammed down the window. "If he doesn't watch out, I'll throw a chamber pot at him."

She sat up, her white-blond hair falling loose over her shoulders. "I love you, Lucas."

He came toward her, smiling, his eyes clear blue, shining. "My *tovarka*. My treasure."

"Lucas!" The countess pounded at the door. "That mad Cossack is out on the street with a mandolin!"

"Balalaika," he corrected her, falling on Tatiana. She giggled, collapsing beneath him on the featherbed.

"What's that you say?"

"It's not a mandolin. It's a balalaika. He is singing an ode he has composed in your honor." He kissed her mouth, soft and sweet as a rose.

"I don't care what it is; I only want it to stop! He will wake the whole neighborhood! You have got to do *something*!"

"I intend to," said Lucas, as Tatiana slowly, gingerly, pulled down his breeches. He moved his mouth to her breast, caught his breath as her fingers tightened on his hard manhood. "Oh. My dear love—"

"Shall we dance, milord?" Tatiana whispered.

They waltzed together for a very long time.

Epilogue

Somerleigh House, June, 1815.

"LOOK HERE," SAID Lucas, and passed the *Post* to Tatiana across the bedclothes. "The Duke of Cumberland has just made another sizable contribution to Russian relief."

"How much?" she demanded, and scanned the article he pointed out. "Only a thousand pounds! Why, that bastard!"

"Mind your tongue," he chided, and licked a bit of jam from the corner of her mouth. "That makes nearly ten thousand altogether. He is getting there."

"Aye, and being lauded as a great humanitarian for it!" Tatiana scowled at the item. " 'When asked the reason for his devotion to the Russian people, His Grace said simply, "Any Christian soul must feel for a nation that has endured so much.' " I'd like to take his bloody Christian soul and—"

Lucas laid a finger on her lip. "He is keeping his word. And you're safe. Nothing matters more than that."

There was a knock at the door, and Carruthers bore in a fresh pot of coffee. For a moment she contemplated the breakfast tray on Tatiana's lap; then she clucked her tongue. "That won't do at all, m'lady," she said briskly. "You finish up that porridge, now, there's a good girl."

"What precisely is it about my state," Tatiana muttered ruefully, "that makes everyone treat me so condescendingly?"

Carruthers rolled her eyes. "You tell her, m'lord."

"Eat your porridge," Lucas obliged, his eyes alight with laughter.

"I *hate* porridge. I should like some eggs, and some bacon, and—"

"Ooh, no, m'lady! Sure to bring on the retching, you are, with rich foods such as that!"

"I never retch," she said archly, and swiped a bit of bacon from Lucas's tray. "Bring me two coddled eggs right now, or I'll dismiss you without references."

"Hmph! Like to see you try," Carruthers sniffed. She set the coffee down and left.

"*One* coddled egg?" Tatiana called after her pleadingly. Lucas snickered, and she elbowed him sharply. "What is so amusing?"

"To think she once was so timid and compliant! It seems that serving a countess has gone to her head."

"I should not have told her."

He caressed her gently swelling belly, and then her breasts. "She'd have guessed by now anyway."

"I really do hate porridge," she said again, sadly.

"You may have my eggs and bacon. *If,*" he added, as she lunged for them eagerly, "you will share with me."

"Tek ar uf it," she said through a huge mouthful, thrusting the porridge bowl at him.

"That wasn't what I had in mind."

Tatiana swallowed. "No?"

"No." He waited patiently while she devoured his breakfast, then set the trays aside and tugged at the ribbons of her nightdress. "I had in mind this."

"If you give me your toast, too," she bargained.

"Greedy girl." But he handed it over. She'd just finished the last bite and turned to him with an enticing, if somewhat crumb-strewn, smile, when another knock sounded. "Go away!" he said curtly.

But Tatiana hushed him. "It may be Carruthers. Perhaps she relented on the eggs. Come in!" she sang out, and Lucas laughed at the way her face fell when it was only Timkins, hands behind his back.

"Beggin' yer pardon, m'lord, m'lady," the gardener stammered, seeing Tatiana's expression.

"It's nothing personal," Lucas assured him. "Her Ladyship would only be glad to see you if you had a slice of ham in your pocket."

"I don't suppose you do," Tatiana sighed.

Timkins's one eye twinkled. "Nah. Somethin' better."

"Pork pie?" she asked, brightening.

He snorted, then drew forth a silver vase containing a single rose blossom—snow-white, richly petaled, quartered, with a button of green at its heart. "Permit me to present Lady Tatiana Strathmere. Ye asked, m'lord, for the first bloom that opened."

"Oh!" Tatiana breathed, all thought of food forgotten. "Oh, Lucas! Oh, Timkins! It is lovely! Isn't it lovely?"

"Exquisite," Lucas said, and kissed her. "I knew it would be."

"What about the fragrance?" she demanded.

"Try it for yerself."

Tatiana buried her nose in the petals, inhaled, then passed the vase to Lucas anxiously, watching his face. He sniffed the bloom, raised his head, sniffed again.

"Beyond imagining, as I predicted," he finally announced. "It smells just like ham."

She moved to hit him, and he blocked her fist. "No, really, Lucas! What do you think?"

"I think it has the perfume of musk and magic," he said solemnly. "Like you." His long, strong fingers parted the petals with professional care. "And it is green-eyed, too."

"Will ye send a description to the Rose Society, m'lord?" Timkins asked then.

Lucas twisted the bloom into Tatiana's thick blond hair. "No. We'll keep this one in the family. Unless . . . should I, Tatiana? It could be your best chance at immortality."

"Oh, no," she demurred, her hand on her belly. "I have *him* for that."

"Her," said Lucas.

"Him," said Tatiana.

Timkins was grinning, watching them like a doting mother hen. His keen eye had not missed Tatiana's unbound bodice ribbons. "Well. I'll leave it here, then, 'n' leave ye twain to it."

"To what?" Tatiana asked, startled.

The gardener bowed. "Why, to yer breakfast, m'lady." But he winked at his master as he turned for the door.

"Cheeky," Tatiana grumbled as it closed behind him.

"That's what I like about him. Down-to-earth. No pretenses. Rather like you that way." Lucas had recommenced where he'd left off, and was stroking her breasts. She lay back, her breath coming faster as his tongue traced the curves of her ear.

"Oh, love—"

"Husband," he corrected her proudly.

"Love," she reiterated. "It's rare enough these days that they should be the same. You should not complain." She reached beneath the covers for his manhood, making him shudder with longing—just as yet another knock sounded at the door.

"Go *away!*" Lucas moaned, lost in the heady sensation of her silken touch, her sweet, warm scent, her blue-veined skin. . . .

"I do beg your pardon, milord." Smithers, as dour as ever. "But the Dowager Countess has just arrived. You asked to be informed."

"I'll lock the door," Lucas whispered. But before he could move, the portal sprang open and Dulcie was upon them, with a flurry of yapping spaniels close at her heels.

"Darlings!" she exclaimed, hurrying to the bedside. "I came the *instant* I heard!"

"She really did this time," Lucas muttered, making Tatiana giggle. And it was true; the note they'd sent regarding her condition could not have reached London more than three days past.

"I am absolutely, positively—oh, I am beyond *words!*" the countess gushed.

"That's God's truth," said her son. "Would you get those dogs away from our breakfast trays?"

"Never mind that," Dulcie said briskly, settling herself onto the coverlet beside Tatiana. "My darling, how are you feeling? A touch of nausea, Carruthers tells me. Best thing in the *world* for you. You must watch your diet, you know. It would not do at *all* for you to become fat." And she prodded Tatiana's stomach.

"Mother, please!" Lucas rolled his eyes.

"Oh, we cannot expect a *man* to understand these matters, my dear, can we? But your woes are over. I am here. And I have come to stay."

"Stay?" Tatiana echoed faintly.

"Why, for the length of your confinement! How could you imagine I'd do anything else?"

"How indeed," Lucas said with a sigh.

"Besides attending to your health, there are so many other decisions to make! Take the nursery, for example—it will have to be done over. And the christening gown! I've brought swatches with me. Madame Descoux is just in ecstasy! And all of London is abuzz at the notion of me, a grandmother—at my age!" She preened at her hair. "Now, so long as you *have* finished breakfast, suppose we get right down to it. The birth announcements should not be a problem—I've selected those already, at Hartin's, and we have only to inform them of the birth date and name. Have you given any thought to names? Should it be a girl, I assume, naturally, you will want to call it after *me*. After all—"

"Mother," said Lucas.

"Where would the two of you be now," the countess forged on brightly, "if not for my help? But if it is a boy, there are several considerations. The Admiral, God rest his soul, always favored—"

"Get out," Lucas told her.

"Biblical names. I thought perhaps Benjamin. Or Israel. Or Zebediah."

"Zebediah?" Tatiana smothered another giggle.

"But then again, you *might* choose to honor the Regent—who has informed me, incidentally, that he is entirely willing to stand as godfather. Isn't that splendid of him?"

Lucas sat up in the bed, delivering a not-quite-accidental kick to a spaniel who was lapping cream from the porridge bowl. "Get out," he said sternly, "or we'll name the baby Harry if it's a boy. Or Jane if it's a girl."

"You wouldn't!" Dulcie cried in horror.

"Oh, yes. We would."

"But—"

He pointed to the door. "*Out. Now!*"

She went—surprisingly meekly. "Not Jane, my dears. Not Harry. Such terribly common names! It would not sit well at *all*. Come, my little ones!" She clapped her hands at the spaniels, who ignored her, eagerly ravaging the breakfast scraps. *"Come!"* she said then, in a terrible voice that instantly brought them all to her side. "We'll talk more just as soon as I am settled in," she assured Tatiana with a glorious smile. "But you have made me *so* happy. Really, I cannot say how ecstatic I am." She withdrew with a fluttering wave of her gloved hand.

They waited for a moment in silence, like victims of a horrendous storm, staring in her wake. Then Tatiana burst out laughing. "Harry?" she said, tears of merriment running down her cheeks. *"Jane?"*

"The only threat I could think of. But it seems to have sufficed."

Tatiana grew solemn. "She is right, you know. Where *would* we be without her?"

"Here," he said, and arched over her. "We would be right here."

"No, we wouldn't," she countered.

"Sooner or later we would," he grunted.

"I *like* the name Dulcibella."

"So do I," he admitted. "But it will be a boy."

"You said you wanted a girl."

"I have reconsidered." He lowered himself inside her, catching his breath at the flood of sensation, the immense surge of love he felt for her and always would.

"You have?"

"I have. Absolutely. We shall have only boys. One Dulcibella Strathmere is all the world can bear." Slowly he withdrew. She pulled him to her, hands at the small of his back.

"You must long sometimes for the days when you were a recluse," she whispered, kissing the arch of his neck.

"Never," he swore, a hitch in his voice as his manhood thrust again into her welcoming sheath.

"Never?" she repeated, staring into his eyes, made stormy only by love now.

The door flew open. "Timkins said you had a hankering for pork pie, m'lady, so I had Cook—oh, my!" Carruthers blushed red as her hair as she saw the entwined couple in the bed.

"Almost never," Lucas amended with a sigh, and got up to bolt the door at last.

Author's Note

OF ALL KING George III's disreputable sons, Ernest Augustus, the Duke of Cumberland, was, in one historian's words, "the least wholesome," and in another's phrase, "the ablest." The combination was a dangerous one. He fomented a great deal of turmoil in his troubled family; among the unsavory but persistent rumors concerning him was that he had an incestuous relationship with his sister, the Princess Sophia. It is true that his valet, Joseph Sellis, was found dead in the duke's apartments. Though the jury at the inquest concluded that Sellis had killed himself after attacking his master, at least one expert witness testified that while Sellis was left-handed, his wounds had been inflicted by a right-handed man. (Some gossips claimed Sellis and the duke had had a homosexual relationship, and Cumberland killed his valet for trying to blackmail him.) At any rate, those who knew Cumberland certainly thought him capable of murder, and for days after the incident the ton visited his apartments to view the bloodstained walls. So while the tale in this book of the duke's ravishment of the Grand Duchess of Oldenburg is fiction, the behavior would not have been out of character.

The visit of Tsar Alexander, his sister the Grand Duchess, Hetman Matvei Platov, and the other foreign luminaries to London in June of 1814 caused a grand sensation; crowds trailed them everywhere they went, eager for glimpses of the Regent's exotic guests. It is true that the Tsar and the Prince Regent took an instant dislike to one another, and that the Grand Duchess went out of her way to make herself disagreeable to her host. Public opinion blamed her for the breakup of Princess Charlotte's betrothal to William of Orange, which resulted in Charlotte's subsequent marriage to Prince Leopold of Saxe-Coburg.

While it does not excuse his outrageous debauchery, the interminable wait suffered by Prince George to ascend to the throne does present some interesting parallels to the current British royal house.

My grandfather, who grew up on a horse farm in Russia, used to tell us how he and his brothers would hitch a wolf-hound to a sleigh, let a cat out of a basket, and enjoy the breakneck ride!